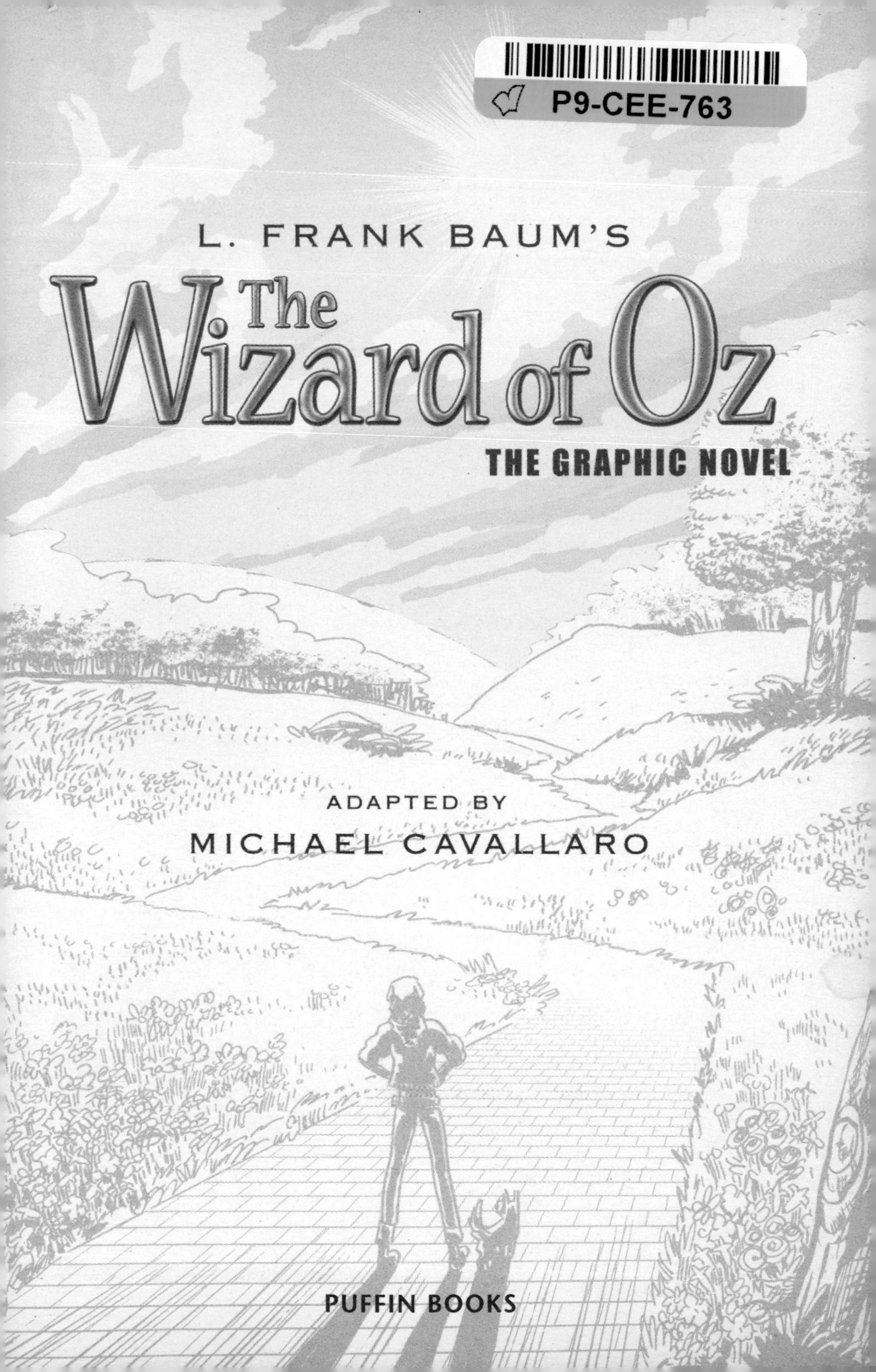

L. FRANK BAUM'S

The Wizard of Oz

THE GRAPHIC NOVEL

ADAPTED BY

MICHAEL CAVALLARO

PUFFIN BOOKS

PUFFIN BOOKS
Published by the Penguin Group
Penguin Young Readers Group,
345 Hudson Street, New York, NY 10014 U.S.A.
Penguin Group (Canada). 10 Alcorn Avenue, Toronto, Ontario, Canada M4V 3B2
(a division of Pearson Penguin Canada Inc.)
Penguin Books Ltd, 80 Strand, London WC2R 0RL, England
Penguin Ireland, 25 St. Stephen's Green, Dublin 2, Ireland
(a division of Penguin Books Ltd)
Penguin Group (Australia), 250 Camberwell Road, Camberwell, Victoria 3124,
Australia (a division of Pearson Australia Group Pty Ltd)
Penguin Books India Pvt Ltd, 11 Community Centre, Panchsheel Park,
New Delhi – 110 017, India
Penguin Group (NZ), Cnr Airborne and Rosedale Roads, Albany, Auckland 1310,
New Zealand (a division of Pearson New Zealand Ltd)
Penguin Books (South Africa) (Pty) Ltd, 24 Sturdee Avenue, Rosebank,
Johannesburg 2196, South Africa

Registered Offices: Penguin Books Ltd, 80 Strand, London WC2R 0RL, England

First published by Puffin Books, a division of Penguin Young Readers Group, 2005

Copyright © Byron Preiss Visual Publications, 2005
All rights reserved

A Byron Preiss Book
Byron Preiss Visual Publications
24 West 25th Street, New York, NY 10010

Adapted by Michael Cavallaro
Cover art by Michael Cavallaro
Series Editor: Dwight Jon Zimmerman
Series Assistant Editor: April Isaacs
Interior design by Raul Carvajal and Gilda Hannah
Cover design by Raul Carvajal

Puffin Books ISBN 0-14-240471-3

Printed in the United States of America

Except in the United States of America, this book is sold subject to the
condition that it shall not, by way of trade or otherwise, be lent, re-sold, hired
out, or otherwise circulated without the publisher's prior consent in any form of
binding or cover other than that in which it is published and without a similar
condition including this condition being imposed on the subsequent purchaser.

The publisher does not have any control over and does not assume any
responsibility for author or third-party Web sites or their content.

L. FRANK BAUM'S

The Wizard of Oz

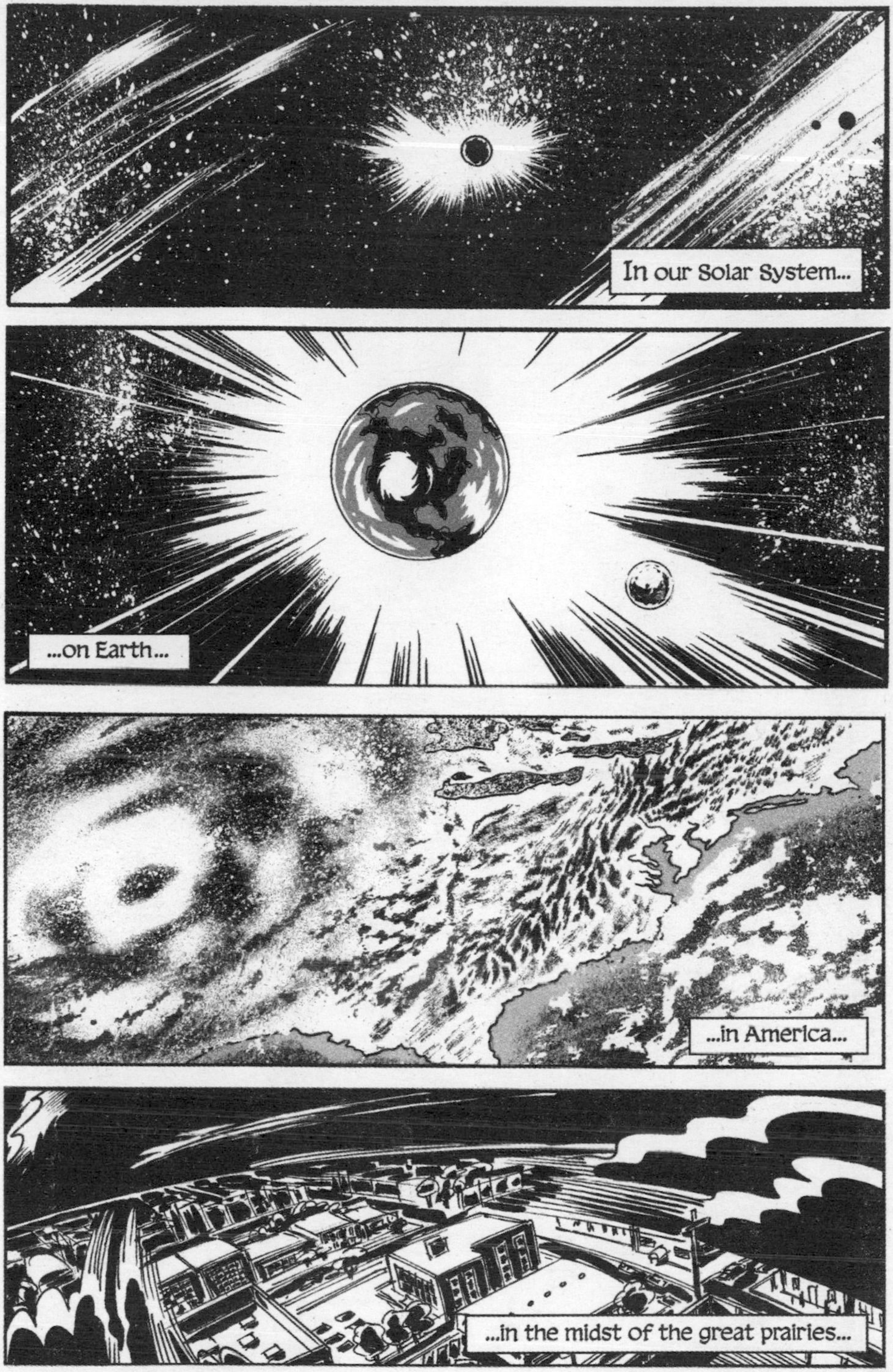
In our Solar System...
...on Earth...
...in America...
...in the midst of the great prairies...

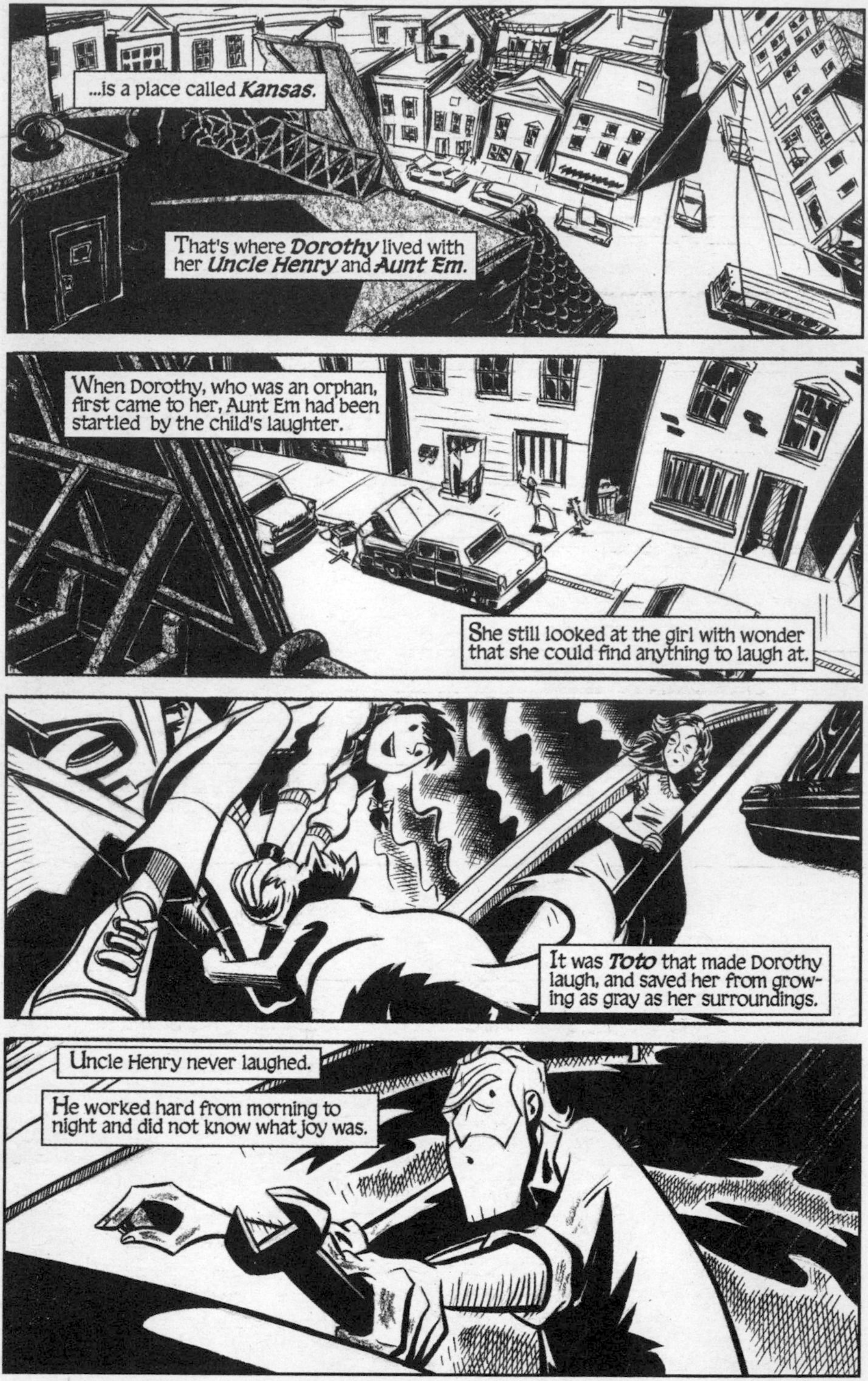
...is a place called *Kansas*.
That's where *Dorothy* lived with her *Uncle Henry* and *Aunt Em*.
When Dorothy, who was an orphan, first came to her, Aunt Em had been startled by the child's laughter.
She still looked at the girl with wonder that she could find anything to laugh at.
It was *Toto* that made Dorothy laugh, and saved her from growing as gray as her surroundings.
Uncle Henry never laughed.
He worked hard from morning to night and did not know what joy was.

EM!
DOROTHY!
THERE'S A CYCLONE COMING!
RUN FOR THE CELLAR!

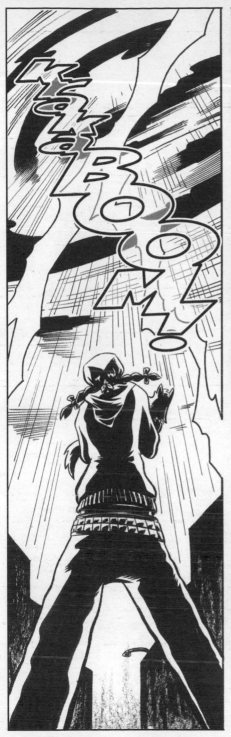

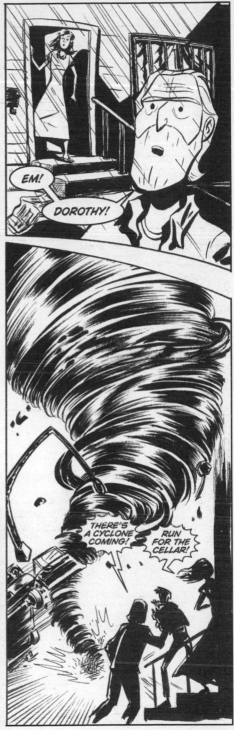

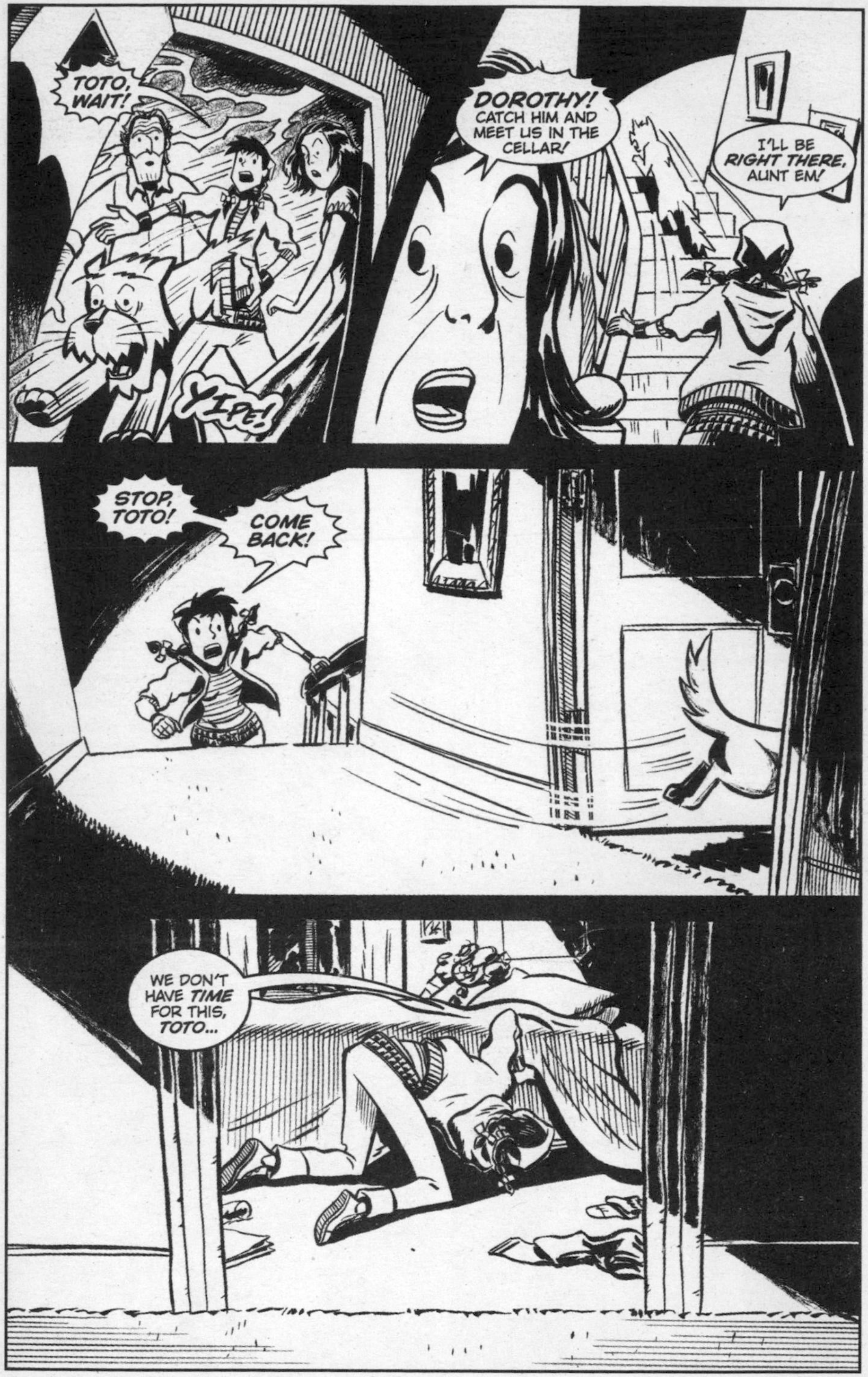
TOTO, WAIT!
YIPE!
DOROTHY! CATCH HIM AND MEET US IN THE CELLAR!
I'LL BE RIGHT THERE, AUNT EM!
STOP, TOTO!
COME BACK!
WE DON'T HAVE TIME FOR THIS, TOTO...

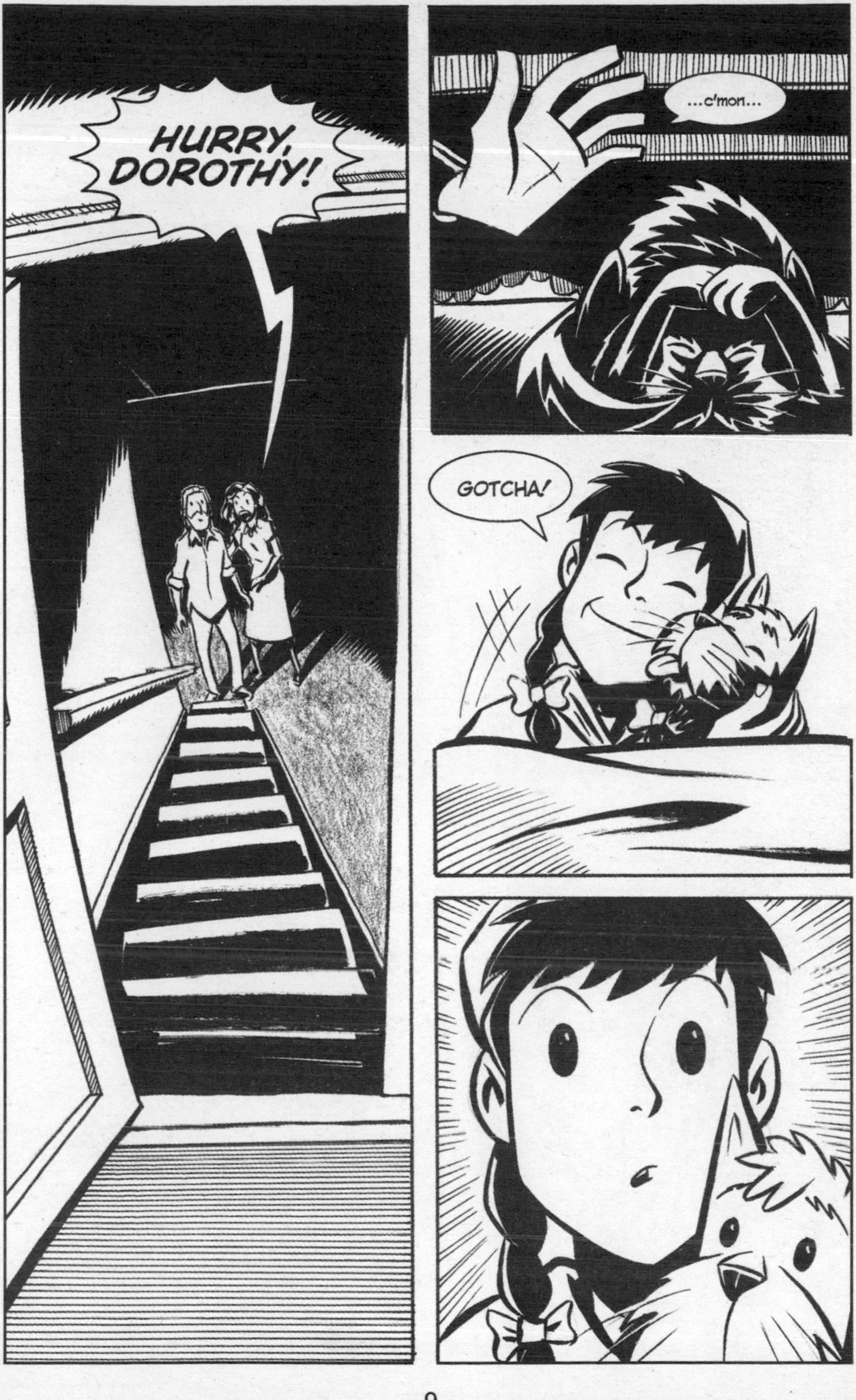
HURRY, DOROTHY!
...c'mon...
GOTCHA!

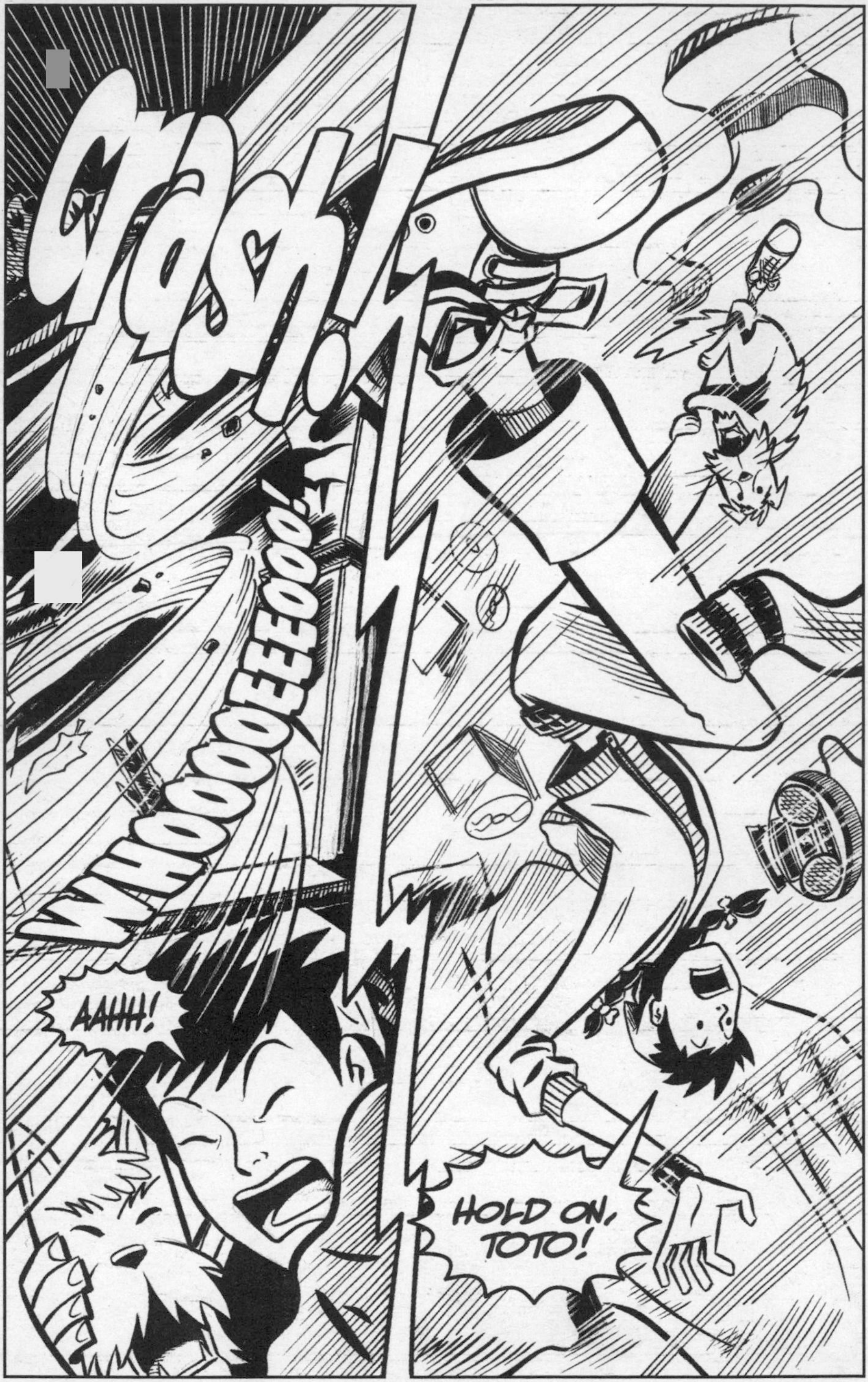
Crash!
WHOOOOOEEEOOOO!
AAHH!
HOLD ON, TOTO!

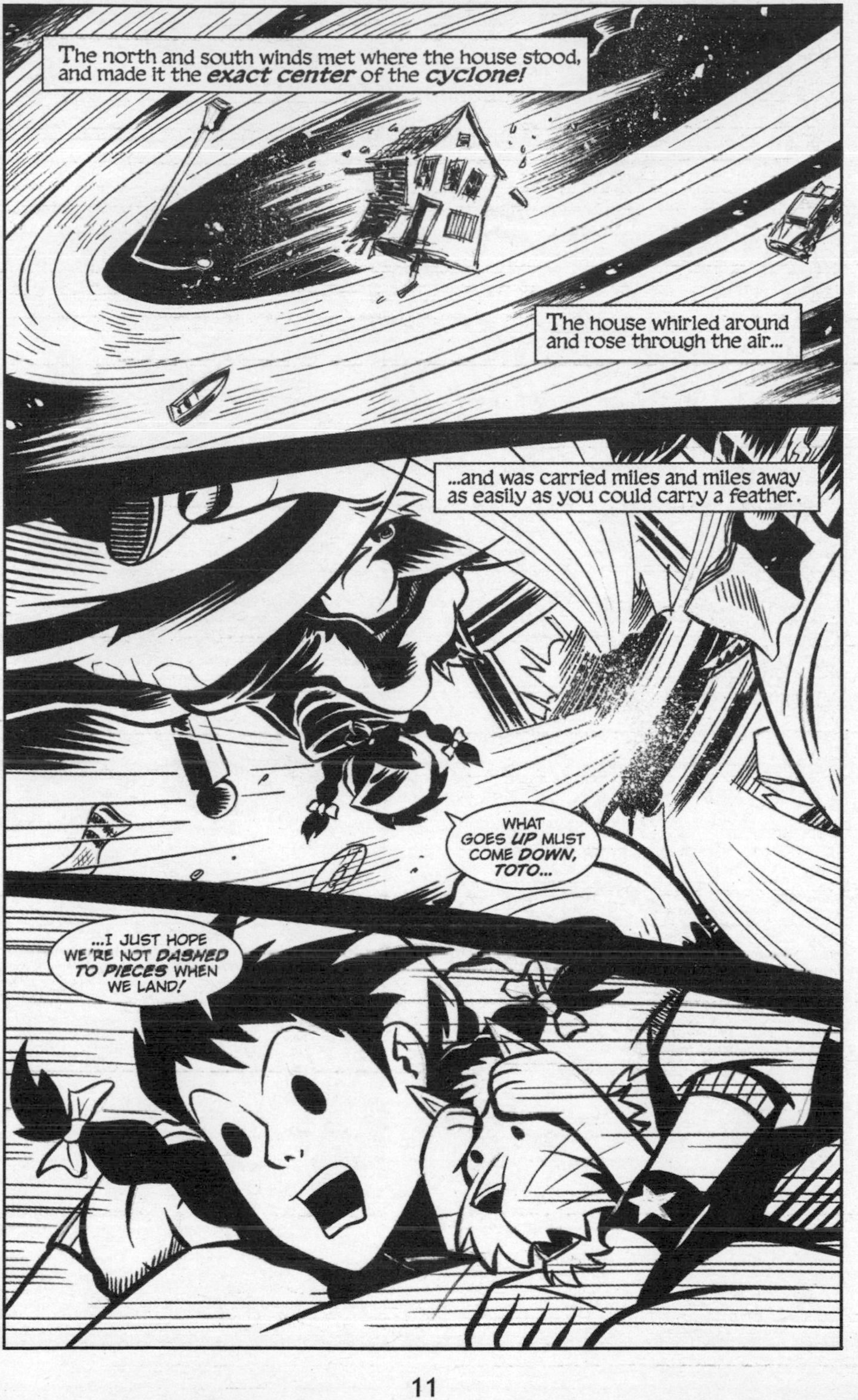
The north and south winds met where the house stood, and made it the exact center of the cyclone!
The house whirled around and rose through the air...
...and was carried miles and miles away as easily as you could carry a feather.
WHAT GOES UP MUST COME DOWN, TOTO...
...I JUST HOPE WE'RE NOT DASHED TO PIECES WHEN WE LAND!

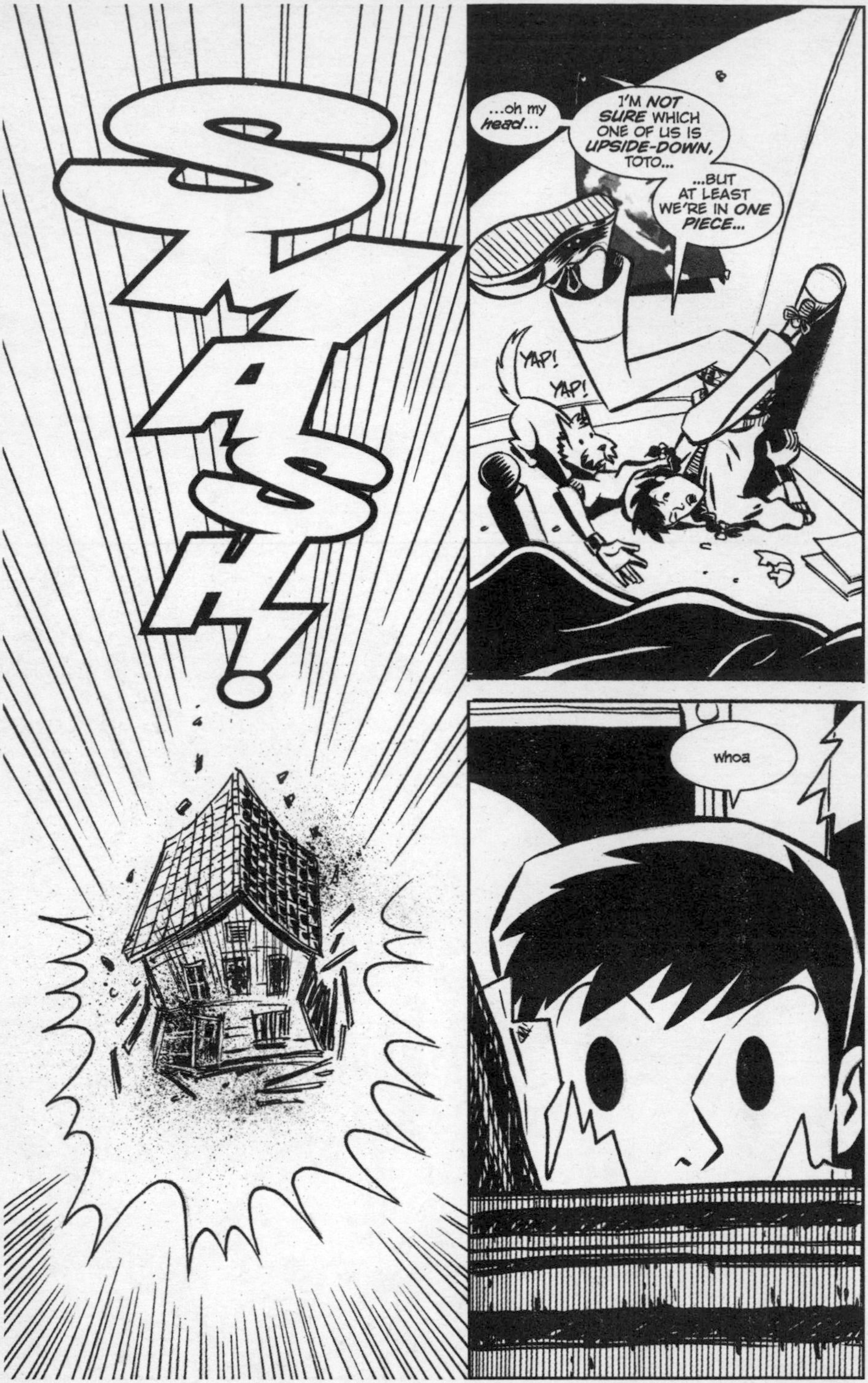
SMASH!
...oh my head...
I'M NOT SURE WHICH ONE OF US IS UPSIDE-DOWN, TOTO...
...BUT AT LEAST WE'RE IN ONE PIECE...
YAP!
YAP!
whoa

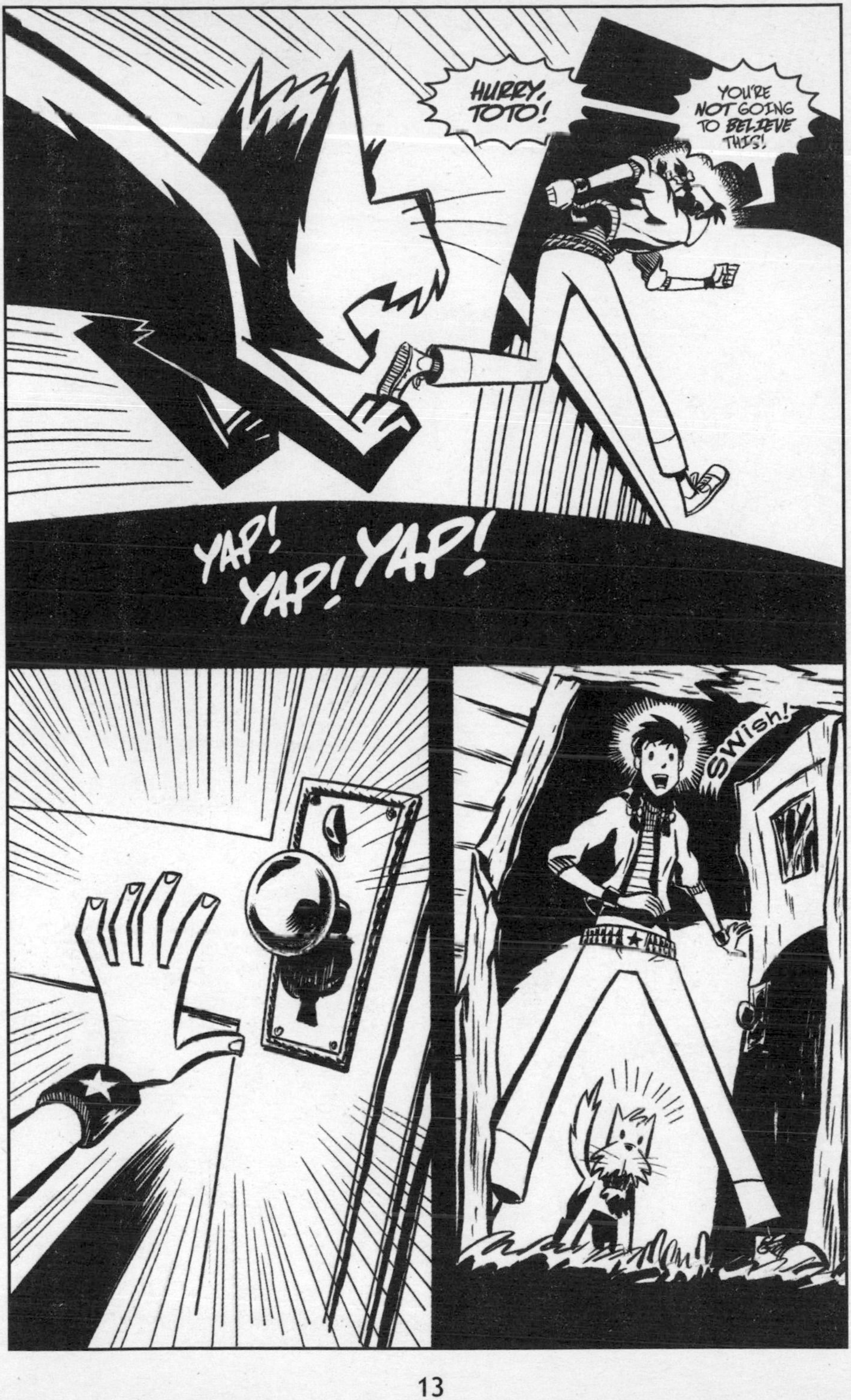
HURRY, TOTO!
YOU'RE NOT GOING TO BELIEVE THIS!
YAP! YAP! YAP!
SWish!

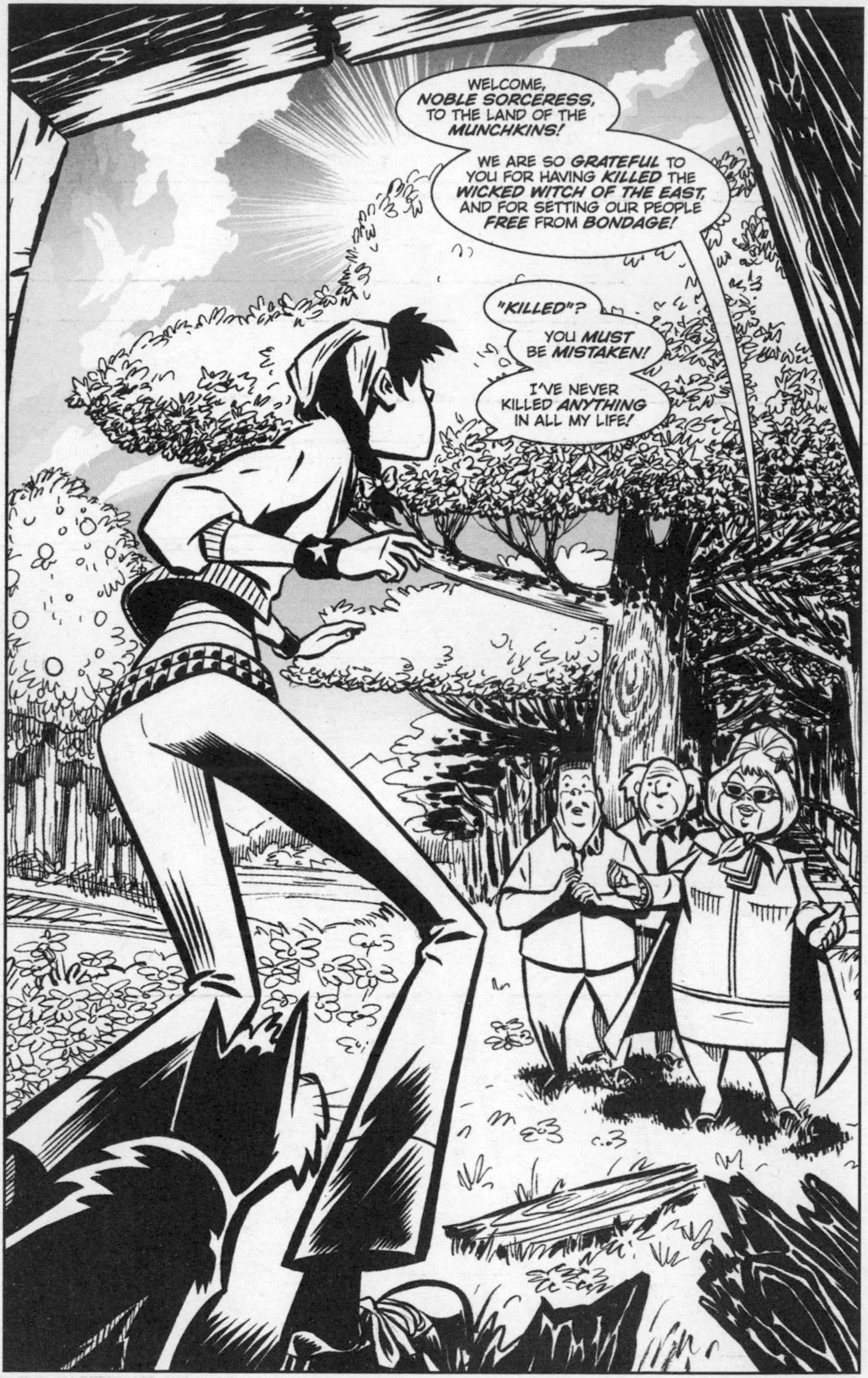
WELCOME, NOBLE SORCERESS, TO THE LAND OF THE MUNCHKINS!
WE ARE SO GRATEFUL TO YOU FOR HAVING KILLED THE WICKED WITCH OF THE EAST, AND FOR SETTING OUR PEOPLE FREE FROM BONDAGE!
"KILLED"?
YOU MUST BE MISTAKEN!
I'VE NEVER KILLED ANYTHING IN ALL MY LIFE!

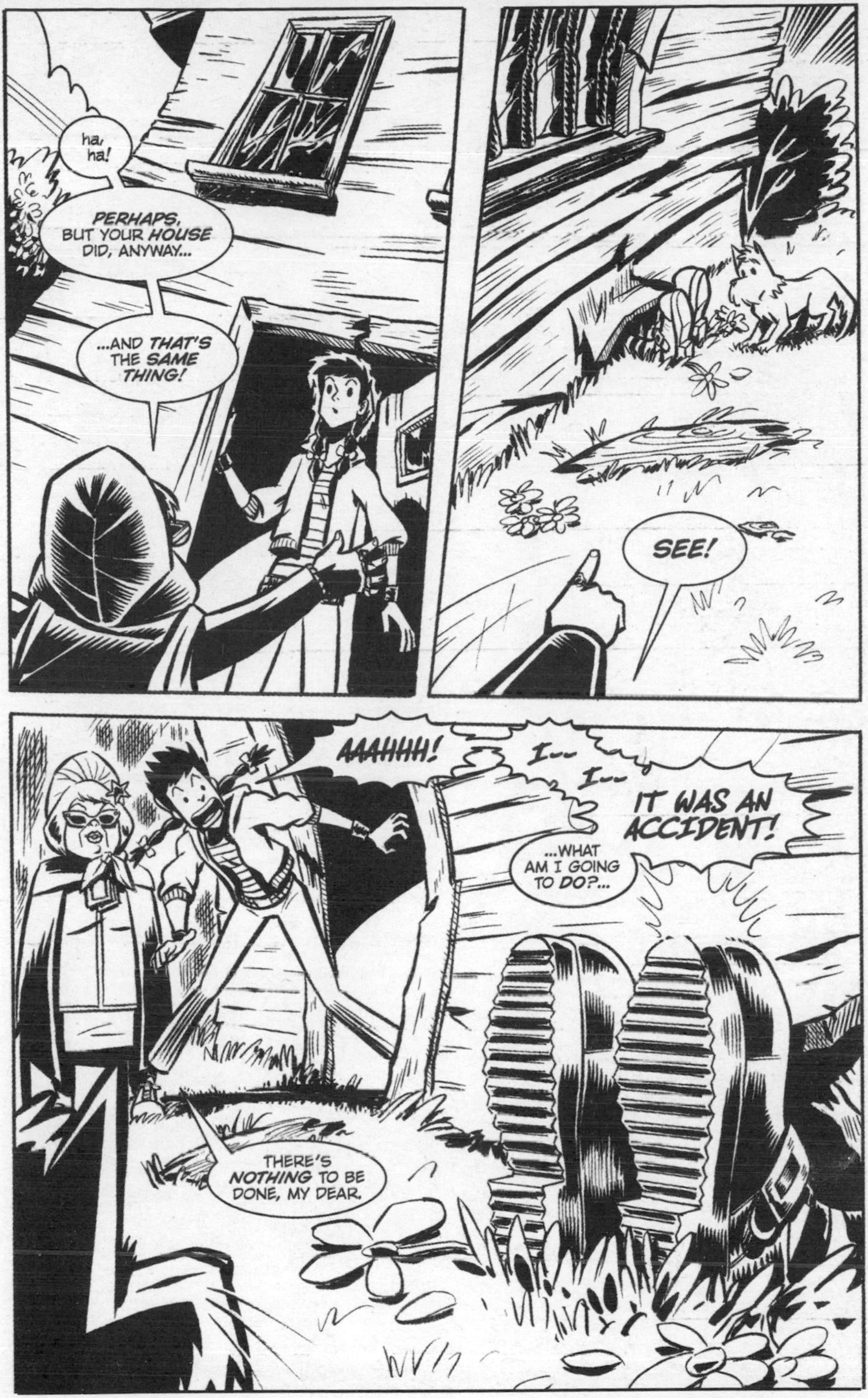
ha, ha!
PERHAPS, BUT YOUR HOUSE DID, ANYWAY...
...AND THAT'S THE SAME THING!
SEE!
AAAHHH!
I-- I-- IT WAS AN ACCIDENT!
...WHAT AM I GOING TO DO?...
THERE'S NOTHING TO BE DONE, MY DEAR.

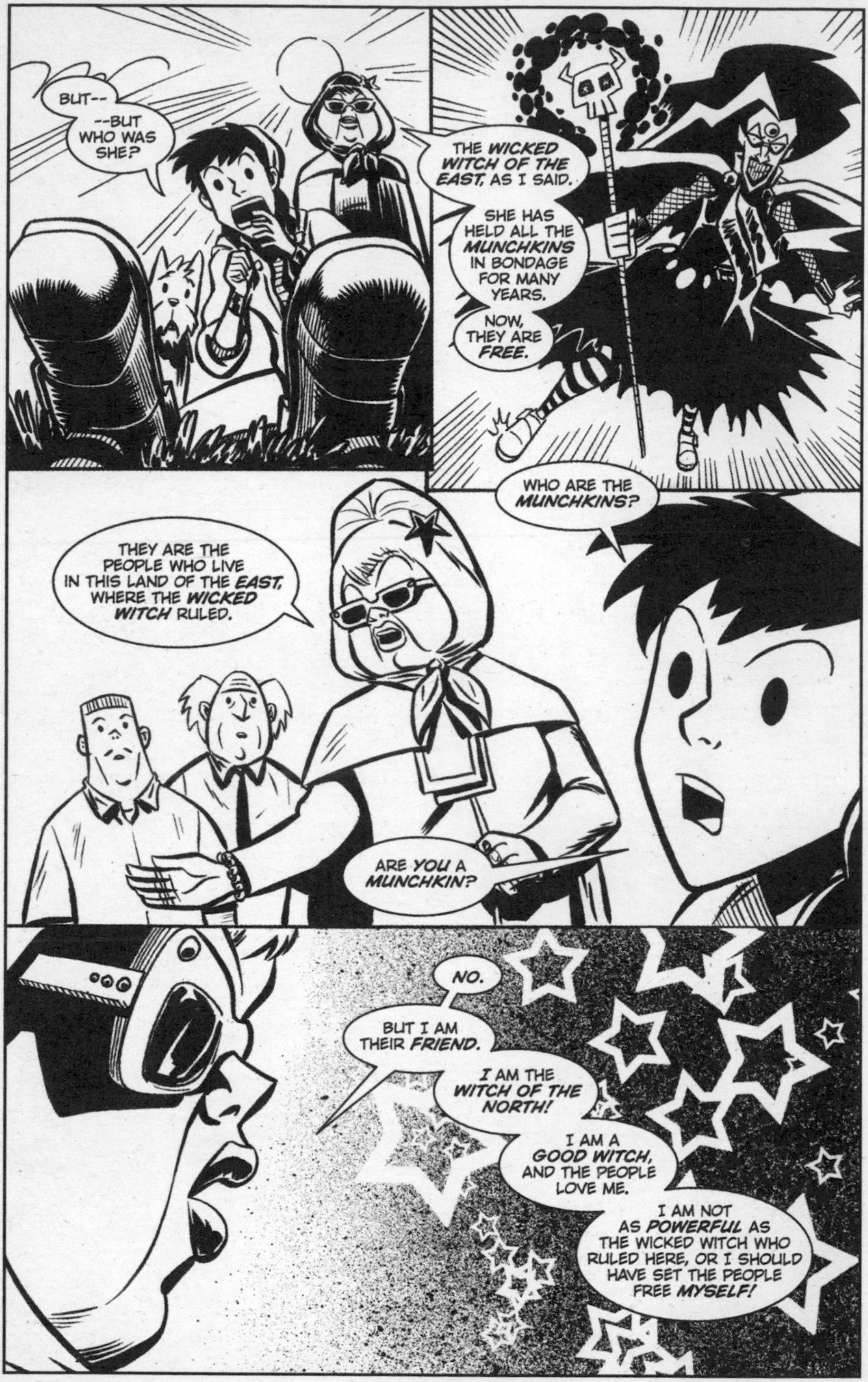
BUT--
--BUT WHO WAS SHE?
THE WICKED WITCH OF THE EAST, AS I SAID.
SHE HAS HELD ALL THE MUNCHKINS IN BONDAGE FOR MANY YEARS.
NOW, THEY ARE FREE.
WHO ARE THE MUNCHKINS?
THEY ARE THE PEOPLE WHO LIVE IN THIS LAND OF THE EAST, WHERE THE WICKED WITCH RULED.
ARE YOU A MUNCHKIN?
NO.
BUT I AM THEIR FRIEND.
I AM THE WITCH OF THE NORTH!
I AM A GOOD WITCH, AND THE PEOPLE LOVE ME.
I AM NOT AS POWERFUL AS THE WICKED WITCH WHO RULED HERE, OR I SHOULD HAVE SET THE PEOPLE FREE MYSELF!

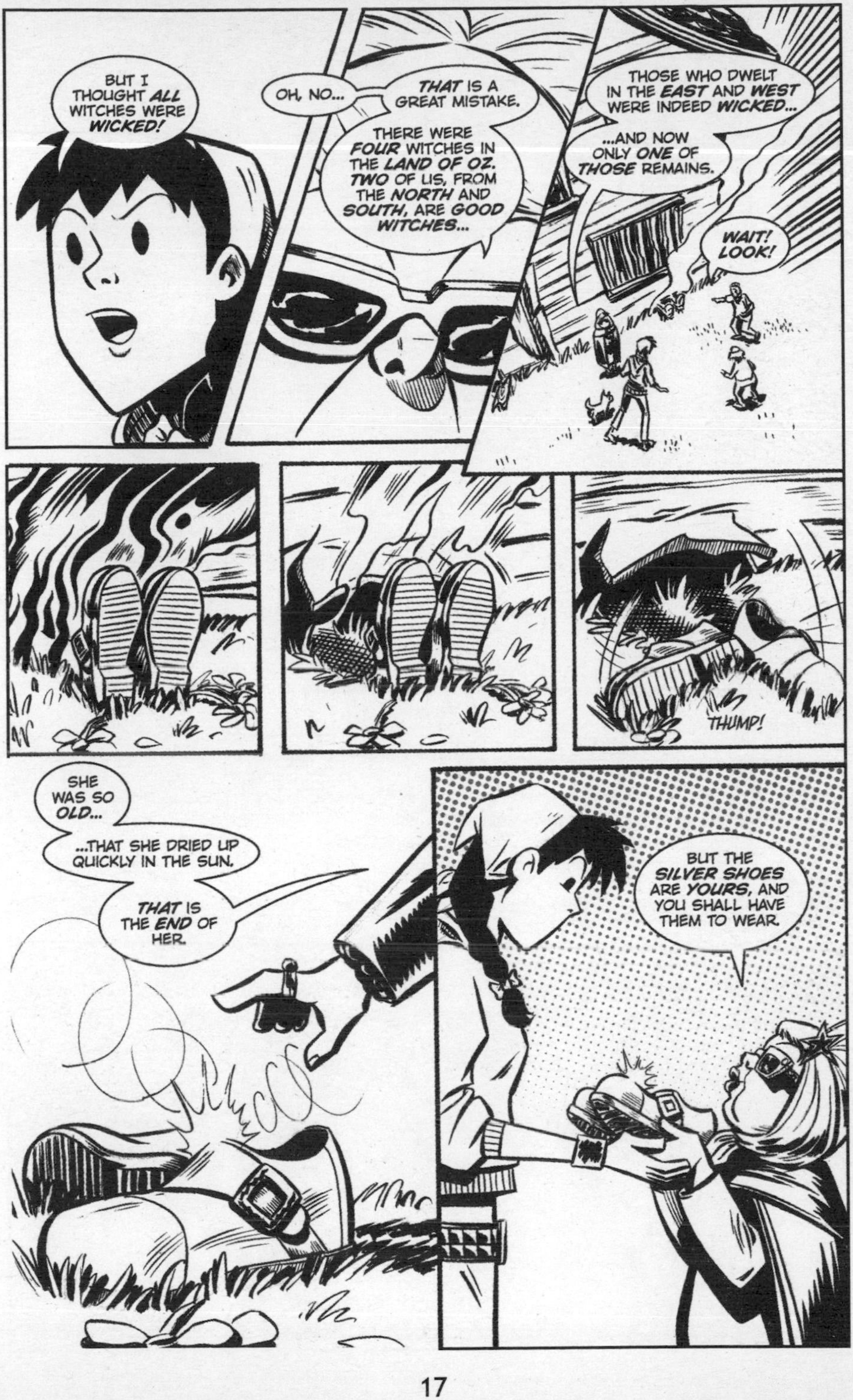
BUT I THOUGHT ALL WITCHES WERE WICKED!
OH, NO...
THAT IS A GREAT MISTAKE.
THERE WERE FOUR WITCHES IN THE LAND OF OZ. TWO OF US, FROM THE NORTH AND SOUTH, ARE GOOD WITCHES...
THOSE WHO DWELT IN THE EAST AND WEST WERE INDEED WICKED...
...AND NOW ONLY ONE OF THOSE REMAINS.
WAIT! LOOK!
THUMP!
SHE WAS SO OLD...
...THAT SHE DRIED UP QUICKLY IN THE SUN.
THAT IS THE END OF HER.
BUT THE SILVER SHOES ARE YOURS, AND YOU SHALL HAVE THEM TO WEAR.

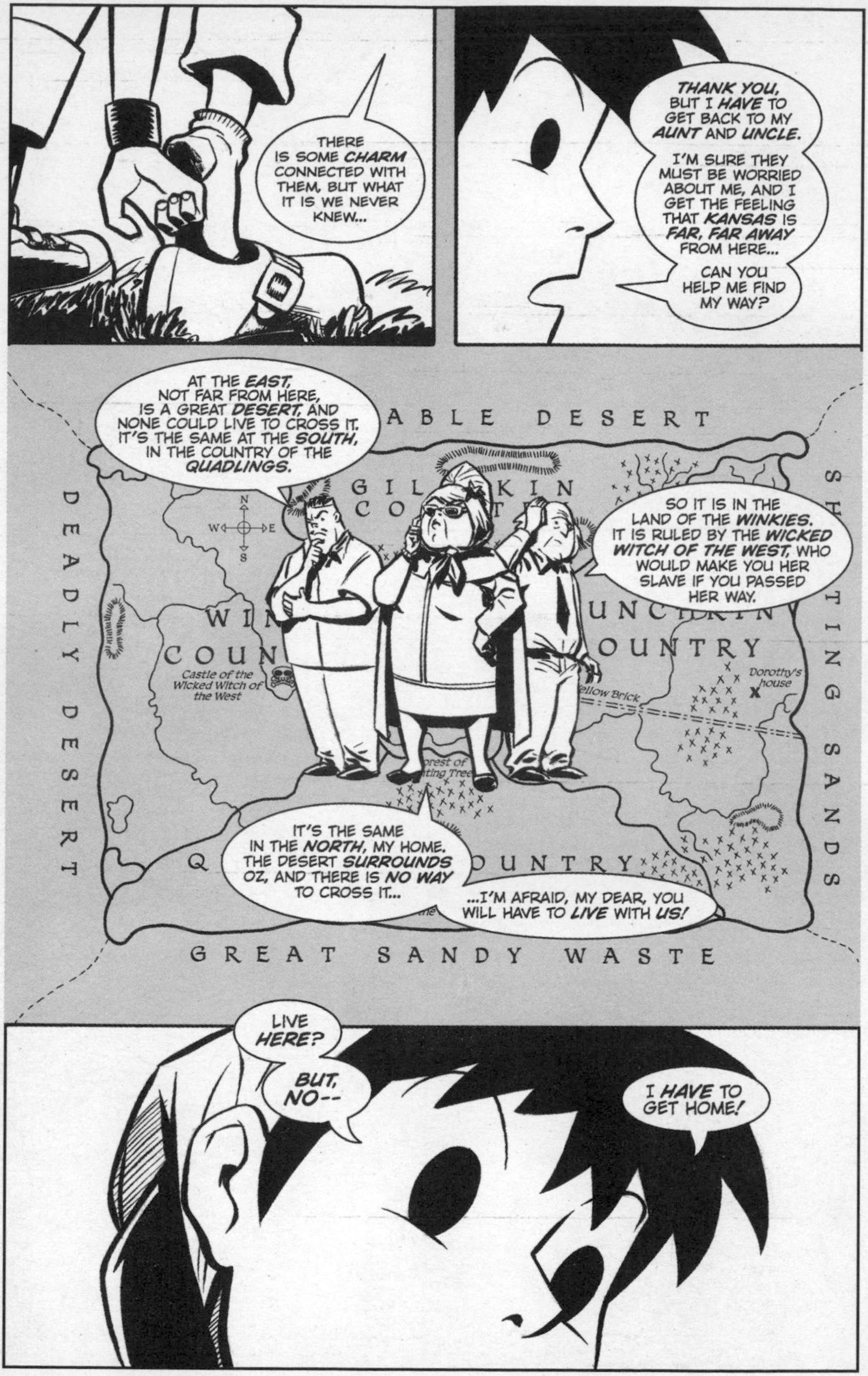
THERE IS SOME *CHARM* CONNECTED WITH THEM, BUT WHAT IT IS WE NEVER KNEW...
THANK YOU, BUT I *HAVE* TO GET BACK TO MY *AUNT* AND *UNCLE.*
I'M SURE THEY MUST BE WORRIED ABOUT ME, AND I GET THE FEELING THAT *KANSAS* IS *FAR, FAR AWAY* FROM HERE...
CAN YOU HELP ME FIND MY WAY?
AT THE *EAST,* NOT FAR FROM HERE, IS A GREAT *DESERT,* AND NONE COULD LIVE TO CROSS IT. IT'S THE SAME AT THE *SOUTH,* IN THE COUNTRY OF THE *QUADLINGS.*
SO IT IS IN THE LAND OF THE *WINKIES.* IT IS RULED BY THE *WICKED WITCH OF THE WEST,* WHO WOULD MAKE YOU HER SLAVE IF YOU PASSED HER WAY.
IT'S THE SAME IN THE *NORTH,* MY HOME. THE DESERT *SURROUNDS* OZ, AND THERE IS *NO WAY* TO CROSS IT...
...I'M AFRAID, MY DEAR, YOU WILL HAVE TO *LIVE* WITH *US!*
DEADLY DESERT
GREAT SANDY WASTE
Castle of the Wicked Witch of the West
Dorothy's house
N
W
E
S
LIVE *HERE?*
BUT, NO--
I *HAVE* TO GET HOME!

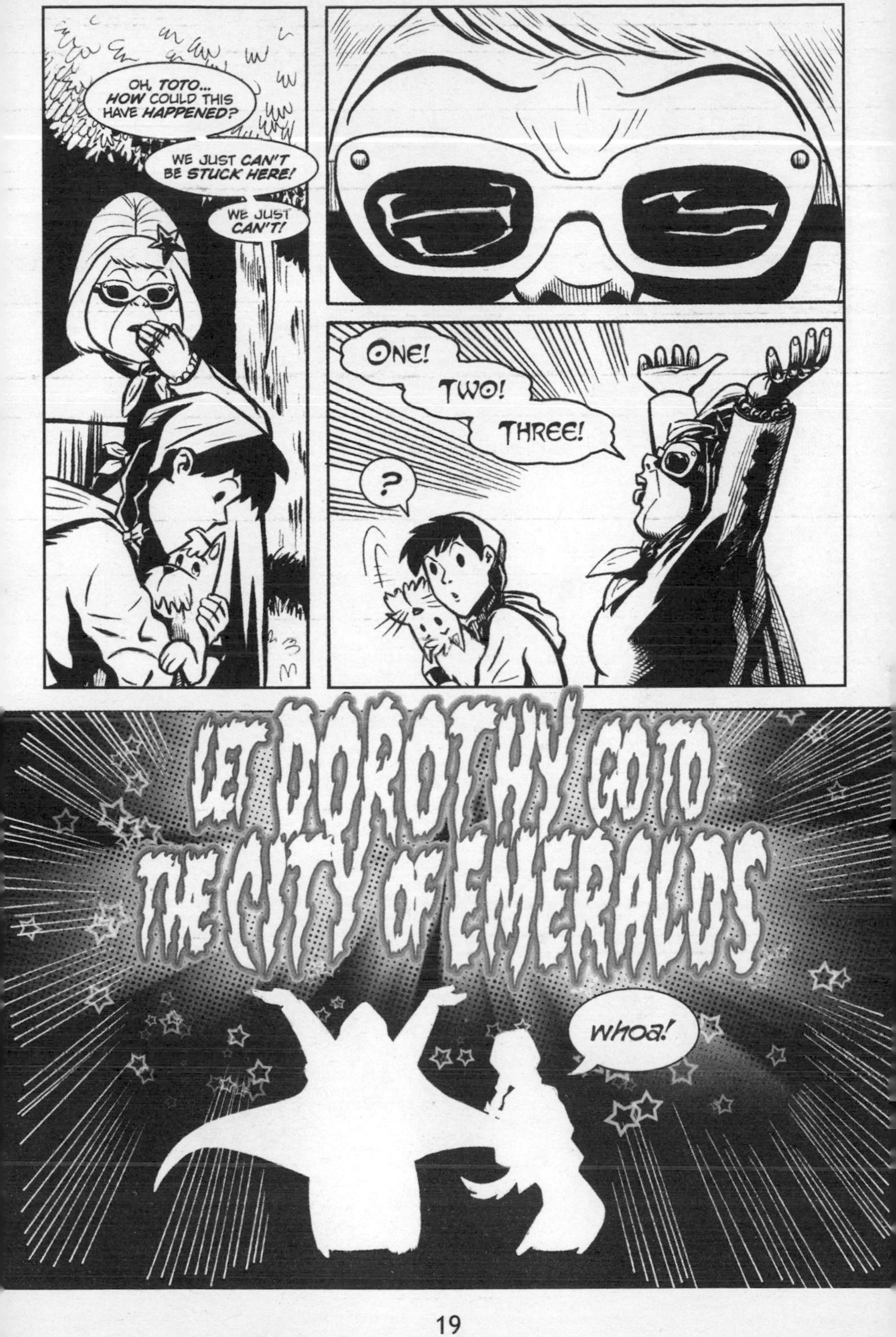
OH, TOTO... HOW COULD THIS HAVE HAPPENED?
WE JUST CAN'T BE STUCK HERE!
WE JUST CAN'T!
ONE!
TWO!
THREE!
?
LET DOROTHY GO TO THE CITY OF EMERALDS
whoa!

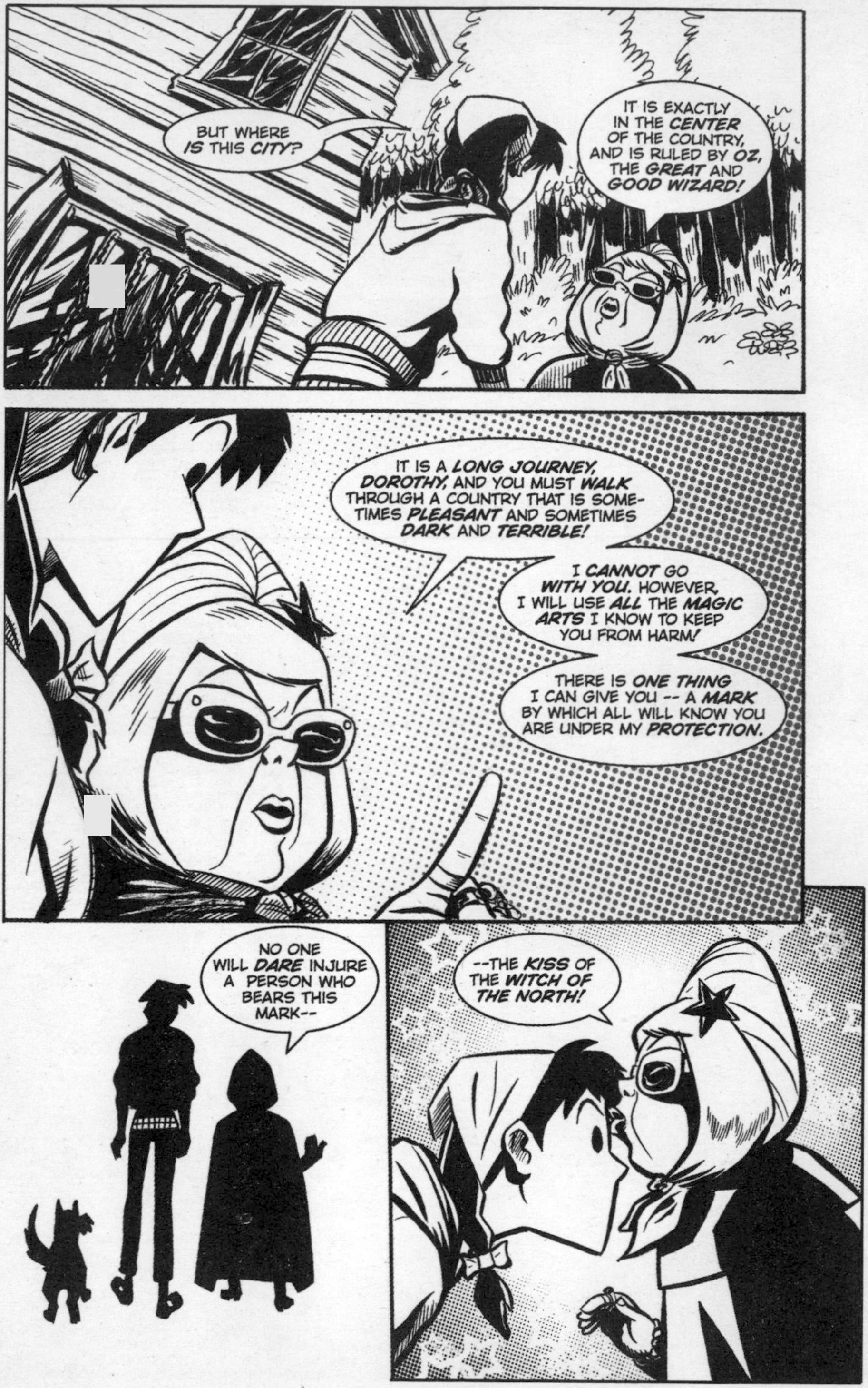
BUT WHERE IS THIS CITY?
IT IS EXACTLY IN THE CENTER OF THE COUNTRY, AND IS RULED BY OZ, THE GREAT AND GOOD WIZARD!
IT IS A LONG JOURNEY, DOROTHY, AND YOU MUST WALK THROUGH A COUNTRY THAT IS SOMETIMES PLEASANT AND SOMETIMES DARK AND TERRIBLE!
I CANNOT GO WITH YOU. HOWEVER, I WILL USE ALL THE MAGIC ARTS I KNOW TO KEEP YOU FROM HARM!
THERE IS ONE THING I CAN GIVE YOU -- A MARK BY WHICH ALL WILL KNOW YOU ARE UNDER MY PROTECTION.
NO ONE WILL DARE INJURE A PERSON WHO BEARS THIS MARK--
--THE KISS OF THE WITCH OF THE NORTH!

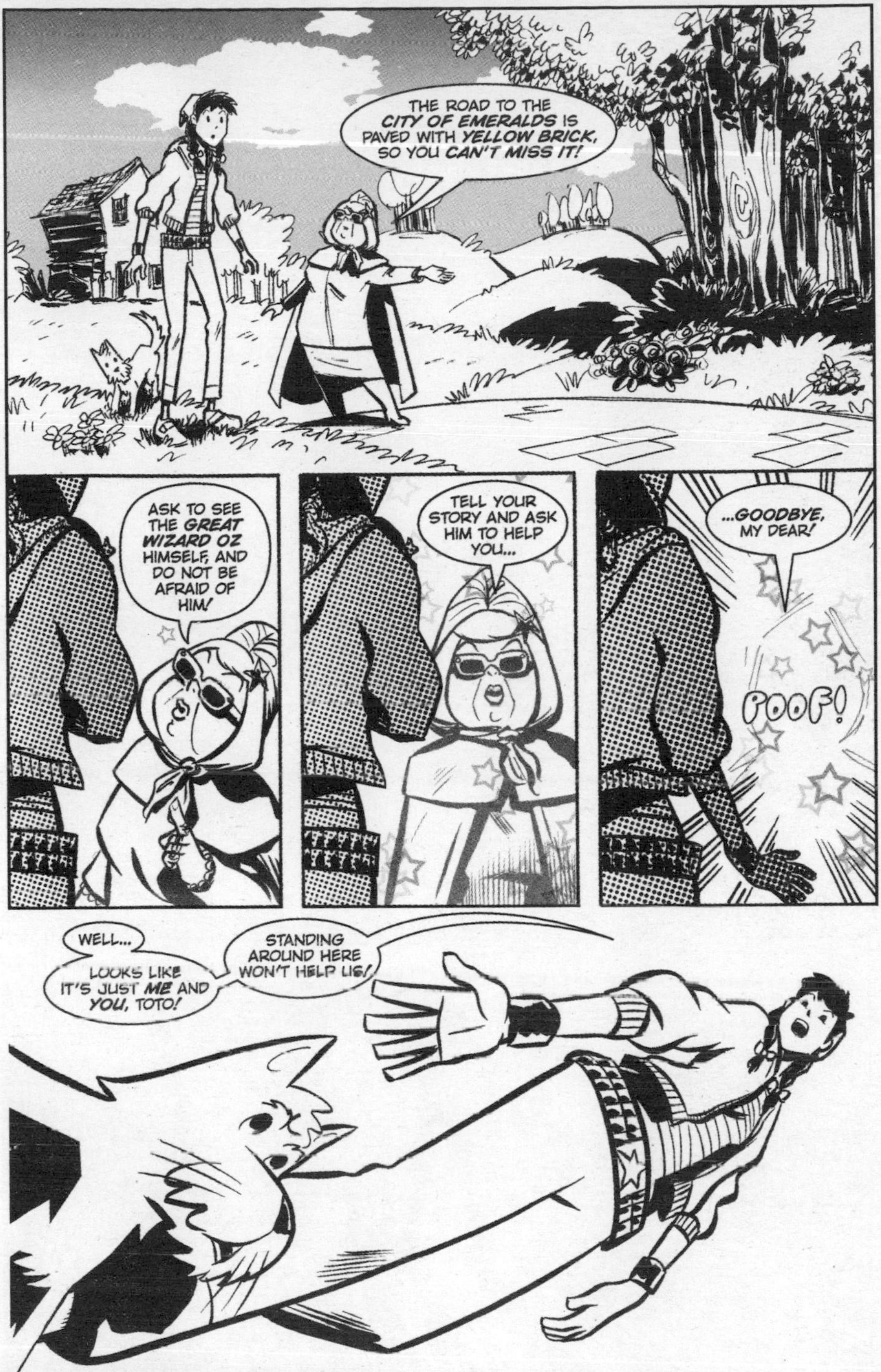
THE ROAD TO THE CITY OF EMERALDS IS PAVED WITH YELLOW BRICK, SO YOU CAN'T MISS IT!
ASK TO SEE THE GREAT WIZARD OZ HIMSELF, AND DO NOT BE AFRAID OF HIM!
TELL YOUR STORY AND ASK HIM TO HELP YOU...
...GOODBYE, MY DEAR!
POOF!
WELL...
LOOKS LIKE IT'S JUST ME AND YOU, TOTO!
STANDING AROUND HERE WON'T HELP US!

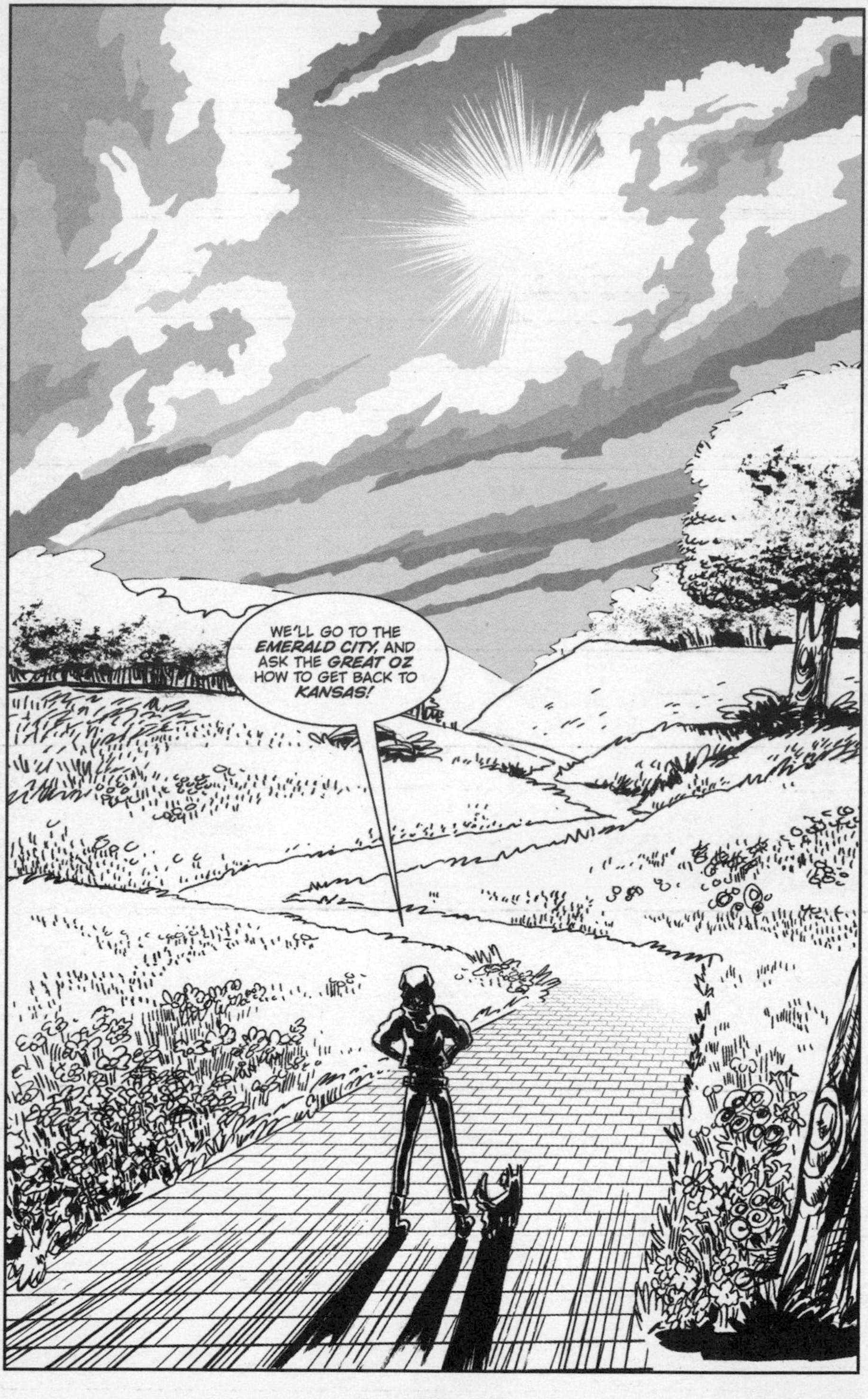
WE'LL GO TO THE EMERALD CITY, AND ASK THE GREAT OZ HOW TO GET BACK TO KANSAS!

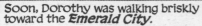

Soon, Dorothy was walking briskly toward the *Emerald City*.

Along the way people bowed to her, for she had been the means of destroying the Wicked Witch.

Dorothy was greeted kindly and invited to supper...

...and given a room to rest in.

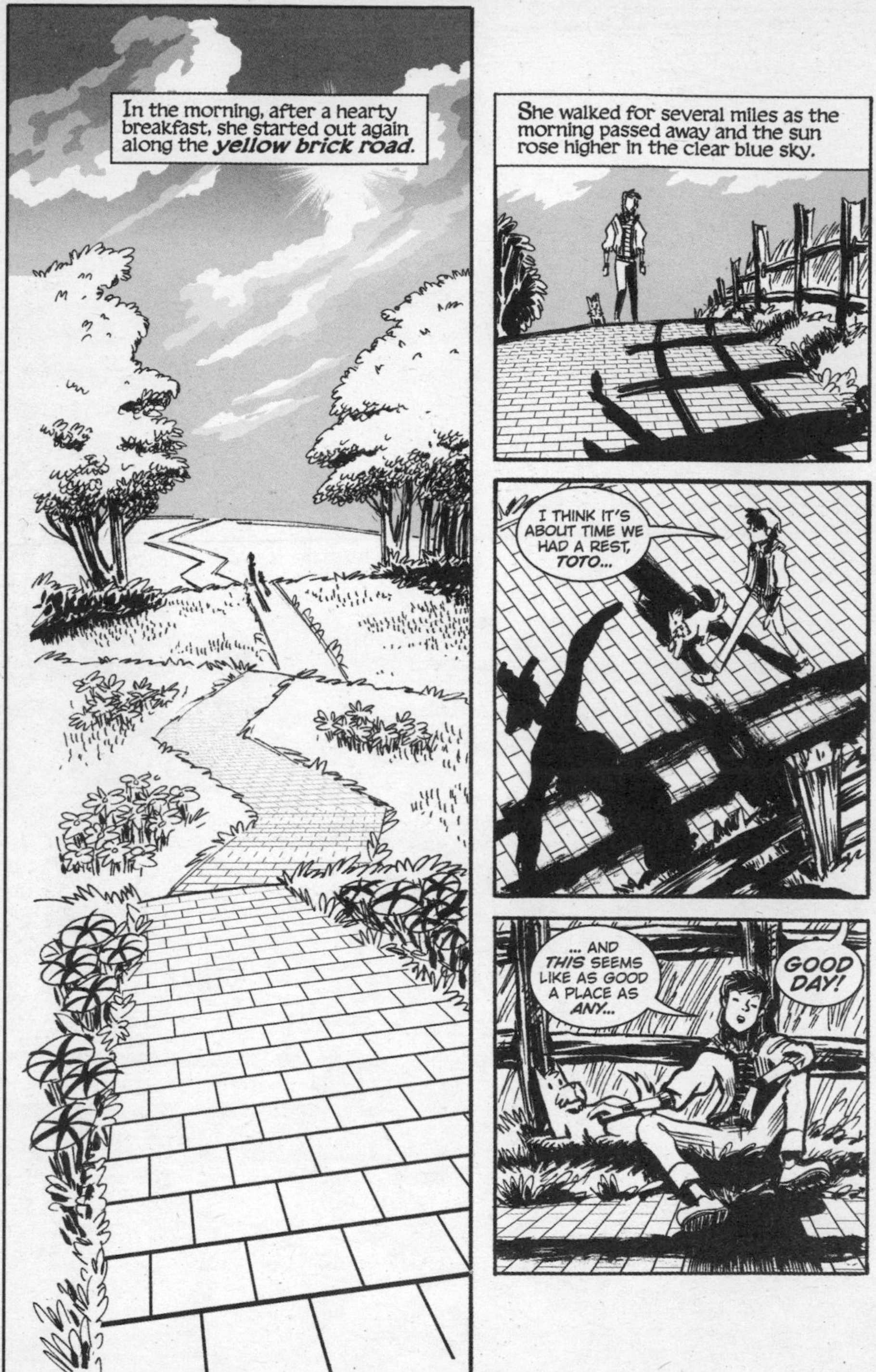
In the morning, after a hearty breakfast, she started out again along the *yellow brick road*.
She walked for several miles as the morning passed away and the sun rose higher in the clear blue sky.
I THINK IT'S ABOUT TIME WE HAD A REST, *TOTO*...
... AND *THIS* SEEMS LIKE AS GOOD A PLACE AS *ANY*...
GOOD DAY!

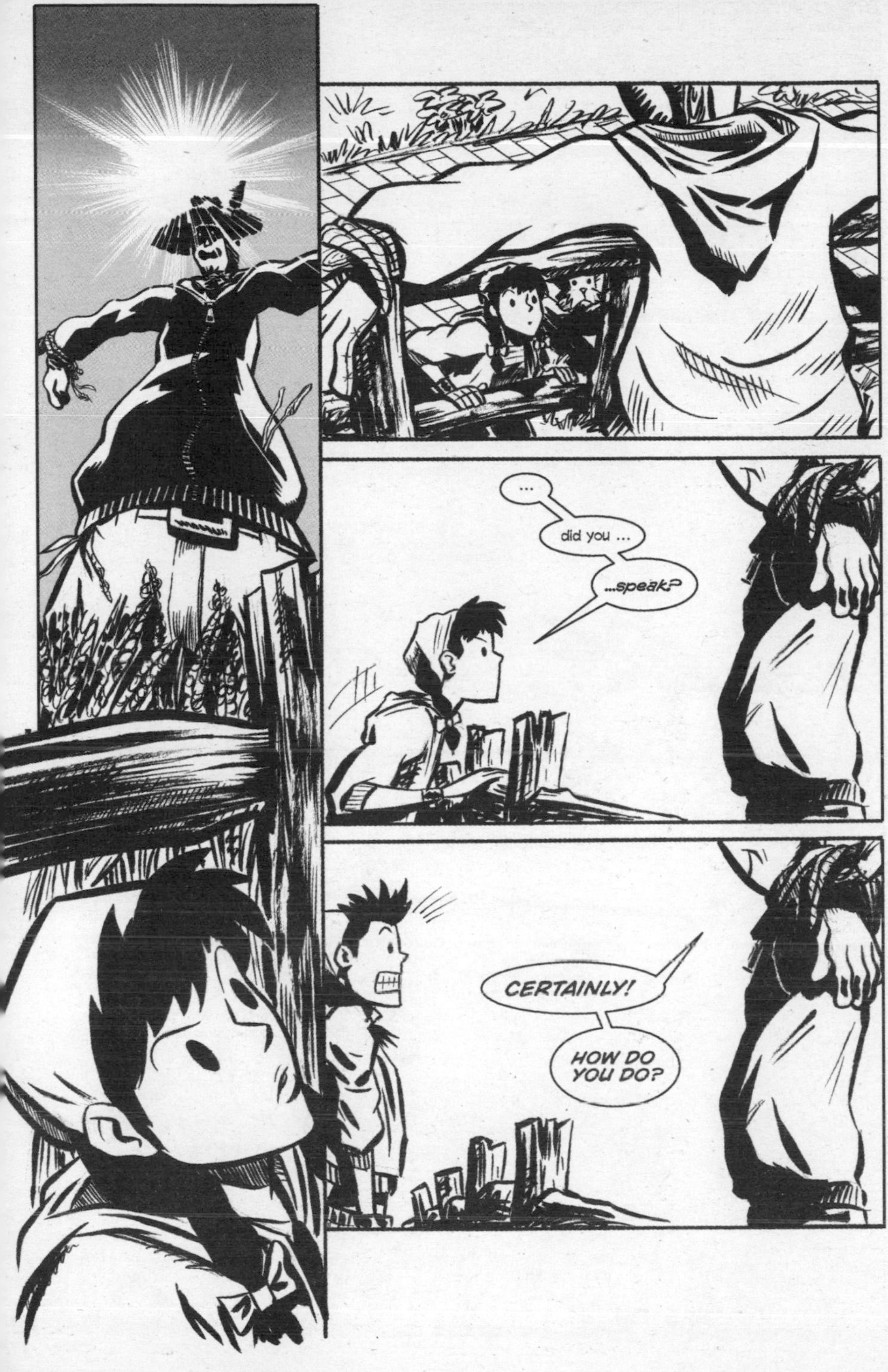
...
did you ...
...speak?
CERTAINLY!
HOW DO YOU DO?

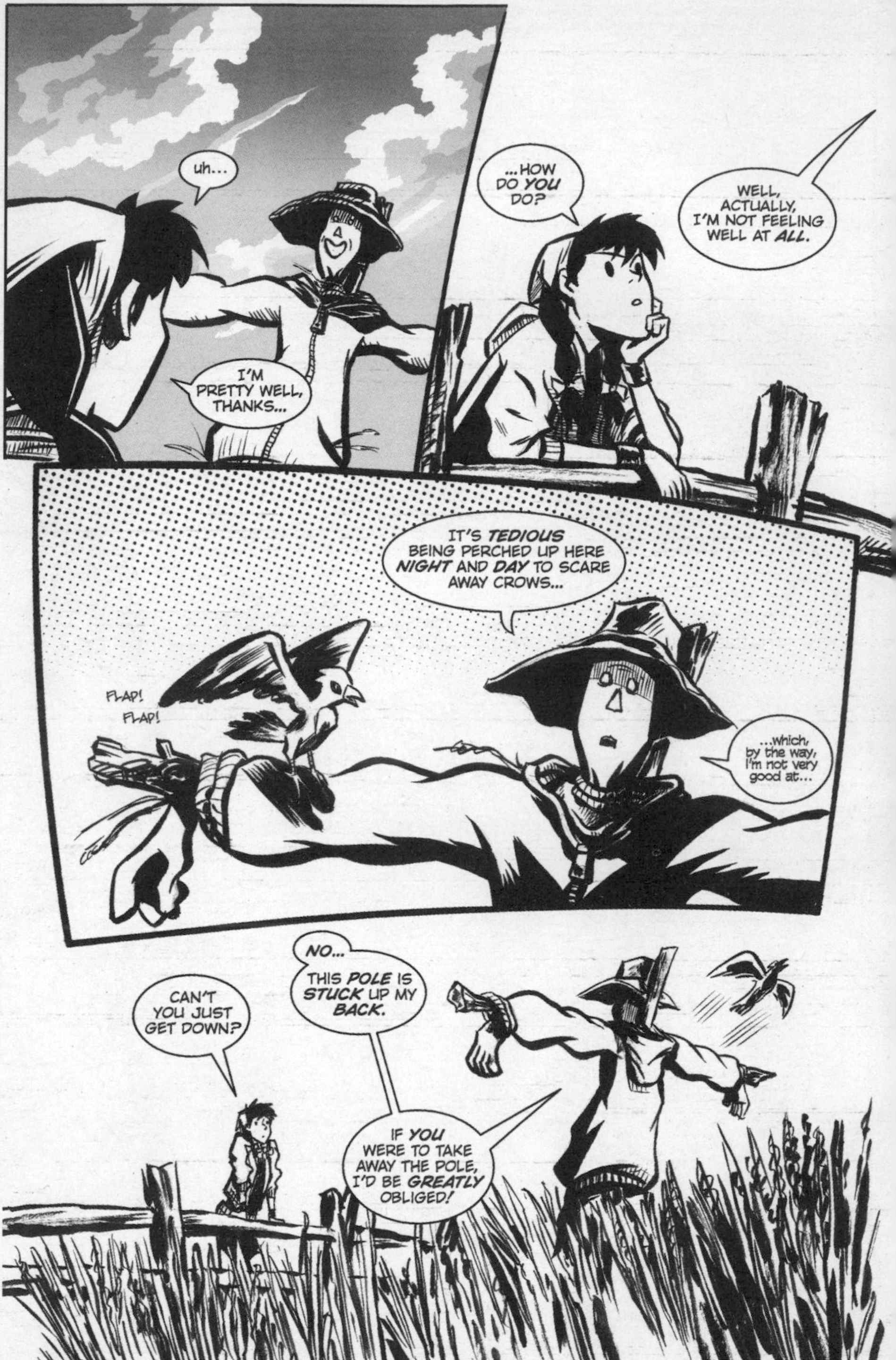
uh...
I'M PRETTY WELL, THANKS...
...HOW DO YOU DO?
WELL, ACTUALLY, I'M NOT FEELING WELL AT ALL.
IT'S TEDIOUS BEING PERCHED UP HERE NIGHT AND DAY TO SCARE AWAY CROWS...
FLAP!
FLAP!
...which, by the way, I'm not very good at...
CAN'T YOU JUST GET DOWN?
NO...
THIS POLE IS STUCK UP MY BACK.
IF YOU WERE TO TAKE AWAY THE POLE, I'D BE GREATLY OBLIGED!

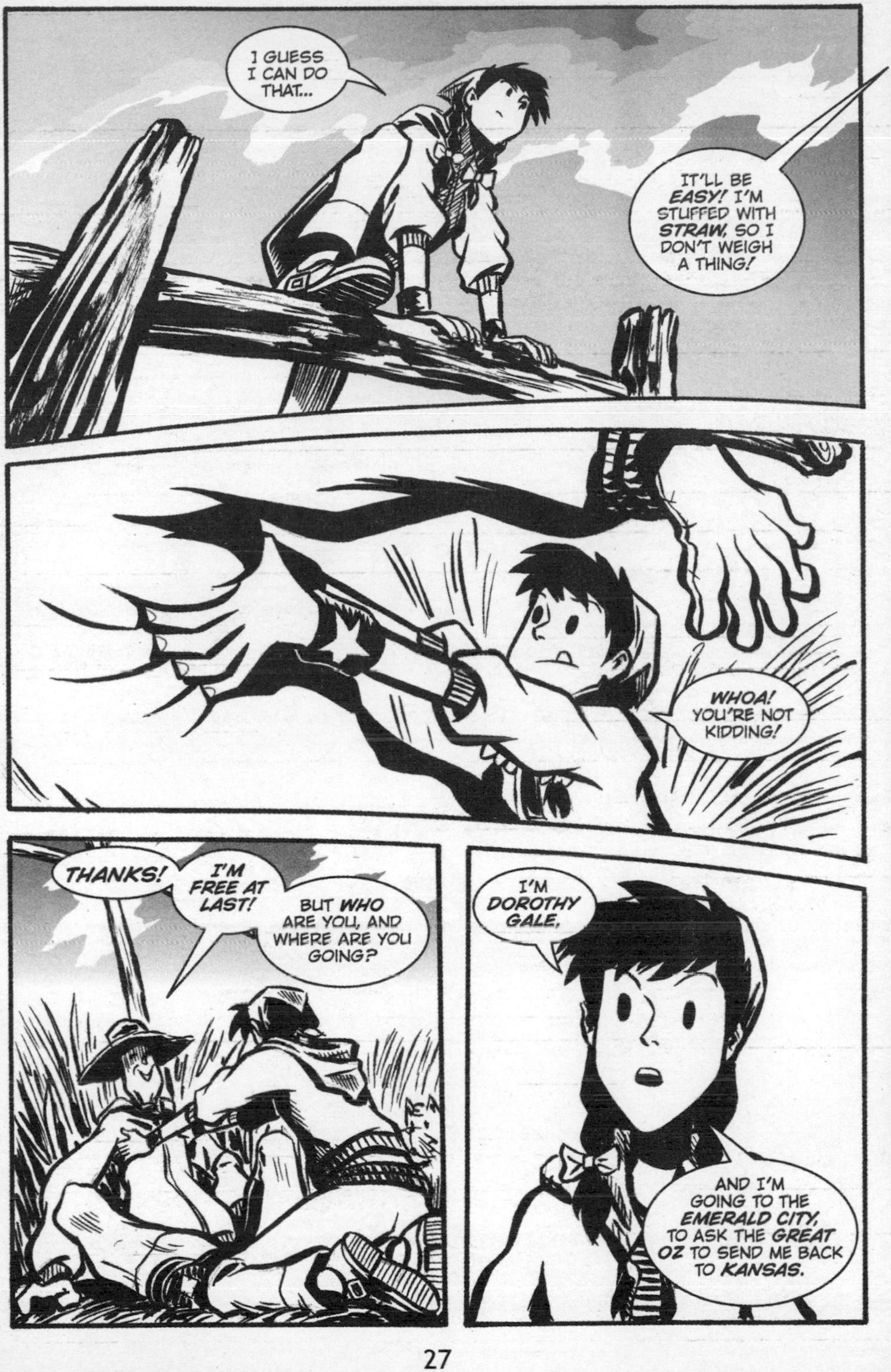
I GUESS I CAN DO THAT...
IT'LL BE EASY! I'M STUFFED WITH STRAW, SO I DON'T WEIGH A THING!
WHOA! YOU'RE NOT KIDDING!
THANKS!
I'M FREE AT LAST!
BUT WHO ARE YOU, AND WHERE ARE YOU GOING?
I'M DOROTHY GALE,
AND I'M GOING TO THE EMERALD CITY, TO ASK THE GREAT OZ TO SEND ME BACK TO KANSAS.

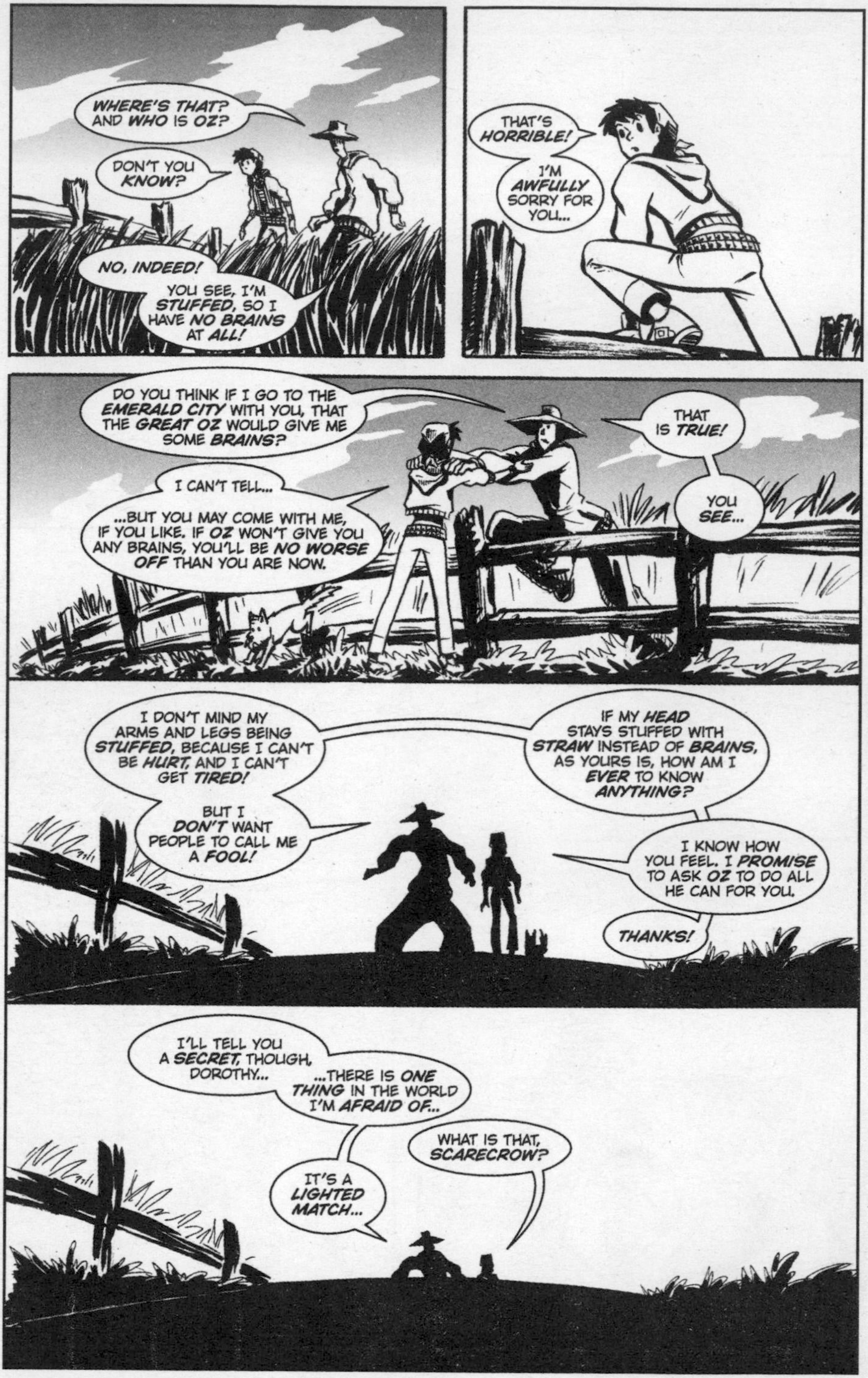

WHERE'S THAT? AND WHO IS OZ?
DON'T YOU KNOW?
NO, INDEED!
YOU SEE, I'M STUFFED, SO I HAVE NO BRAINS AT ALL!
THAT'S HORRIBLE!
I'M AWFULLY SORRY FOR YOU...
DO YOU THINK IF I GO TO THE EMERALD CITY WITH YOU, THAT THE GREAT OZ WOULD GIVE ME SOME BRAINS?
I CAN'T TELL...
...BUT YOU MAY COME WITH ME, IF YOU LIKE. IF OZ WON'T GIVE YOU ANY BRAINS, YOU'LL BE NO WORSE OFF THAN YOU ARE NOW.
THAT IS TRUE!
YOU SEE...
I DON'T MIND MY ARMS AND LEGS BEING STUFFED, BECAUSE I CAN'T BE HURT, AND I CAN'T GET TIRED!
BUT I DON'T WANT PEOPLE TO CALL ME A FOOL!
IF MY HEAD STAYS STUFFED WITH STRAW INSTEAD OF BRAINS, AS YOURS IS, HOW AM I EVER TO KNOW ANYTHING?
I KNOW HOW YOU FEEL. I PROMISE TO ASK OZ TO DO ALL HE CAN FOR YOU.
THANKS!
I'LL TELL YOU A SECRET, THOUGH, DOROTHY...
...THERE IS ONE THING IN THE WORLD I'M AFRAID OF...
WHAT IS THAT, SCARECROW?
IT'S A LIGHTED MATCH...

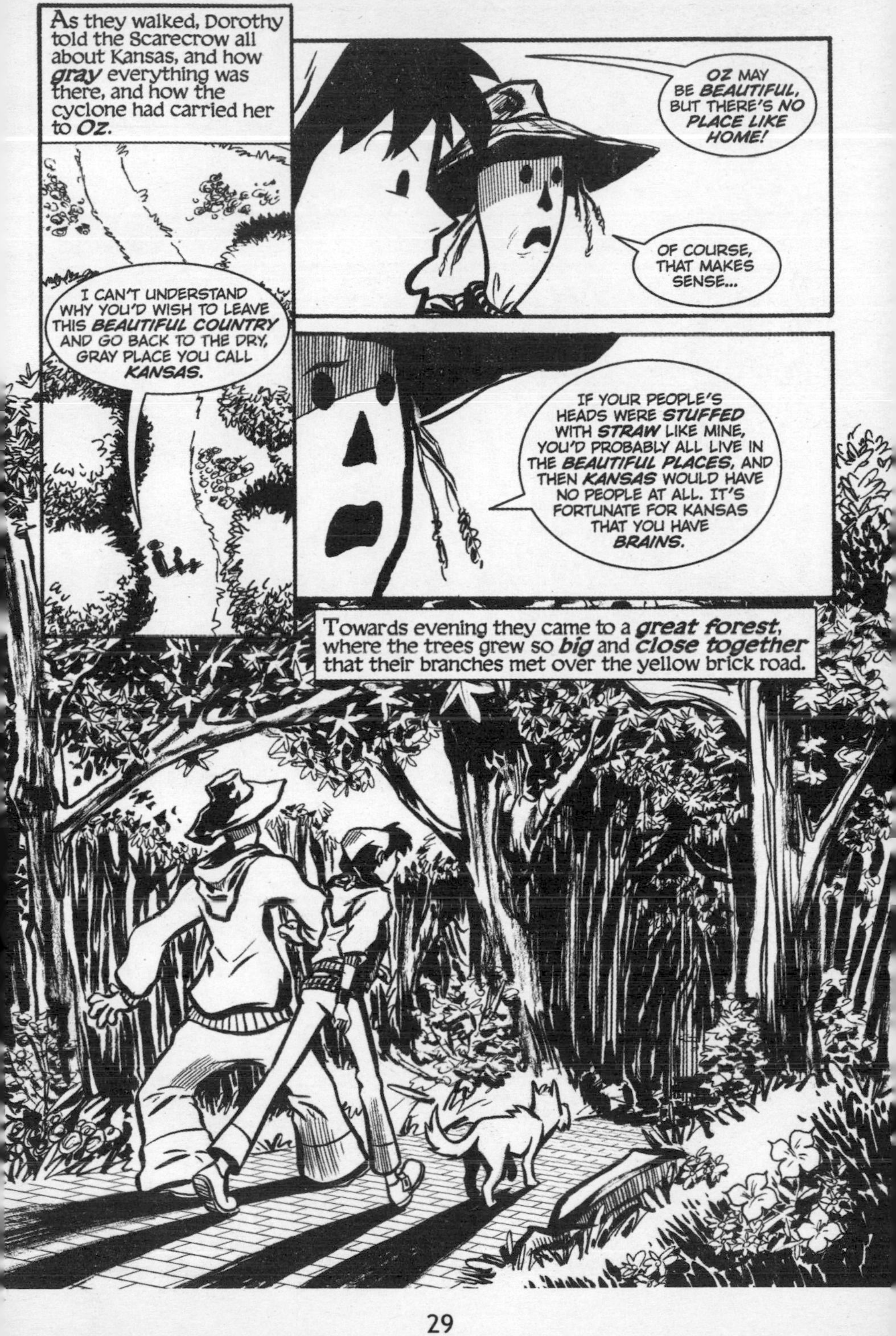
As they walked, Dorothy told the Scarecrow all about Kansas, and how *gray* everything was there, and how the cyclone had carried her to *Oz*.
OZ MAY BE BEAUTIFUL, BUT THERE'S NO PLACE LIKE HOME!
OF COURSE, THAT MAKES SENSE...
I CAN'T UNDERSTAND WHY YOU'D WISH TO LEAVE THIS BEAUTIFUL COUNTRY AND GO BACK TO THE DRY, GRAY PLACE YOU CALL KANSAS.
IF YOUR PEOPLE'S HEADS WERE STUFFED WITH STRAW LIKE MINE, YOU'D PROBABLY ALL LIVE IN THE BEAUTIFUL PLACES, AND THEN KANSAS WOULD HAVE NO PEOPLE AT ALL. IT'S FORTUNATE FOR KANSAS THAT YOU HAVE BRAINS.
Towards evening they came to a *great forest*, where the trees grew so *big* and *close together* that their branches met over the yellow brick road.

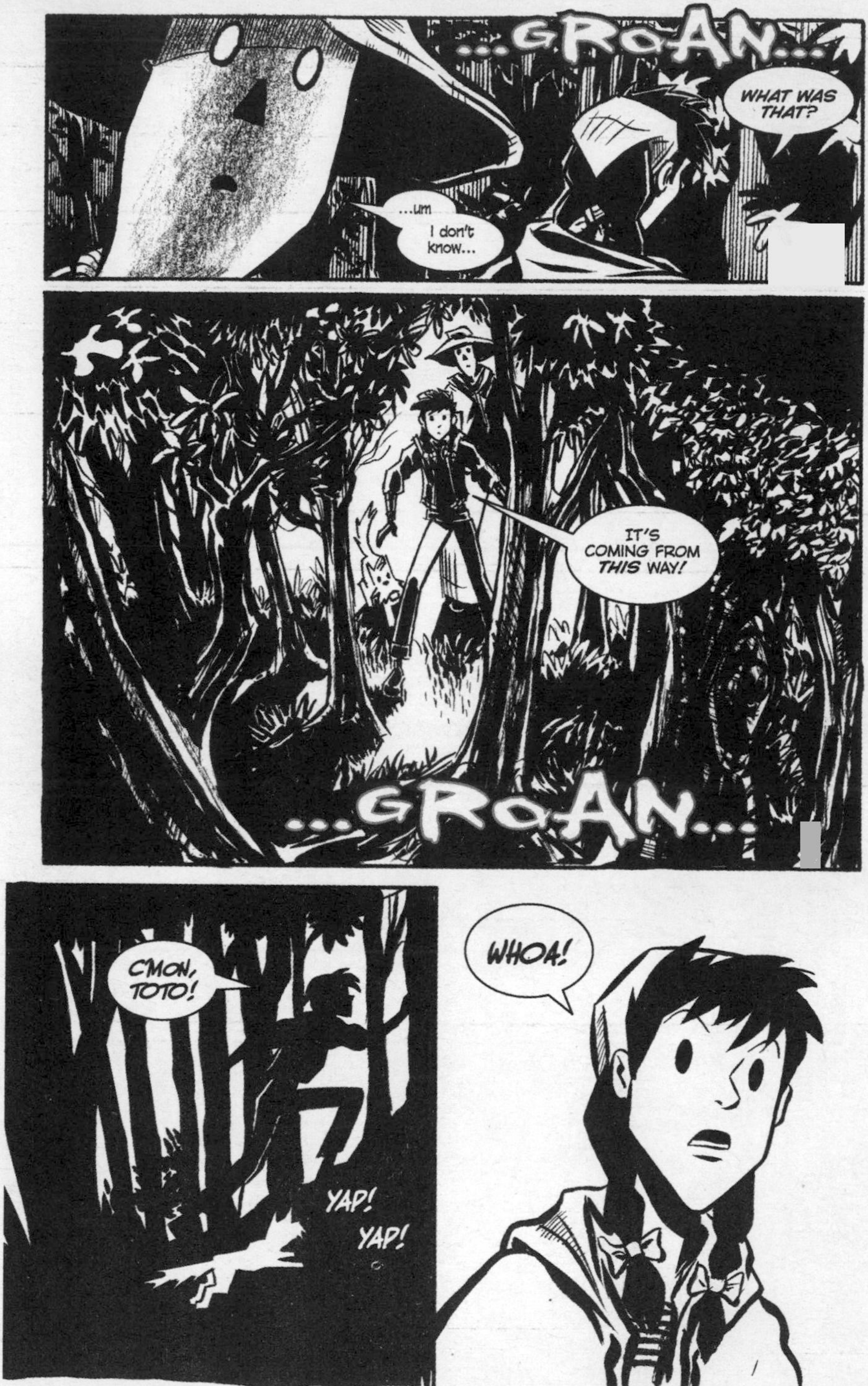
...GROAN...
WHAT WAS THAT?
...um
I don't know...
IT'S COMING FROM THIS WAY!
...GROAN...
C'MON, TOTO!
YAP!
YAP!
WHOA!

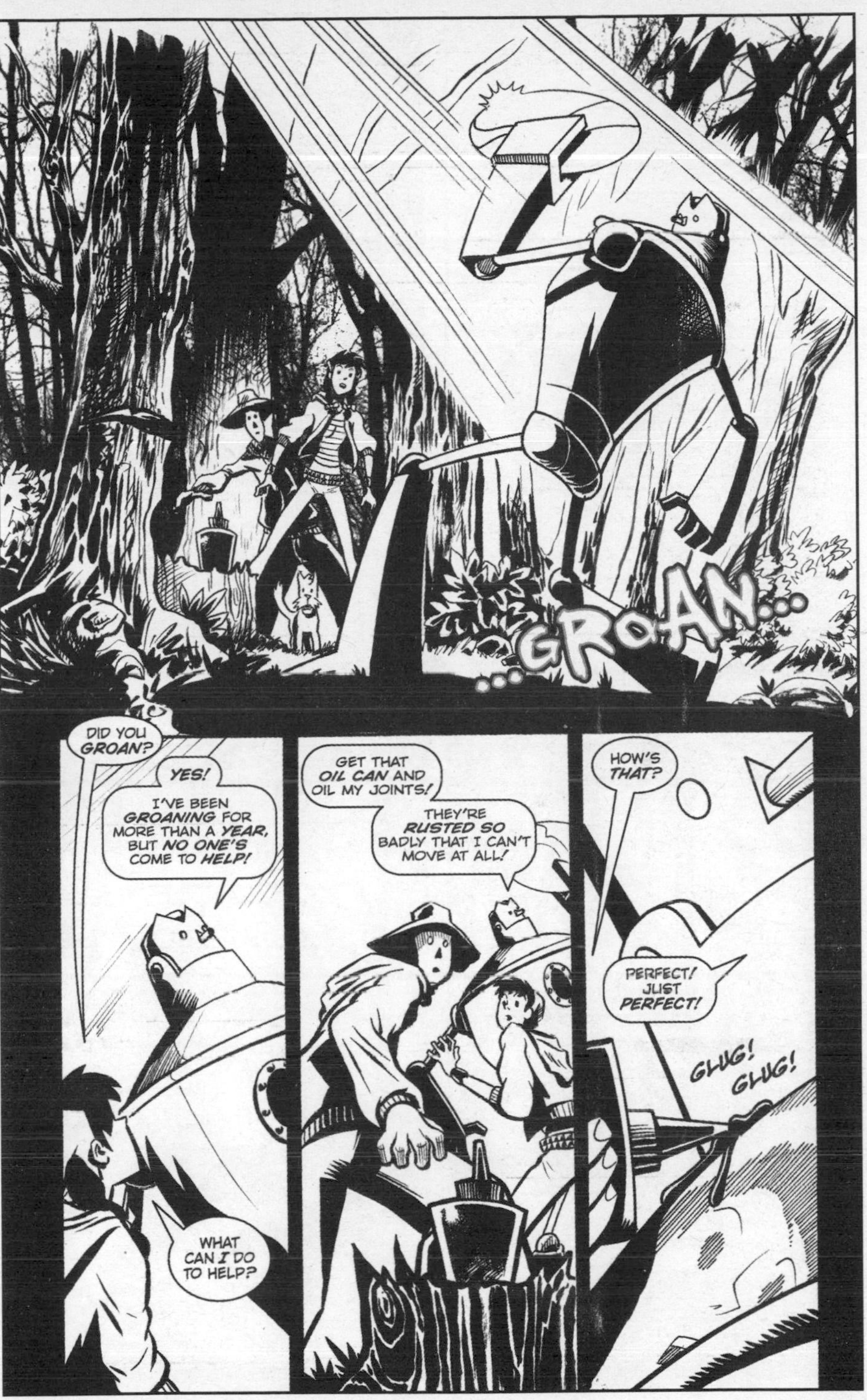
...GROAN...
DID YOU GROAN?
YES!
I'VE BEEN GROANING FOR MORE THAN A YEAR, BUT NO ONE'S COME TO HELP!
WHAT CAN I DO TO HELP?
GET THAT OIL CAN AND OIL MY JOINTS!
THEY'RE RUSTED SO BADLY THAT I CAN'T MOVE AT ALL!
HOW'S THAT?
PERFECT! JUST PERFECT!
GLUG! GLUG!

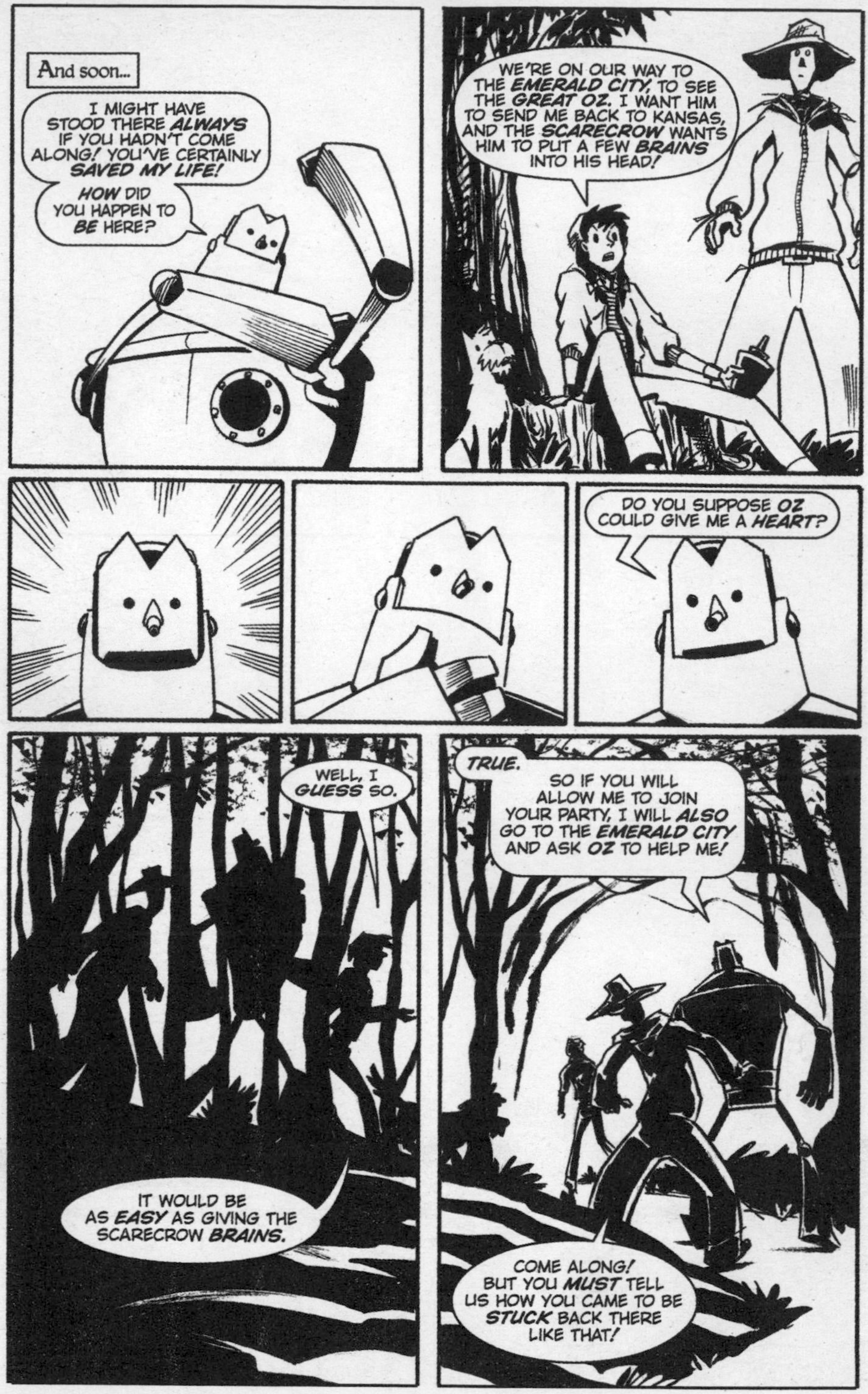
And soon...
I MIGHT HAVE STOOD THERE ALWAYS IF YOU HADN'T COME ALONG! YOU'VE CERTAINLY SAVED MY LIFE!
HOW DID YOU HAPPEN TO BE HERE?
WE'RE ON OUR WAY TO THE EMERALD CITY, TO SEE THE GREAT OZ. I WANT HIM TO SEND ME BACK TO KANSAS, AND THE SCARECROW WANTS HIM TO PUT A FEW BRAINS INTO HIS HEAD!
DO YOU SUPPOSE OZ COULD GIVE ME A HEART?
WELL, I GUESS SO.
IT WOULD BE AS EASY AS GIVING THE SCARECROW BRAINS.
TRUE.
SO IF YOU WILL ALLOW ME TO JOIN YOUR PARTY, I WILL ALSO GO TO THE EMERALD CITY AND ASK OZ TO HELP ME!
COME ALONG! BUT YOU MUST TELL US HOW YOU CAME TO BE STUCK BACK THERE LIKE THAT!

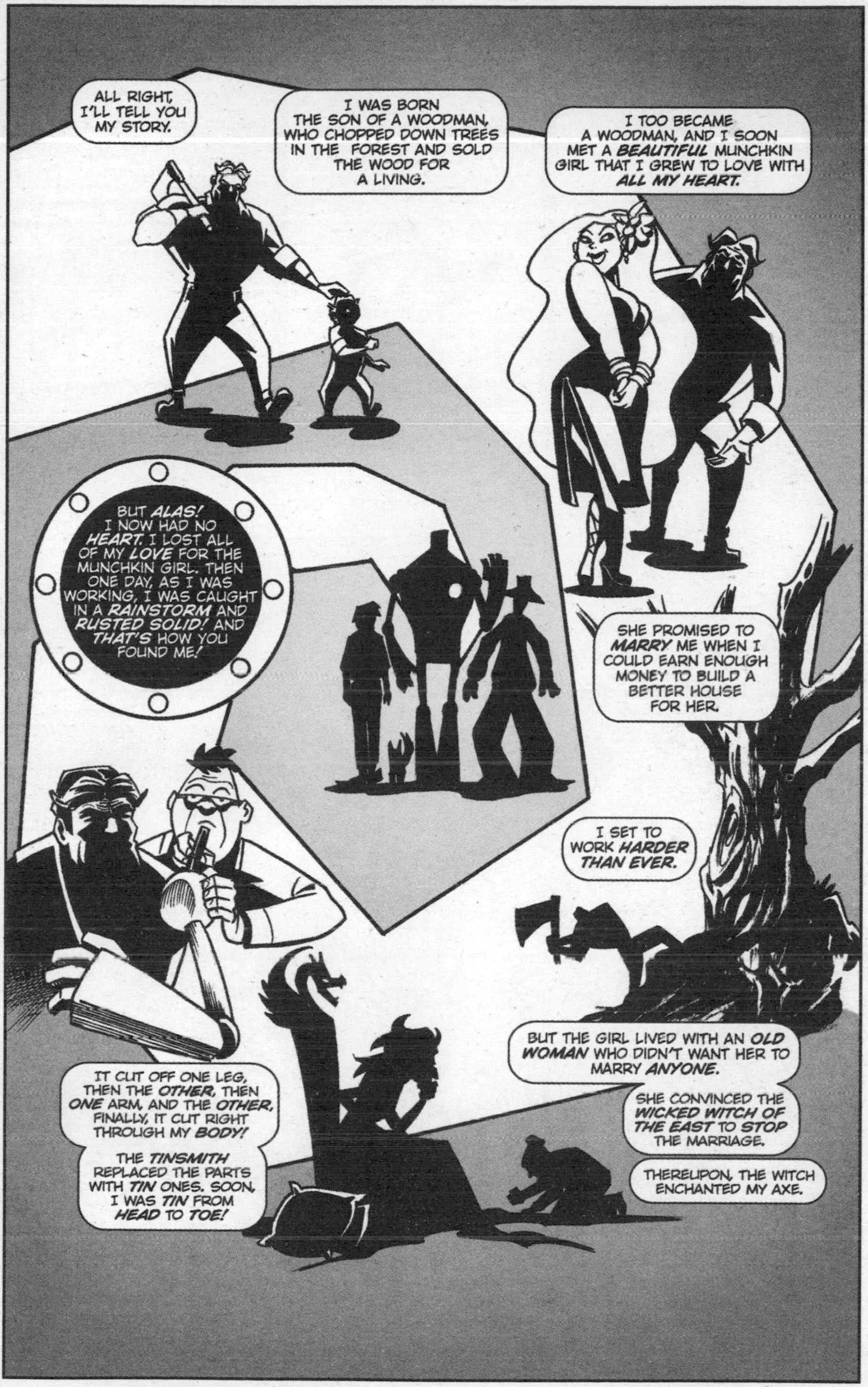

ALL RIGHT, I'LL TELL YOU MY STORY.
I WAS BORN THE SON OF A WOODMAN, WHO CHOPPED DOWN TREES IN THE FOREST AND SOLD THE WOOD FOR A LIVING.
I TOO BECAME A WOODMAN, AND I SOON MET A BEAUTIFUL MUNCHKIN GIRL THAT I GREW TO LOVE WITH ALL MY HEART.
SHE PROMISED TO MARRY ME WHEN I COULD EARN ENOUGH MONEY TO BUILD A BETTER HOUSE FOR HER.
I SET TO WORK HARDER THAN EVER.
BUT THE GIRL LIVED WITH AN OLD WOMAN WHO DIDN'T WANT HER TO MARRY ANYONE.
SHE CONVINCED THE WICKED WITCH OF THE EAST TO STOP THE MARRIAGE.
THEREUPON, THE WITCH ENCHANTED MY AXE.
IT CUT OFF ONE LEG, THEN THE OTHER, THEN ONE ARM, AND THE OTHER. FINALLY, IT CUT RIGHT THROUGH MY BODY!
THE TINSMITH REPLACED THE PARTS WITH TIN ONES. SOON, I WAS TIN FROM HEAD TO TOE!
BUT ALAS! I NOW HAD NO HEART. I LOST ALL OF MY LOVE FOR THE MUNCHKIN GIRL. THEN ONE DAY, AS I WAS WORKING, I WAS CAUGHT IN A RAINSTORM AND RUSTED SOLID! AND THAT'S HOW YOU FOUND ME!

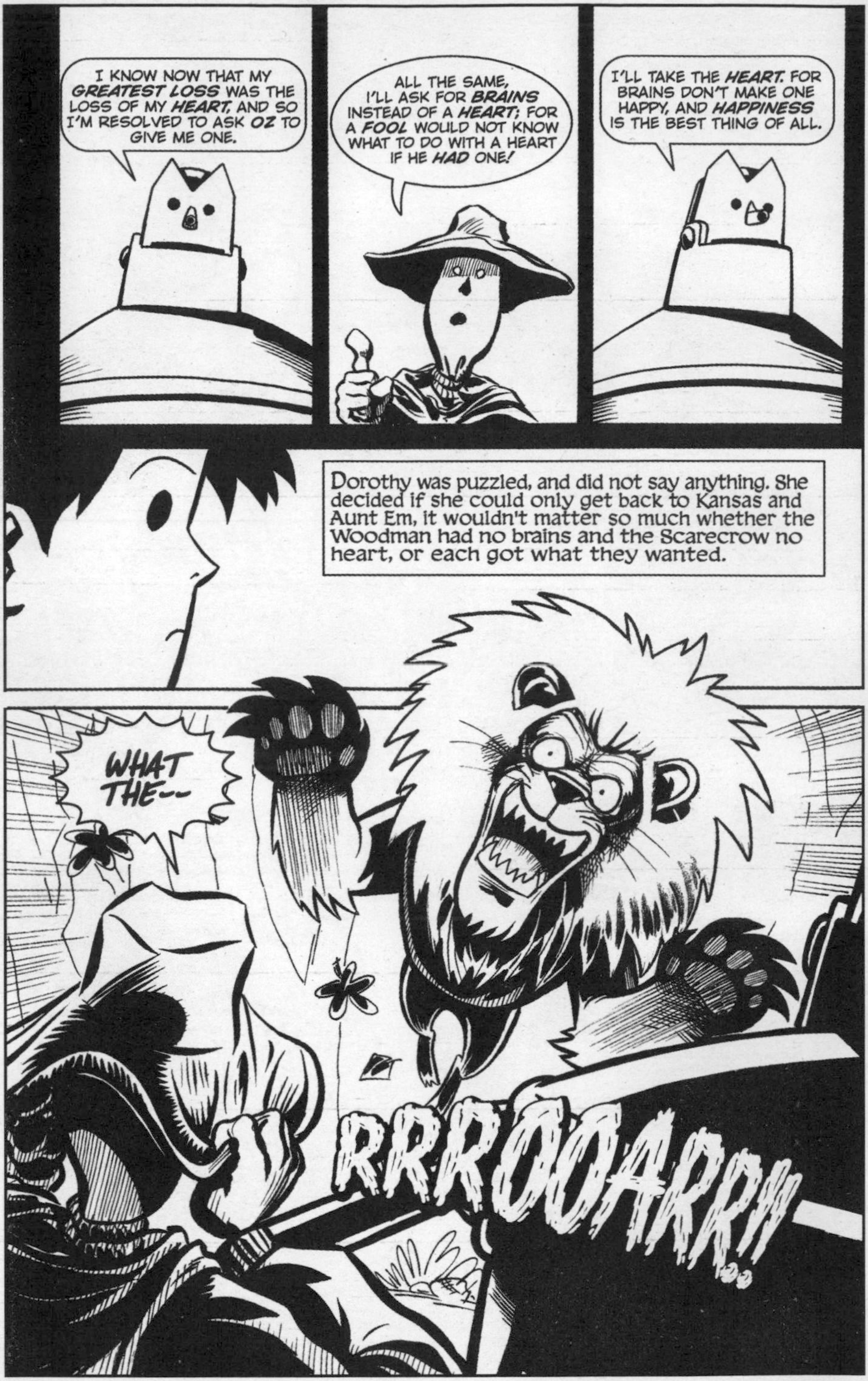
I KNOW NOW THAT MY GREATEST LOSS WAS THE LOSS OF MY HEART, AND SO I'M RESOLVED TO ASK OZ TO GIVE ME ONE.
ALL THE SAME, I'LL ASK FOR BRAINS INSTEAD OF A HEART; FOR A FOOL WOULD NOT KNOW WHAT TO DO WITH A HEART IF HE HAD ONE!
I'LL TAKE THE HEART. FOR BRAINS DON'T MAKE ONE HAPPY, AND HAPPINESS IS THE BEST THING OF ALL.
Dorothy was puzzled, and did not say anything. She decided if she could only get back to Kansas and Aunt Em, it wouldn't matter so much whether the Woodman had no brains and the Scarecrow no heart, or each got what they wanted.
WHAT THE--
RRROOARR!!

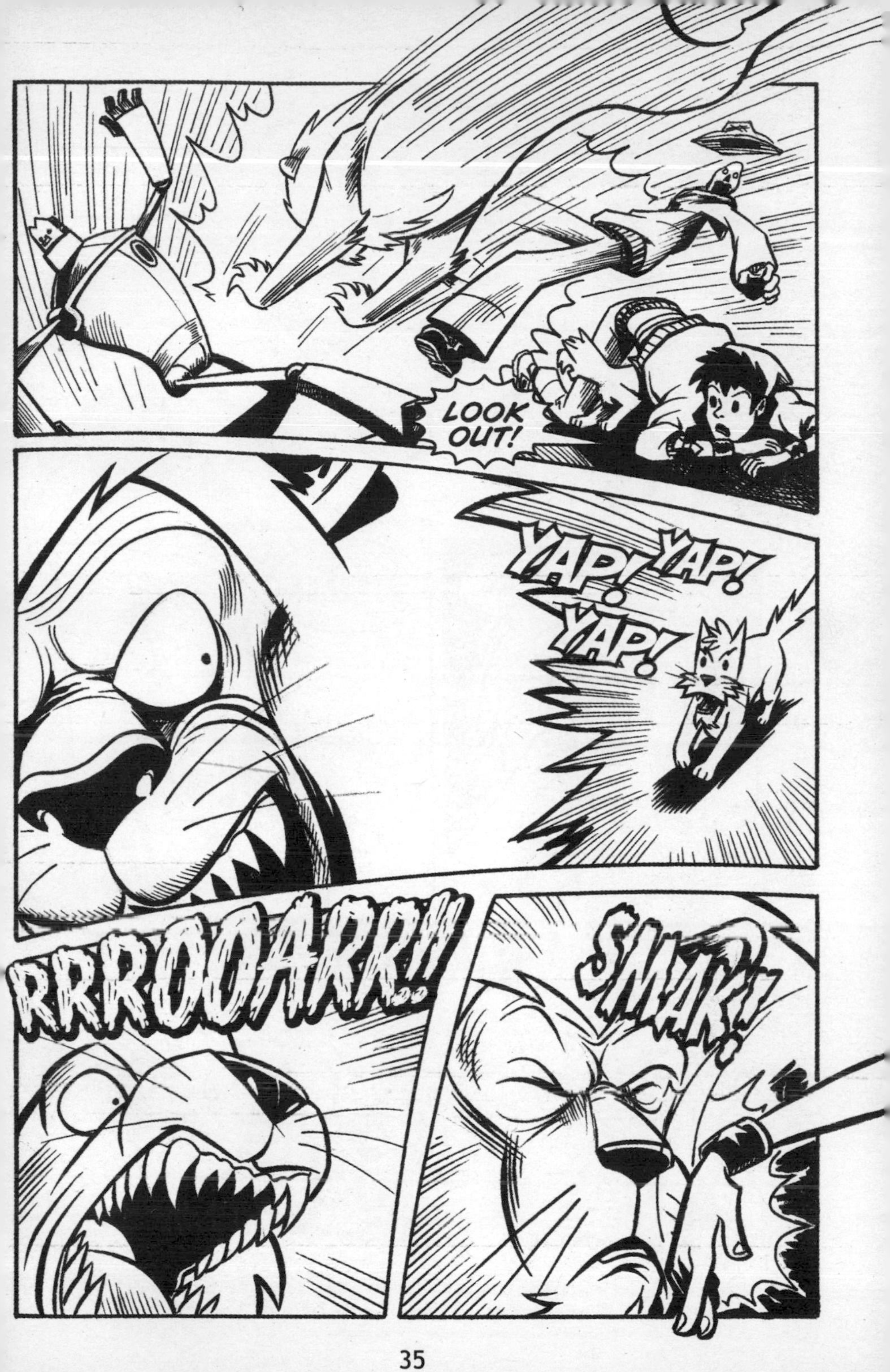
LOOK OUT!
YAP! YAP!
YAP!
RRROOARR!!
SMAK!!

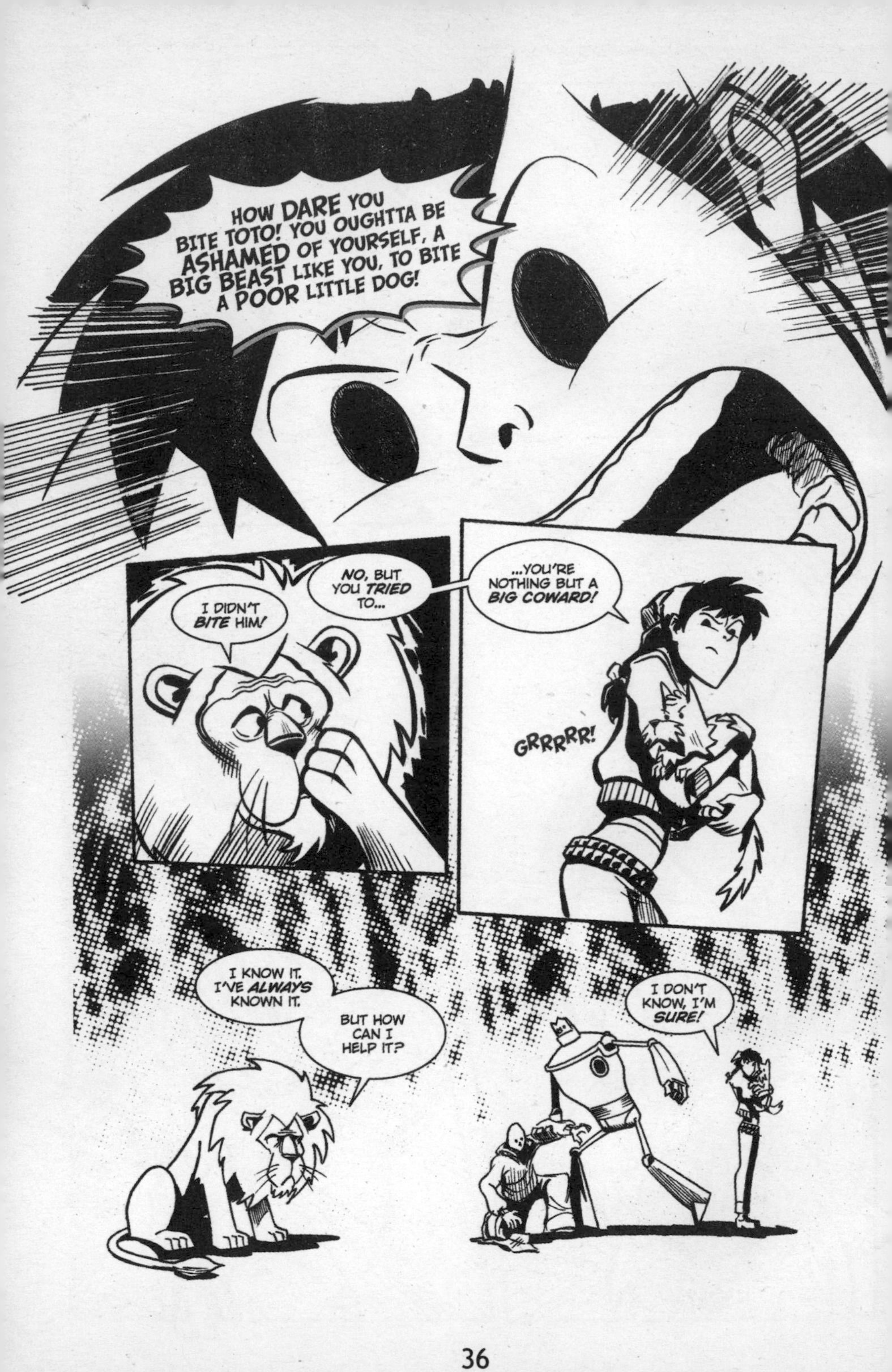
HOW DARE YOU BITE TOTO! YOU OUGHTTA BE ASHAMED OF YOURSELF, A BIG BEAST LIKE YOU, TO BITE A POOR LITTLE DOG!
I DIDN'T BITE HIM!
NO, BUT YOU TRIED TO...
...YOU'RE NOTHING BUT A BIG COWARD!
GRRRRR!
I KNOW IT. I'VE ALWAYS KNOWN IT.
BUT HOW CAN I HELP IT?
I DON'T KNOW, I'M SURE!

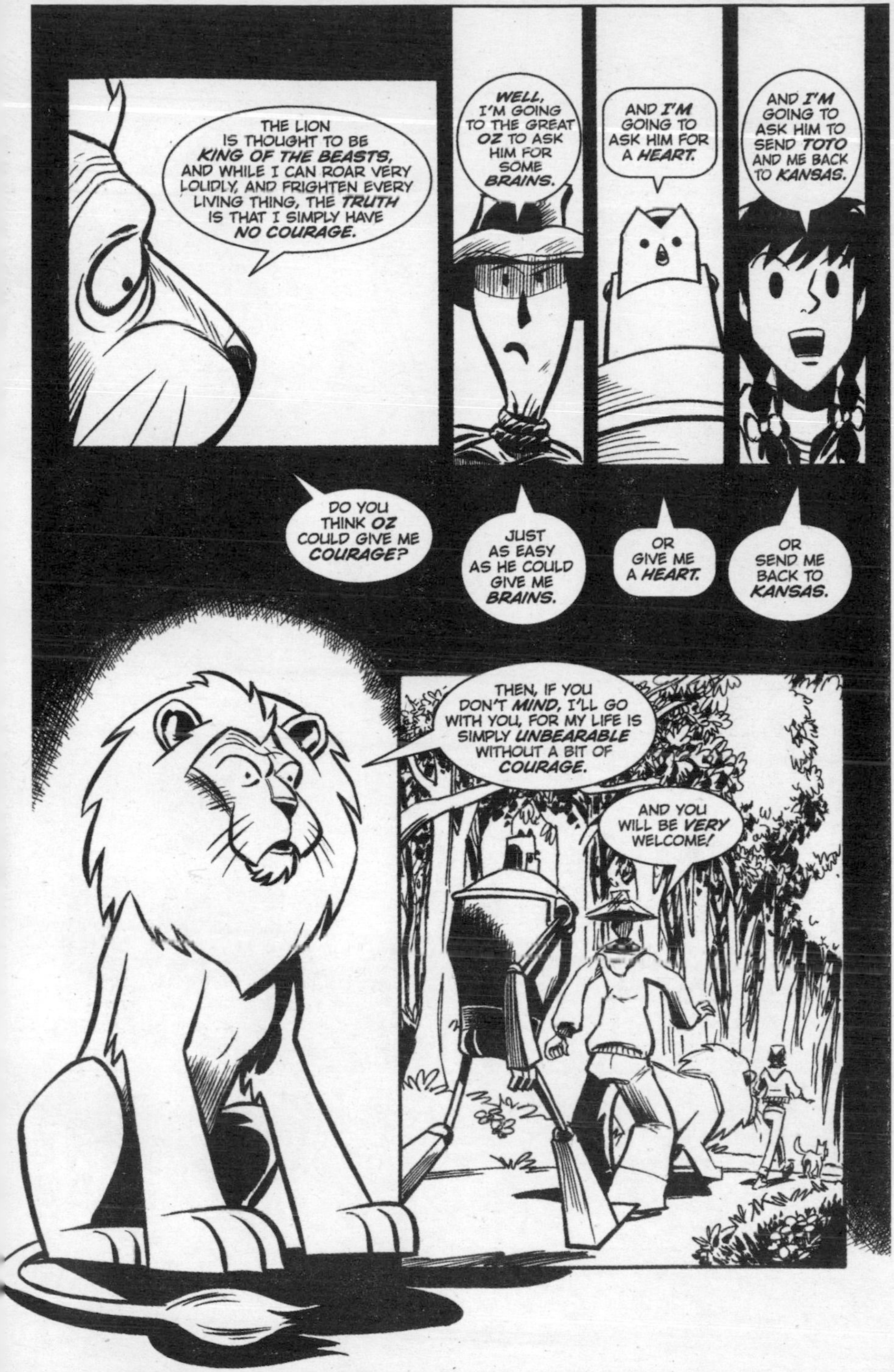
THE LION IS THOUGHT TO BE KING OF THE BEASTS, AND WHILE I CAN ROAR VERY LOUDLY, AND FRIGHTEN EVERY LIVING THING, THE TRUTH IS THAT I SIMPLY HAVE NO COURAGE.
WELL, I'M GOING TO THE GREAT OZ TO ASK HIM FOR SOME BRAINS.
AND I'M GOING TO ASK HIM FOR A HEART.
AND I'M GOING TO ASK HIM TO SEND TOTO AND ME BACK TO KANSAS.
DO YOU THINK OZ COULD GIVE ME COURAGE?
JUST AS EASY AS HE COULD GIVE ME BRAINS.
OR GIVE ME A HEART.
OR SEND ME BACK TO KANSAS.
THEN, IF YOU DON'T MIND, I'LL GO WITH YOU, FOR MY LIFE IS SIMPLY UNBEARABLE WITHOUT A BIT OF COURAGE.
AND YOU WILL BE VERY WELCOME!

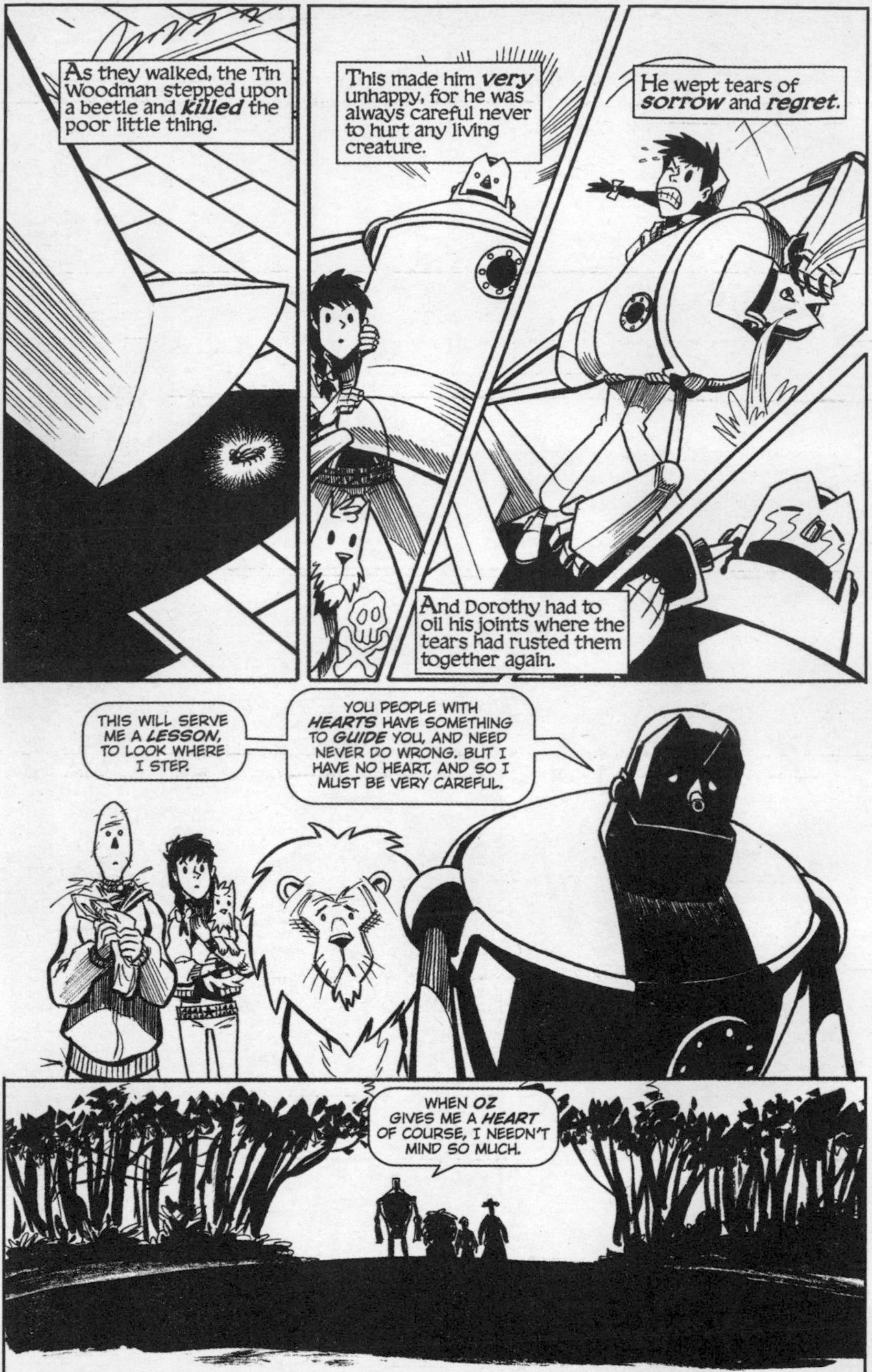
As they walked, the Tin Woodman stepped upon a beetle and killed the poor little thing.
This made him very unhappy, for he was always careful never to hurt any living creature.
He wept tears of sorrow and regret.
And Dorothy had to oil his joints where the tears had rusted them together again.
THIS WILL SERVE ME A LESSON, TO LOOK WHERE I STEP.
YOU PEOPLE WITH HEARTS HAVE SOMETHING TO GUIDE YOU, AND NEED NEVER DO WRONG. BUT I HAVE NO HEART, AND SO I MUST BE VERY CAREFUL.
WHEN OZ GIVES ME A HEART OF COURSE, I NEEDN'T MIND SO MUCH.

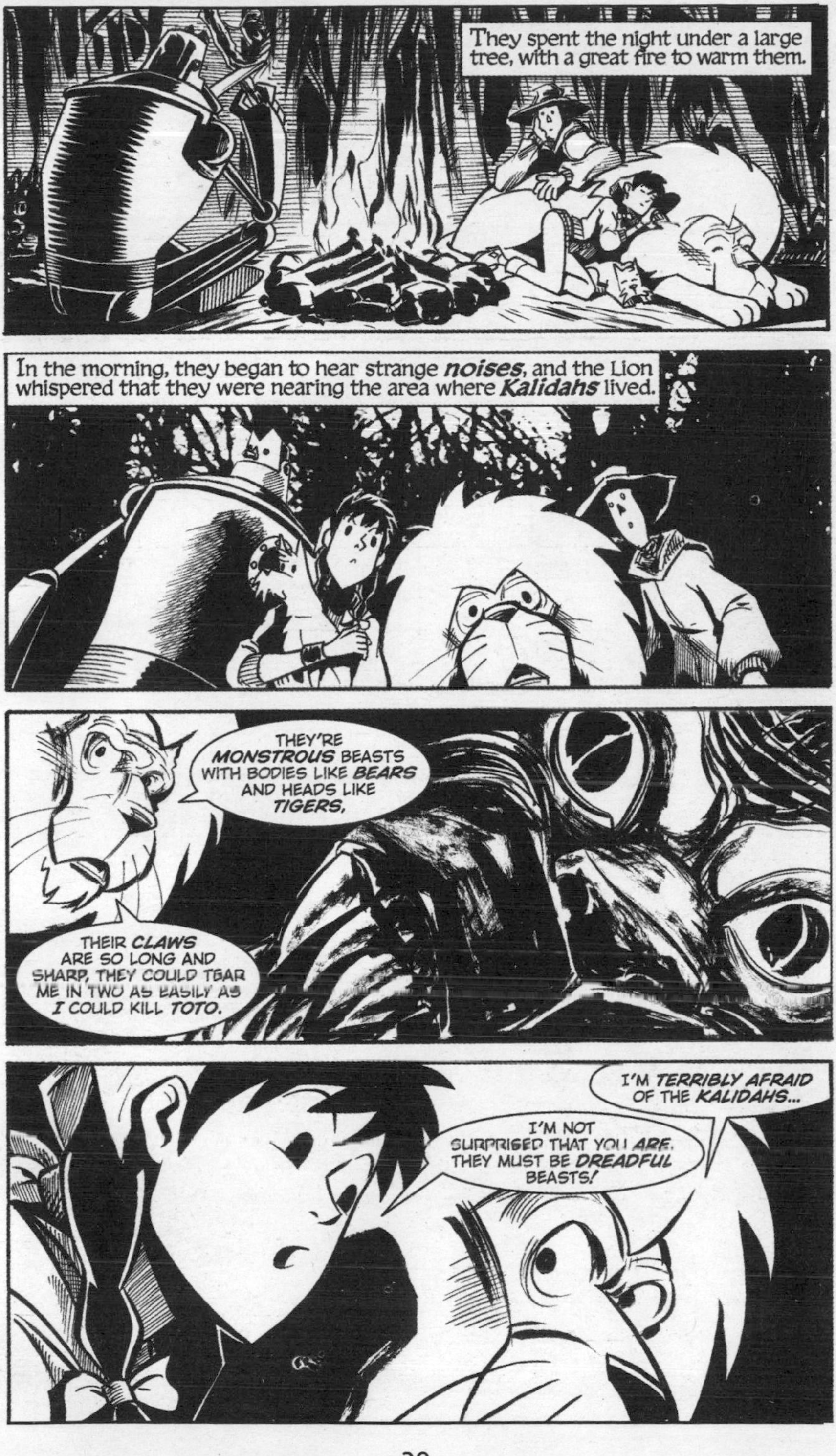
They spent the night under a large tree, with a great fire to warm them.
In the morning, they began to hear strange *noises*, and the Lion whispered that they were nearing the area where *Kalidahs* lived.
THEY'RE *MONSTROUS* BEASTS WITH BODIES LIKE *BEARS* AND HEADS LIKE *TIGERS*,
THEIR *CLAWS* ARE SO LONG AND SHARP, THEY COULD TEAR ME IN TWO AS EASILY AS *I* COULD KILL *TOTO*.
I'M *TERRIBLY AFRAID* OF THE *KALIDAHS*...
I'M NOT SURPRISED THAT YOU *ARE*. THEY MUST BE *DREADFUL* BEASTS!

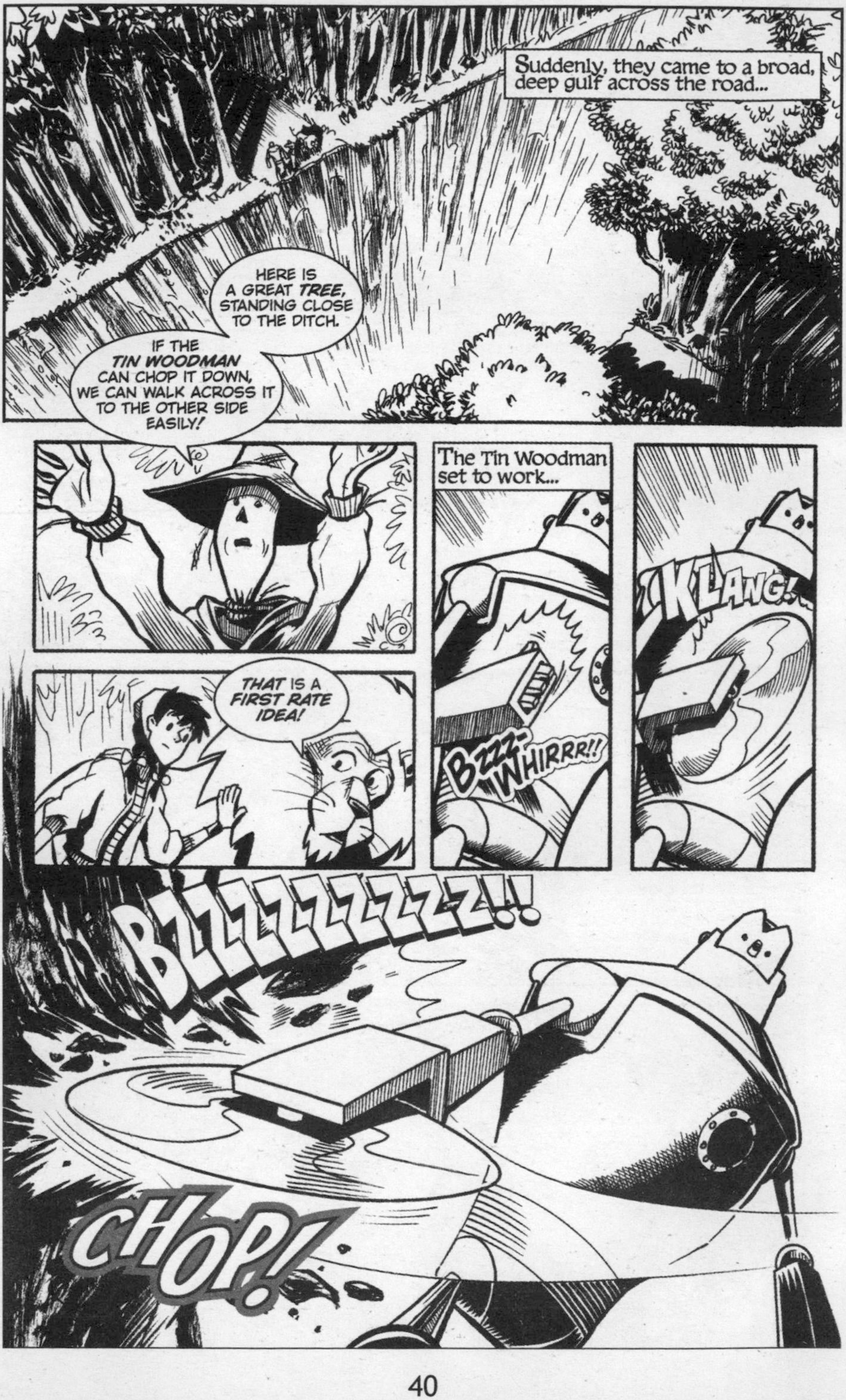
Suddenly, they came to a broad, deep gulf across the road...
HERE IS A GREAT TREE, STANDING CLOSE TO THE DITCH.
IF THE TIN WOODMAN CAN CHOP IT DOWN, WE CAN WALK ACROSS IT TO THE OTHER SIDE EASILY!
THAT IS A FIRST RATE IDEA!
The Tin Woodman set to work...
BZZZ-WHIRRR!!
KLANG!
BZZZZZZZZZZZZ!!
CHOP!

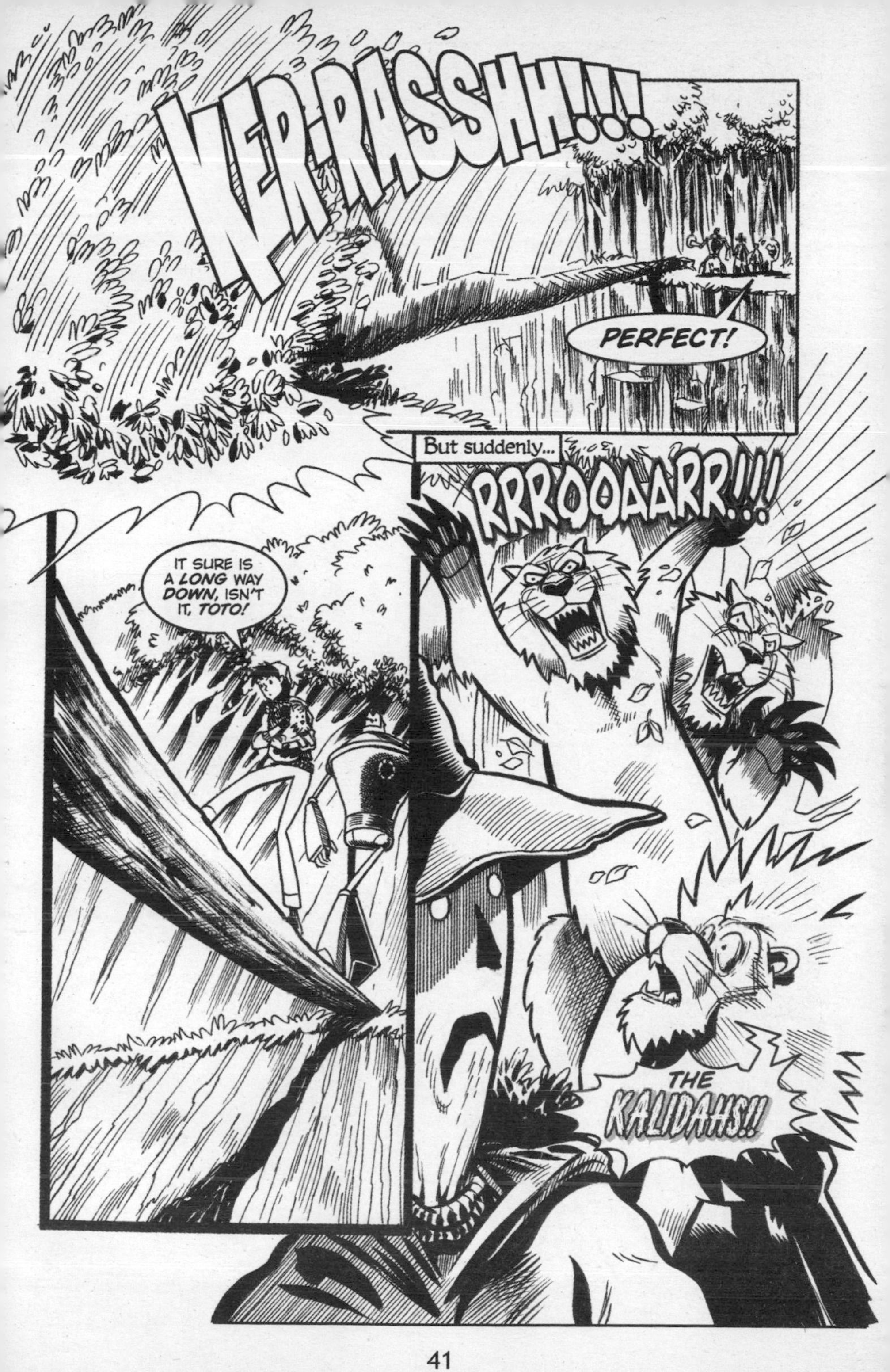

KER-RASSHH!!!
PERFECT!
But suddenly...
RRROOAARR!!!
IT SURE IS A LONG WAY DOWN, ISN'T IT, TOTO!
THE KALIDAHS!!

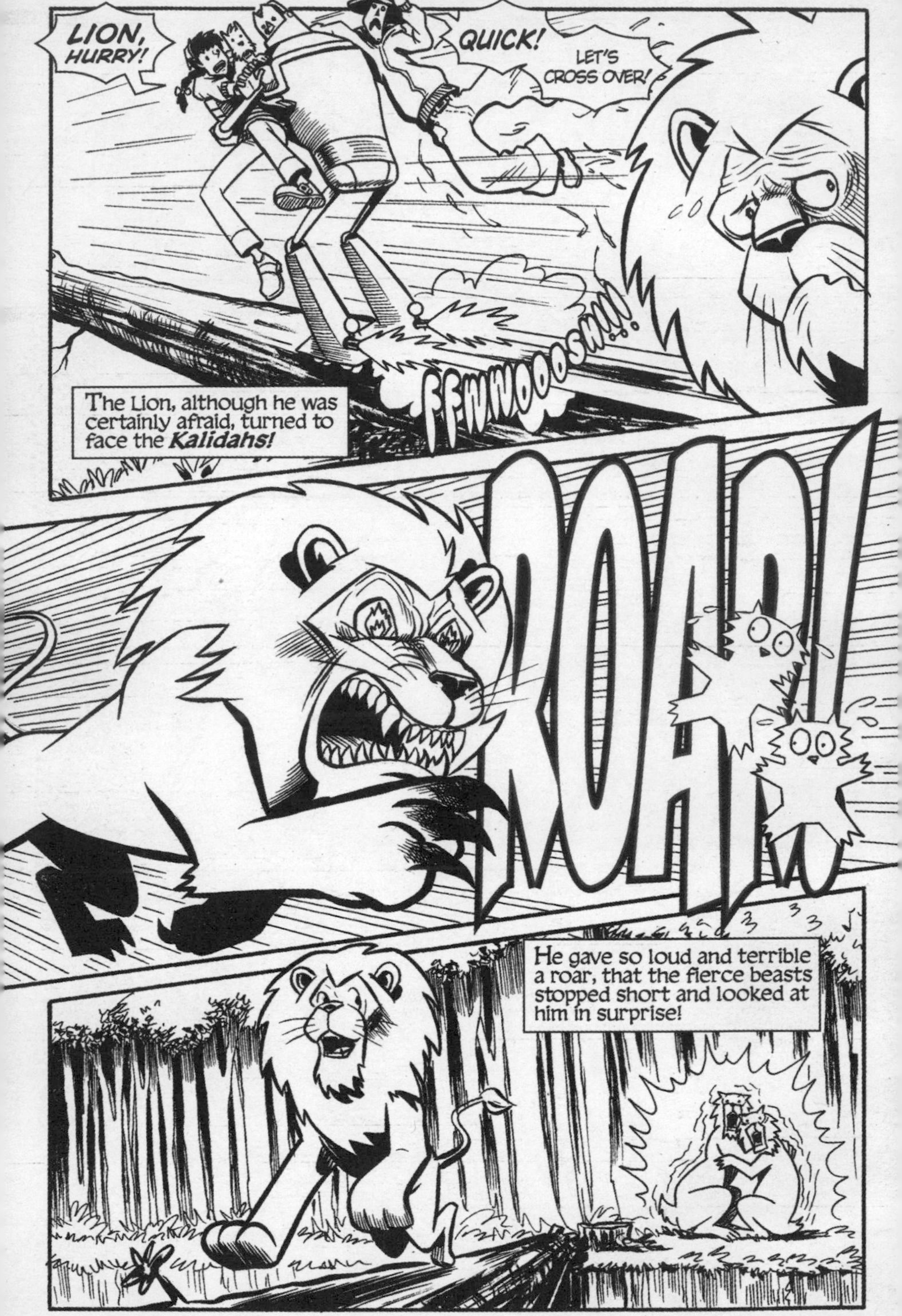
LION, HURRY!
QUICK!
LET'S CROSS OVER!
FFWWOOOSH!!!
The Lion, although he was certainly afraid, turned to face the ***Kalidahs!***
ROAR!
He gave so loud and terrible a roar, that the fierce beasts stopped short and looked at him in surprise!

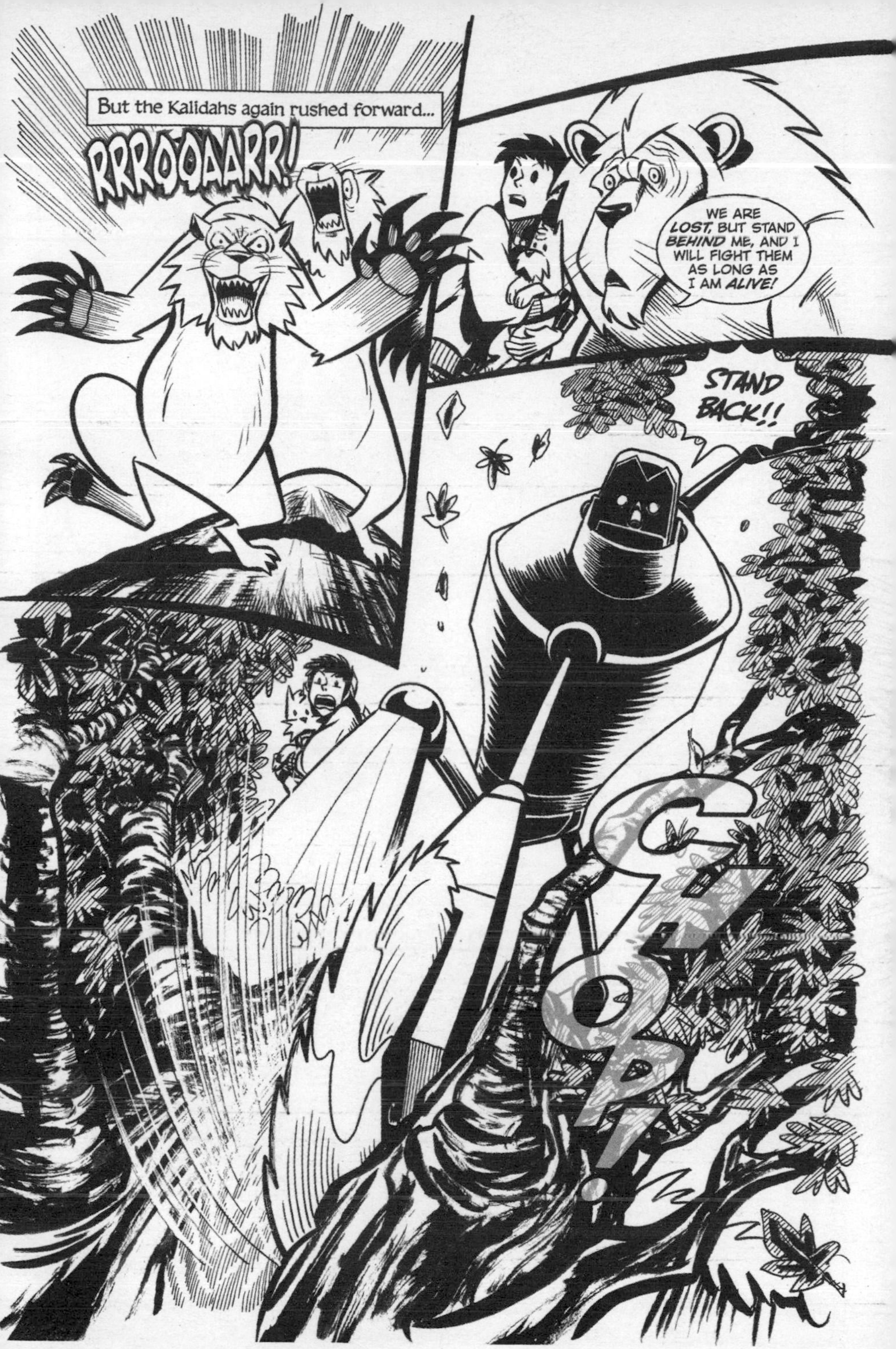

But the Kalidahs again rushed forward...
RRROOAARR!
WE ARE LOST, BUT STAND BEHIND ME, AND I WILL FIGHT THEM AS LONG AS I AM ALIVE!
STAND BACK!!
CHOP!

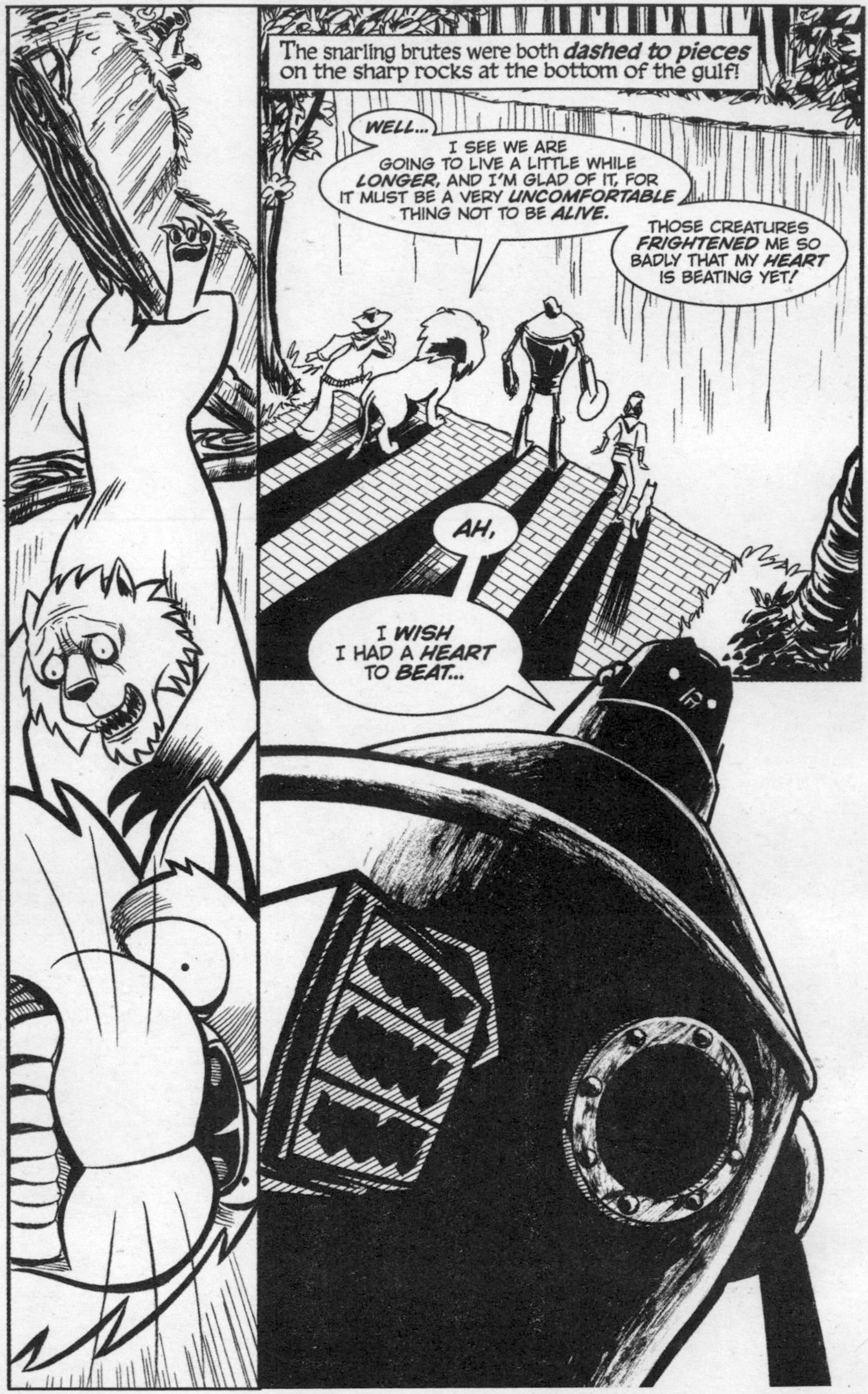
The snarling brutes were both *dashed to pieces* on the sharp rocks at the bottom of the gulf!
WELL...
I SEE WE ARE GOING TO LIVE A LITTLE WHILE LONGER, AND I'M GLAD OF IT, FOR IT MUST BE A VERY UNCOMFORTABLE THING NOT TO BE ALIVE.
THOSE CREATURES FRIGHTENED ME SO BADLY THAT MY HEART IS BEATING YET!
AH,
I WISH I HAD A HEART TO BEAT...

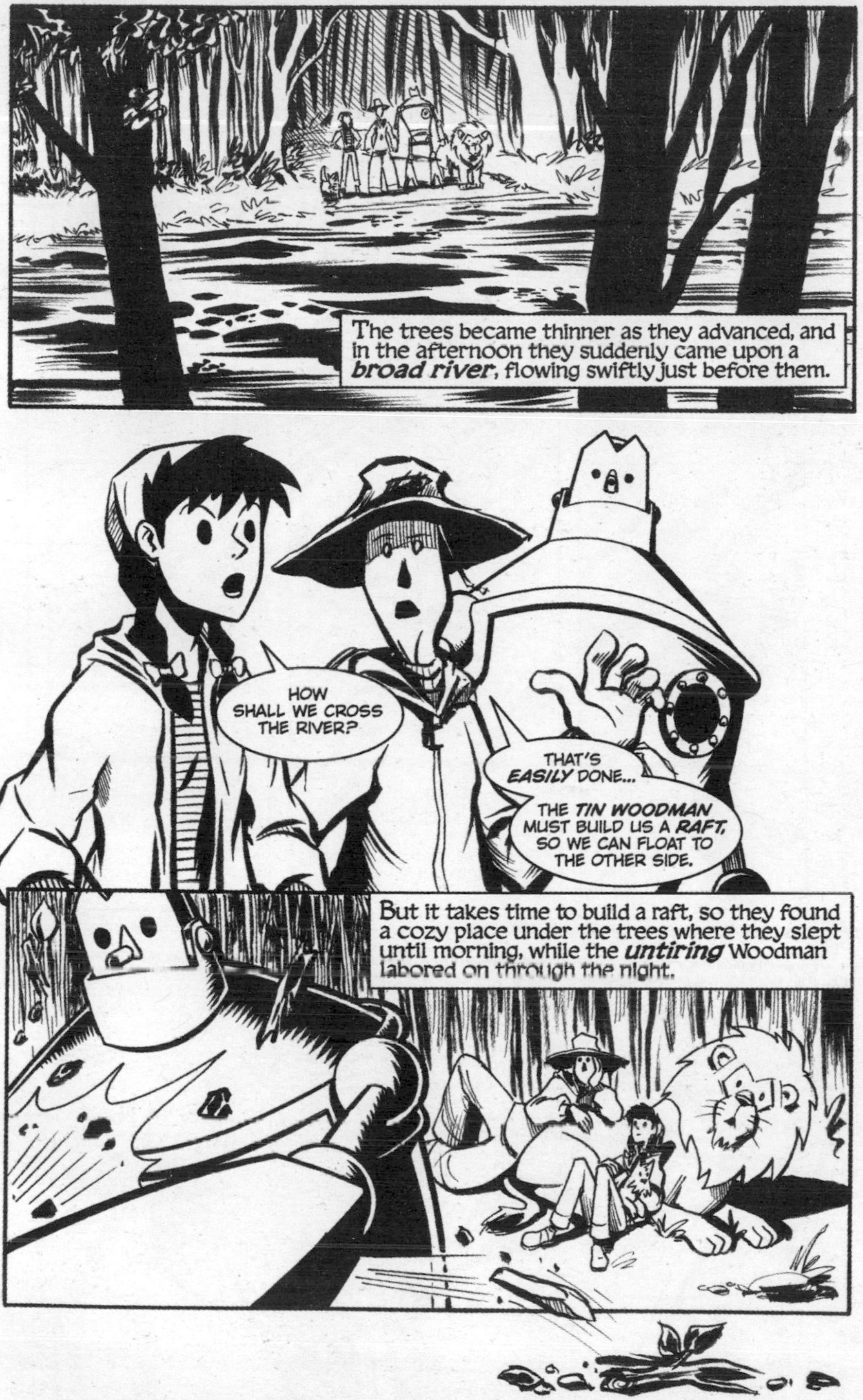

The trees became thinner as they advanced, and in the afternoon they suddenly came upon a *broad river*, flowing swiftly just before them.
HOW SHALL WE CROSS THE RIVER?
THAT'S *EASILY* DONE...
THE *TIN WOODMAN* MUST BUILD US A *RAFT*, SO WE CAN FLOAT TO THE OTHER SIDE.
But it takes time to build a raft, so they found a cozy place under the trees where they slept until morning, while the *untiring* Woodman labored on through the night.

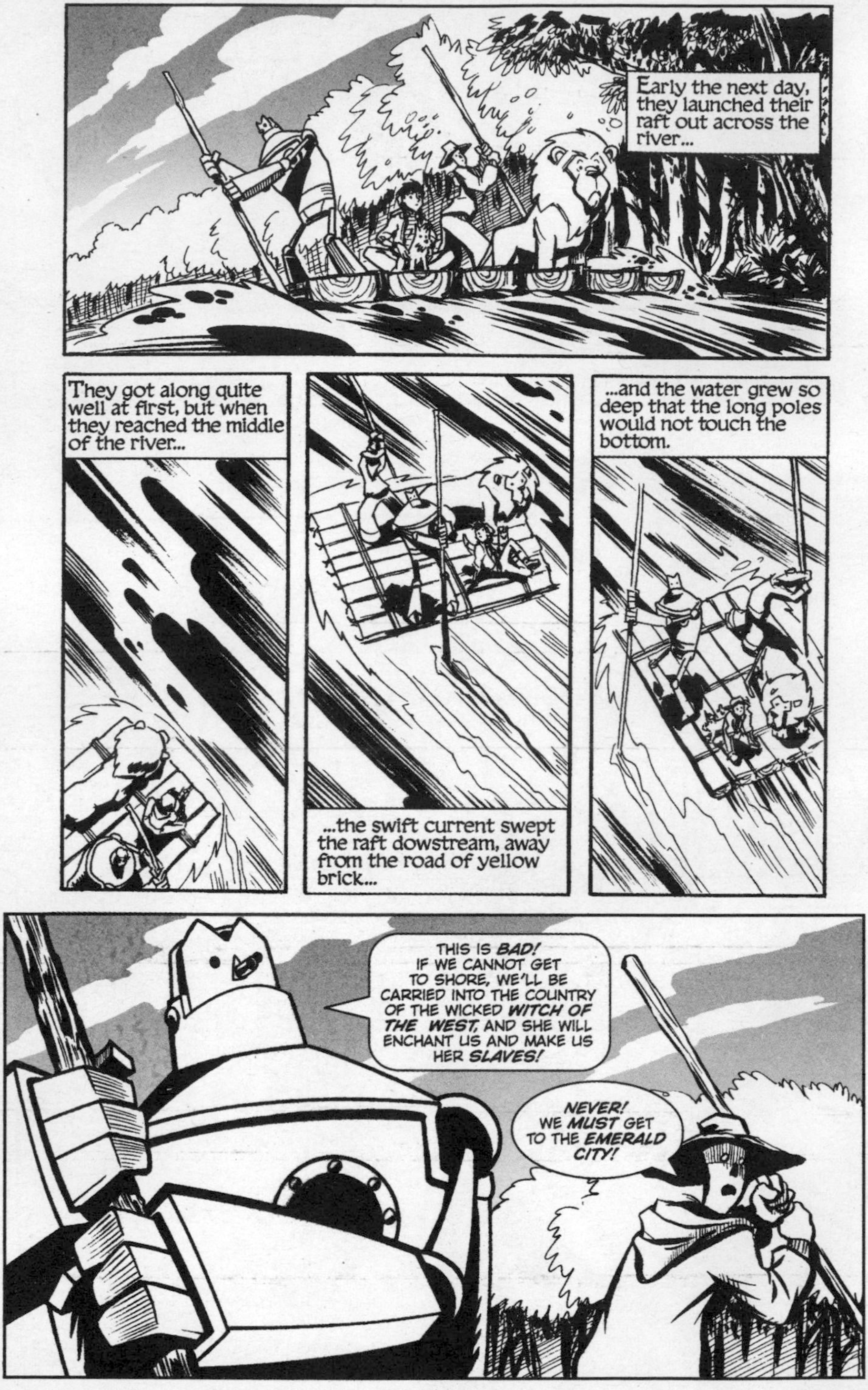
Early the next day, they launched their raft out across the river...
They got along quite well at first, but when they reached the middle of the river...
...the swift current swept the raft dowstream, away from the road of yellow brick...
...and the water grew so deep that the long poles would not touch the bottom.
THIS IS BAD! IF WE CANNOT GET TO SHORE, WE'LL BE CARRIED INTO THE COUNTRY OF THE WICKED WITCH OF THE WEST, AND SHE WILL ENCHANT US AND MAKE US HER SLAVES!
NEVER! WE MUST GET TO THE EMERALD CITY!

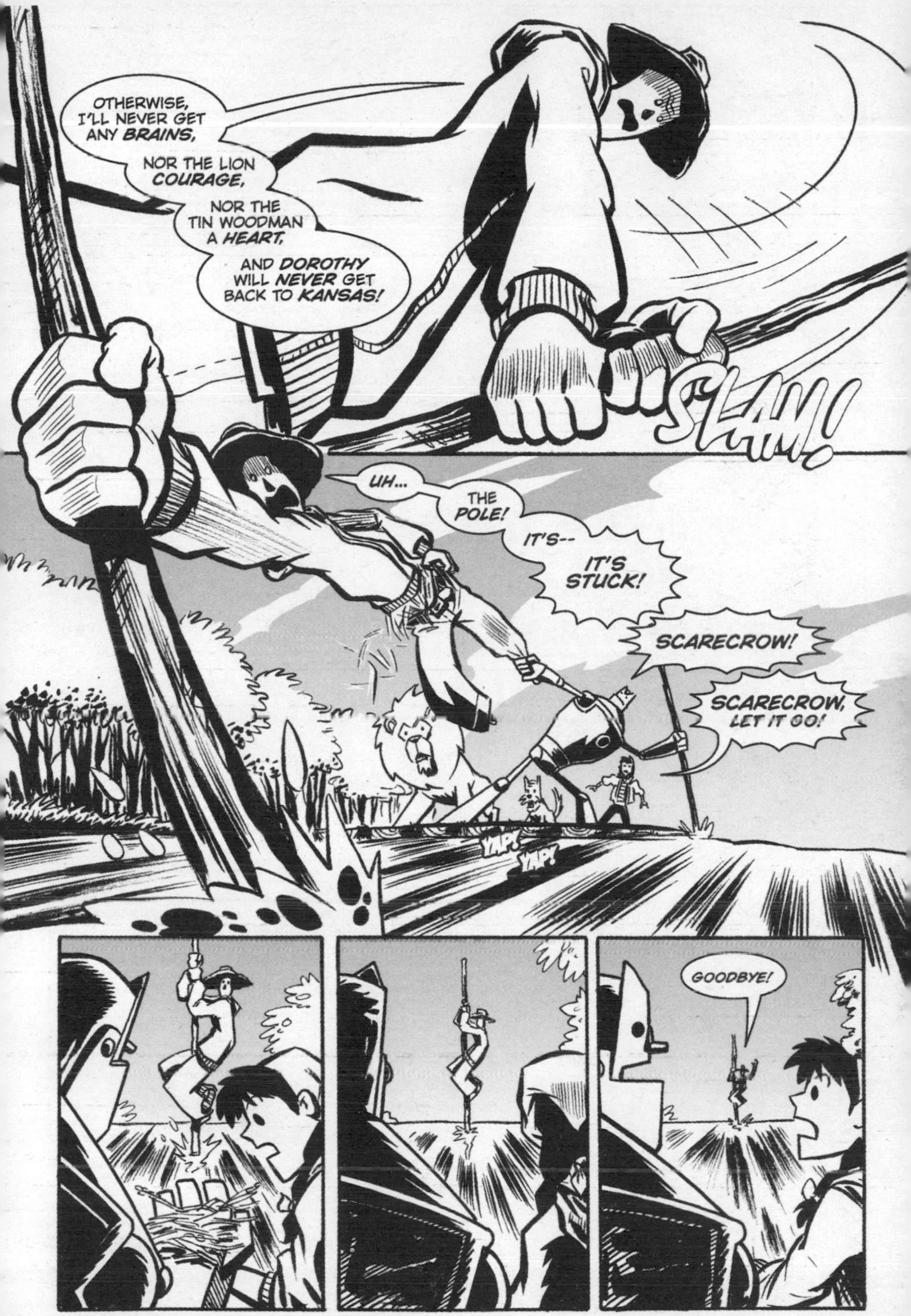
OTHERWISE, I'LL NEVER GET ANY BRAINS,
NOR THE LION COURAGE,
NOR THE TIN WOODMAN A HEART,
AND DOROTHY WILL NEVER GET BACK TO KANSAS!
SLAM!
UH...
THE POLE!
IT'S--
IT'S STUCK!
SCARECROW!
SCARECROW, LET IT GO!
YAP!
YAP!
GOODBYE!

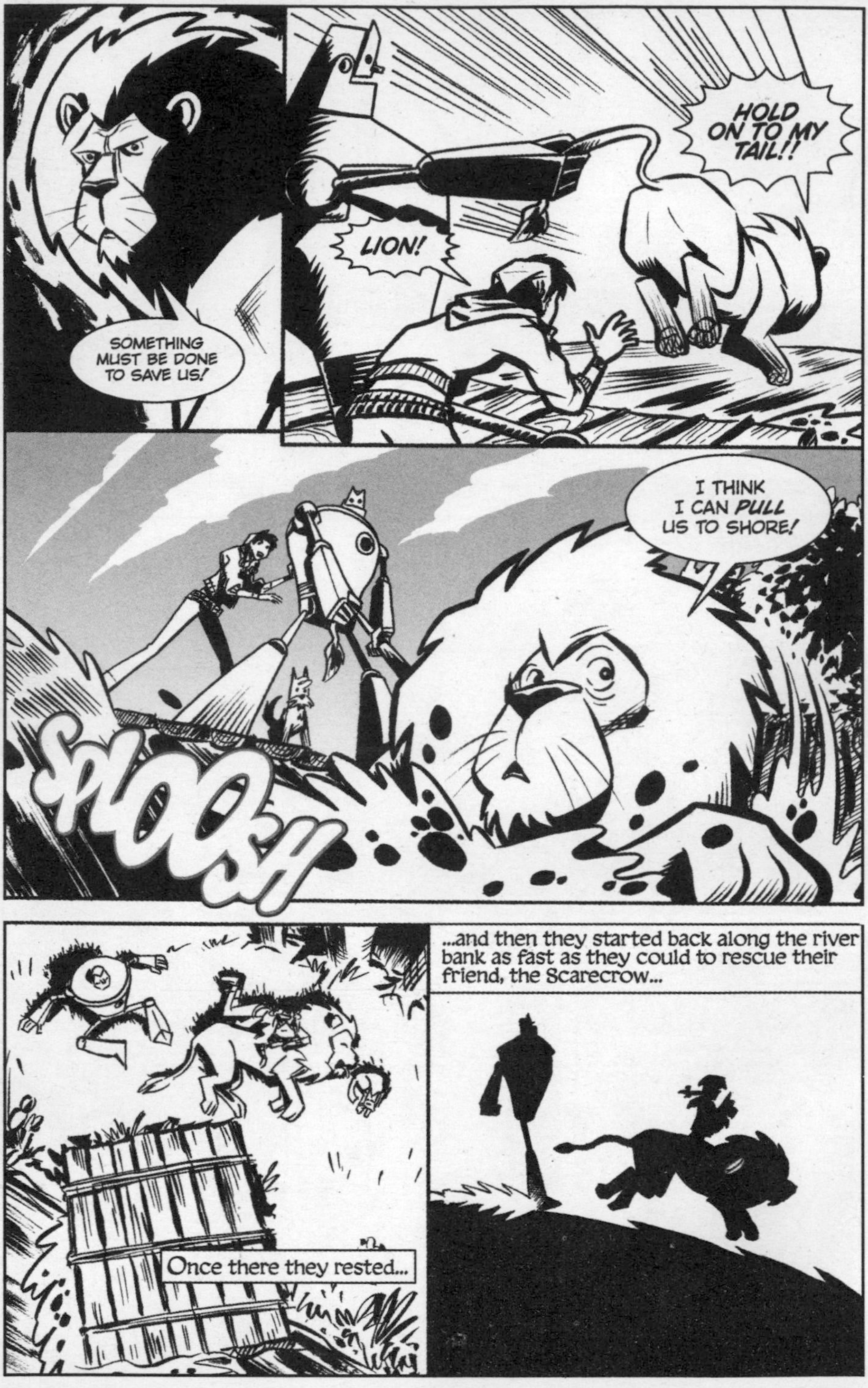
HOLD ON TO MY TAIL!!
LION!
SOMETHING MUST BE DONE TO SAVE US!
I THINK I CAN PULL US TO SHORE!
SPLOOSH
Once there they rested...
...and then they started back along the river bank as fast as they could to rescue their friend, the Scarecrow...

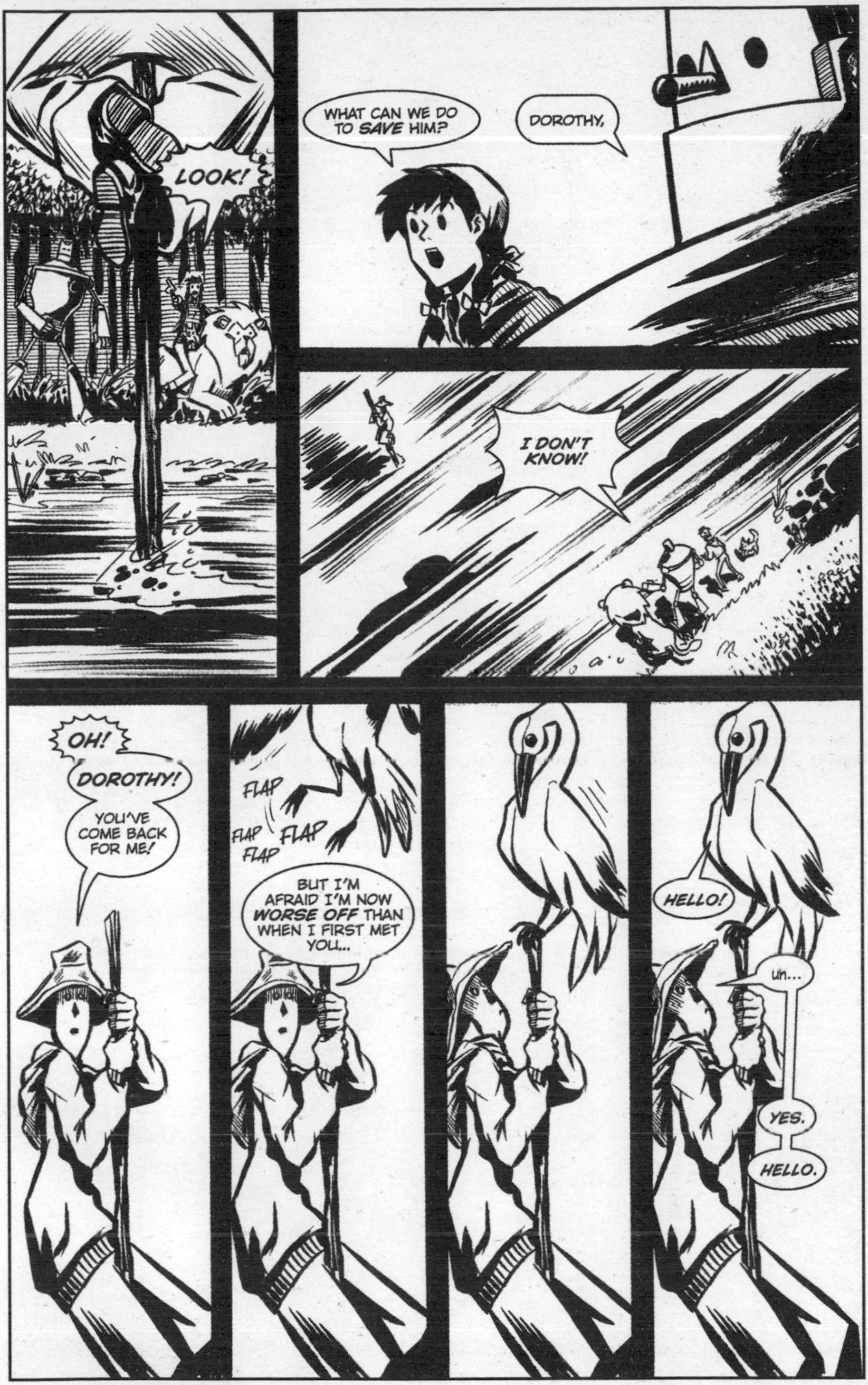
LOOK!
WHAT CAN WE DO TO SAVE HIM?
DOROTHY,
I DON'T KNOW!
OH!
DOROTHY!
YOU'VE COME BACK FOR ME!
FLAP
FLAP FLAP
FLAP
BUT I'M AFRAID I'M NOW WORSE OFF THAN WHEN I FIRST MET YOU...
HELLO!
uh...
YES.
HELLO.

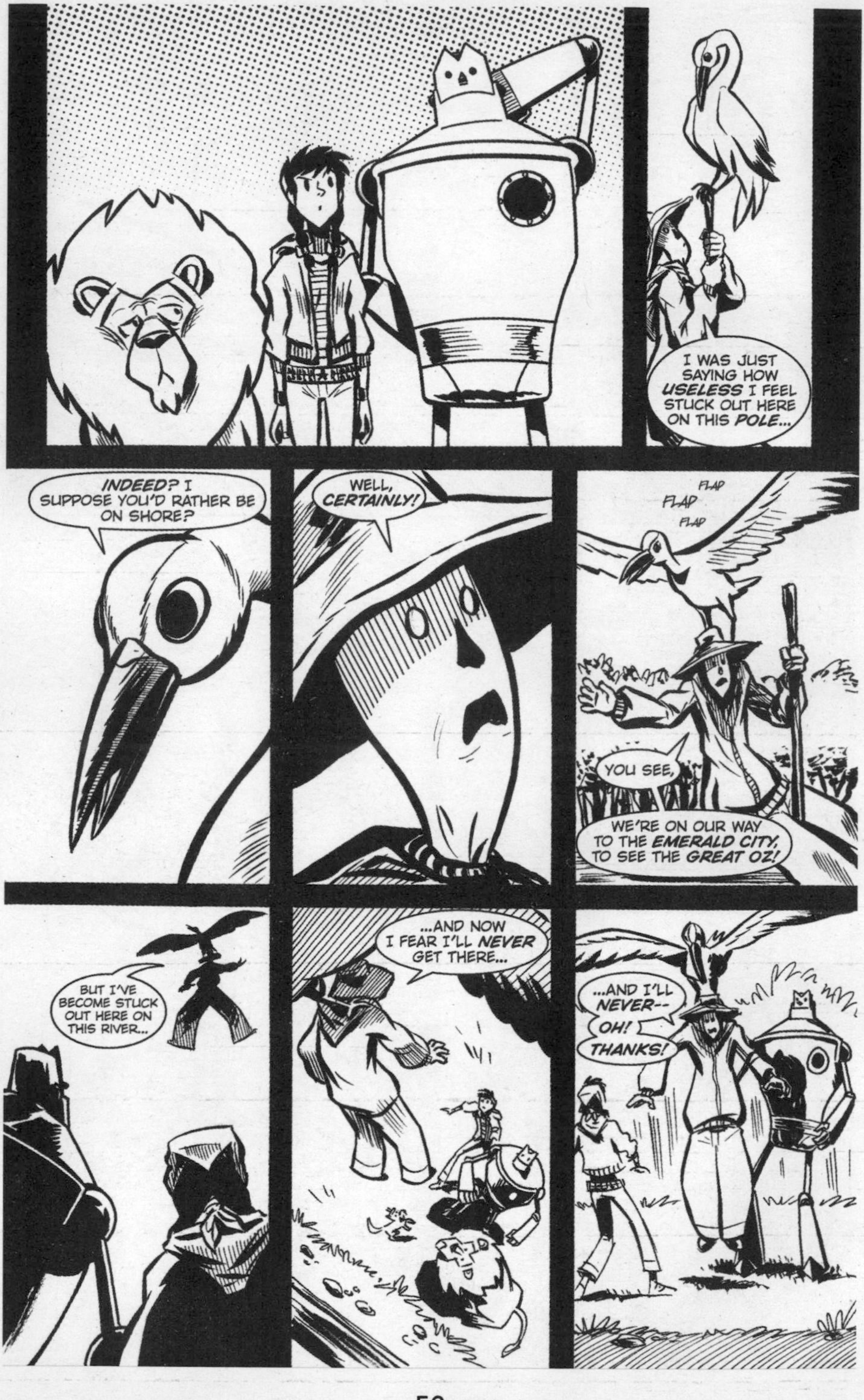
I WAS JUST SAYING HOW USELESS I FEEL STUCK OUT HERE ON THIS POLE...
INDEED? I SUPPOSE YOU'D RATHER BE ON SHORE?
WELL, CERTAINLY!
FLAP
FLAP
FLAP
YOU SEE,
WE'RE ON OUR WAY TO THE EMERALD CITY, TO SEE THE GREAT OZ!
BUT I'VE BECOME STUCK OUT HERE ON THIS RIVER...
...AND NOW I FEAR I'LL NEVER GET THERE...
...AND I'LL NEVER--
OH!
THANKS!

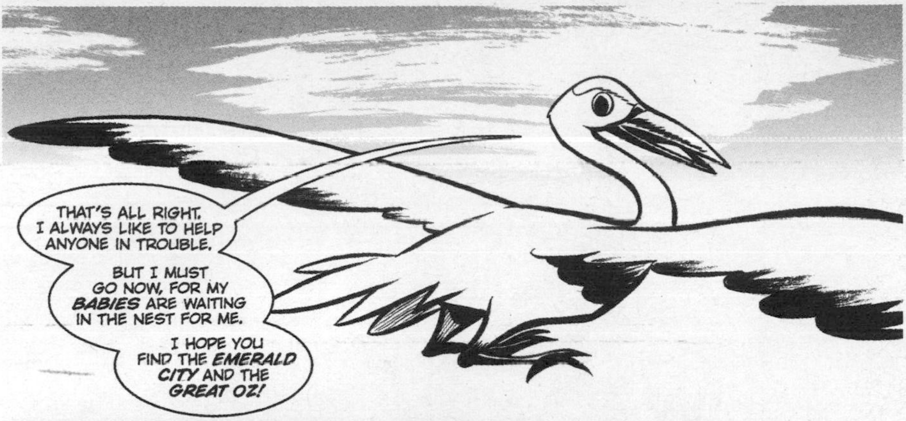
THAT'S ALL RIGHT. I ALWAYS LIKE TO HELP ANYONE IN TROUBLE.
BUT I MUST GO NOW, FOR MY BABIES ARE WAITING IN THE NEST FOR ME.
I HOPE YOU FIND THE EMERALD CITY AND THE GREAT OZ!

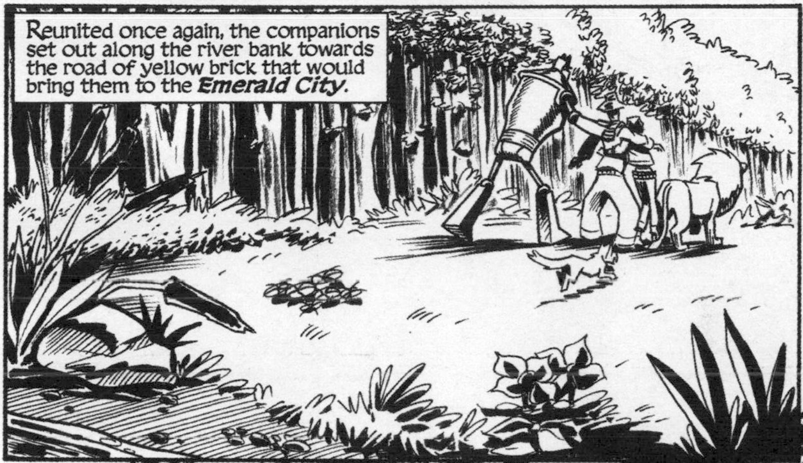
Reunited once again, the companions set out along the river bank towards the road of yellow brick that would bring them to the Emerald City.

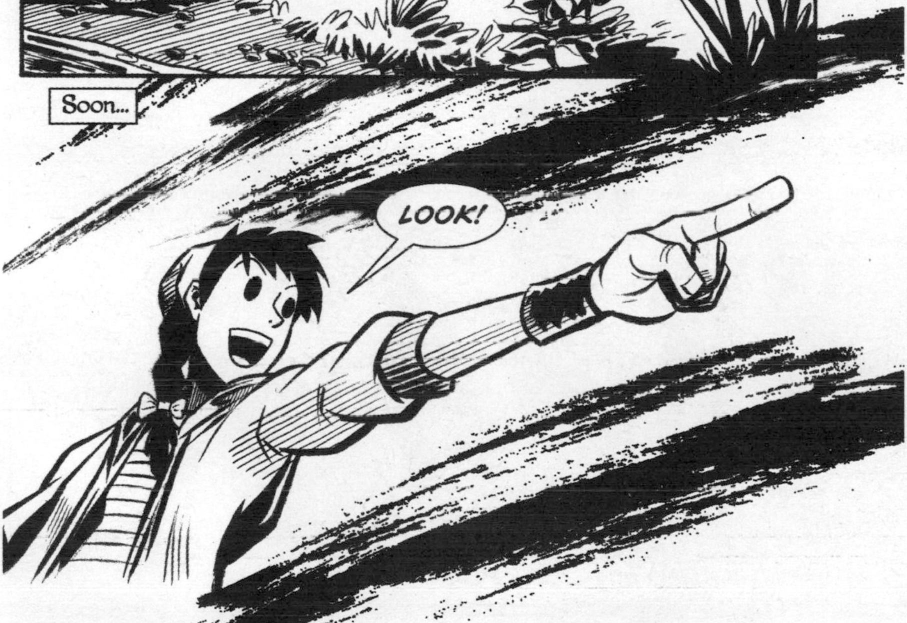
Soon...
LOOK!

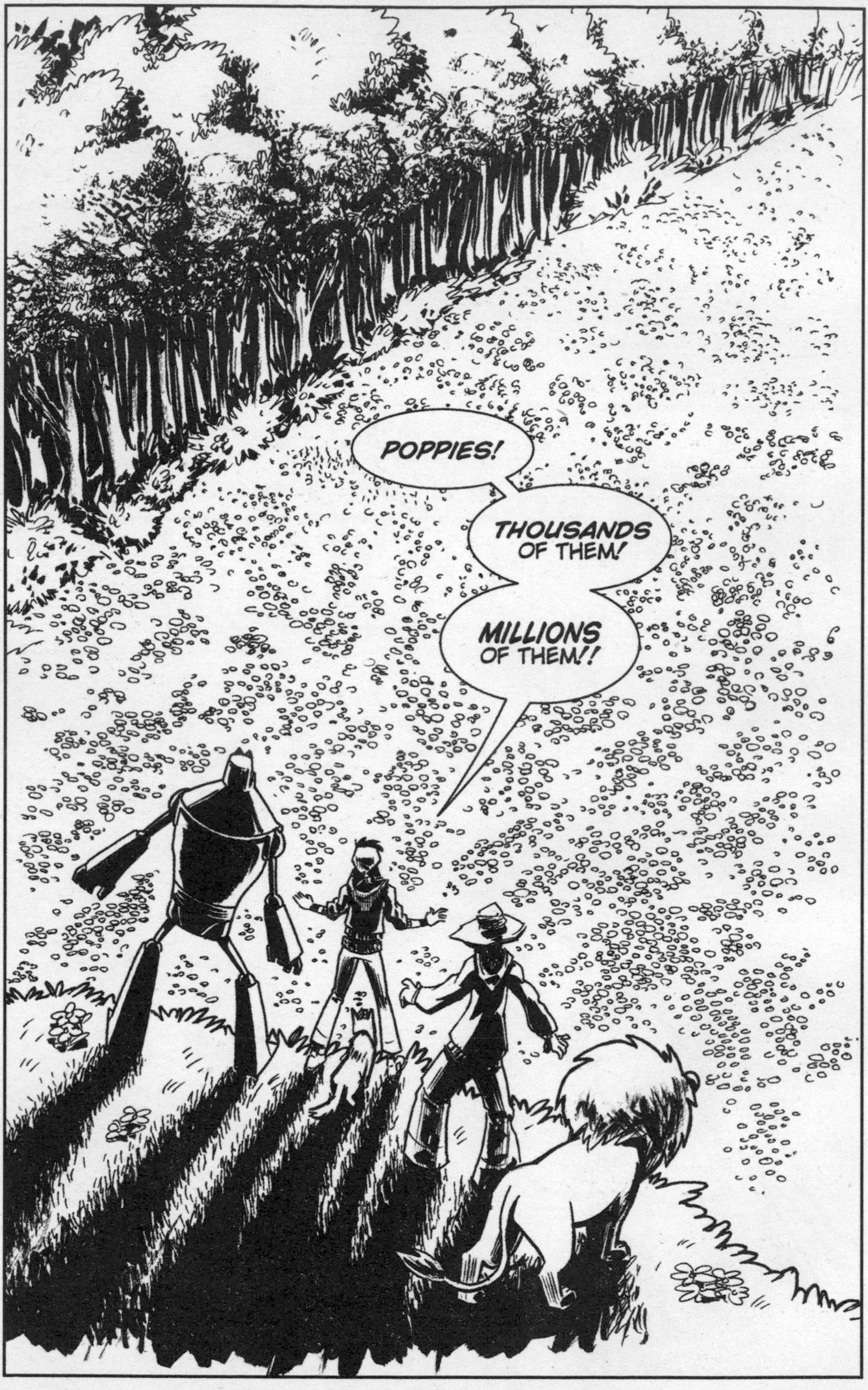
POPPIES!
THOUSANDS OF THEM!
MILLIONS OF THEM!!

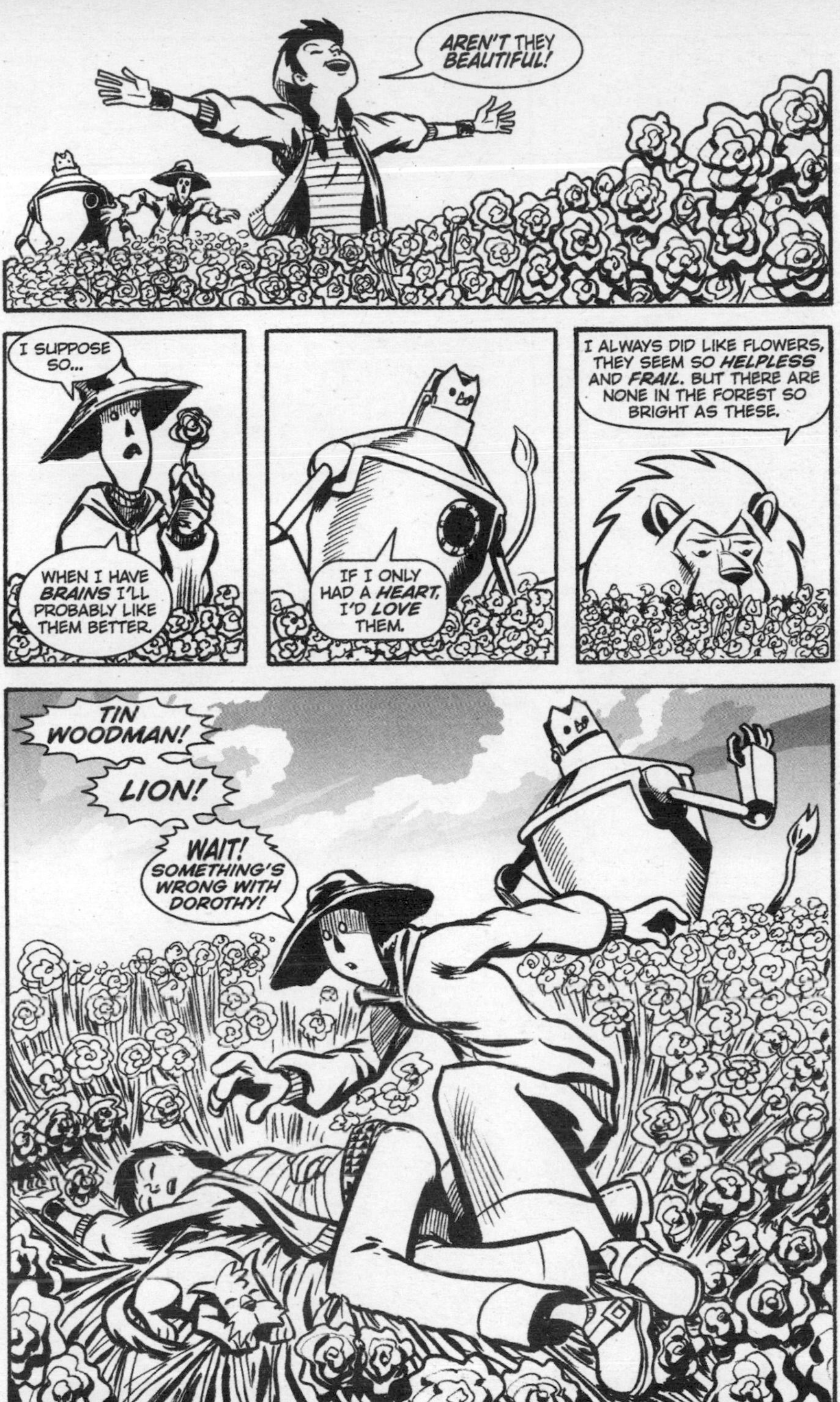

AREN'T THEY BEAUTIFUL!
I SUPPOSE SO...
WHEN I HAVE BRAINS I'LL PROBABLY LIKE THEM BETTER.
IF I ONLY HAD A HEART, I'D LOVE THEM.
I ALWAYS DID LIKE FLOWERS, THEY SEEM SO HELPLESS AND FRAIL. BUT THERE ARE NONE IN THE FOREST SO BRIGHT AS THESE.
TIN WOODMAN!
LION!
WAIT! SOMETHING'S WRONG WITH DOROTHY!

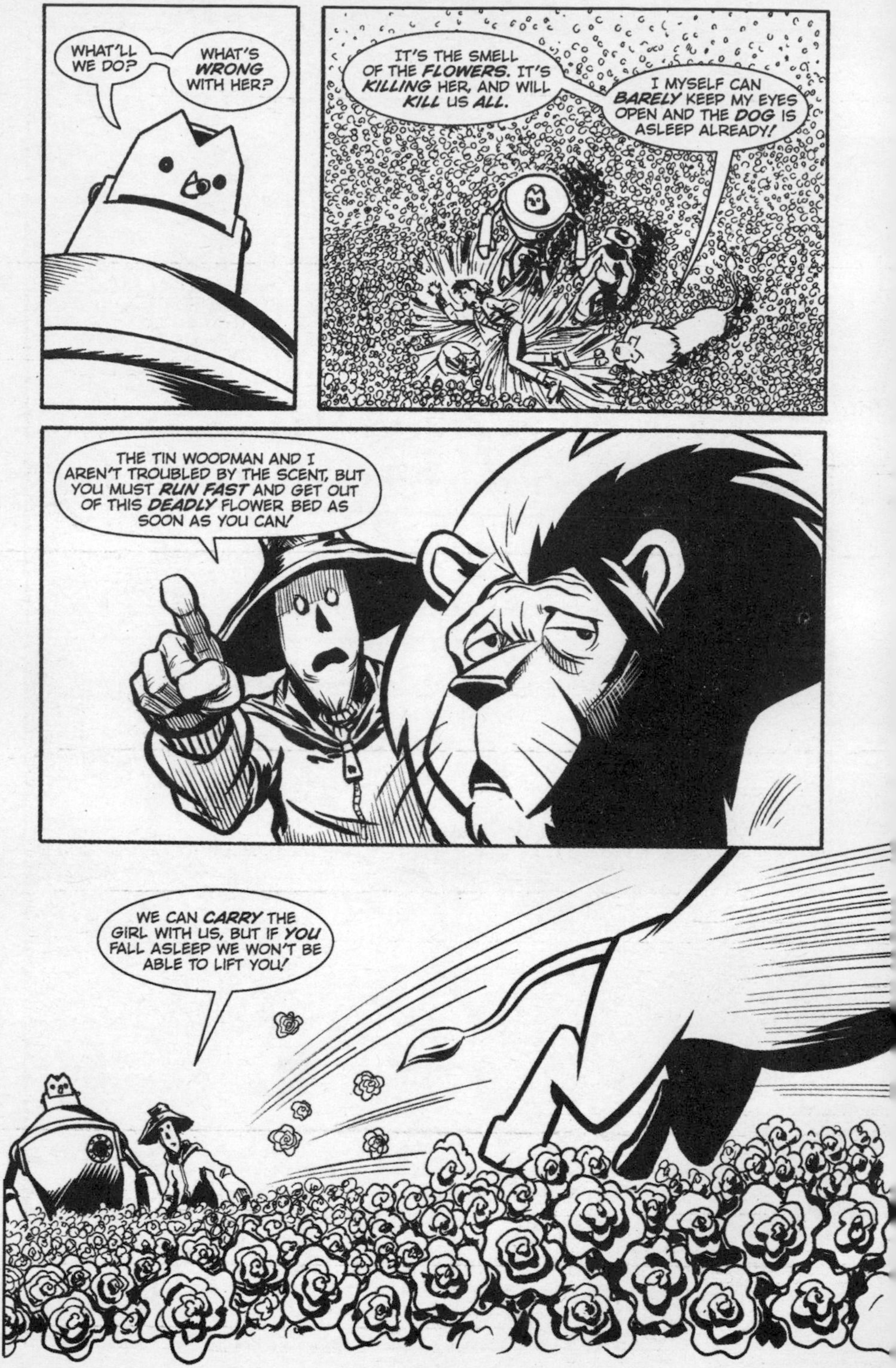

WHAT'LL WE DO?
WHAT'S WRONG WITH HER?
IT'S THE SMELL OF THE FLOWERS. IT'S KILLING HER, AND WILL KILL US ALL.
I MYSELF CAN BARELY KEEP MY EYES OPEN AND THE DOG IS ASLEEP ALREADY!
THE TIN WOODMAN AND I AREN'T TROUBLED BY THE SCENT, BUT YOU MUST RUN FAST AND GET OUT OF THIS DEADLY FLOWER BED AS SOON AS YOU CAN!
WE CAN CARRY THE GIRL WITH US, BUT IF YOU FALL ASLEEP WE WON'T BE ABLE TO LIFT YOU!

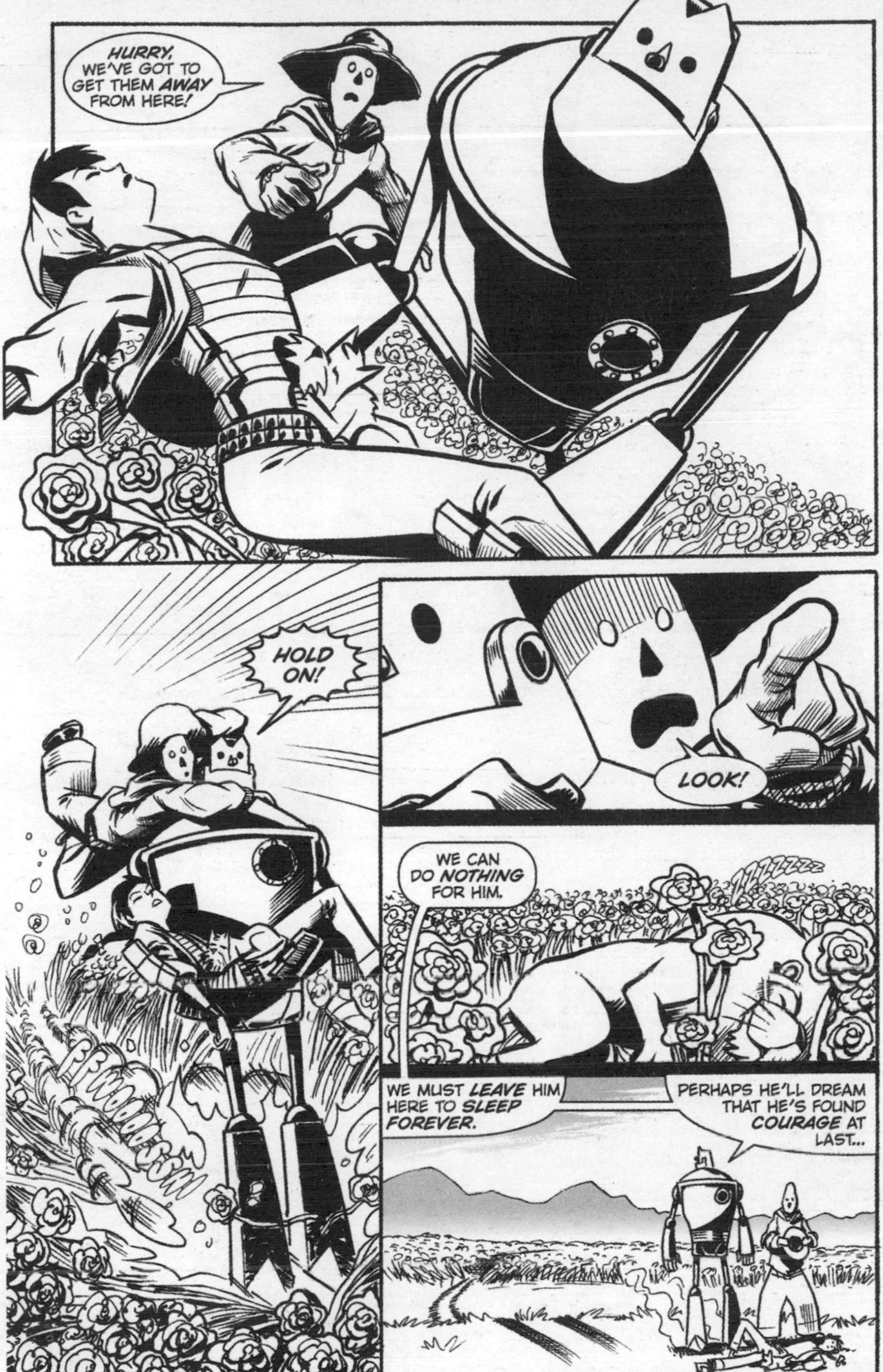
HURRY, WE'VE GOT TO GET THEM AWAY FROM HERE!
HOLD ON!
LOOK!
WE CAN DO NOTHING FOR HIM.
WE MUST LEAVE HIM HERE TO SLEEP FOREVER.
PERHAPS HE'LL DREAM THAT HE'S FOUND COURAGE AT LAST...

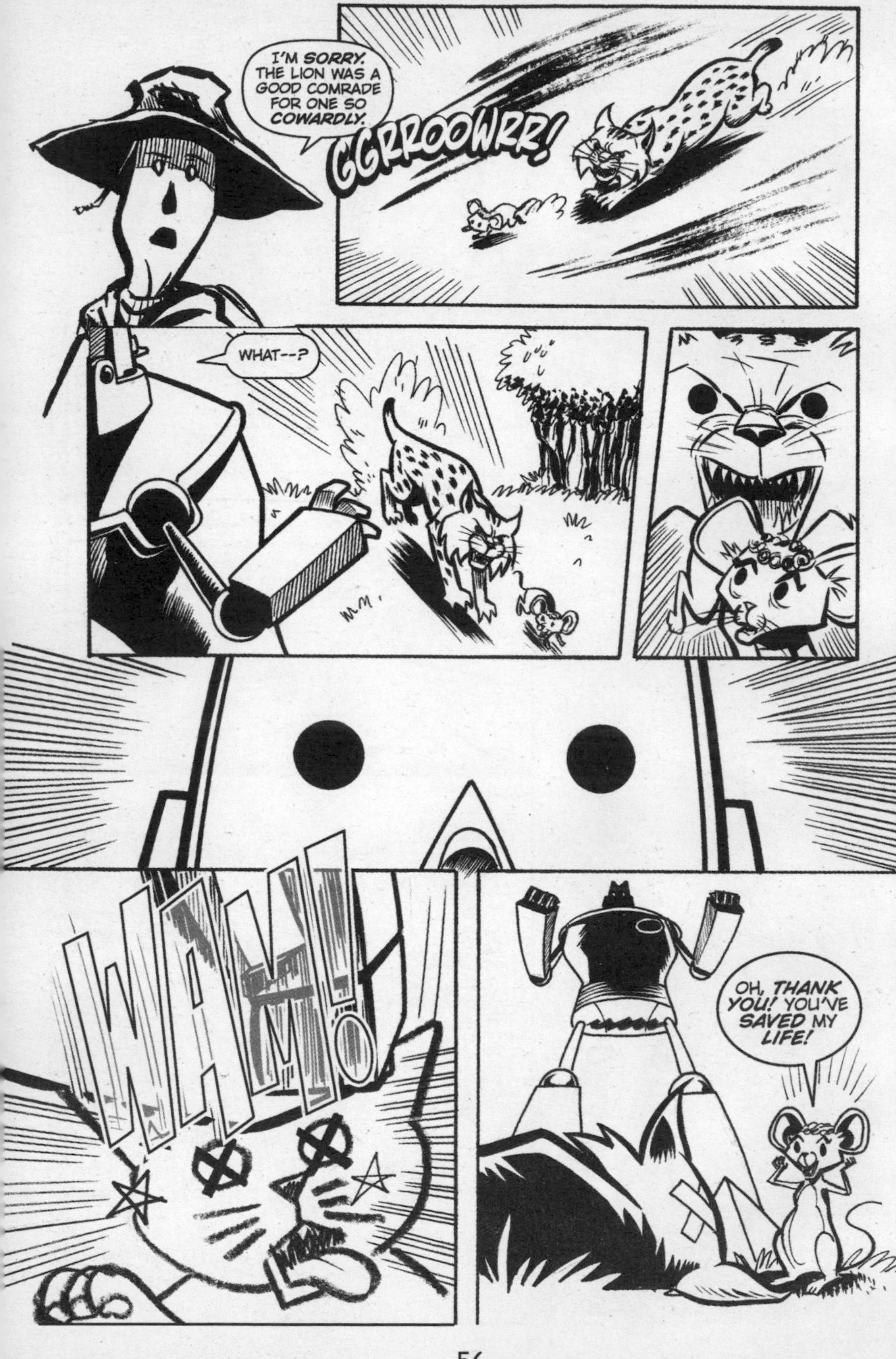
I'M SORRY. THE LION WAS A GOOD COMRADE FOR ONE SO COWARDLY.
GGRROOWRR!
WHAT--?
WAM!
OH, THANK YOU! YOU'VE SAVED MY LIFE!

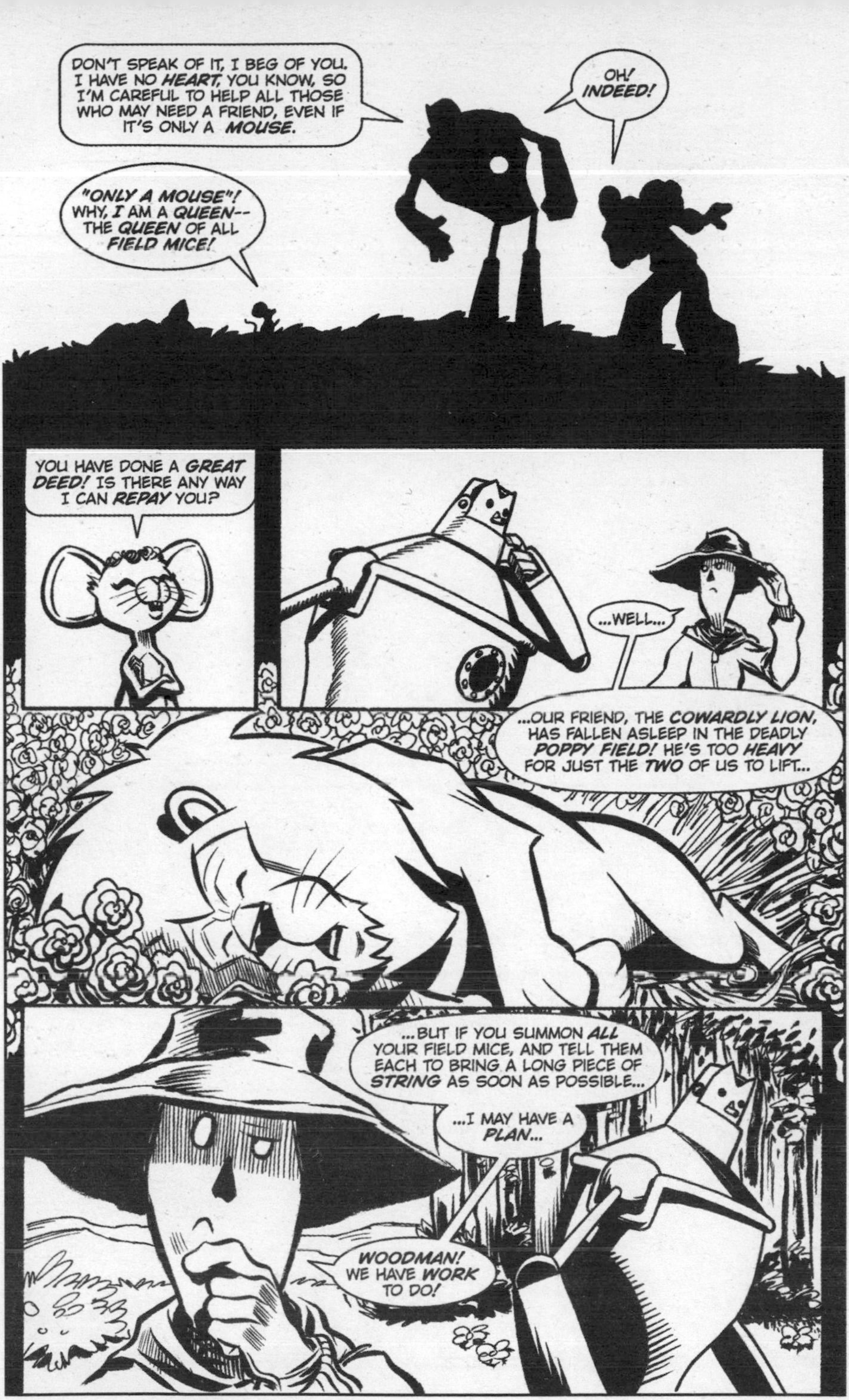
DON'T SPEAK OF IT, I BEG OF YOU. I HAVE NO HEART, YOU KNOW, SO I'M CAREFUL TO HELP ALL THOSE WHO MAY NEED A FRIEND, EVEN IF IT'S ONLY A MOUSE.
OH! INDEED!
"ONLY A MOUSE"! WHY, I AM A QUEEN-- THE QUEEN OF ALL FIELD MICE!
YOU HAVE DONE A GREAT DEED! IS THERE ANY WAY I CAN REPAY YOU?
...WELL...
...OUR FRIEND, THE COWARDLY LION, HAS FALLEN ASLEEP IN THE DEADLY POPPY FIELD! HE'S TOO HEAVY FOR JUST THE TWO OF US TO LIFT...
...BUT IF YOU SUMMON ALL YOUR FIELD MICE, AND TELL THEM EACH TO BRING A LONG PIECE OF STRING AS SOON AS POSSIBLE...
...I MAY HAVE A PLAN...
WOODMAN! WE HAVE WORK TO DO!

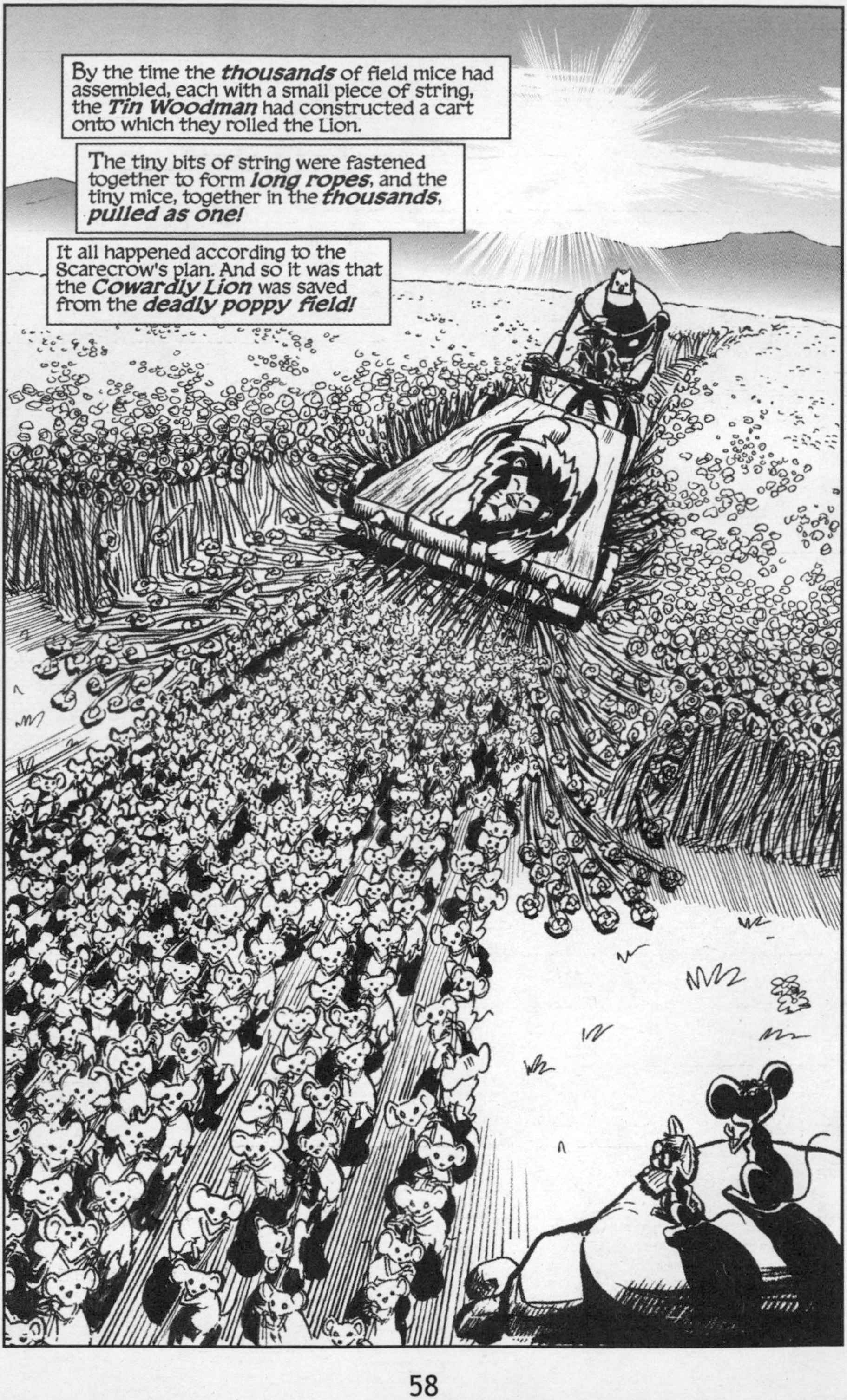
By the time the *thousands* of field mice had assembled, each with a small piece of string, the *Tin Woodman* had constructed a cart onto which they rolled the Lion.
The tiny bits of string were fastened together to form *long ropes*, and the tiny mice, together in the *thousands*, *pulled as one!*
It all happened according to the Scarecrow's plan. And so it was that the *Cowardly Lion* was saved from the *deadly poppy field!*

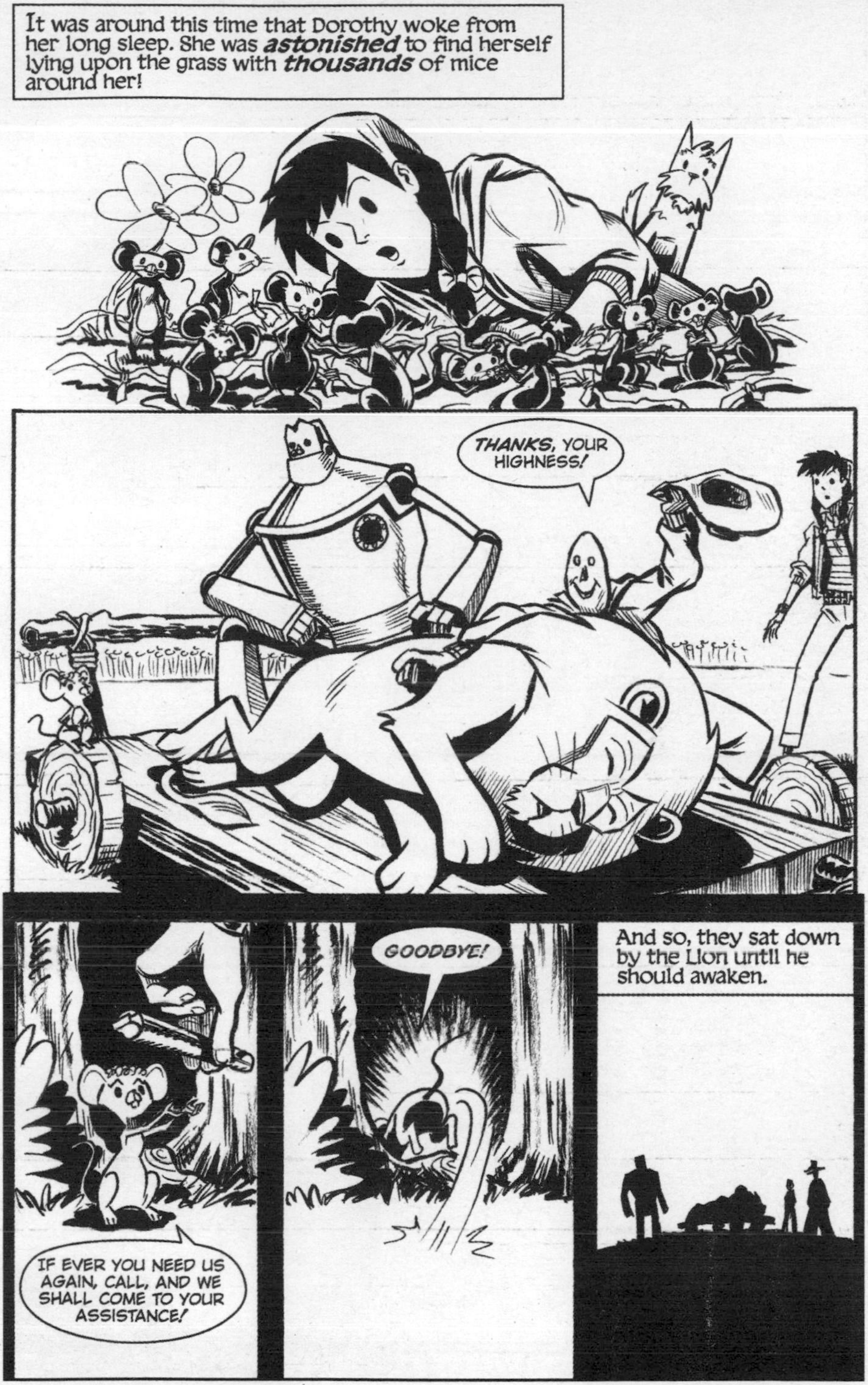
It was around this time that Dorothy woke from her long sleep. She was *astonished* to find herself lying upon the grass with *thousands* of mice around her!
THANKS, YOUR HIGHNESS!
IF EVER YOU NEED US AGAIN, CALL, AND WE SHALL COME TO YOUR ASSISTANCE!
GOODBYE!
And so, they sat down by the Lion until he should awaken.

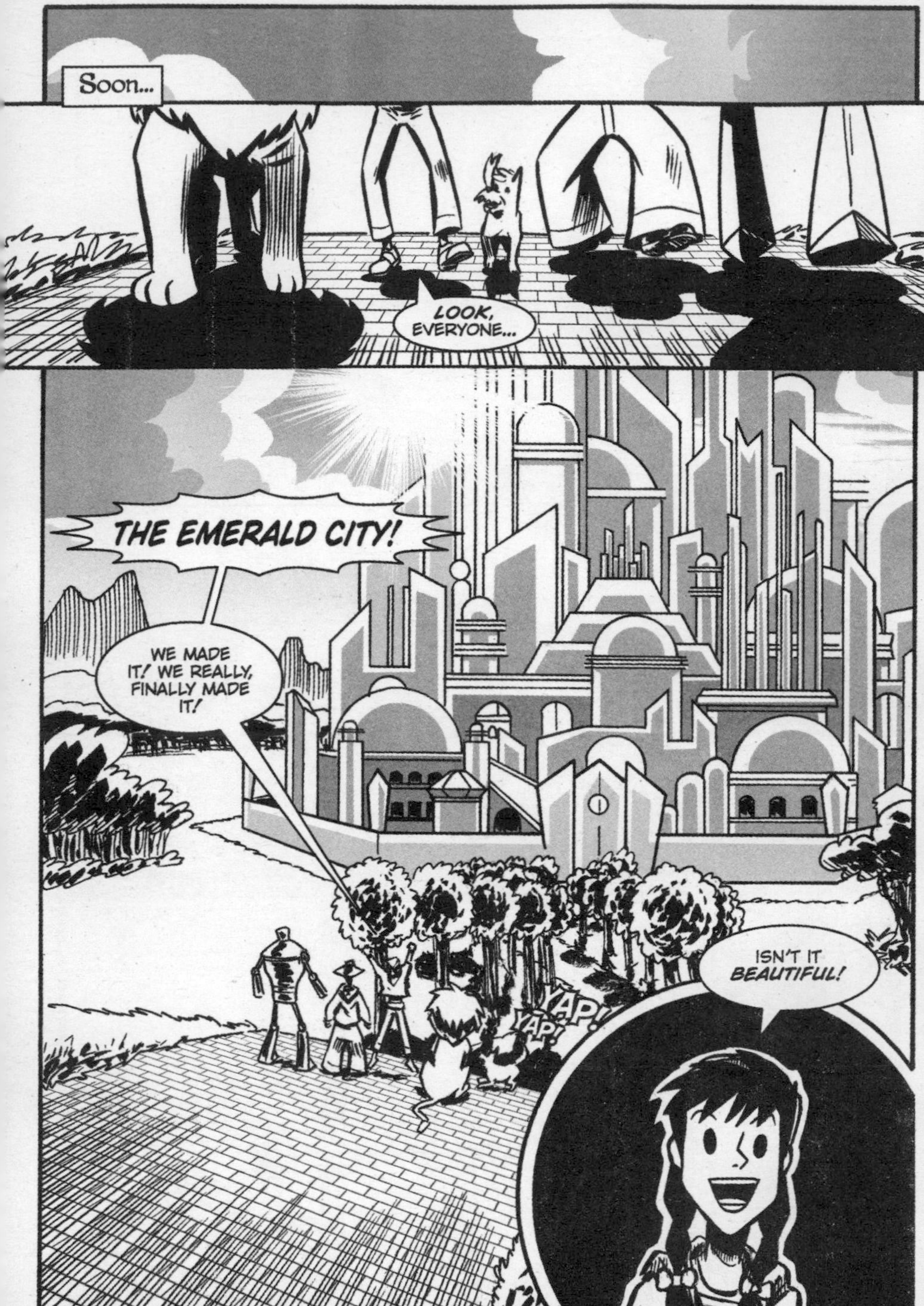

Soon...
LOOK, EVERYONE...
THE EMERALD CITY!
WE MADE IT! WE REALLY, FINALLY MADE IT!
YAP! YAP!
ISN'T IT BEAUTIFUL!

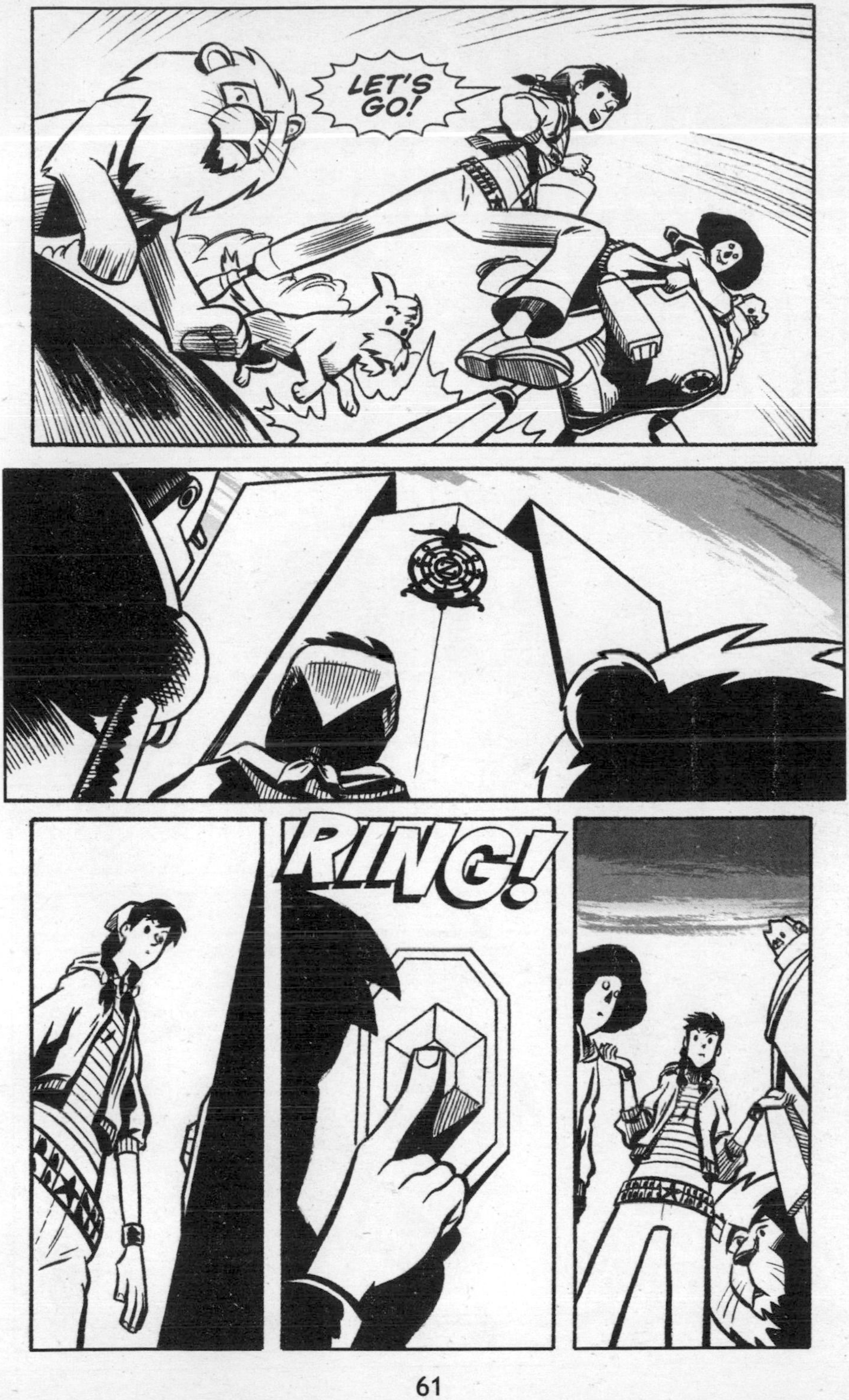
LET'S GO!
RING!

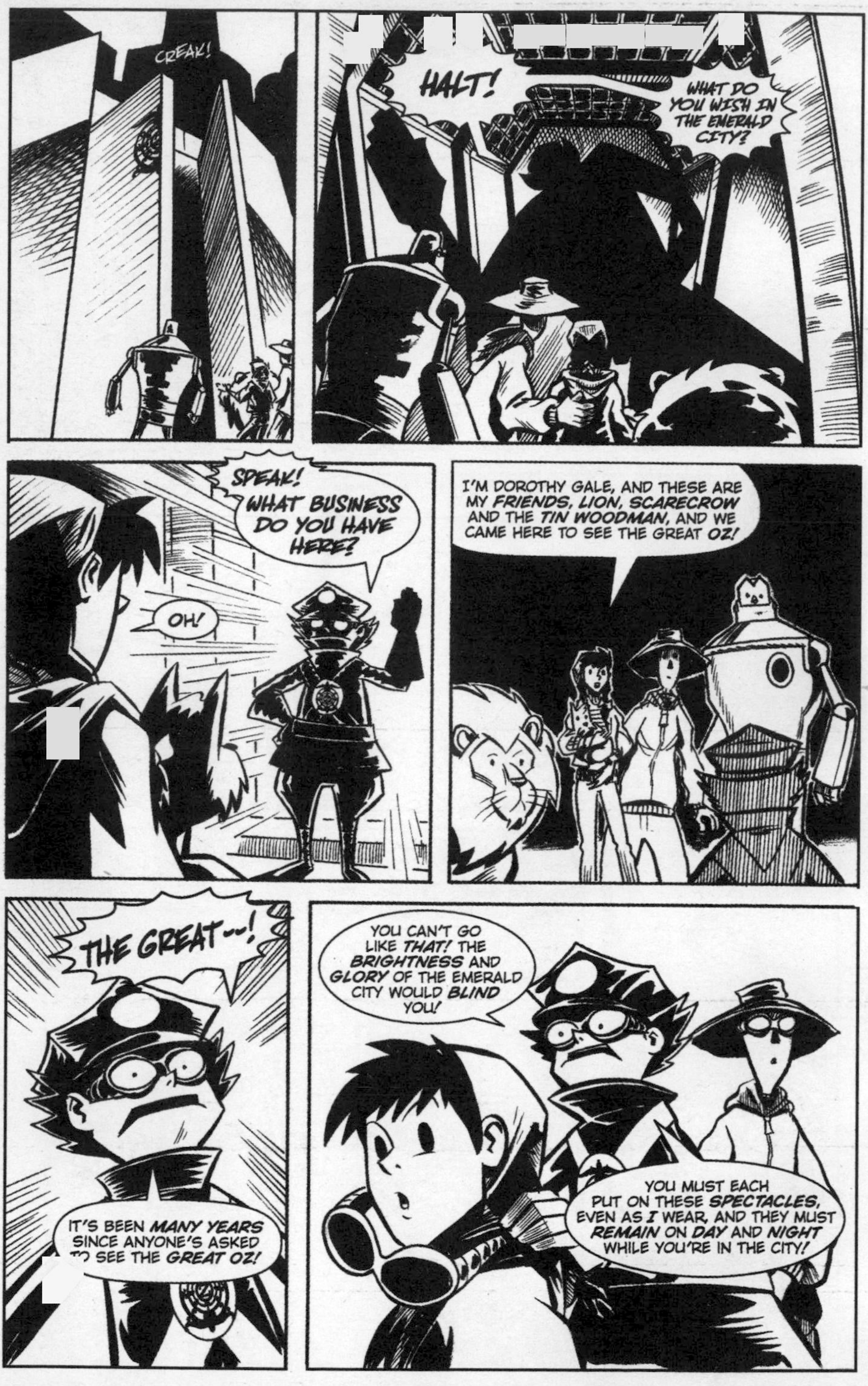
CREAK!
HALT!
WHAT DO YOU WISH IN THE EMERALD CITY?
SPEAK! WHAT BUSINESS DO YOU HAVE HERE?
OH!
I'M DOROTHY GALE, AND THESE ARE MY FRIENDS, LION, SCARECROW AND THE TIN WOODMAN, AND WE CAME HERE TO SEE THE GREAT OZ!
THE GREAT--!
IT'S BEEN MANY YEARS SINCE ANYONE'S ASKED TO SEE THE GREAT OZ!
YOU CAN'T GO LIKE THAT! THE BRIGHTNESS AND GLORY OF THE EMERALD CITY WOULD BLIND YOU!
YOU MUST EACH PUT ON THESE SPECTACLES, EVEN AS I WEAR, AND THEY MUST REMAIN ON DAY AND NIGHT WHILE YOU'RE IN THE CITY!

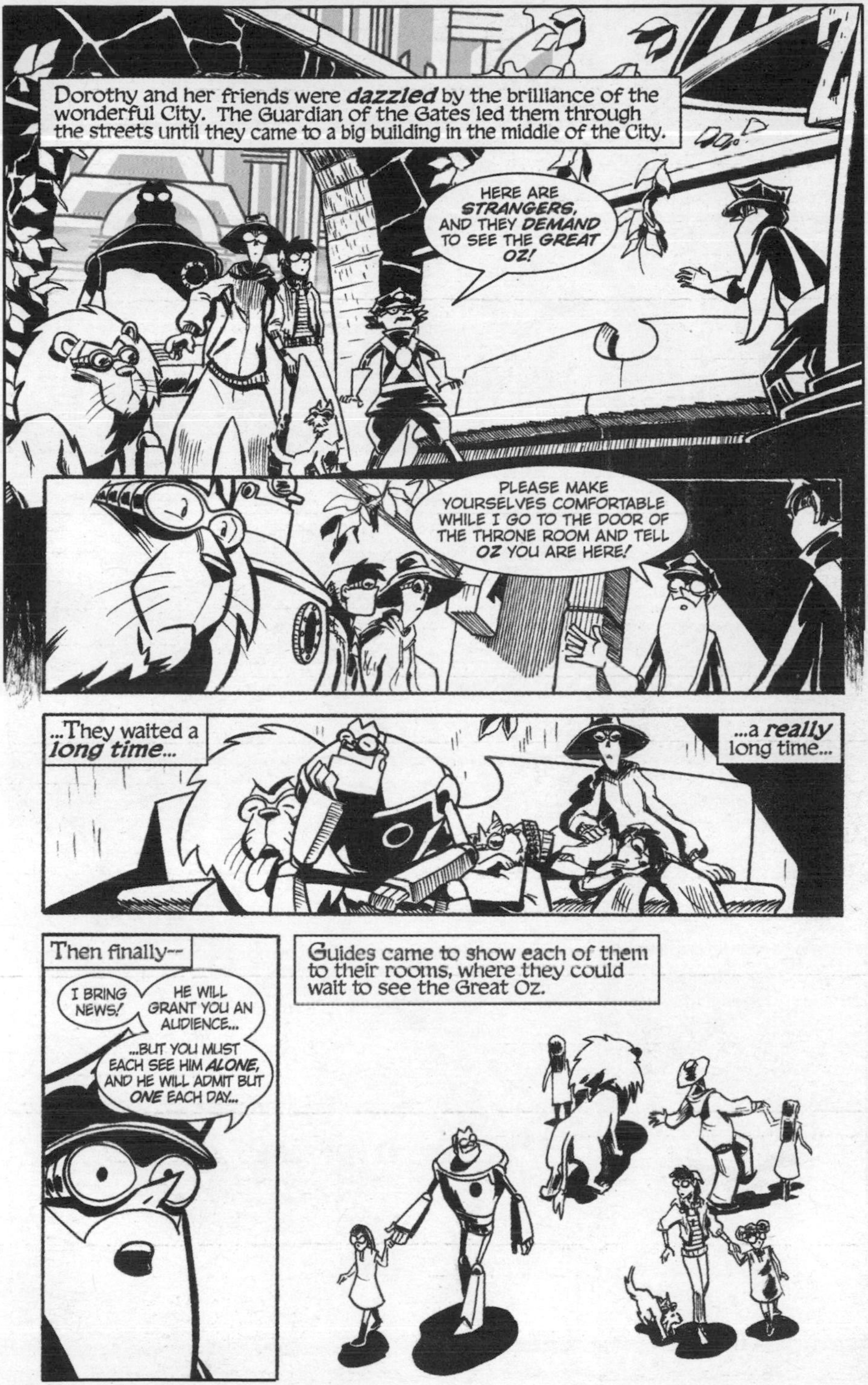
Dorothy and her friends were dazzled by the brilliance of the wonderful City. The Guardian of the Gates led them through the streets until they came to a big building in the middle of the City.
HERE ARE STRANGERS, AND THEY DEMAND TO SEE THE GREAT OZ!
PLEASE MAKE YOURSELVES COMFORTABLE WHILE I GO TO THE DOOR OF THE THRONE ROOM AND TELL OZ YOU ARE HERE!
...They waited a long time...
...a really long time...
Then finally--
I BRING NEWS!
HE WILL GRANT YOU AN AUDIENCE...
...BUT YOU MUST EACH SEE HIM ALONE, AND HE WILL ADMIT BUT ONE EACH DAY...
Guides came to show each of them to their rooms, where they could wait to see the Great Oz.

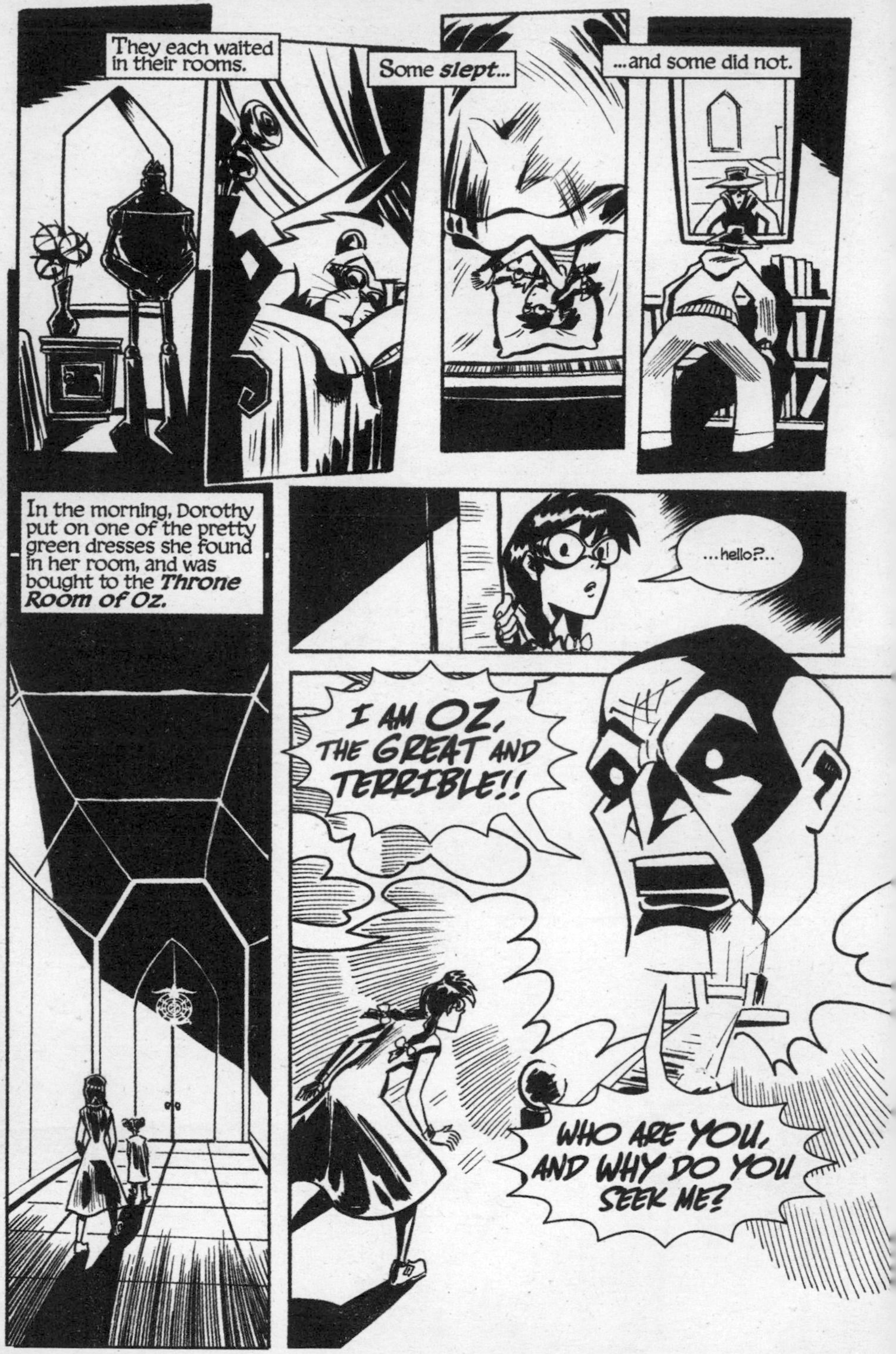

They each waited in their rooms.
Some *slept*...
...and some did not.
In the morning, Dorothy put on one of the pretty green dresses she found in her room, and was bought to the *Throne Room of Oz.*
...hello?...
I AM OZ, THE GREAT AND TERRIBLE!!
WHO ARE YOU, AND WHY DO YOU SEEK ME?

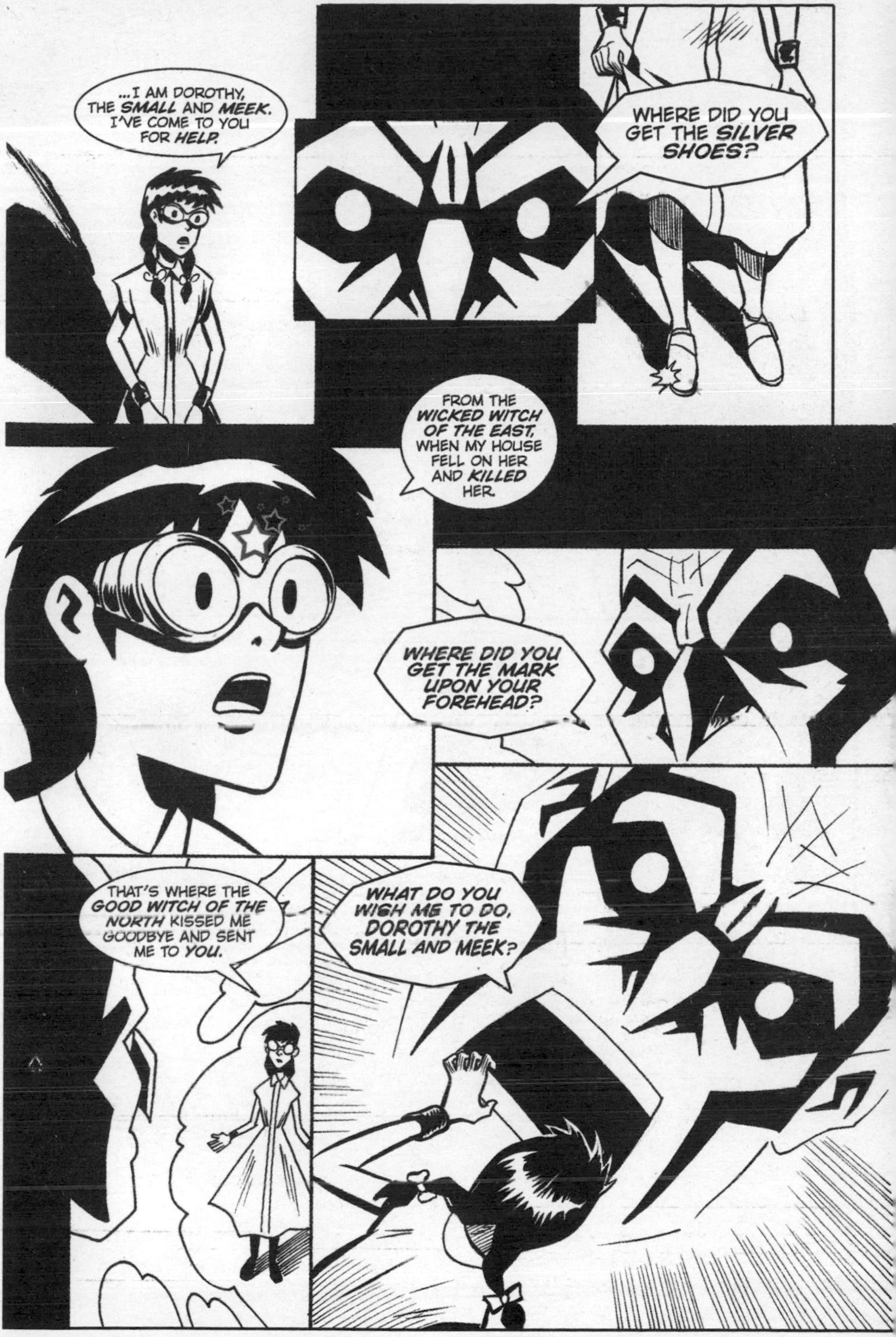

...I AM DOROTHY, THE SMALL AND MEEK. I'VE COME TO YOU FOR HELP.
WHERE DID YOU GET THE SILVER SHOES?
FROM THE WICKED WITCH OF THE EAST, WHEN MY HOUSE FELL ON HER AND KILLED HER.
WHERE DID YOU GET THE MARK UPON YOUR FOREHEAD?
THAT'S WHERE THE GOOD WITCH OF THE NORTH KISSED ME GOODBYE AND SENT ME TO YOU.
WHAT DO YOU WISH ME TO DO, DOROTHY THE SMALL AND MEEK?

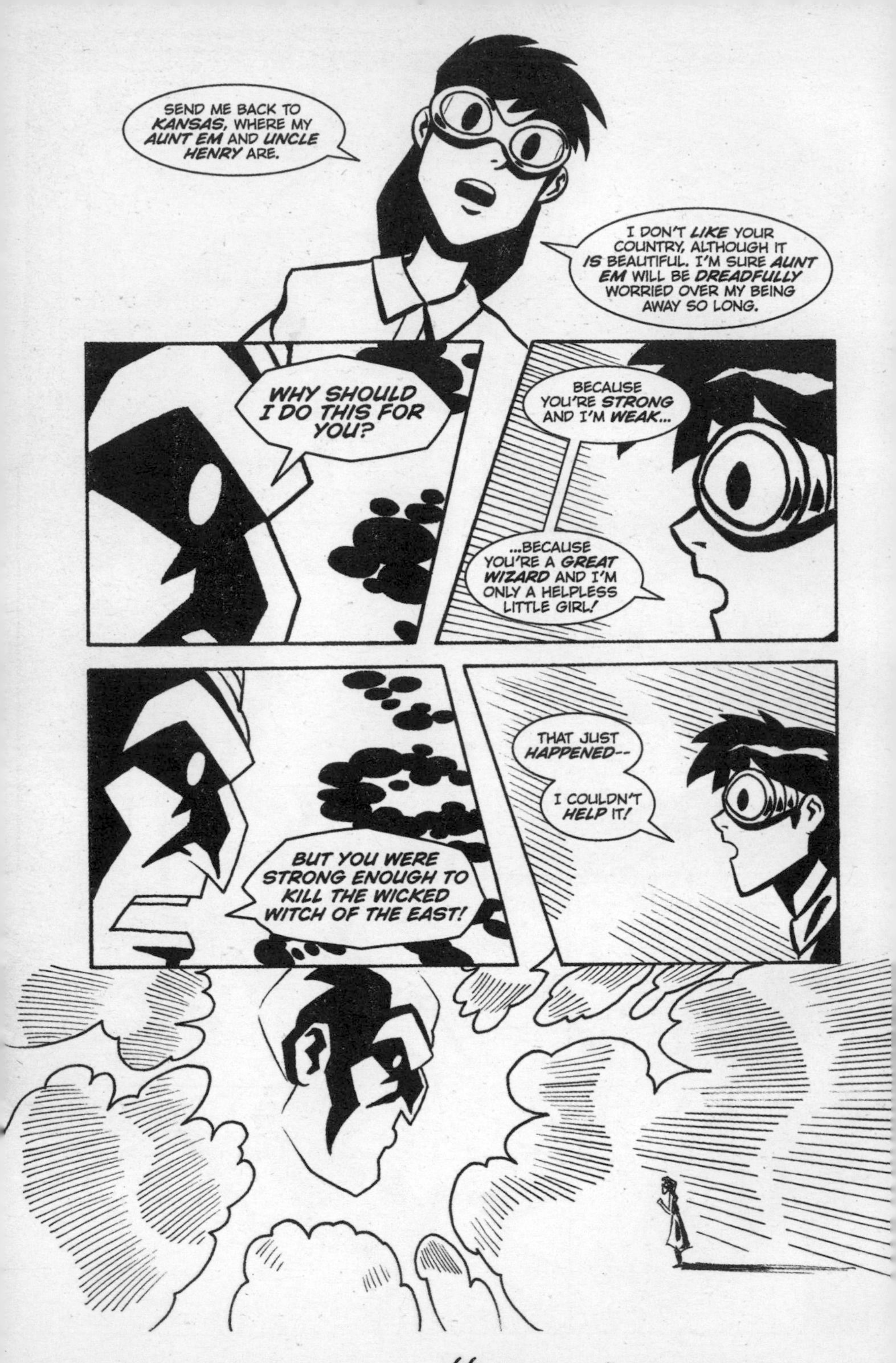
SEND ME BACK TO KANSAS, WHERE MY AUNT EM AND UNCLE HENRY ARE.
I DON'T LIKE YOUR COUNTRY, ALTHOUGH IT IS BEAUTIFUL. I'M SURE AUNT EM WILL BE DREADFULLY WORRIED OVER MY BEING AWAY SO LONG.
WHY SHOULD I DO THIS FOR YOU?
BECAUSE YOU'RE STRONG AND I'M WEAK...
...BECAUSE YOU'RE A GREAT WIZARD AND I'M ONLY A HELPLESS LITTLE GIRL!
BUT YOU WERE STRONG ENOUGH TO KILL THE WICKED WITCH OF THE EAST!
THAT JUST HAPPENED--
I COULDN'T HELP IT!

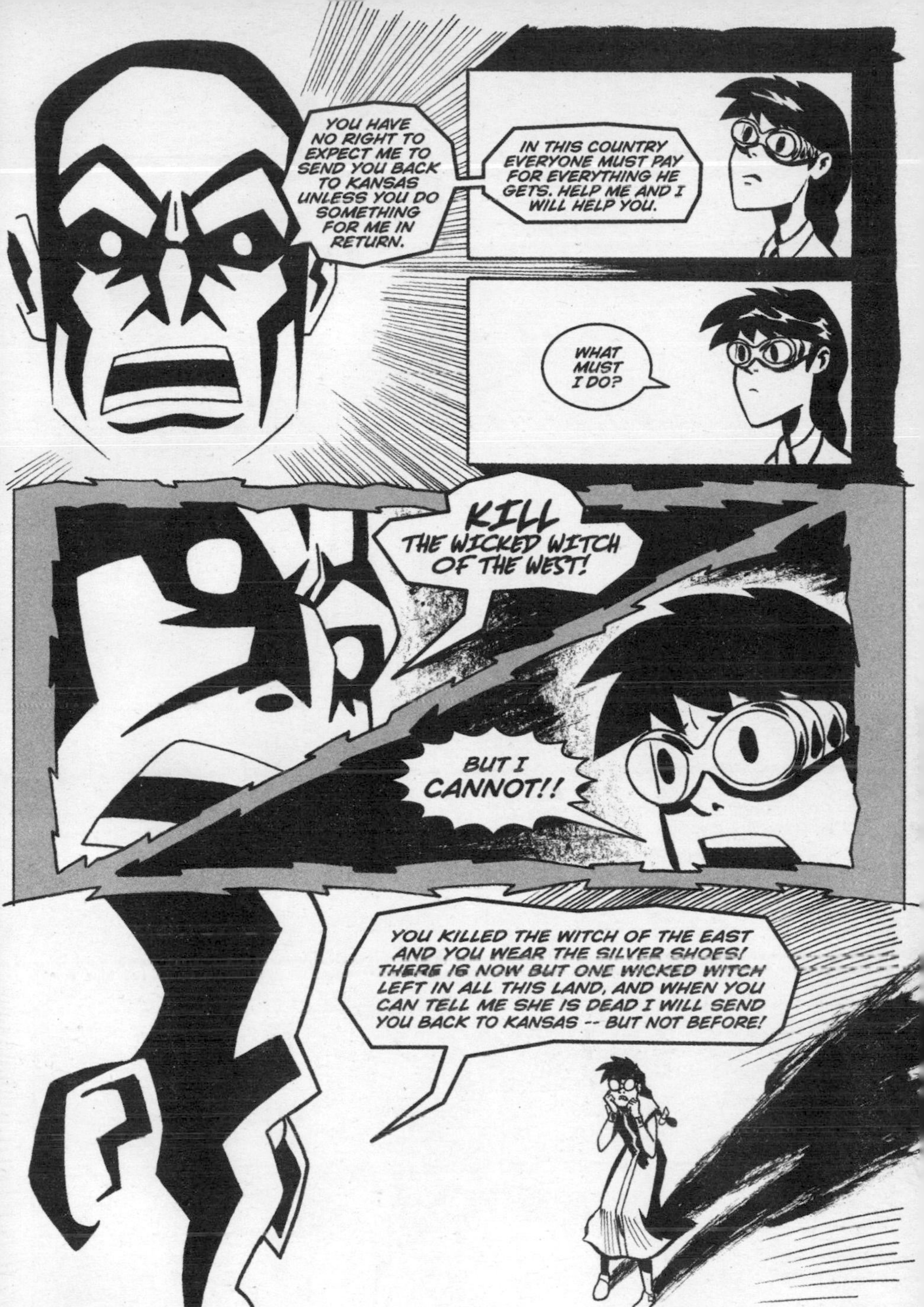
YOU HAVE NO RIGHT TO EXPECT ME TO SEND YOU BACK TO KANSAS UNLESS YOU DO SOMETHING FOR ME IN RETURN.
IN THIS COUNTRY EVERYONE MUST PAY FOR EVERYTHING HE GETS. HELP ME AND I WILL HELP YOU.
WHAT MUST I DO?
KILL THE WICKED WITCH OF THE WEST!
BUT I CANNOT!!
YOU KILLED THE WITCH OF THE EAST AND YOU WEAR THE SILVER SHOES! THERE IS NOW BUT ONE WICKED WITCH LEFT IN ALL THIS LAND, AND WHEN YOU CAN TELL ME SHE IS DEAD I WILL SEND YOU BACK TO KANSAS -- BUT NOT BEFORE!

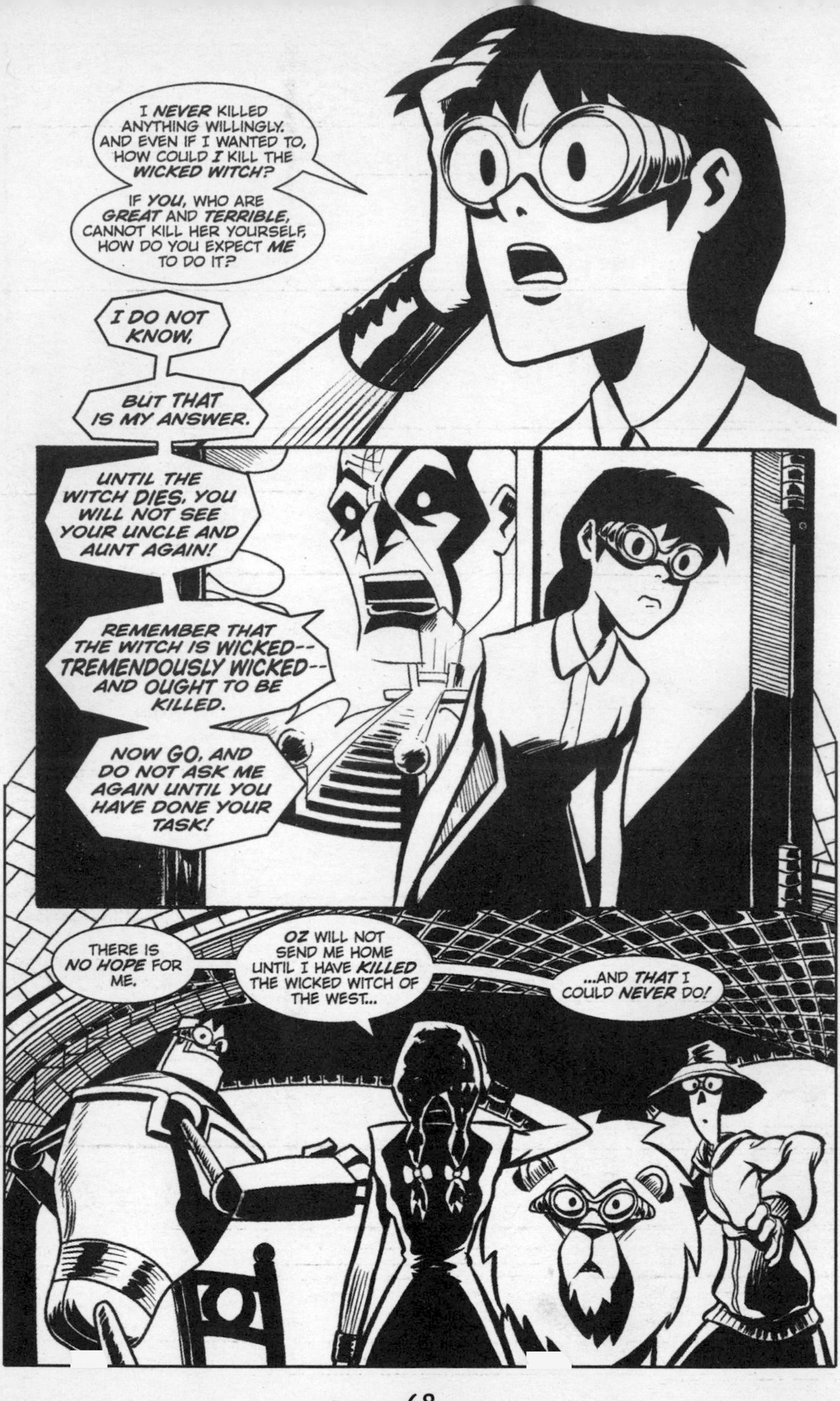
I NEVER KILLED ANYTHING WILLINGLY. AND EVEN IF I WANTED TO, HOW COULD I KILL THE WICKED WITCH?
IF YOU, WHO ARE GREAT AND TERRIBLE, CANNOT KILL HER YOURSELF, HOW DO YOU EXPECT ME TO DO IT?
I DO NOT KNOW,
BUT THAT IS MY ANSWER.
UNTIL THE WITCH DIES, YOU WILL NOT SEE YOUR UNCLE AND AUNT AGAIN!
REMEMBER THAT THE WITCH IS WICKED-- TREMENDOUSLY WICKED-- AND OUGHT TO BE KILLED.
NOW GO, AND DO NOT ASK ME AGAIN UNTIL YOU HAVE DONE YOUR TASK!
THERE IS NO HOPE FOR ME.
OZ WILL NOT SEND ME HOME UNTIL I HAVE KILLED THE WICKED WITCH OF THE WEST...
...AND THAT I COULD NEVER DO!

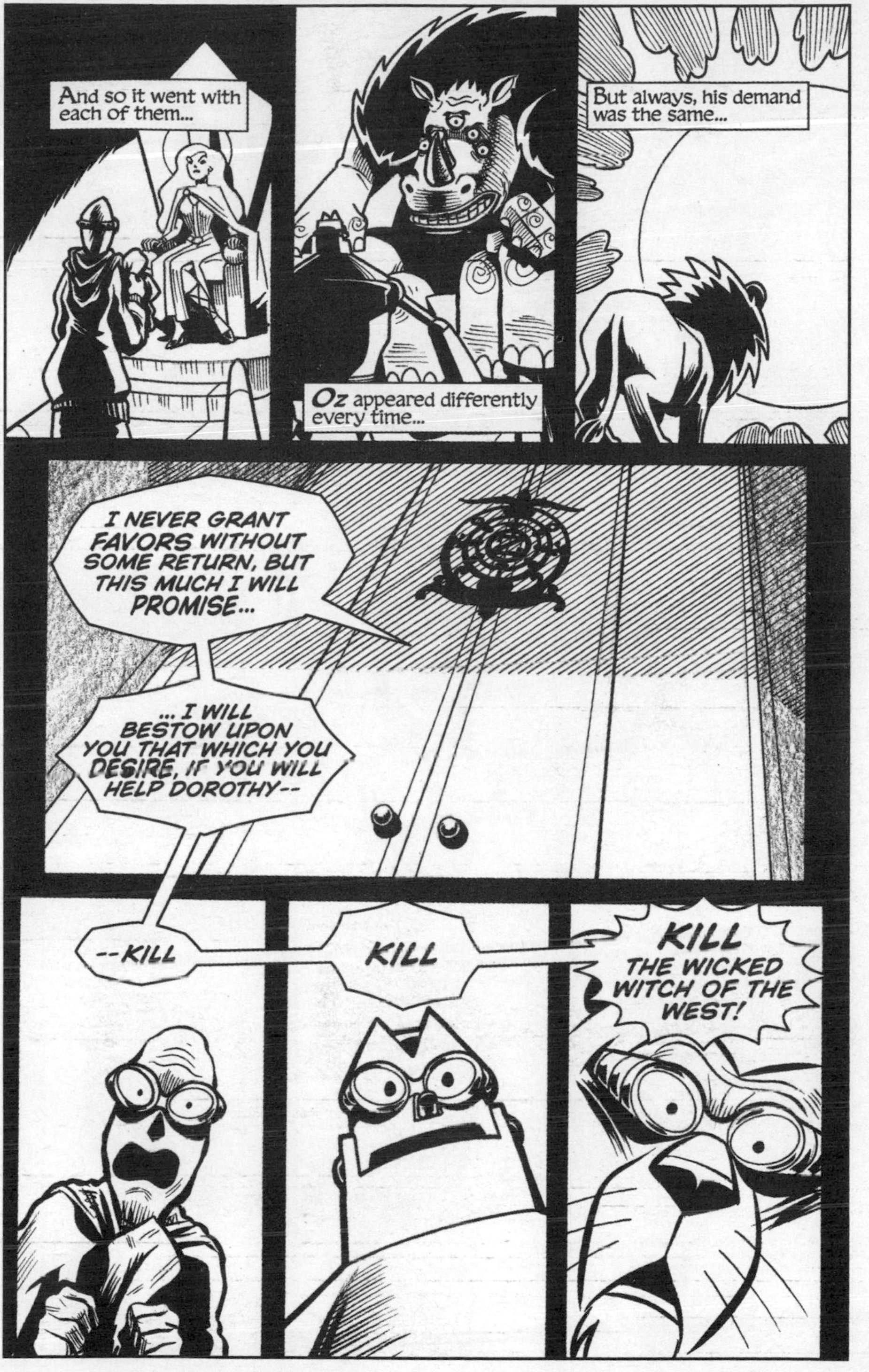
And so it went with each of them...
Oz appeared differently every time...
But always, his demand was the same...
I NEVER GRANT FAVORS WITHOUT SOME RETURN, BUT THIS MUCH I WILL PROMISE...
... I WILL BESTOW UPON YOU THAT WHICH YOU DESIRE, IF YOU WILL HELP DOROTHY--
--KILL
KILL
KILL THE WICKED WITCH OF THE WEST!

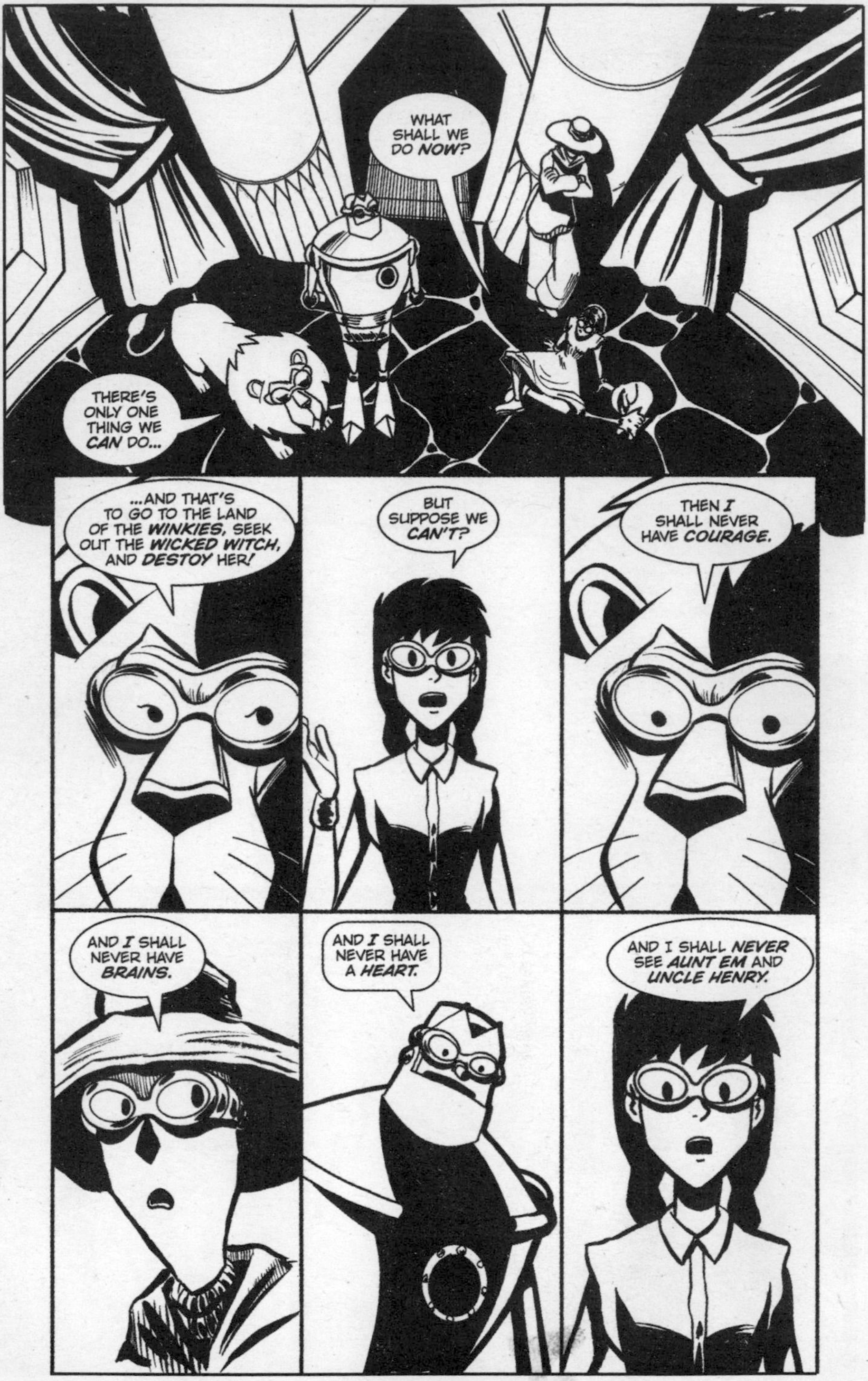
WHAT SHALL WE DO NOW?
THERE'S ONLY ONE THING WE CAN DO...
...AND THAT'S TO GO TO THE LAND OF THE WINKIES, SEEK OUT THE WICKED WITCH, AND DESTOY HER!
BUT SUPPOSE WE CAN'T?
THEN I SHALL NEVER HAVE COURAGE.
AND I SHALL NEVER HAVE BRAINS.
AND I SHALL NEVER HAVE A HEART.
AND I SHALL NEVER SEE AUNT EM AND UNCLE HENRY.

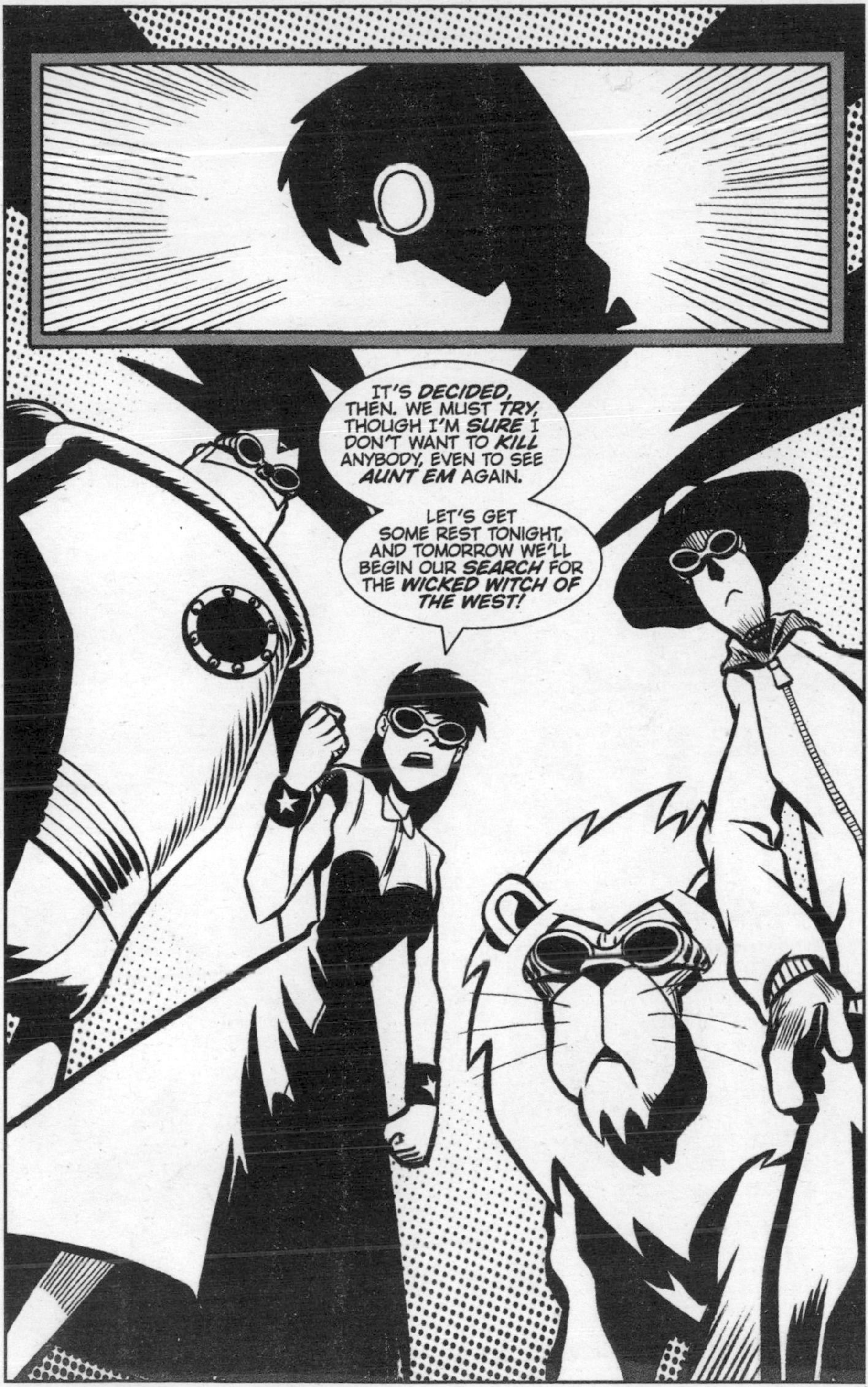
IT'S DECIDED, THEN. WE MUST TRY, THOUGH I'M SURE I DON'T WANT TO KILL ANYBODY, EVEN TO SEE AUNT EM AGAIN.
LET'S GET SOME REST TONIGHT, AND TOMORROW WE'LL BEGIN OUR SEARCH FOR THE WICKED WITCH OF THE WEST!

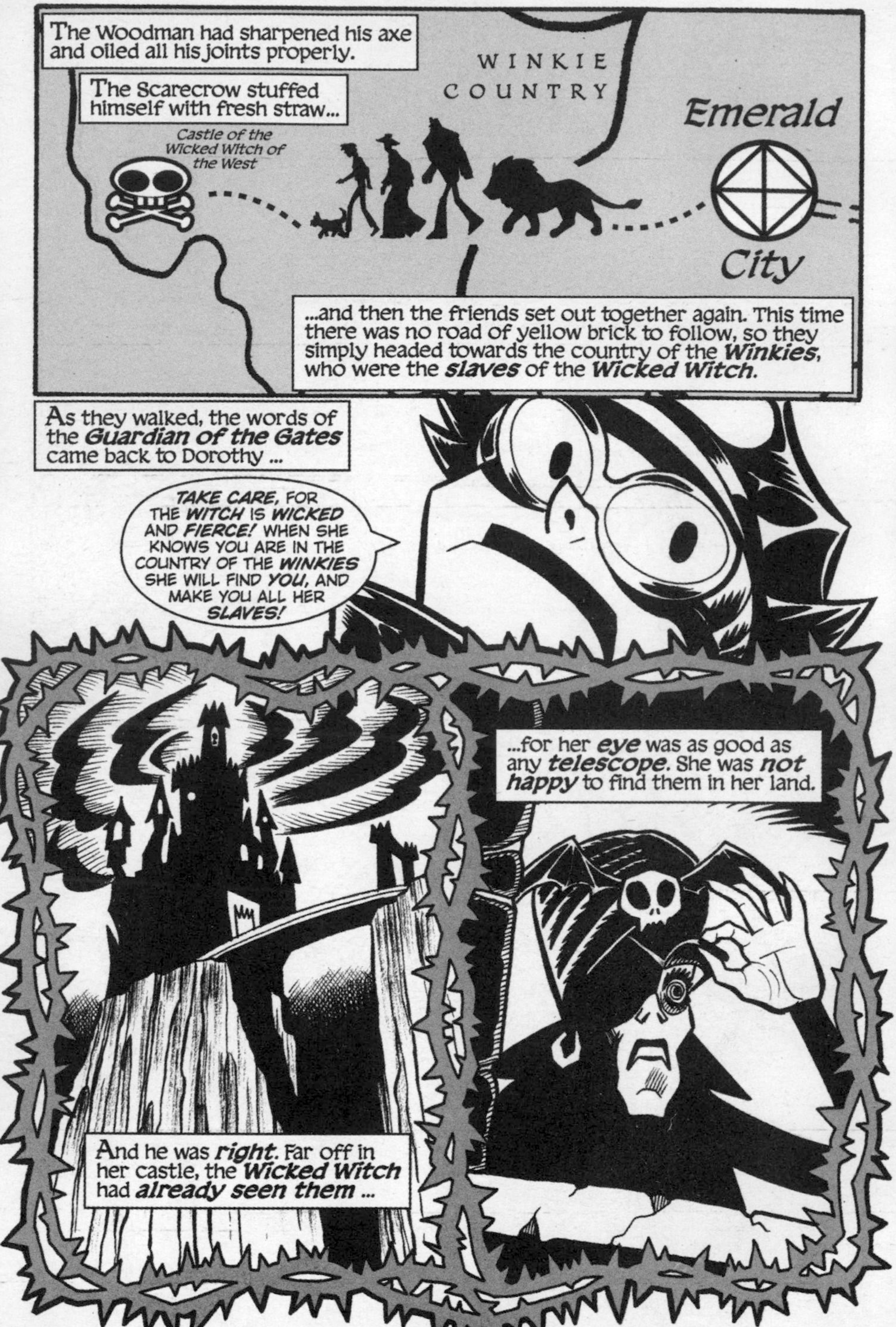
The Woodman had sharpened his axe and oiled all his joints properly.
The Scarecrow stuffed himself with fresh straw...
WINKIE COUNTRY
Emerald City
Castle of the Wicked Witch of the West
...and then the friends set out together again. This time there was no road of yellow brick to follow, so they simply headed towards the country of the Winkies, who were the slaves of the Wicked Witch.
As they walked, the words of the Guardian of the Gates came back to Dorothy ...
TAKE CARE, FOR THE WITCH IS WICKED AND FIERCE! WHEN SHE KNOWS YOU ARE IN THE COUNTRY OF THE WINKIES SHE WILL FIND YOU, AND MAKE YOU ALL HER SLAVES!
And he was right. Far off in her castle, the Wicked Witch had already seen them ...
...for her eye was as good as any telescope. She was not happy to find them in her land.

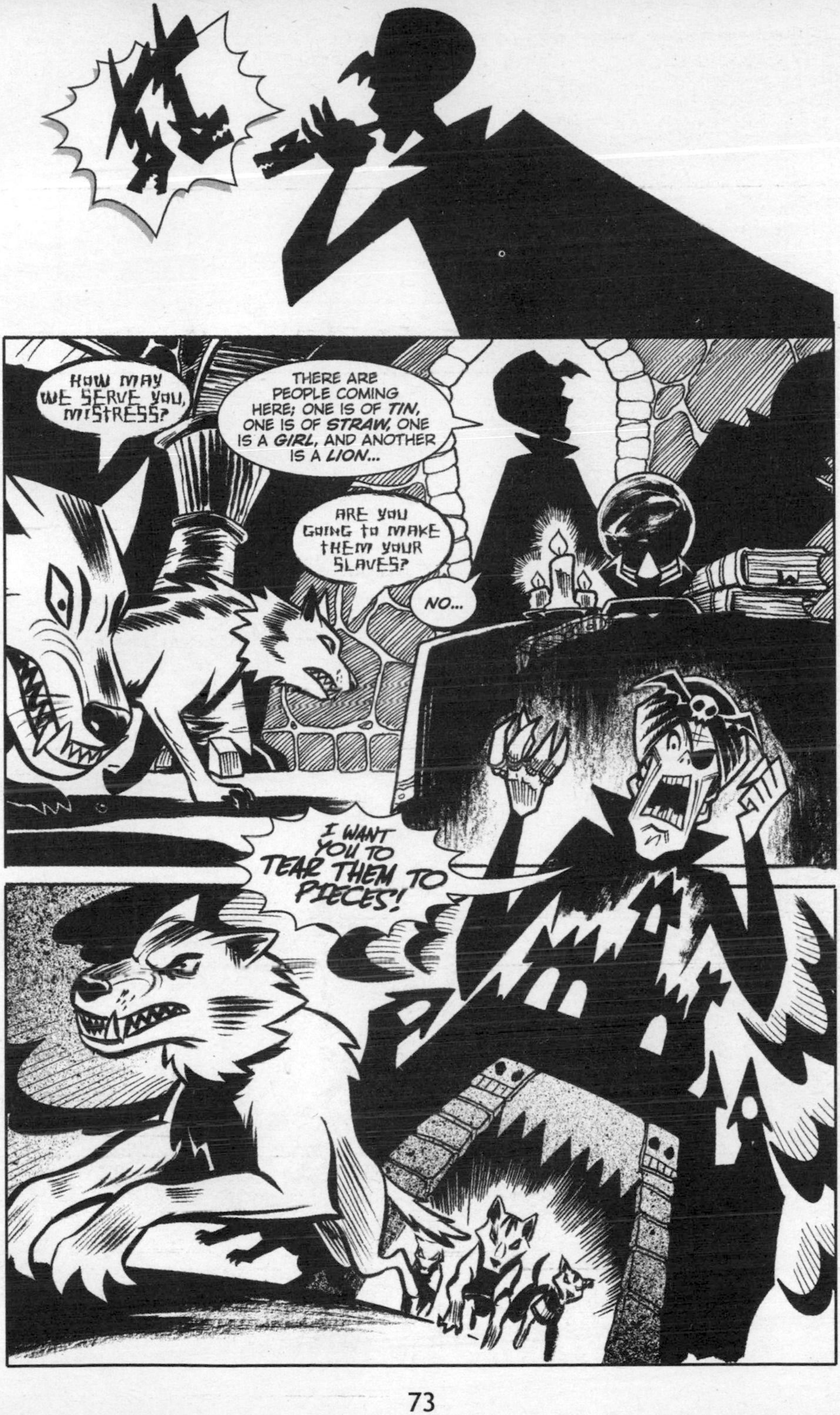
HOW MAY WE SERVE YOU, MISTRESS?
THERE ARE PEOPLE COMING HERE; ONE IS OF *TIN*, ONE IS OF ***STRAW***, ONE IS A *GIRL*, AND ANOTHER IS A *LION*...
ARE YOU GOING TO MAKE THEM YOUR SLAVES?
NO...
I WANT YOU TO **TEAR THEM TO PIECES!**

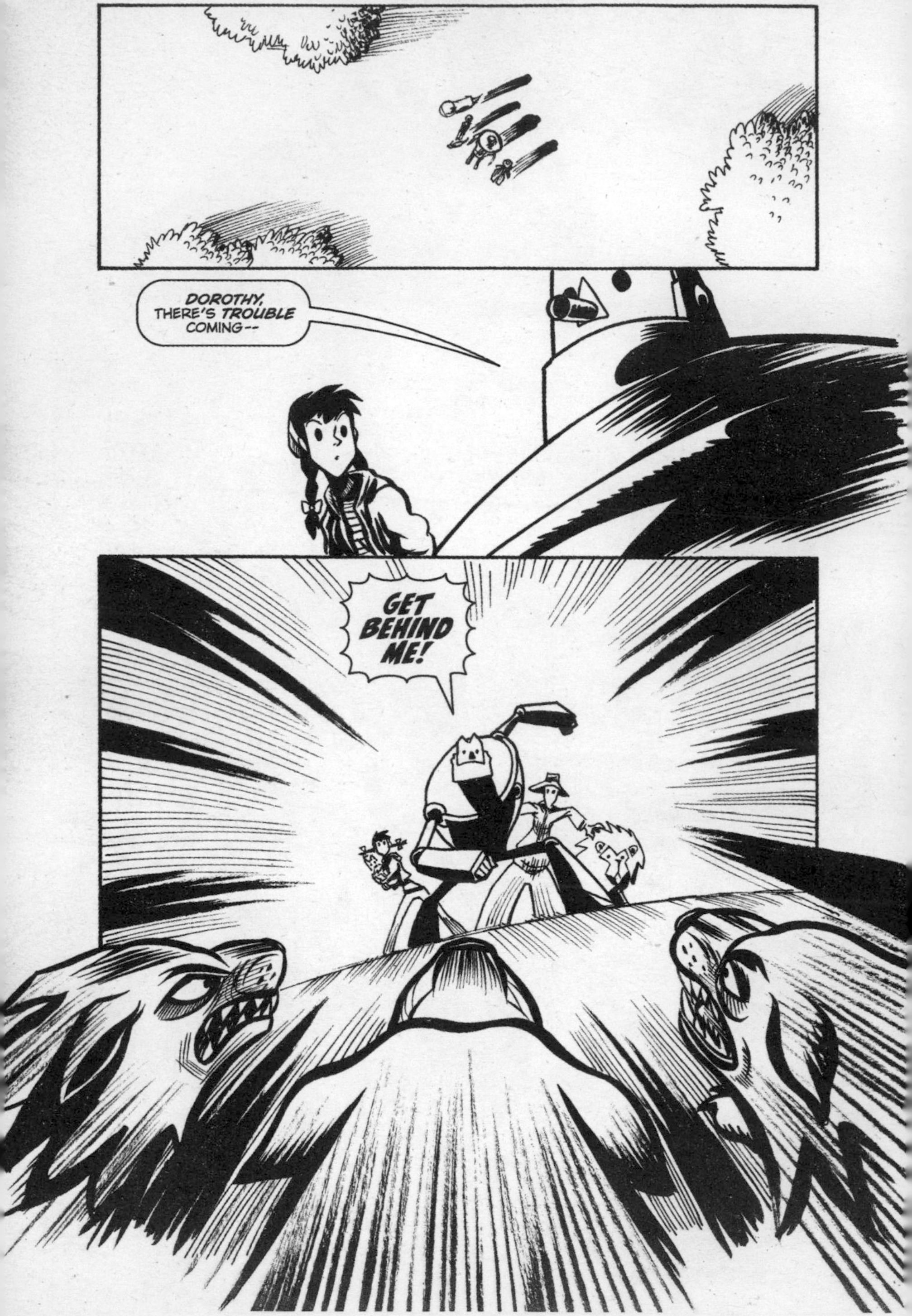
DOROTHY, THERE'S TROUBLE COMING--
GET BEHIND ME!

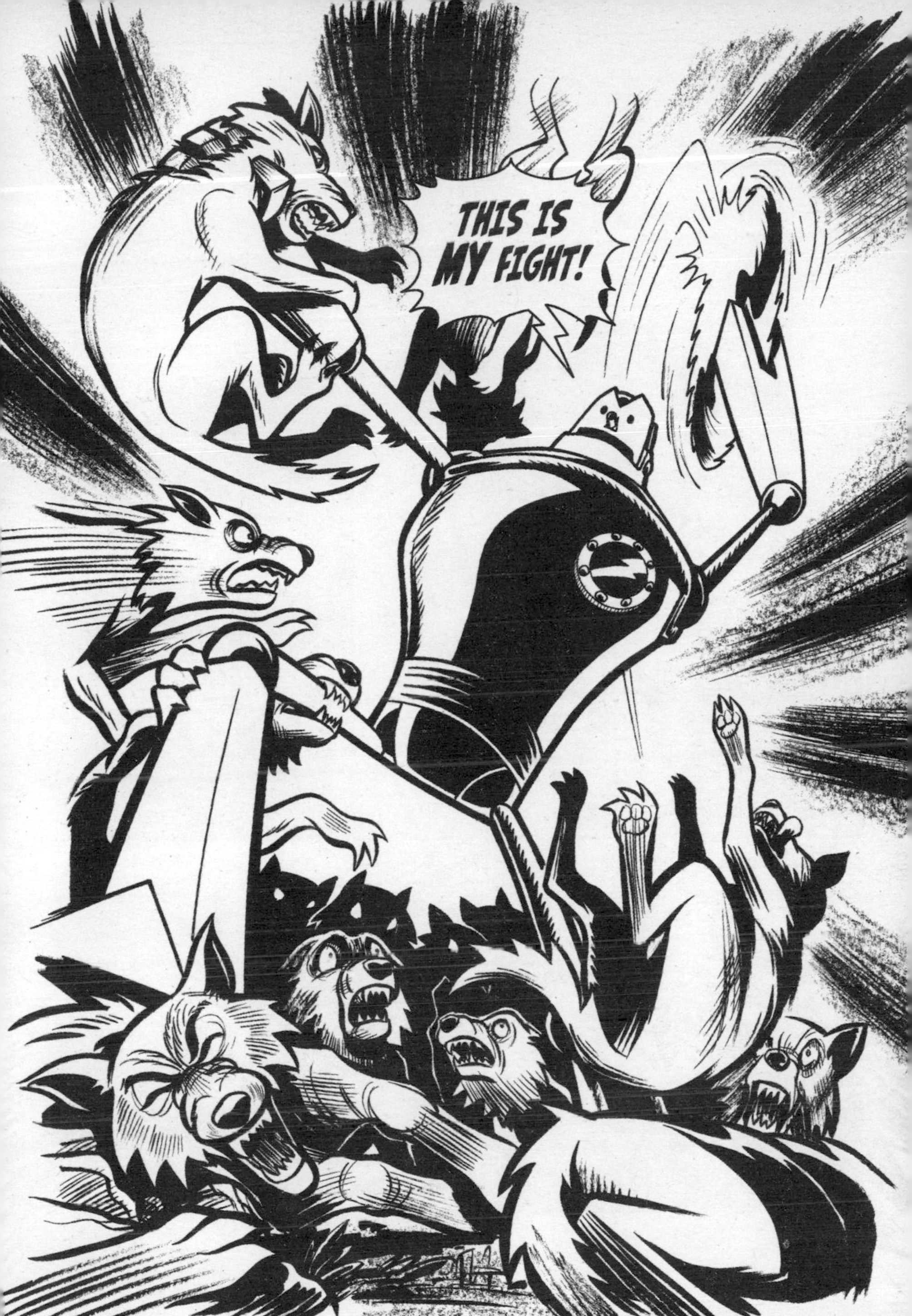
THIS IS MY FIGHT!

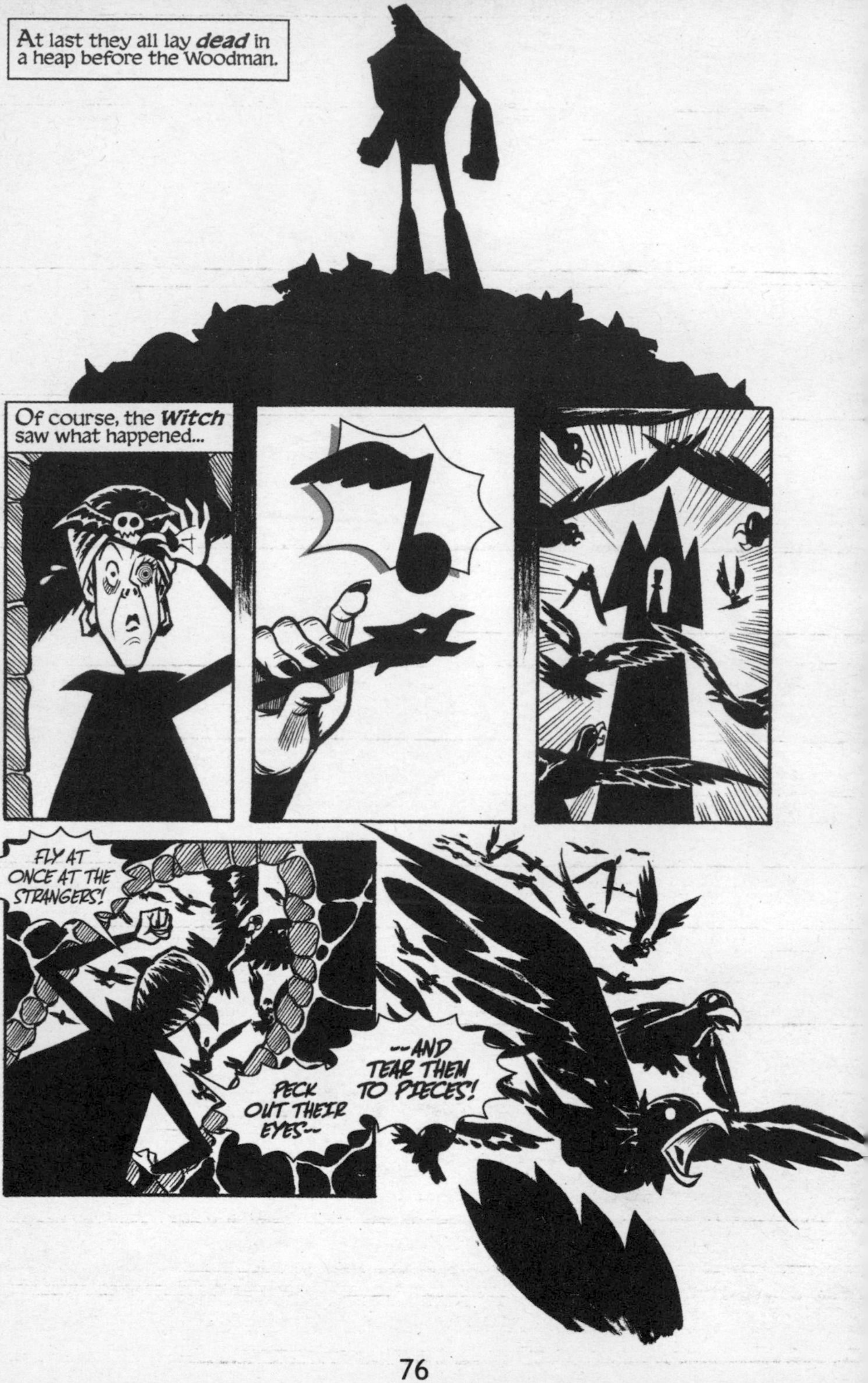
At last they all lay *dead* in a heap before the Woodman.
Of course, the *Witch* saw what happened...
FLY AT ONCE AT THE STRANGERS!
PECK OUT THEIR EYES--
--AND TEAR THEM TO PIECES!

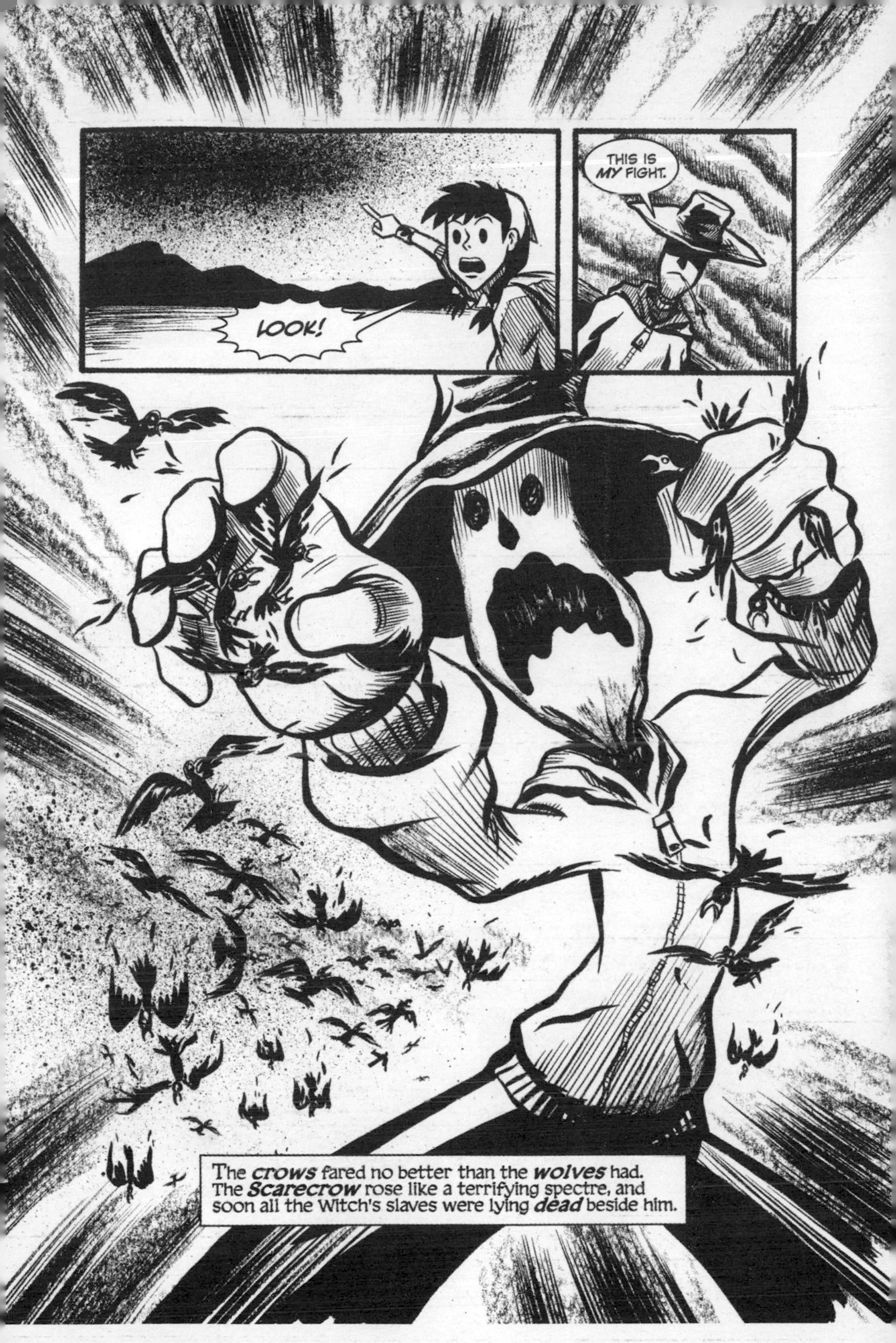
LOOK!
THIS IS MY FIGHT.
The crows fared no better than the wolves had. The Scarecrow rose like a terrifying spectre, and soon all the Witch's slaves were lying dead beside him.

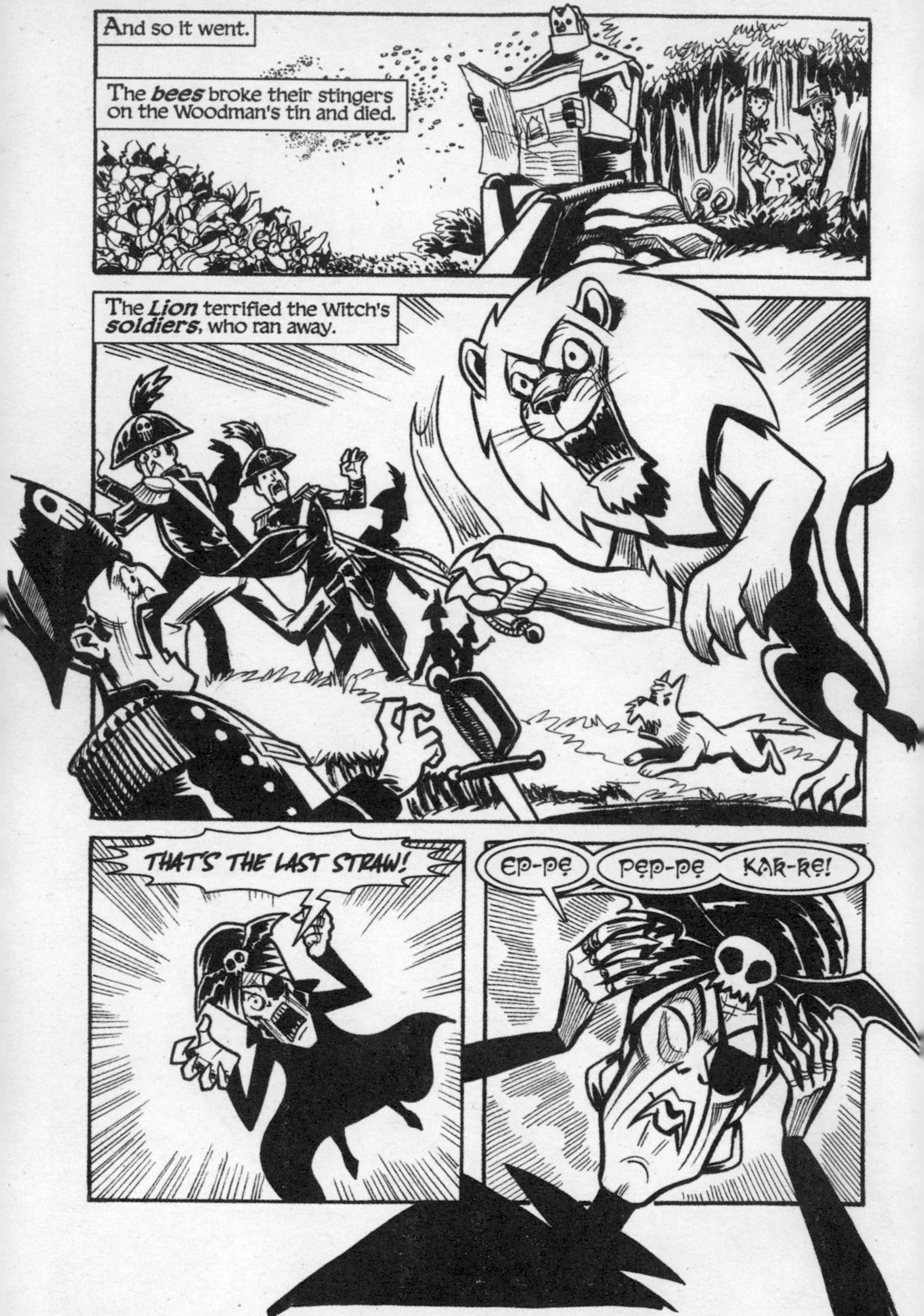
And so it went.
The *bees* broke their stingers on the Woodman's tin and died.
The *Lion* terrified the Witch's *soldiers*, who ran away.
THAT'S THE LAST STRAW!
EP-PE
PEP-PE
KAK-KE!

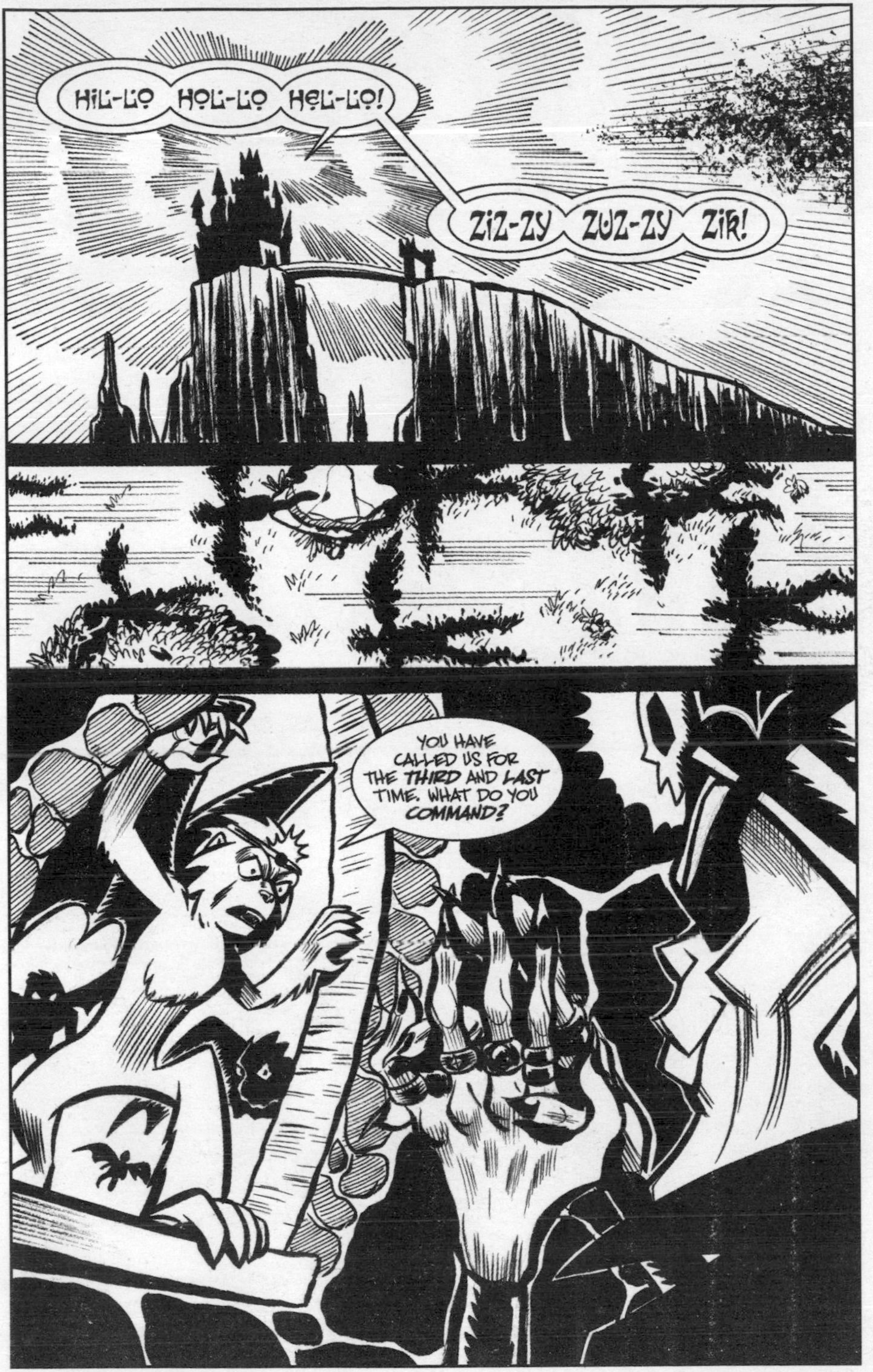
HIL-LO HOL-LO HEL-LO!
ZIZ-ZY ZUZ-ZY ZIK!
YOU HAVE CALLED US FOR THE THIRD AND LAST TIME. WHAT DO YOU COMMAND?

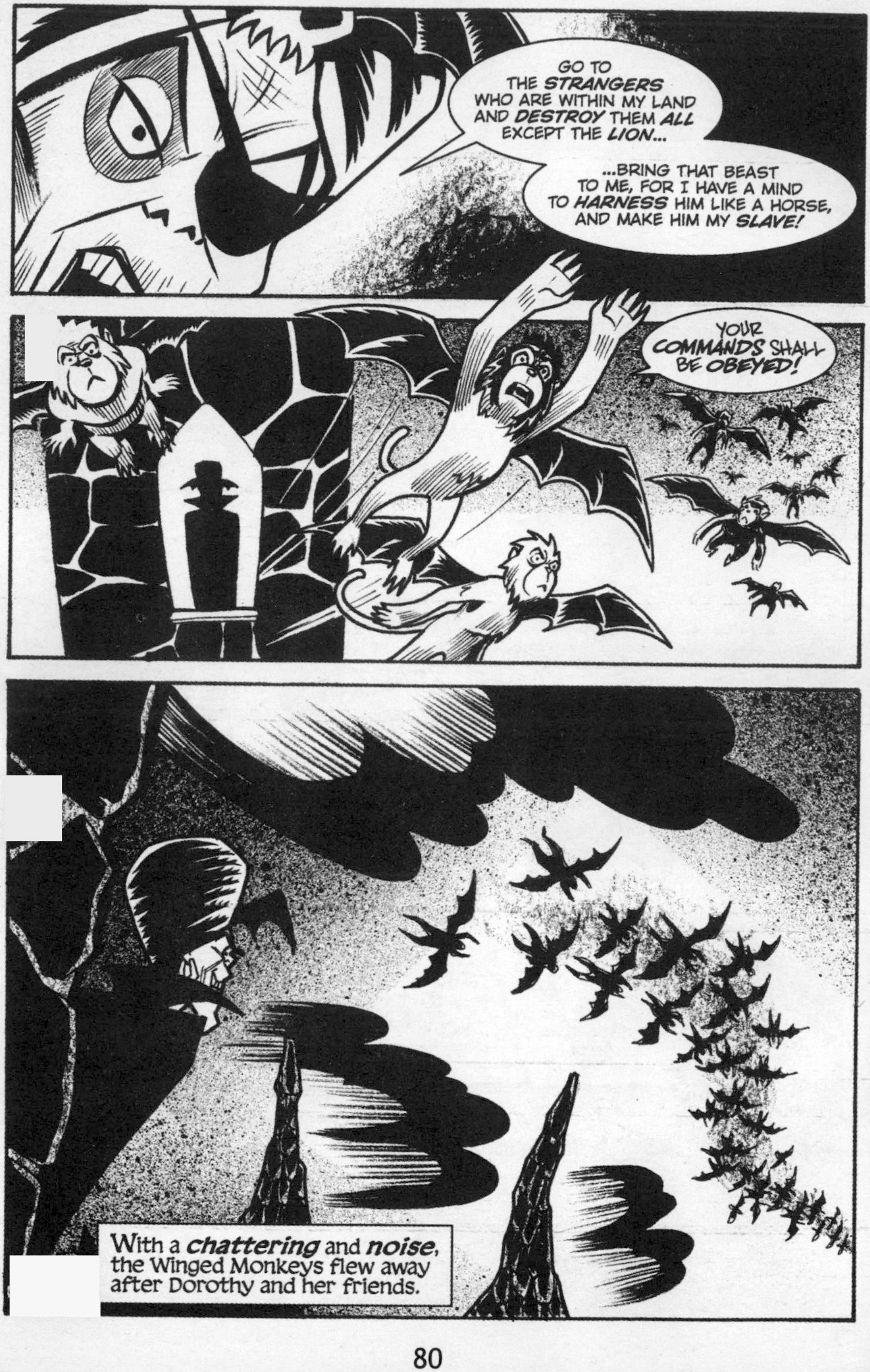
GO TO THE STRANGERS WHO ARE WITHIN MY LAND AND DESTROY THEM ALL EXCEPT THE LION...
...BRING THAT BEAST TO ME, FOR I HAVE A MIND TO HARNESS HIM LIKE A HORSE, AND MAKE HIM MY SLAVE!
YOUR COMMANDS SHALL BE OBEYED!
With a chattering and noise, the Winged Monkeys flew away after Dorothy and her friends.

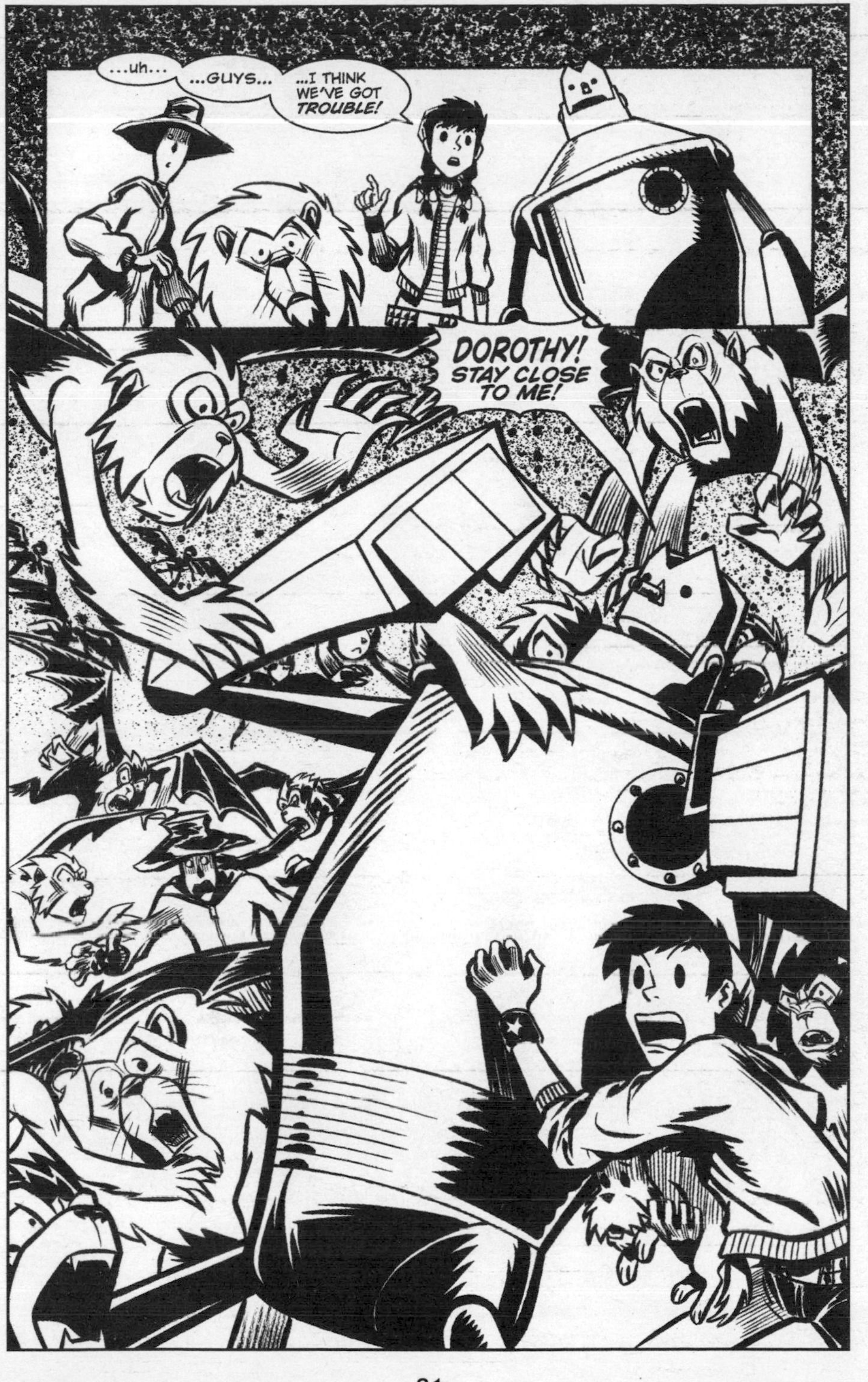
...uh...
...GUYS...
...I THINK WE'VE GOT TROUBLE!
DOROTHY! STAY CLOSE TO ME!

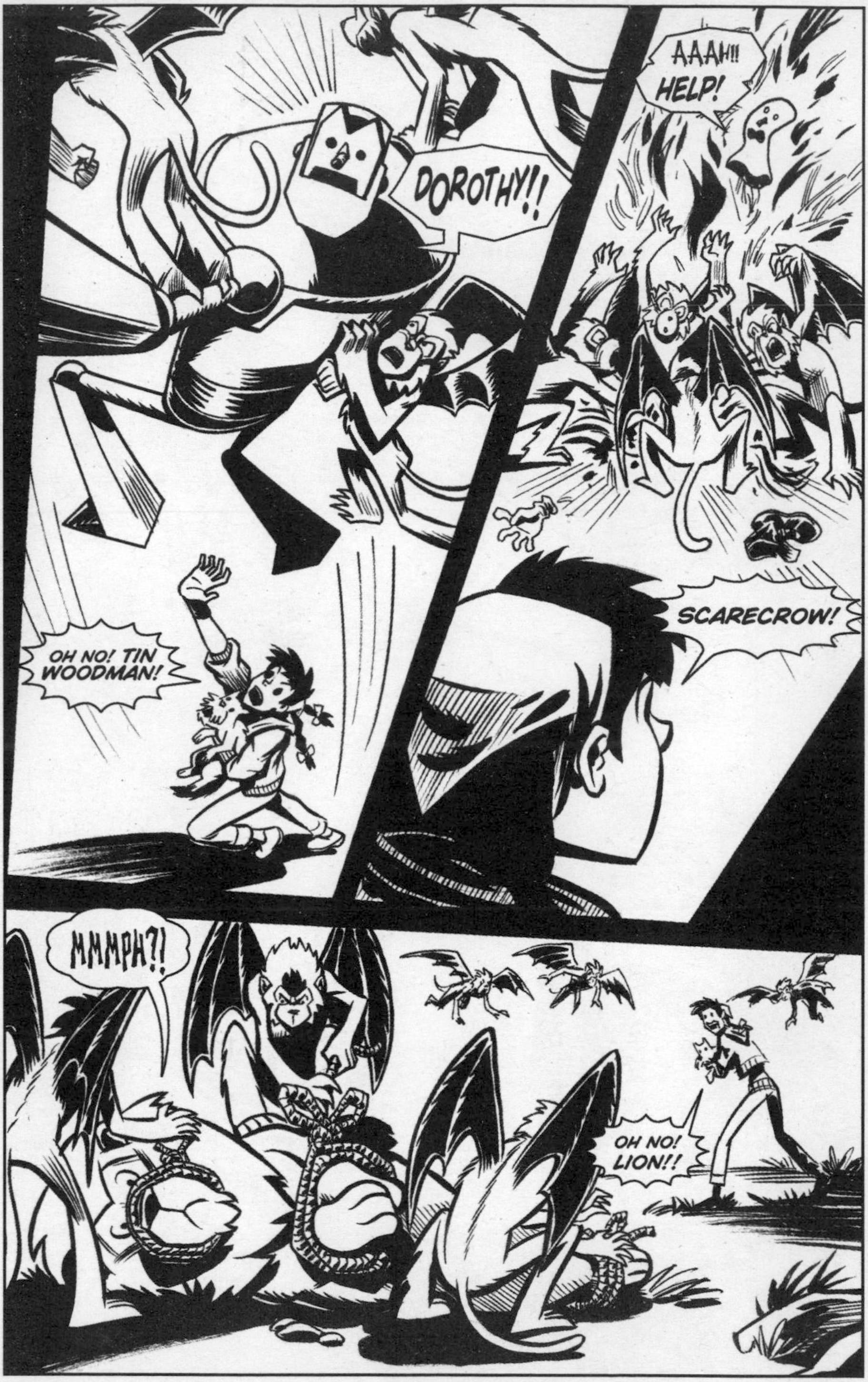
DOROTHY!!
AAAH!! HELP!
OH NO! TIN WOODMAN!
SCARECROW!
MMMPH?!
OH NO! LION!!

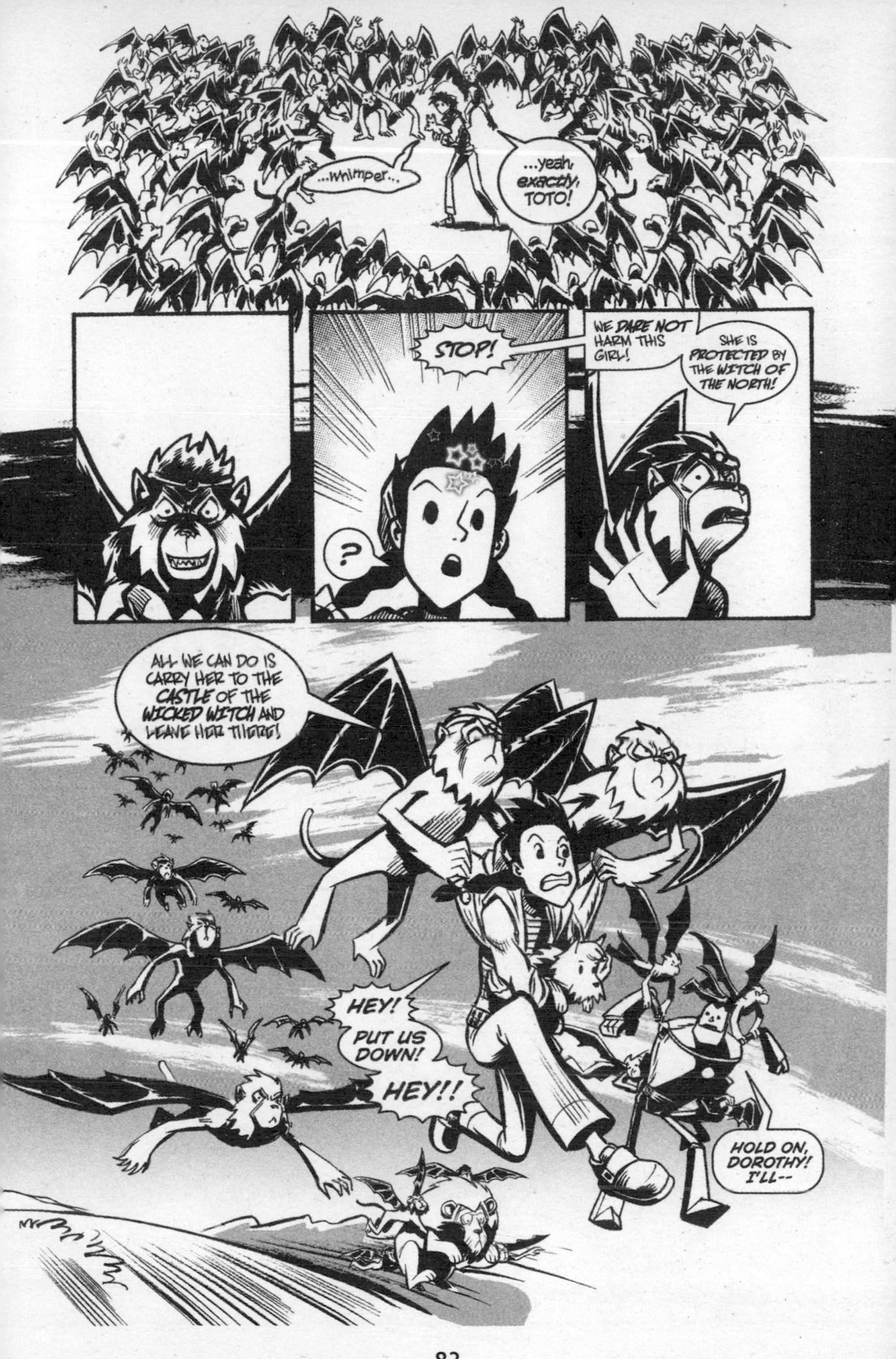
...whimper...
...yeah, exactly, TOTO!
STOP!
?
WE DARE NOT HARM THIS GIRL!
SHE IS PROTECTED BY THE WITCH OF THE NORTH!
ALL WE CAN DO IS CARRY HER TO THE CASTLE OF THE WICKED WITCH AND LEAVE HER THERE!
HEY!
PUT US DOWN!
HEY!!
HOLD ON, DOROTHY! I'LL--

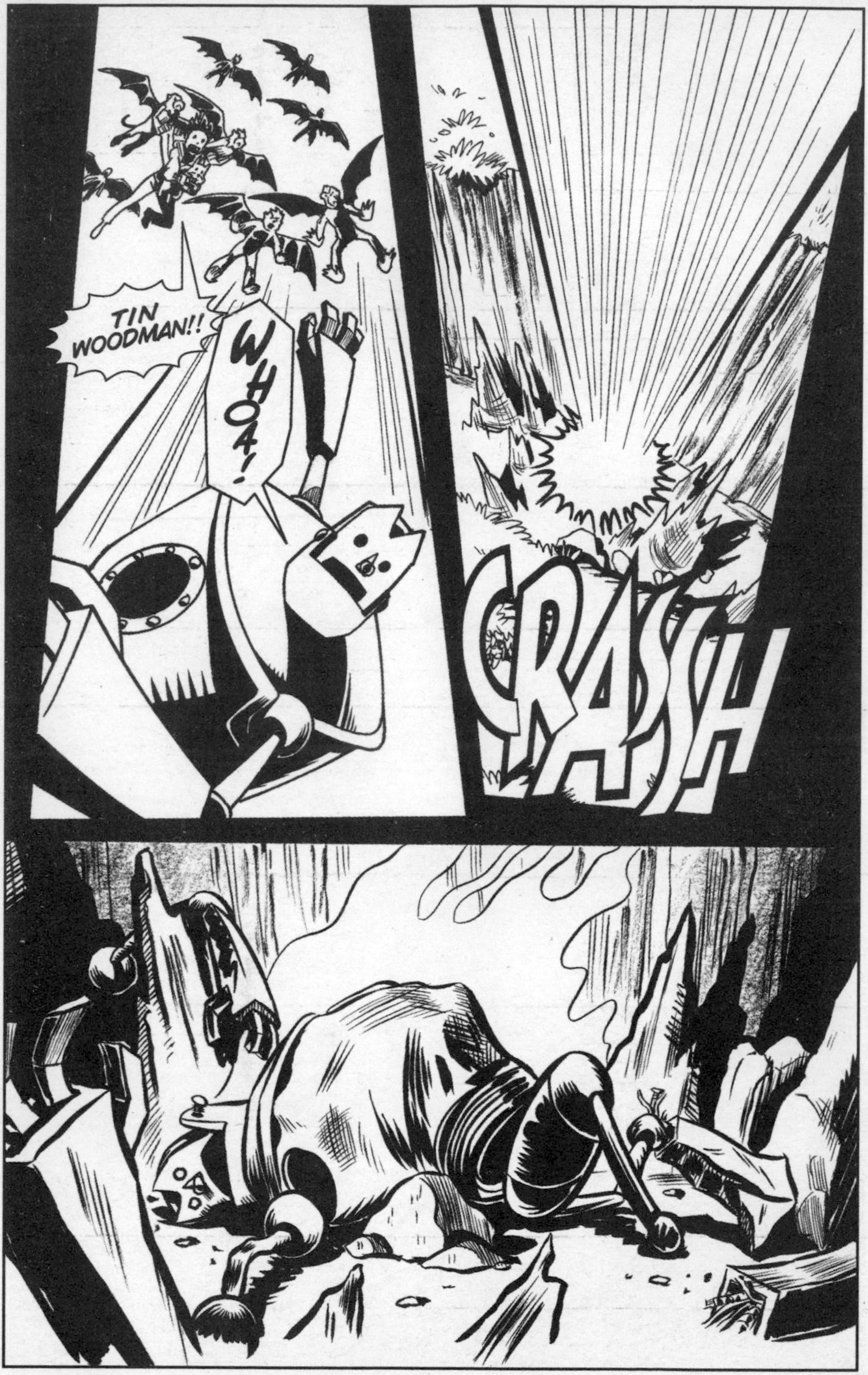
TIN WOODMAN!!
WHOA!
CRASH

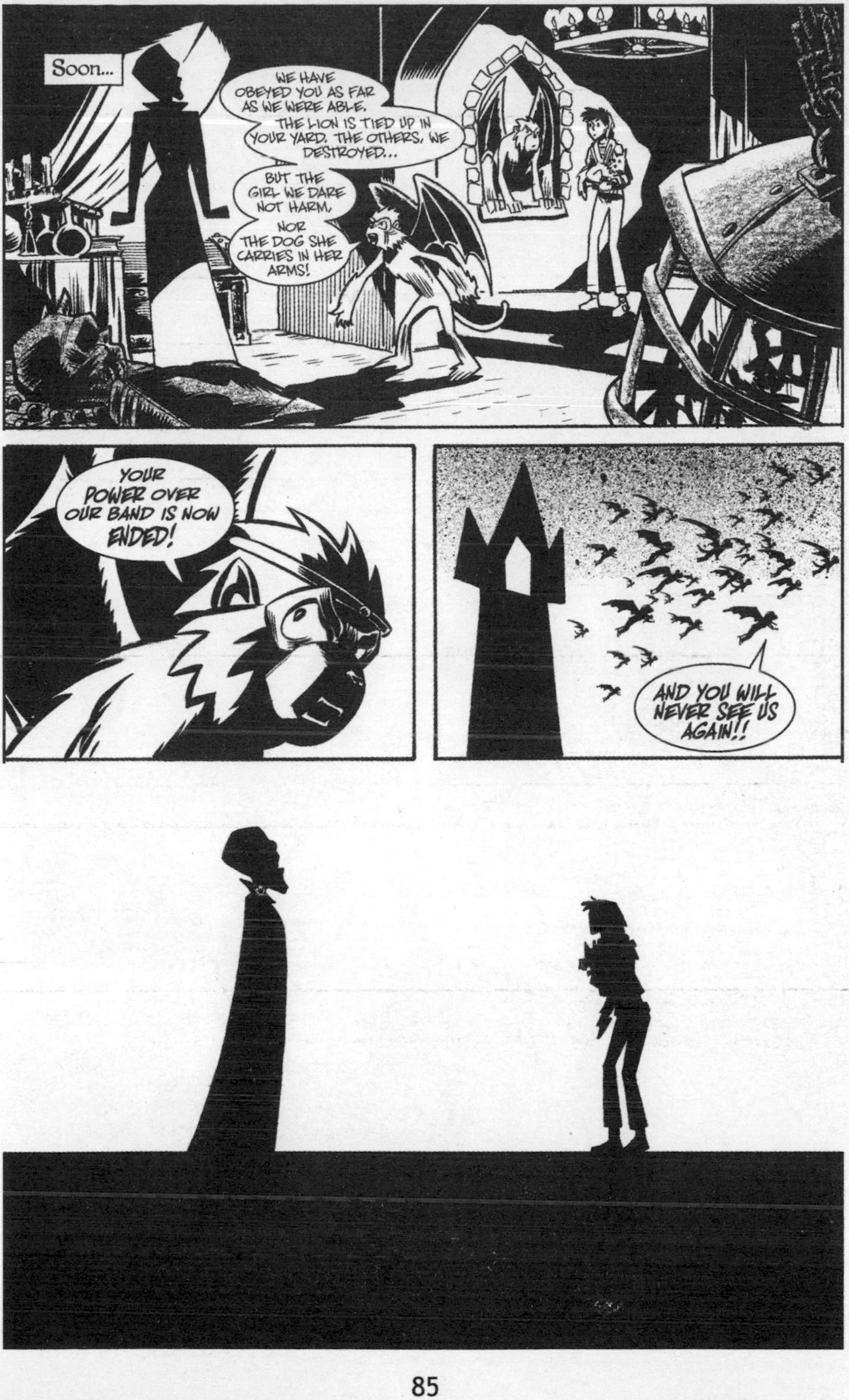
Soon...
WE HAVE OBEYED YOU AS FAR AS WE WERE ABLE.
THE LION IS TIED UP IN YOUR YARD. THE OTHERS, WE DESTROYED...
BUT THE GIRL WE DARE NOT HARM,
NOR THE DOG SHE CARRIES IN HER ARMS!
YOUR POWER OVER OUR BAND IS NOW ENDED!
AND YOU WILL NEVER SEE US AGAIN!!

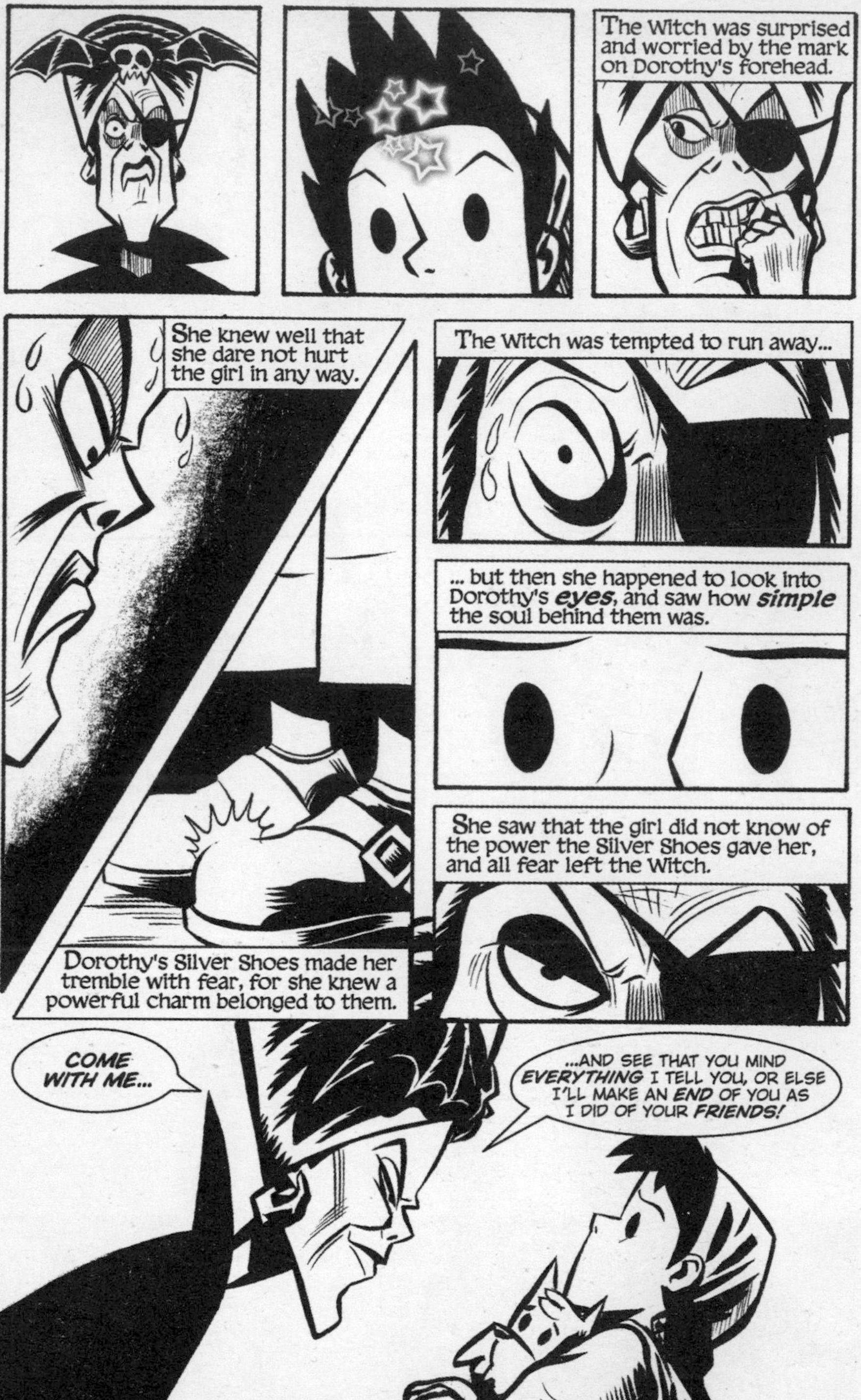

The Witch was surprised and worried by the mark on Dorothy's forehead.
She knew well that she dare not hurt the girl in any way.
Dorothy's Silver Shoes made her tremble with fear, for she knew a powerful charm belonged to them.
The Witch was tempted to run away...
... but then she happened to look into Dorothy's *eyes*, and saw how *simple* the soul behind them was.
She saw that the girl did not know of the power the Silver Shoes gave her, and all fear left the Witch.
COME WITH ME...
...AND SEE THAT YOU MIND *EVERYTHING* I TELL YOU, OR ELSE I'LL MAKE AN *END* OF YOU AS I DID OF YOUR *FRIENDS!*

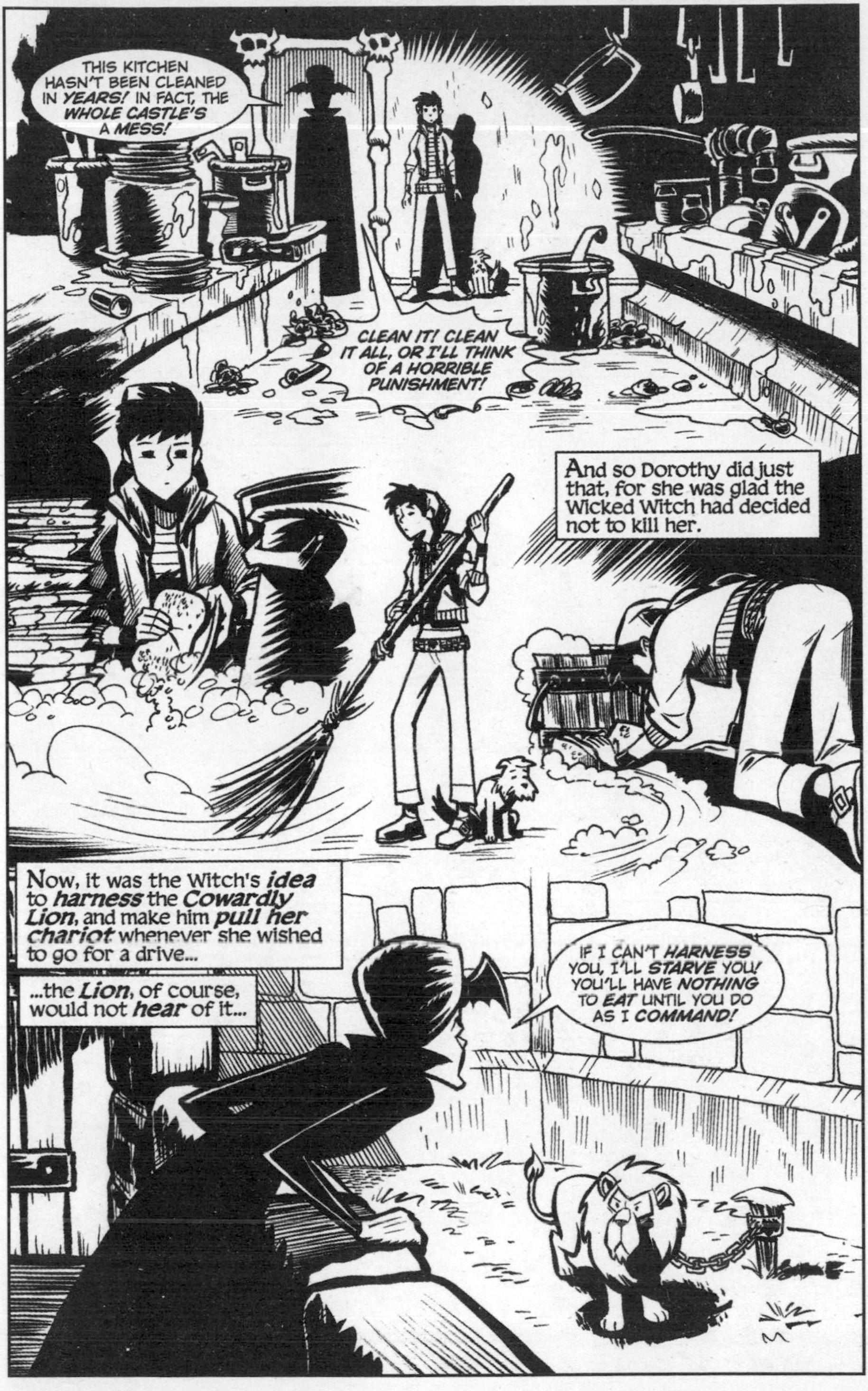
THIS KITCHEN HASN'T BEEN CLEANED IN YEARS! IN FACT, THE WHOLE CASTLE'S A MESS!
CLEAN IT! CLEAN IT ALL, OR I'LL THINK OF A HORRIBLE PUNISHMENT!
And so Dorothy did just that, for she was glad the Wicked Witch had decided not to kill her.
Now, it was the Witch's idea to harness the Cowardly Lion, and make him pull her chariot whenever she wished to go for a drive...
...the Lion, of course, would not hear of it...
IF I CAN'T HARNESS YOU, I'LL STARVE YOU! YOU'LL HAVE NOTHING TO EAT UNTIL YOU DO AS I COMMAND!

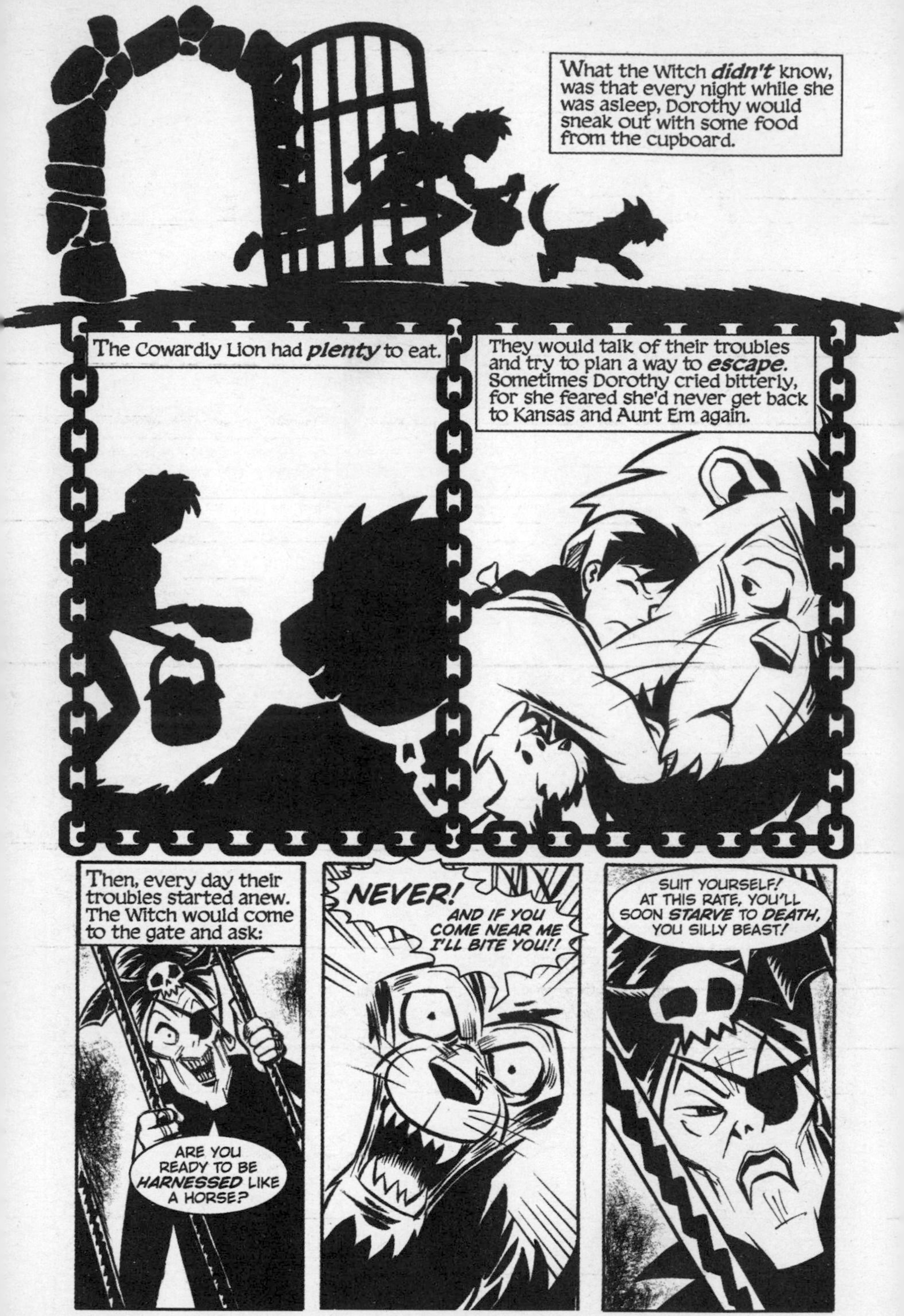
What the Witch didn't know, was that every night while she was asleep, Dorothy would sneak out with some food from the cupboard.
The Cowardly Lion had plenty to eat.
They would talk of their troubles and try to plan a way to escape. Sometimes Dorothy cried bitterly, for she feared she'd never get back to Kansas and Aunt Em again.
Then, every day their troubles started anew. The Witch would come to the gate and ask:
ARE YOU READY TO BE HARNESSED LIKE A HORSE?
NEVER!
AND IF YOU COME NEAR ME I'LL BITE YOU!!
SUIT YOURSELF! AT THIS RATE, YOU'LL SOON STARVE TO DEATH, YOU SILLY BEAST!

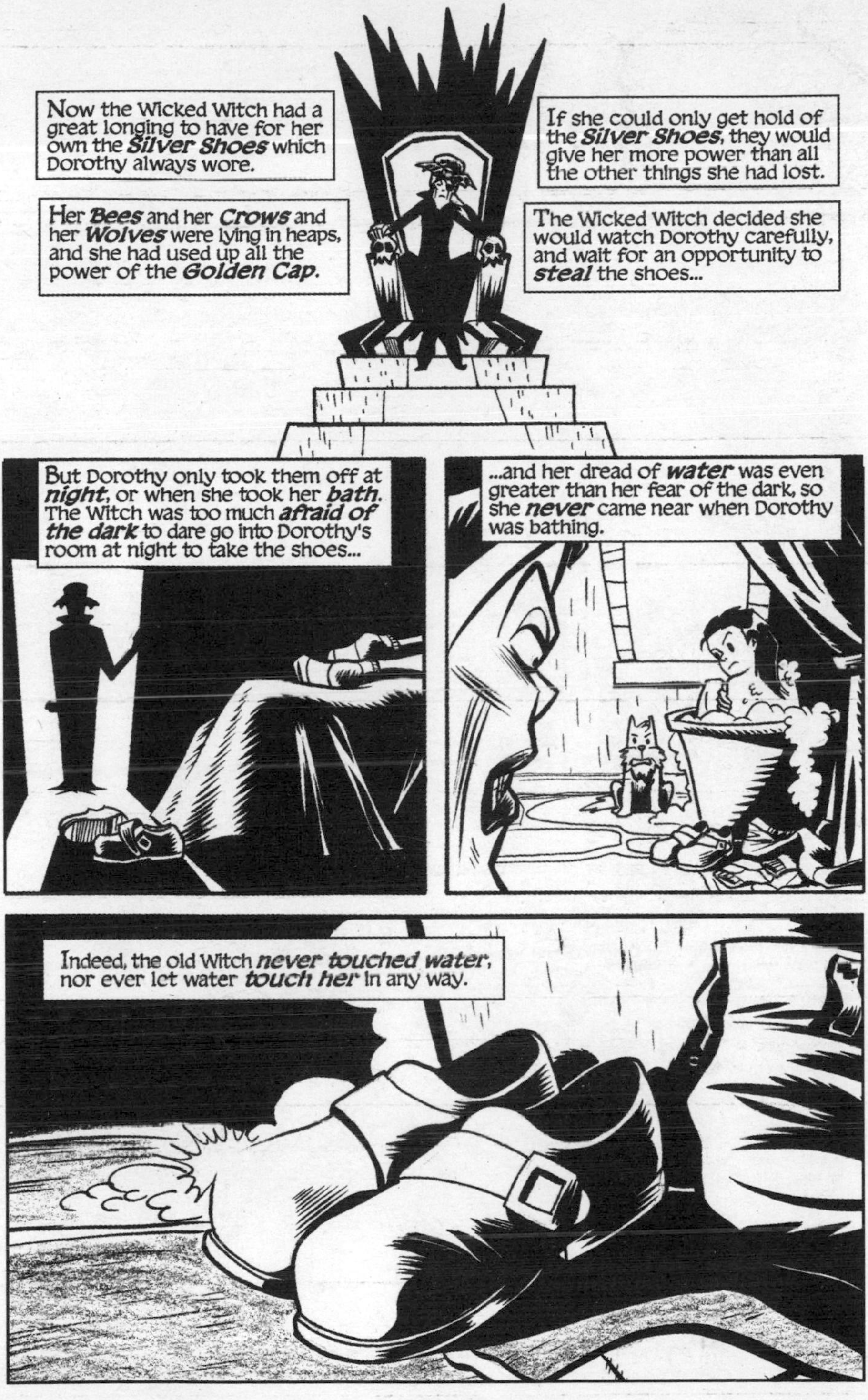
Now the Wicked Witch had a great longing to have for her own the Silver Shoes which Dorothy always wore.
Her Bees and her Crows and her Wolves were lying in heaps, and she had used up all the power of the Golden Cap.
If she could only get hold of the Silver Shoes, they would give her more power than all the other things she had lost.
The Wicked Witch decided she would watch Dorothy carefully, and wait for an opportunity to steal the shoes...
But Dorothy only took them off at night, or when she took her bath. The Witch was too much afraid of the dark to dare go into Dorothy's room at night to take the shoes...
...and her dread of water was even greater than her fear of the dark, so she never came near when Dorothy was bathing.
Indeed, the old Witch never touched water, nor ever let water touch her in any way.

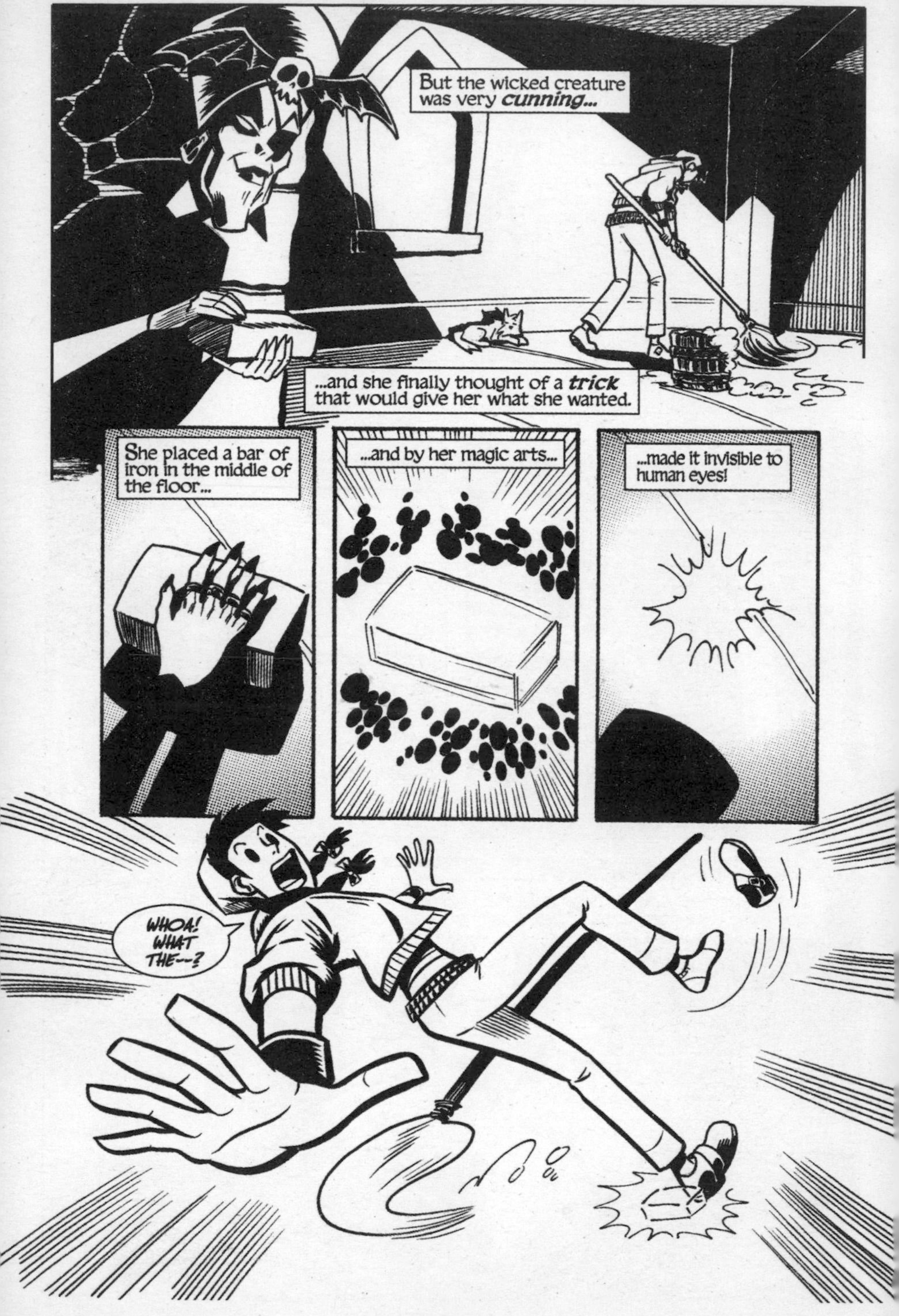

But the wicked creature was very *cunning*...
...and she finally thought of a *trick* that would give her what she wanted.
She placed a bar of iron in the middle of the floor...
...and by her magic arts...
...made it invisible to human eyes!
WHOA! WHAT THE--?

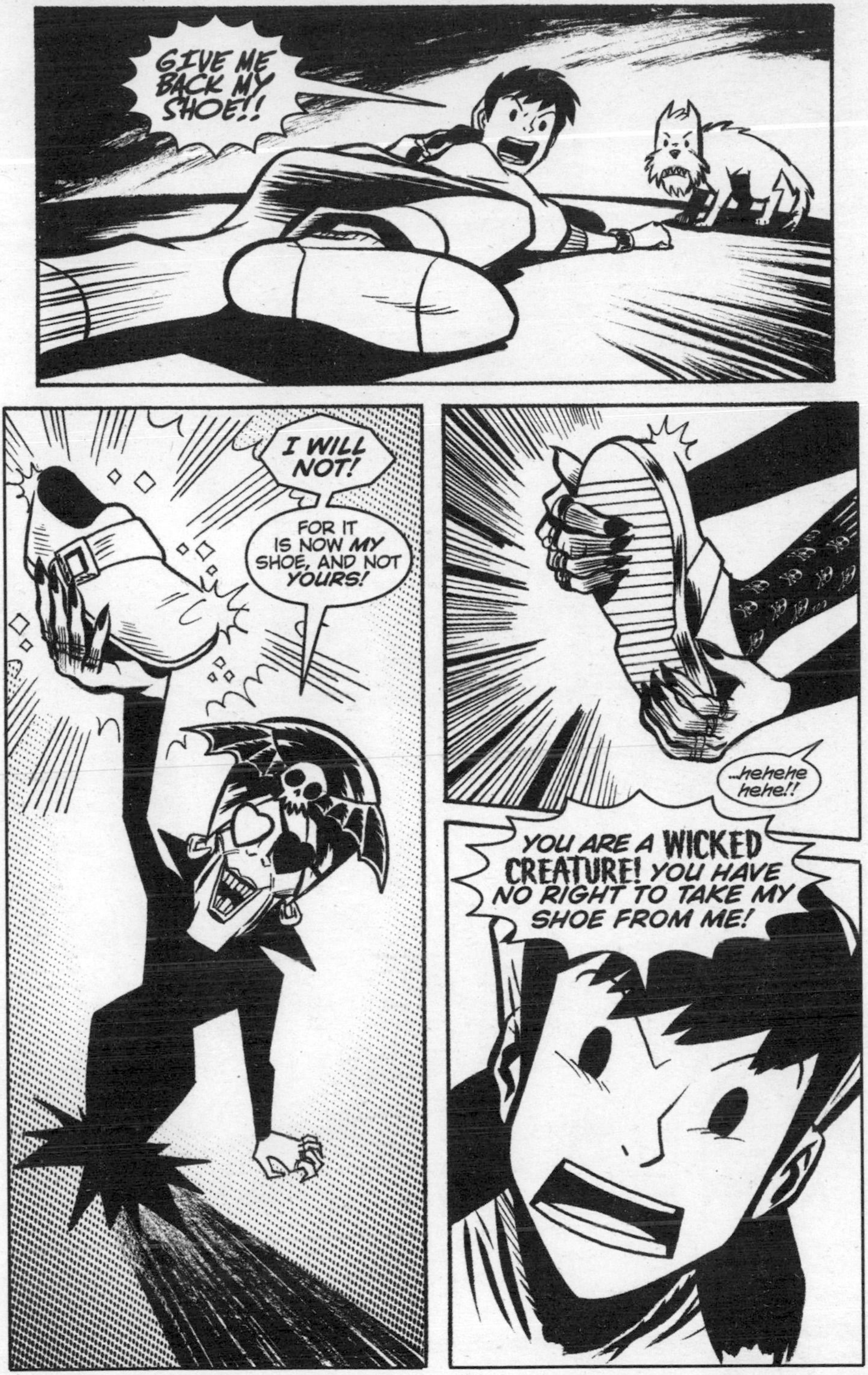
GIVE ME BACK MY SHOE!!
I WILL NOT!
FOR IT IS NOW MY SHOE, AND NOT YOURS!
...hehehe hehe!!
YOU ARE A WICKED CREATURE! YOU HAVE NO RIGHT TO TAKE MY SHOE FROM ME!

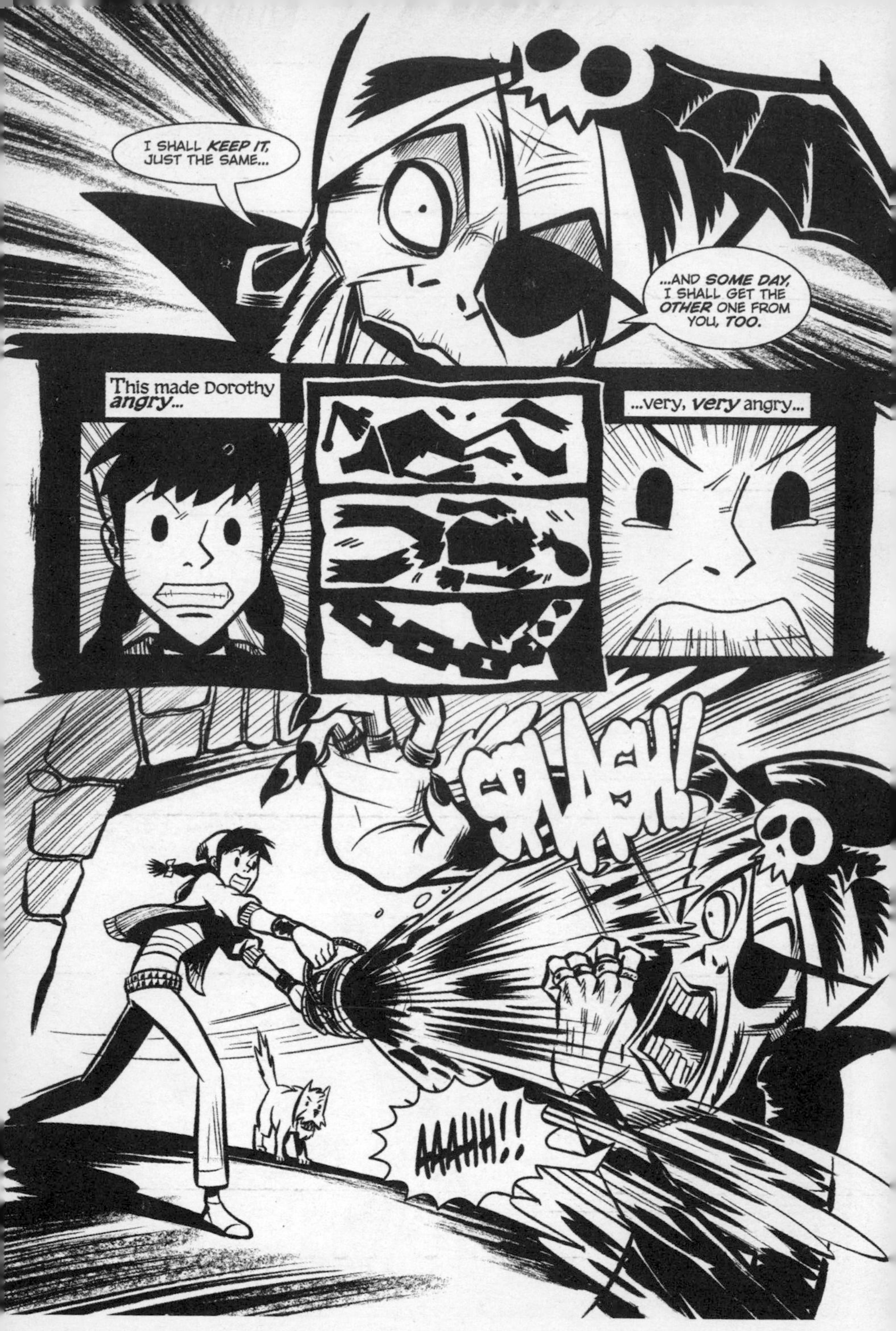
I SHALL KEEP IT, JUST THE SAME...
...AND SOME DAY, I SHALL GET THE OTHER ONE FROM YOU, TOO.
This made Dorothy angry...
...very, very angry...
SPLASH!
AAAHH!!

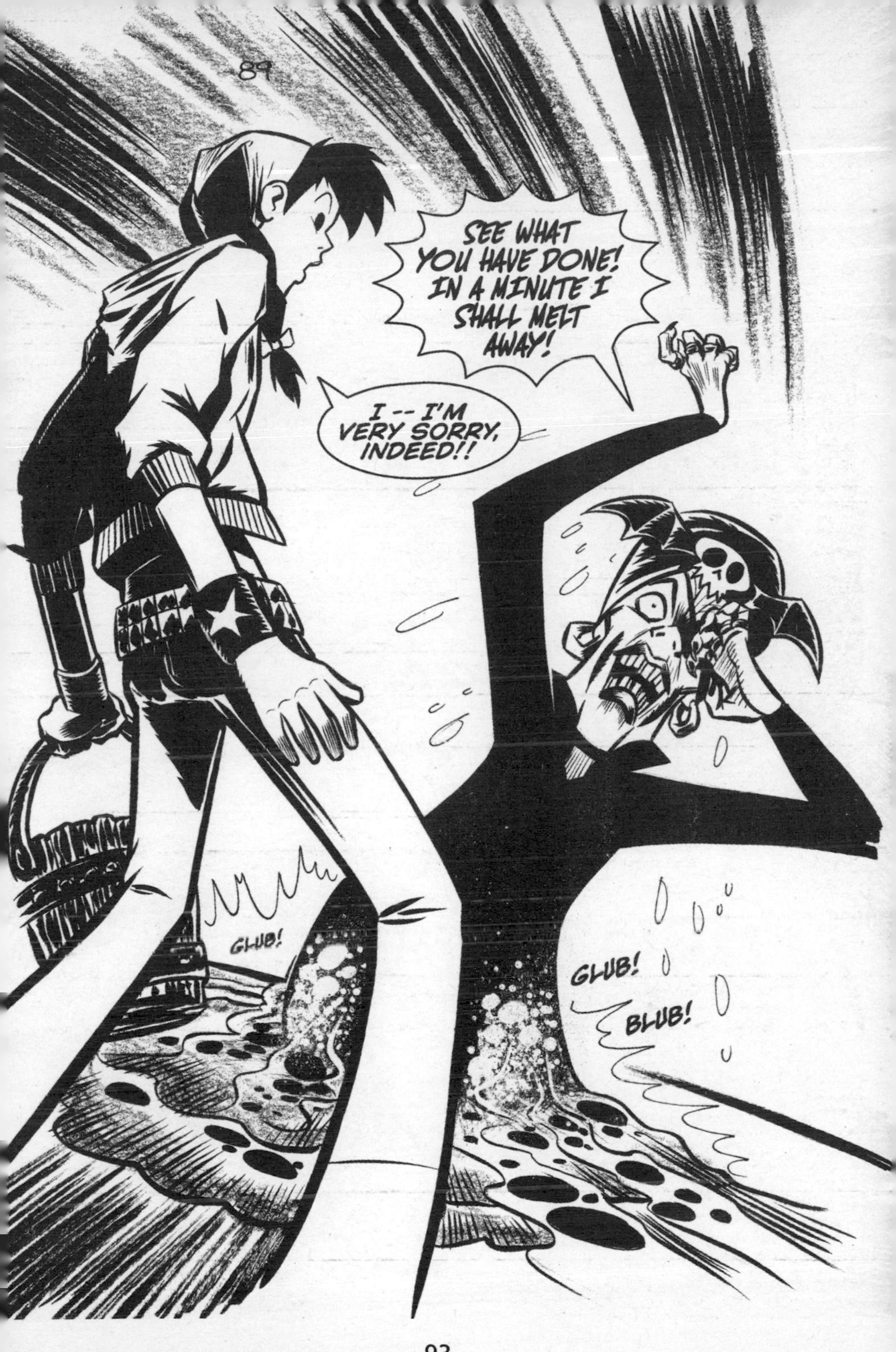
89
SEE WHAT YOU HAVE DONE! IN A MINUTE I SHALL MELT AWAY!
I -- I'M VERY SORRY, INDEED!!
GLUB!
GLUB!
BLUB!

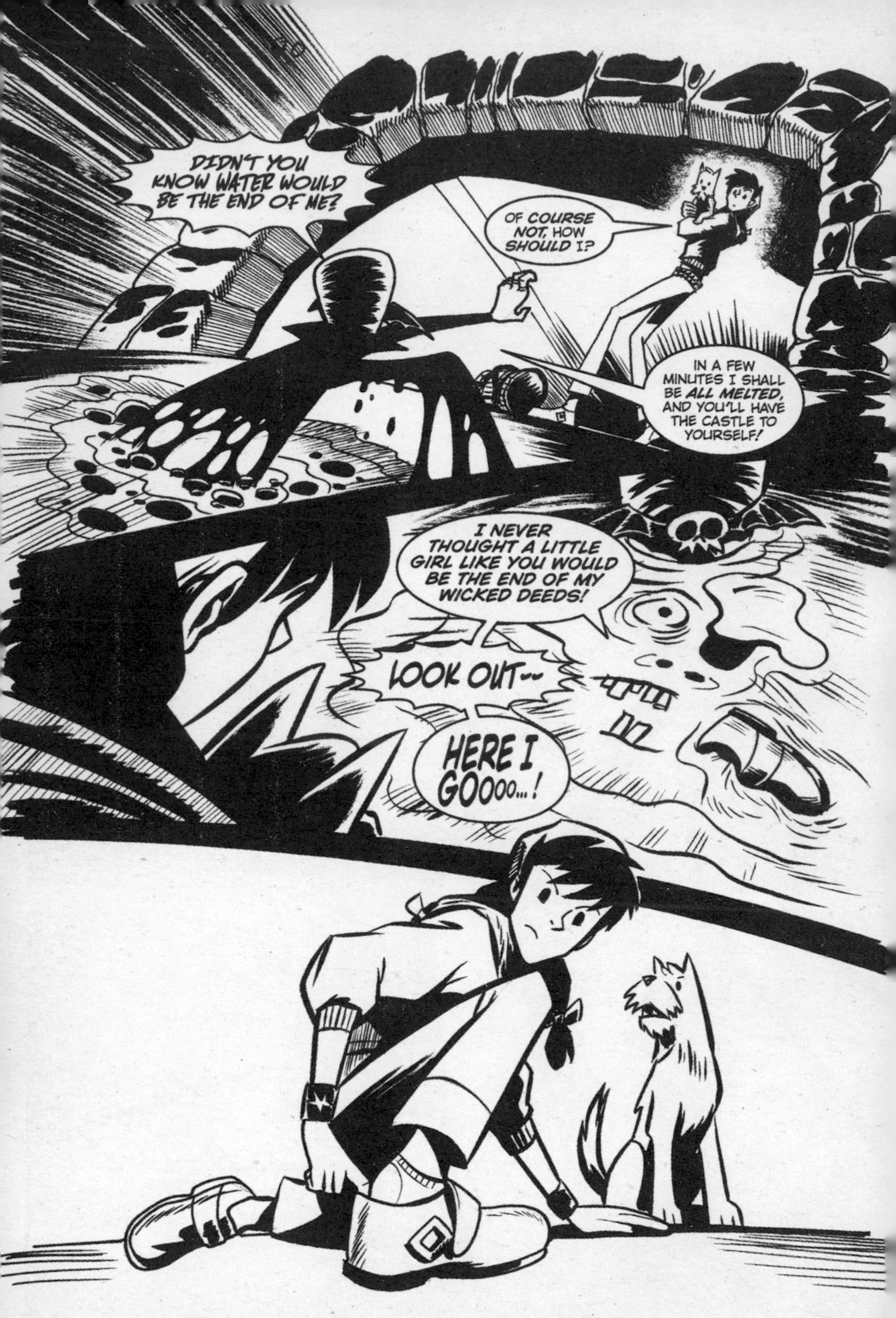
DIDN'T YOU KNOW WATER WOULD BE THE END OF ME?
OF COURSE NOT, HOW SHOULD I?
IN A FEW MINUTES I SHALL BE ALL MELTED, AND YOU'LL HAVE THE CASTLE TO YOURSELF!
I NEVER THOUGHT A LITTLE GIRL LIKE YOU WOULD BE THE END OF MY WICKED DEEDS!
LOOK OUT--
HERE I GOOoo...!

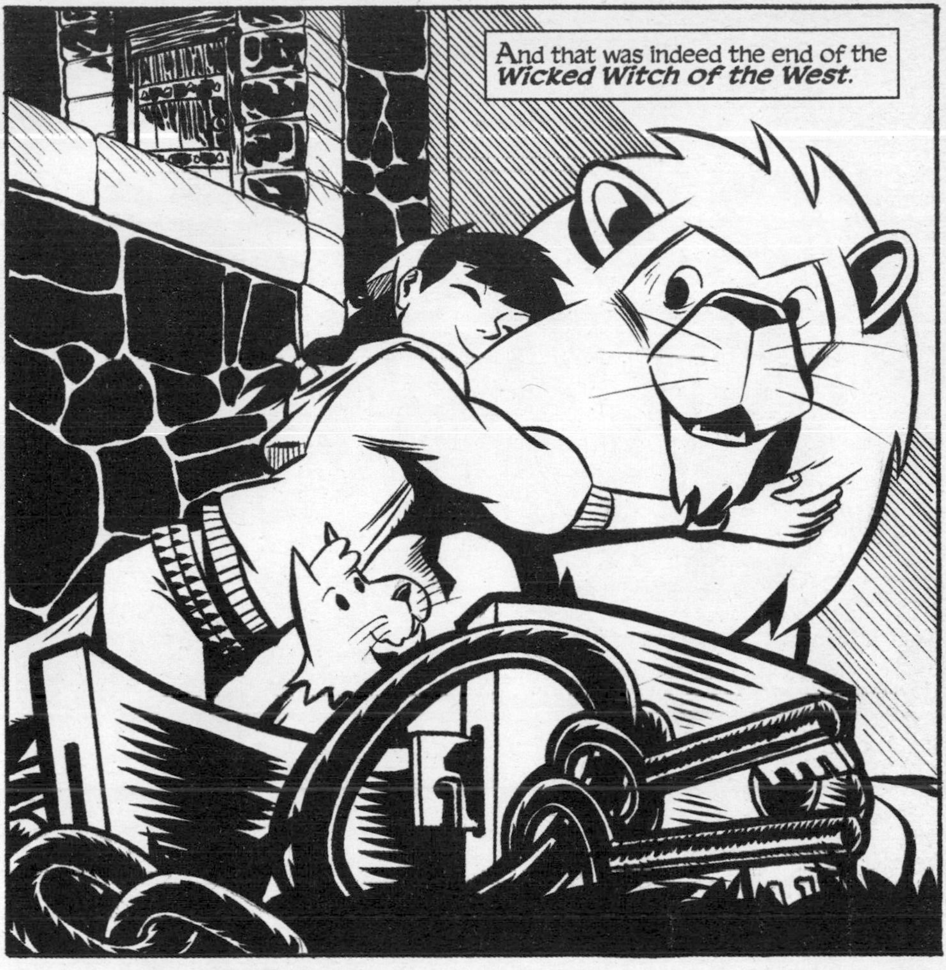
And that was indeed the end of the *Wicked Witch of the West*.

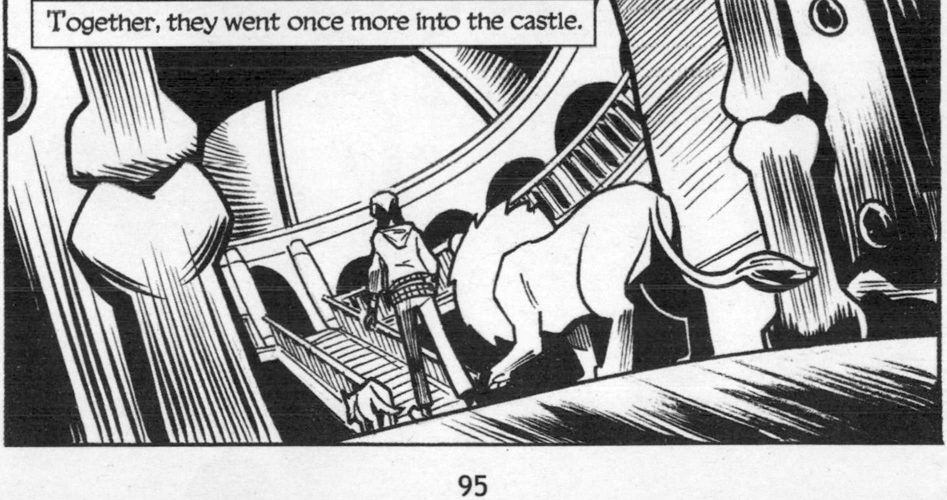
Together, they went once more into the castle.

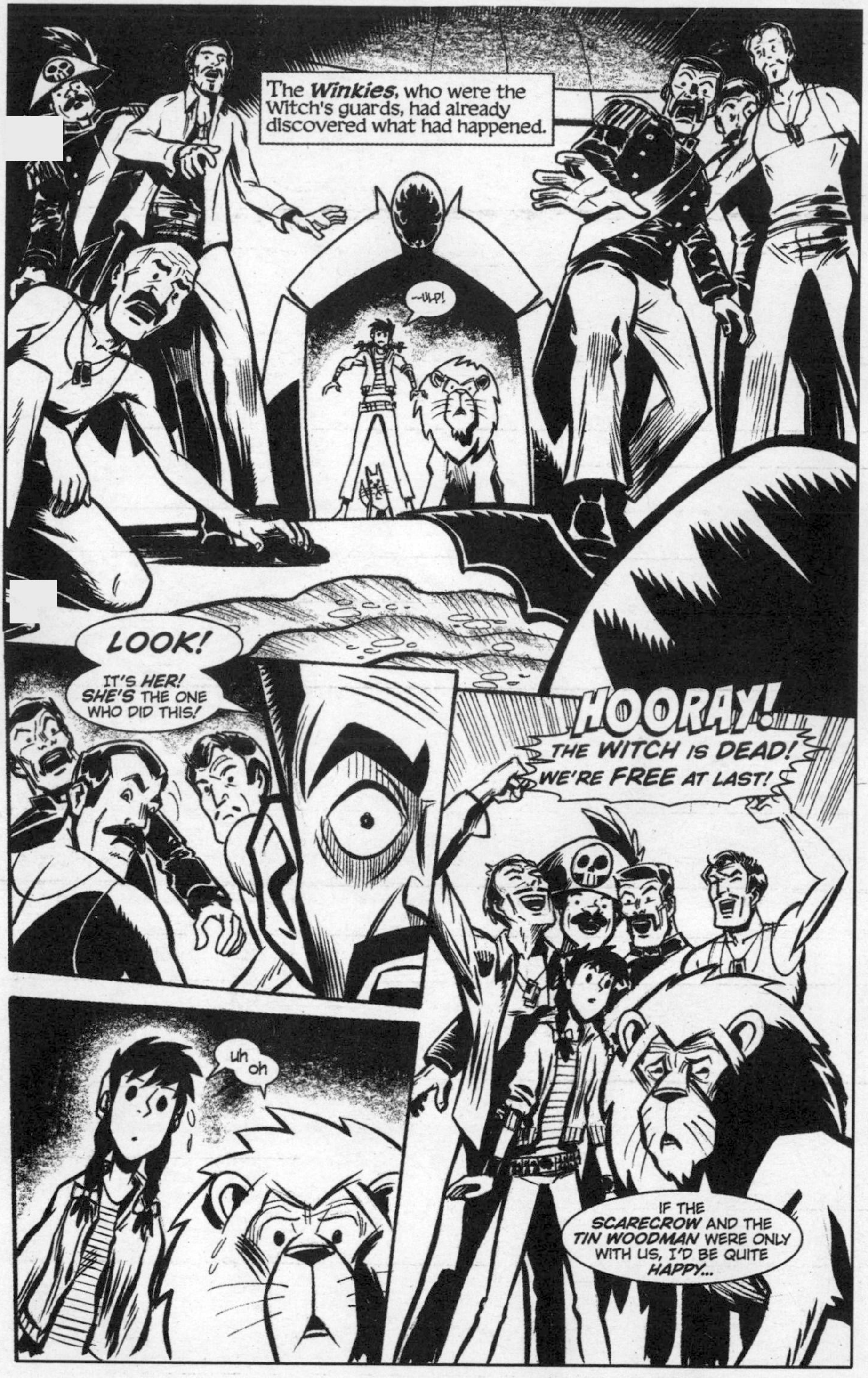

The Winkies, who were the Witch's guards, had already discovered what had happened.
~ULP!
LOOK!
IT'S HER! SHE'S THE ONE WHO DID THIS!
HOORAY!
THE WITCH IS DEAD! WE'RE FREE AT LAST!
uh oh
IF THE SCARECROW AND THE TIN WOODMAN WERE ONLY WITH US, I'D BE QUITE HAPPY...

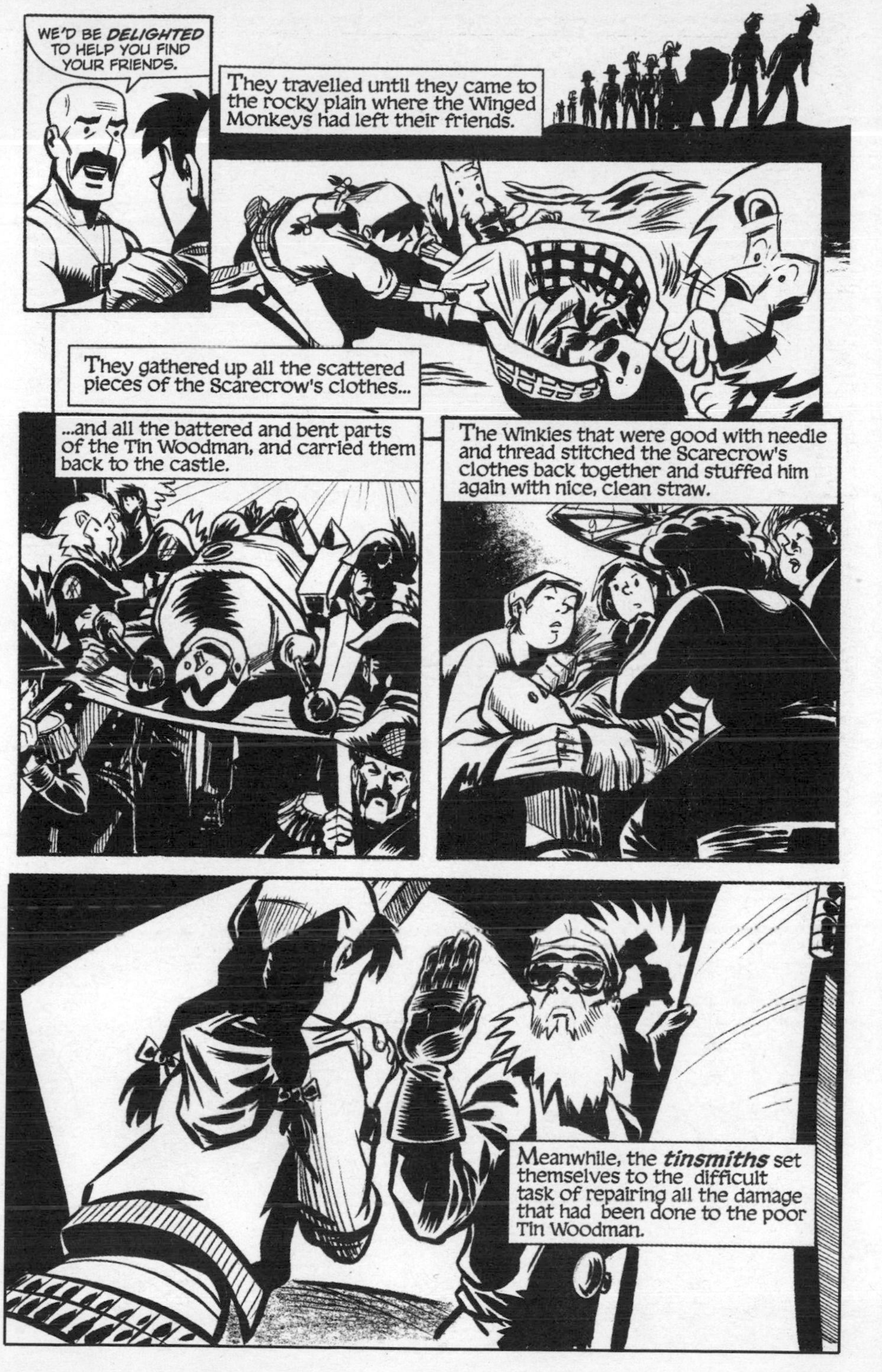
WE'D BE DELIGHTED TO HELP YOU FIND YOUR FRIENDS.
They travelled until they came to the rocky plain where the Winged Monkeys had left their friends.
They gathered up all the scattered pieces of the Scarecrow's clothes...
...and all the battered and bent parts of the Tin Woodman, and carried them back to the castle.
The Winkies that were good with needle and thread stitched the Scarecrow's clothes back together and stuffed him again with nice, clean straw.
Meanwhile, the tinsmiths set themselves to the difficult task of repairing all the damage that had been done to the poor Tin Woodman.

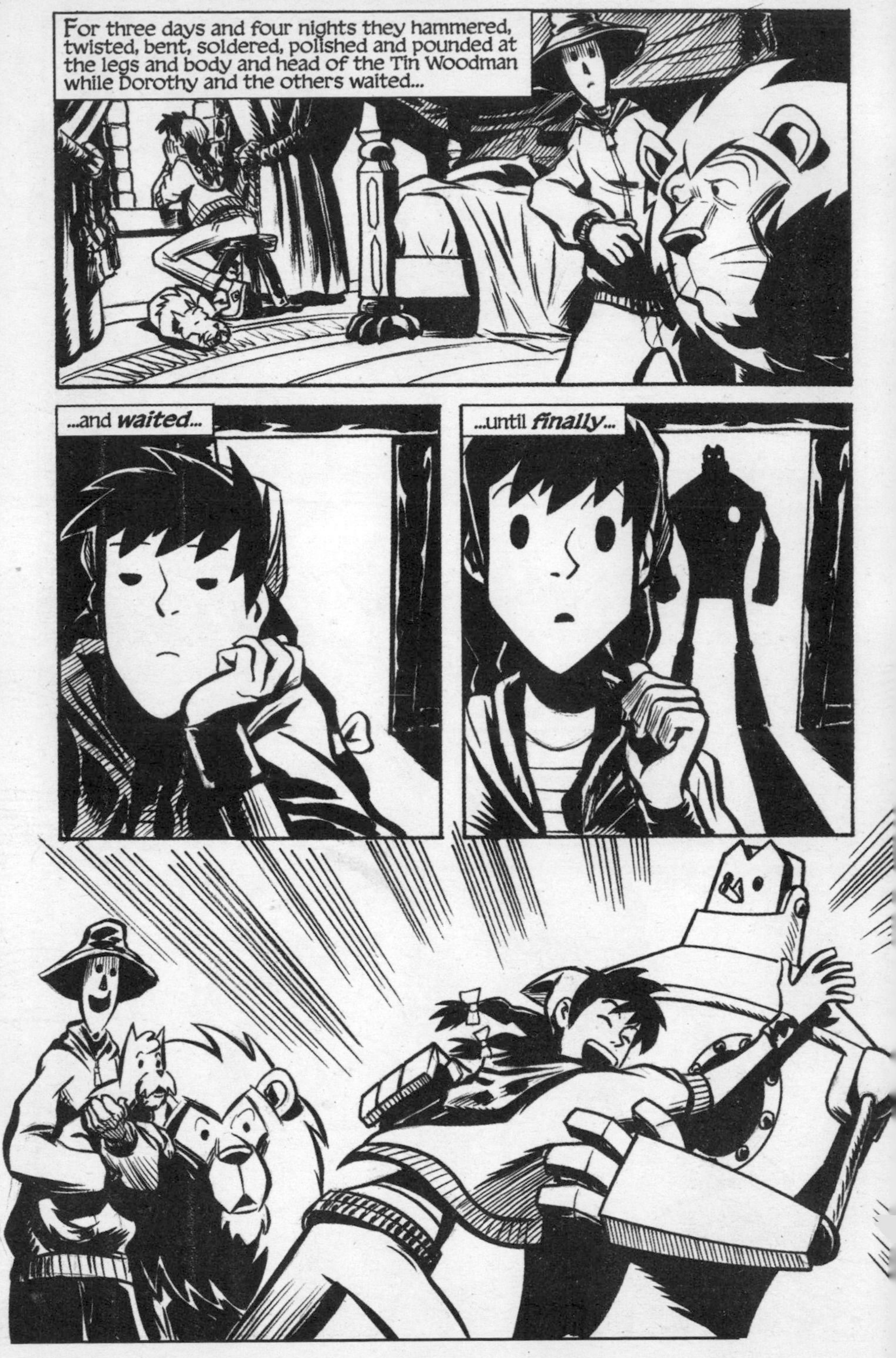
For three days and four nights they hammered, twisted, bent, soldered, polished and pounded at the legs and body and head of the Tin Woodman while Dorothy and the others waited...
...and *waited*...
...until *finally*...

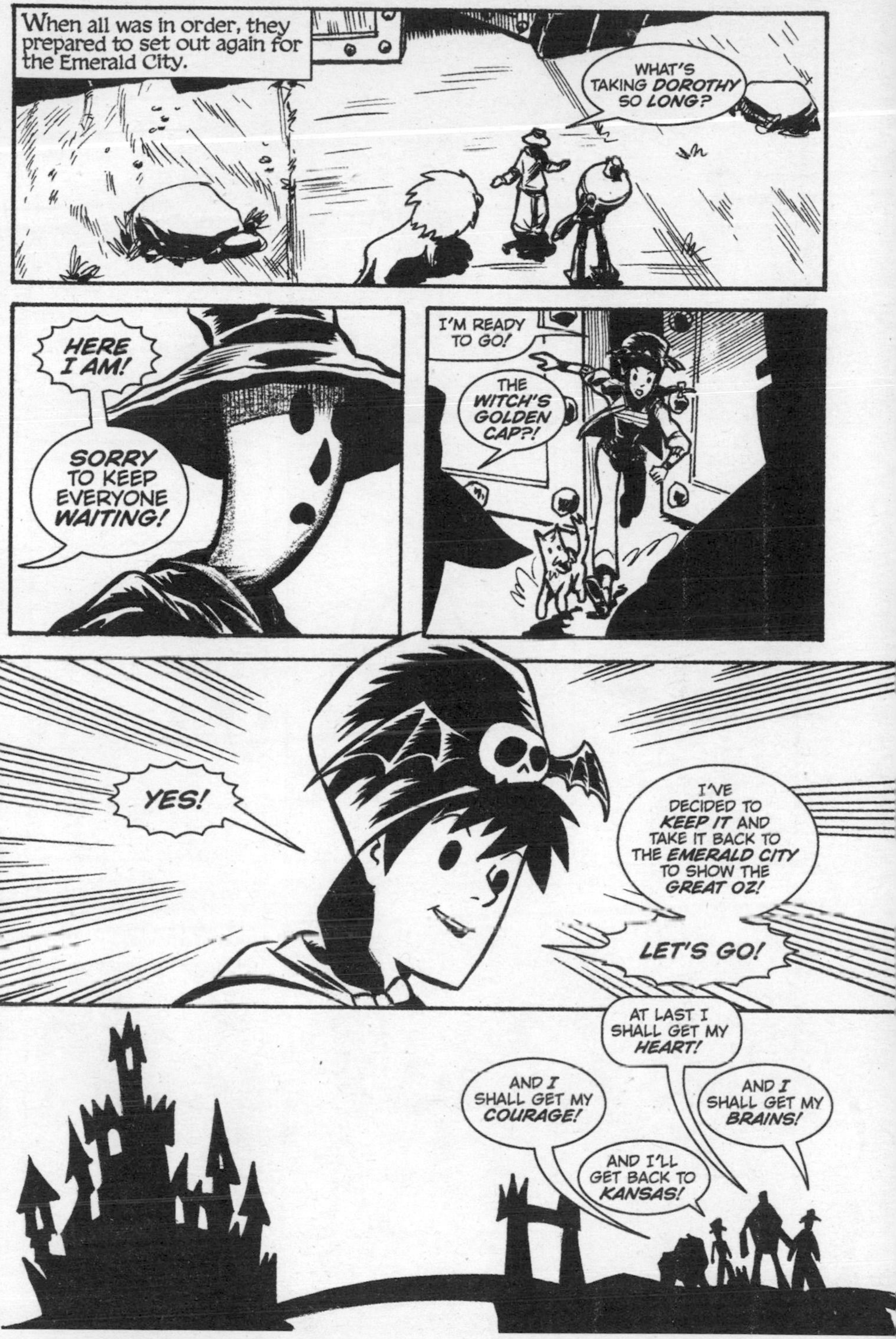
When all was in order, they prepared to set out again for the Emerald City.
WHAT'S TAKING DOROTHY SO LONG?
HERE I AM!
SORRY TO KEEP EVERYONE WAITING!
I'M READY TO GO!
THE WITCH'S GOLDEN CAP?!
YES!
I'VE DECIDED TO KEEP IT AND TAKE IT BACK TO THE EMERALD CITY TO SHOW THE GREAT OZ!
LET'S GO!
AT LAST I SHALL GET MY HEART!
AND I SHALL GET MY COURAGE!
AND I SHALL GET MY BRAINS!
AND I'LL GET BACK TO KANSAS!

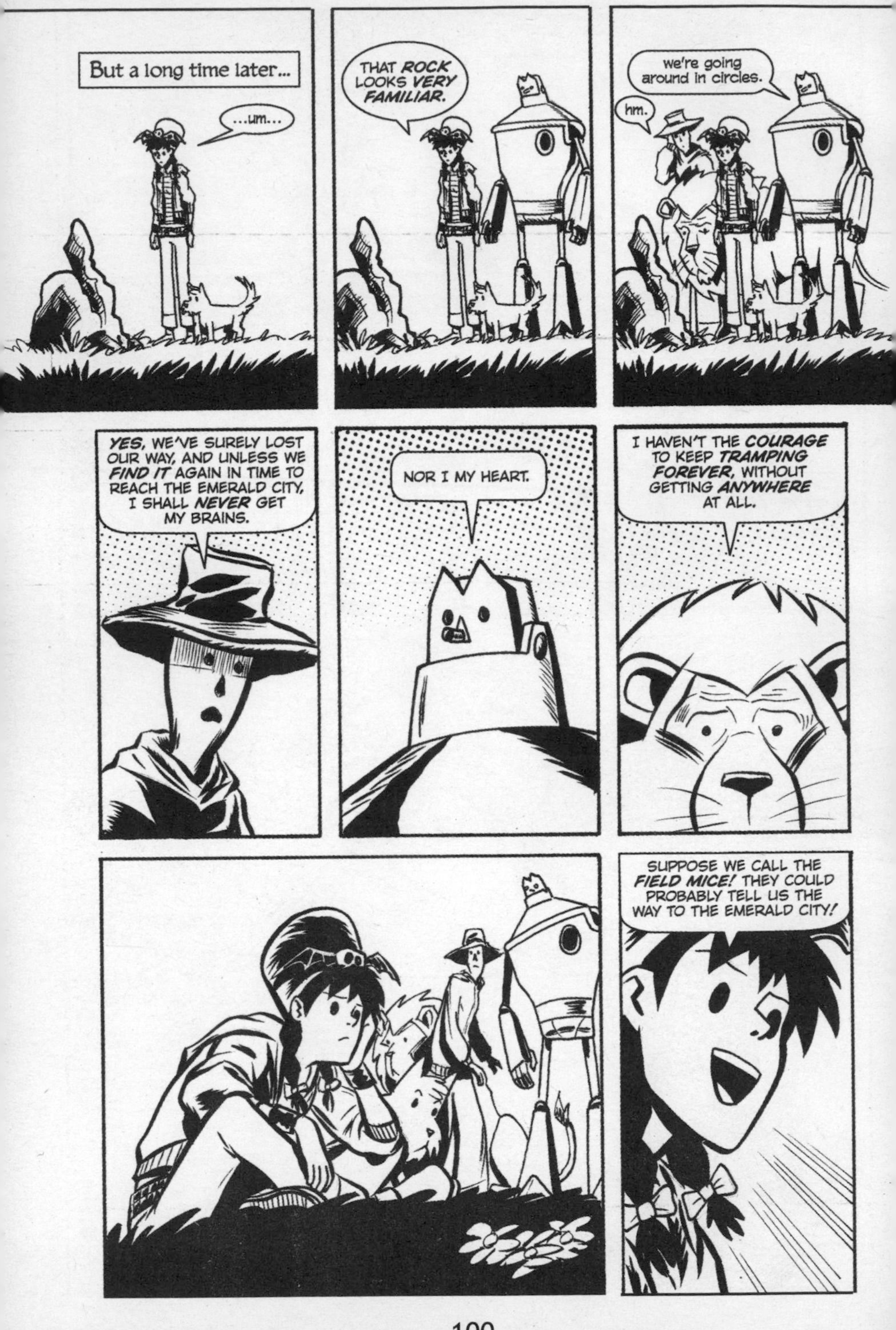
But a long time later...
...um...
THAT ROCK LOOKS VERY FAMILIAR.
we're going around in circles.
hm.
YES, WE'VE SURELY LOST OUR WAY, AND UNLESS WE FIND IT AGAIN IN TIME TO REACH THE EMERALD CITY, I SHALL NEVER GET MY BRAINS.
NOR I MY HEART.
I HAVEN'T THE COURAGE TO KEEP TRAMPING FOREVER, WITHOUT GETTING ANYWHERE AT ALL.
SUPPOSE WE CALL THE FIELD MICE! THEY COULD PROBABLY TELL US THE WAY TO THE EMERALD CITY!

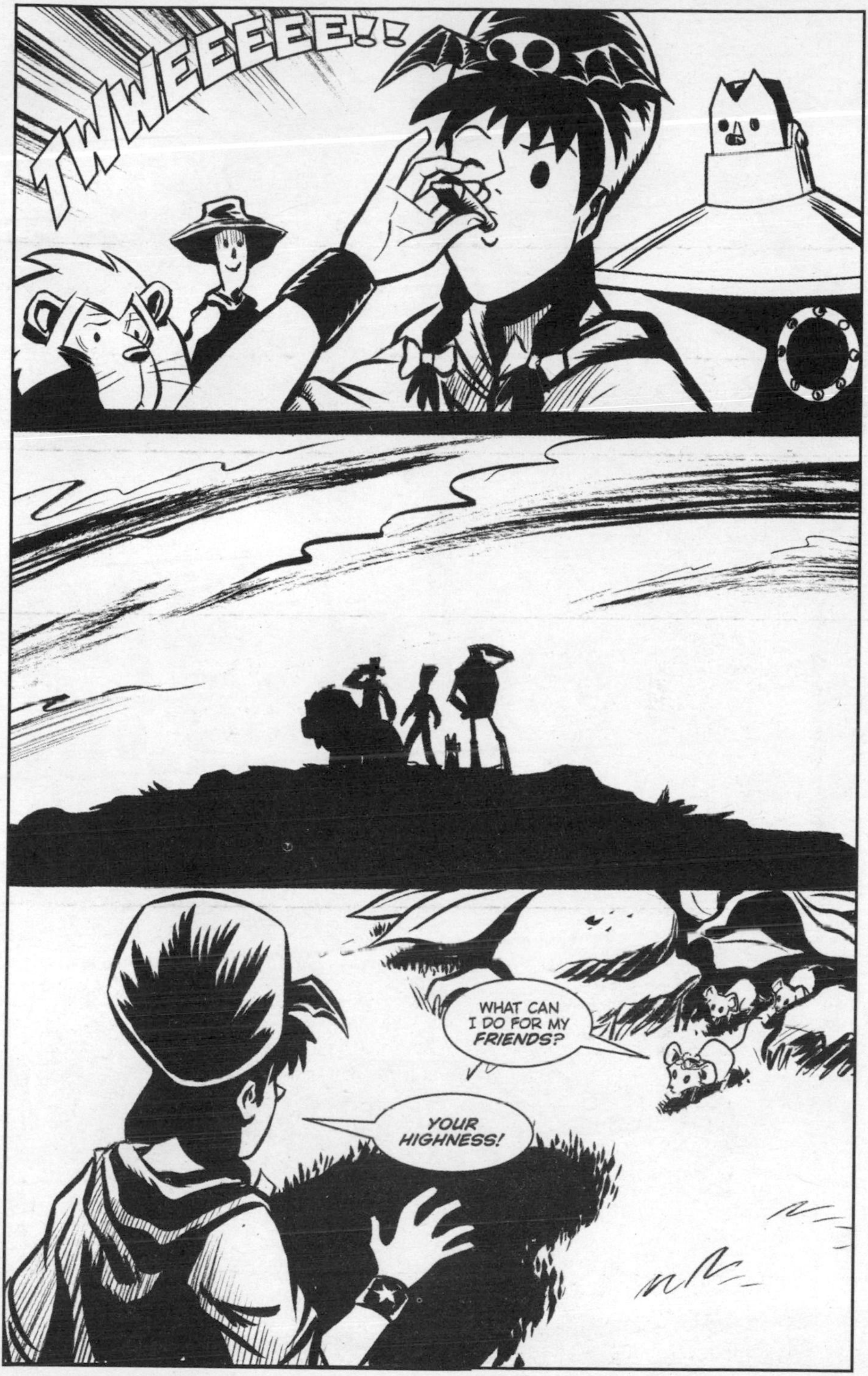
TWWEEEEEE!!
WHAT CAN I DO FOR MY FRIENDS?
YOUR HIGHNESS!

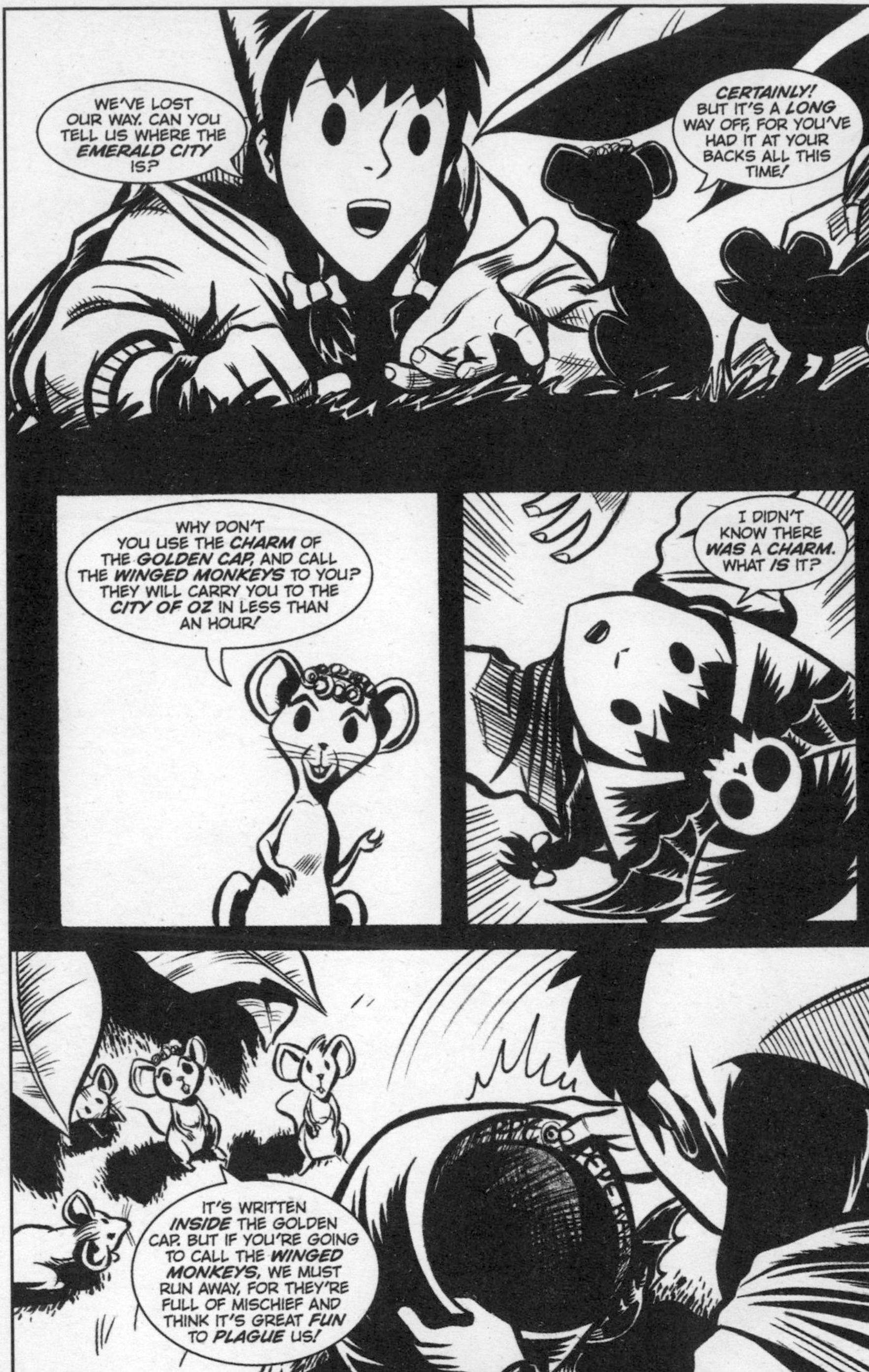
WE'VE LOST OUR WAY. CAN YOU TELL US WHERE THE EMERALD CITY IS?
CERTAINLY! BUT IT'S A LONG WAY OFF, FOR YOU'VE HAD IT AT YOUR BACKS ALL THIS TIME!
WHY DON'T YOU USE THE CHARM OF THE GOLDEN CAP, AND CALL THE WINGED MONKEYS TO YOU? THEY WILL CARRY YOU TO THE CITY OF OZ IN LESS THAN AN HOUR!
I DIDN'T KNOW THERE WAS A CHARM. WHAT IS IT?
IT'S WRITTEN INSIDE THE GOLDEN CAP. BUT IF YOU'RE GOING TO CALL THE WINGED MONKEYS, WE MUST RUN AWAY, FOR THEY'RE FULL OF MISCHIEF AND THINK IT'S GREAT FUN TO PLAGUE US!

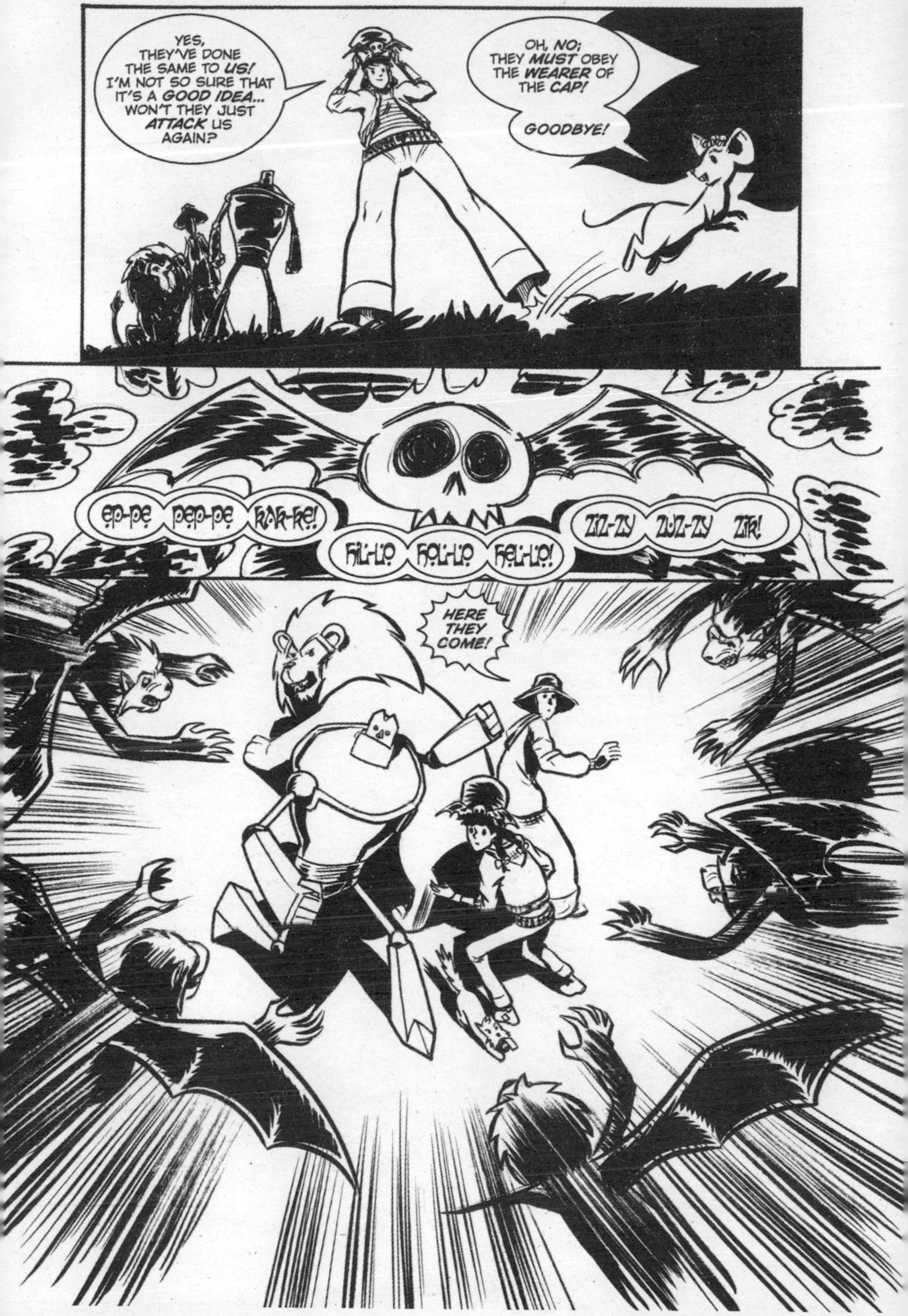
YES, THEY'VE DONE THE SAME TO US! I'M NOT SO SURE THAT IT'S A GOOD IDEA... WON'T THEY JUST ATTACK US AGAIN?
OH, NO; THEY MUST OBEY THE WEARER OF THE CAP!
GOODBYE!
EP-PE PEP-PE KAK-KE!
HIL-LO HOL-LO HEL-LO!
ZIZ-ZY ZUZ-ZY ZIK!
HERE THEY COME!

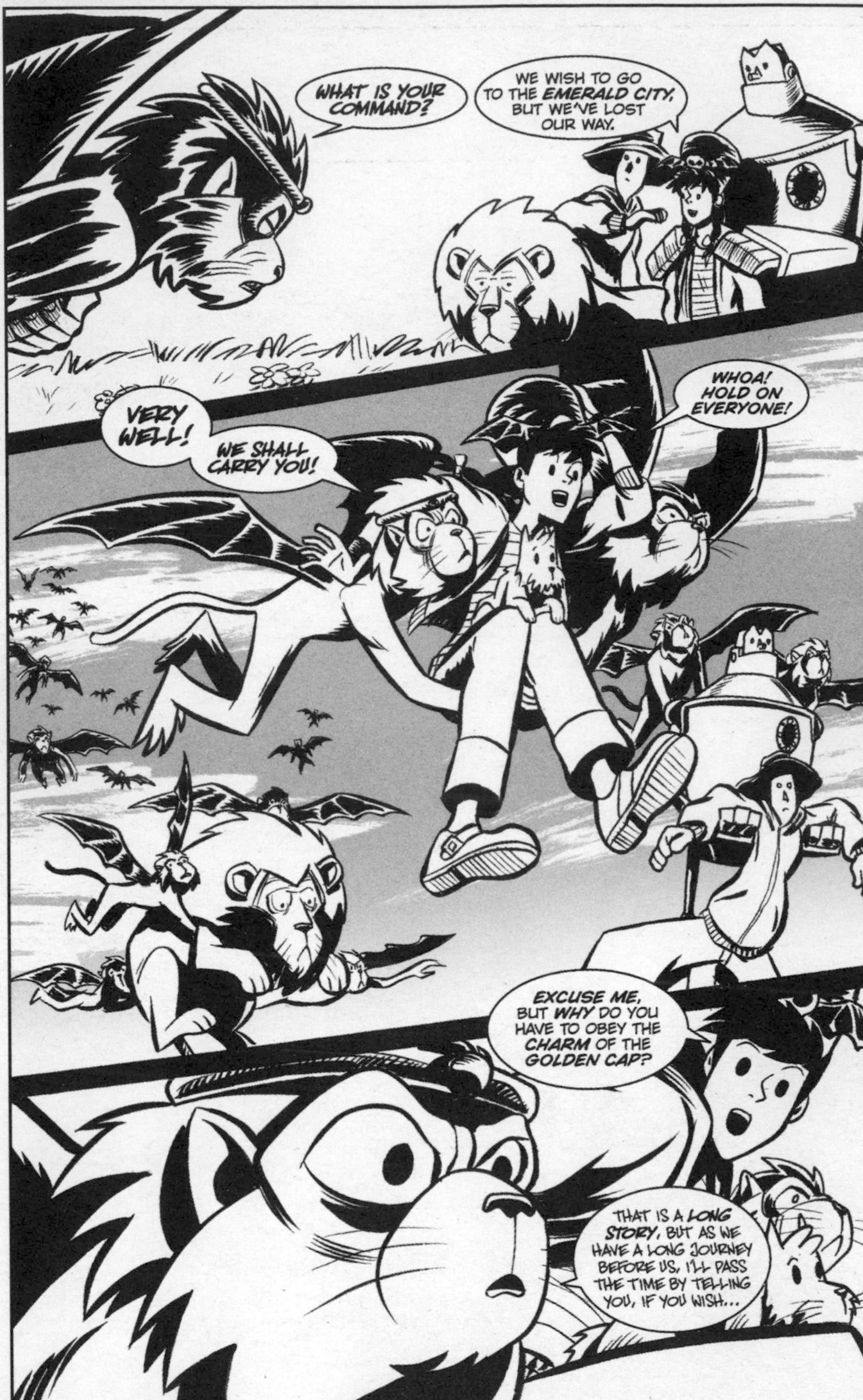
WHAT IS YOUR COMMAND?
WE WISH TO GO TO THE EMERALD CITY, BUT WE'VE LOST OUR WAY.
VERY WELL!
WE SHALL CARRY YOU!
WHOA! HOLD ON EVERYONE!
EXCUSE ME, BUT WHY DO YOU HAVE TO OBEY THE CHARM OF THE GOLDEN CAP?
THAT IS A LONG STORY, BUT AS WE HAVE A LONG JOURNEY BEFORE US, I'LL PASS THE TIME BY TELLING YOU, IF YOU WISH...

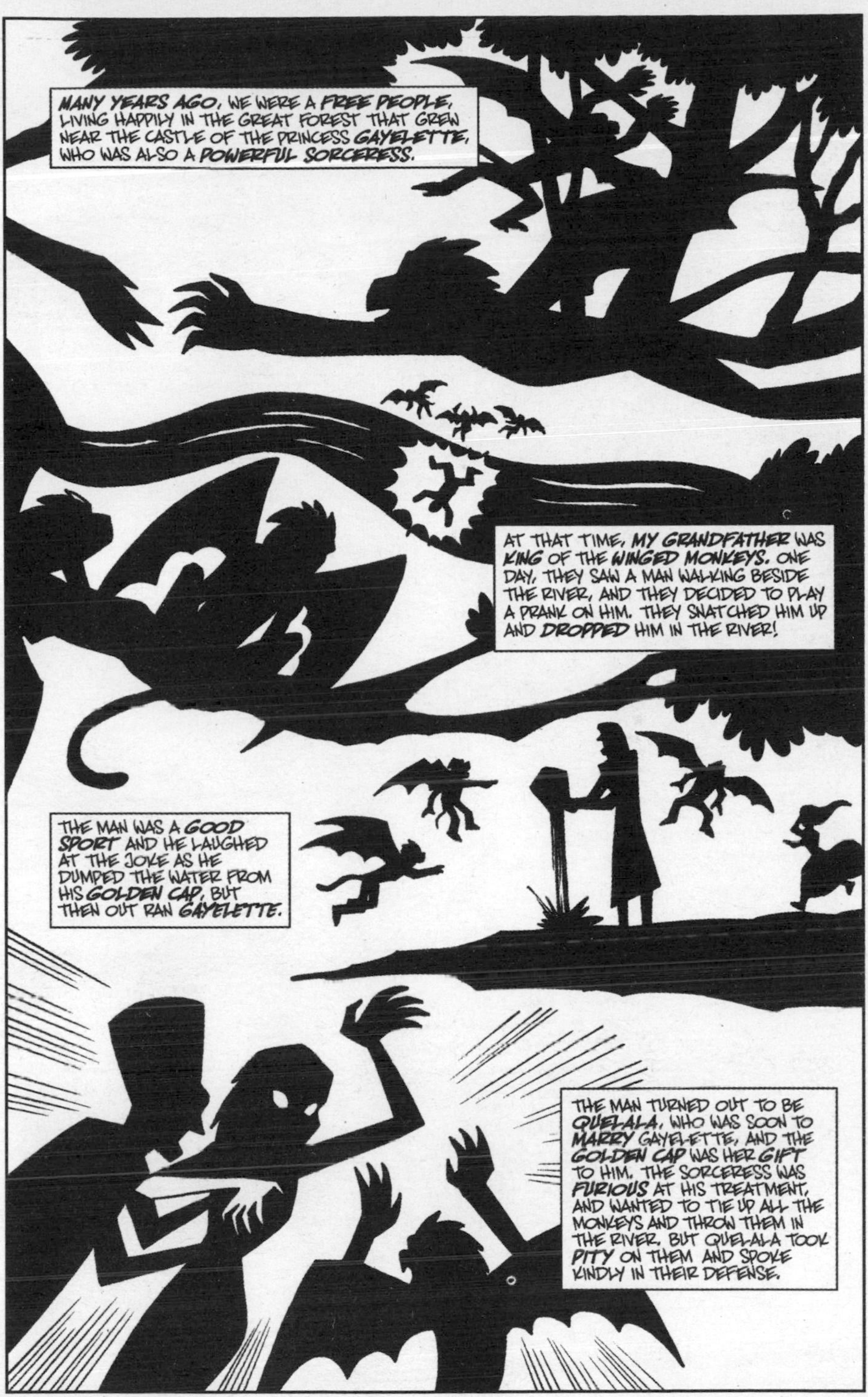
MANY YEARS AGO, WE WERE A FREE PEOPLE, LIVING HAPPILY IN THE GREAT FOREST THAT GREW NEAR THE CASTLE OF THE PRINCESS GAYELETTE, WHO WAS ALSO A POWERFUL SORCERESS.
AT THAT TIME, MY GRANDFATHER WAS KING OF THE WINGED MONKEYS. ONE DAY, THEY SAW A MAN WALKING BESIDE THE RIVER, AND THEY DECIDED TO PLAY A PRANK ON HIM. THEY SNATCHED HIM UP AND DROPPED HIM IN THE RIVER!
THE MAN WAS A GOOD SPORT AND HE LAUGHED AT THE JOKE AS HE DUMPED THE WATER FROM HIS GOLDEN CAP, BUT THEN OUT RAN GAYELETTE.
THE MAN TURNED OUT TO BE QUELALA, WHO WAS SOON TO MARRY GAYELETTE, AND THE GOLDEN CAP WAS HER GIFT TO HIM. THE SORCERESS WAS FURIOUS AT HIS TREATMENT, AND WANTED TO TIE UP ALL THE MONKEYS AND THROW THEM IN THE RIVER. BUT QUELALA TOOK PITY ON THEM AND SPOKE KINDLY IN THEIR DEFENSE.

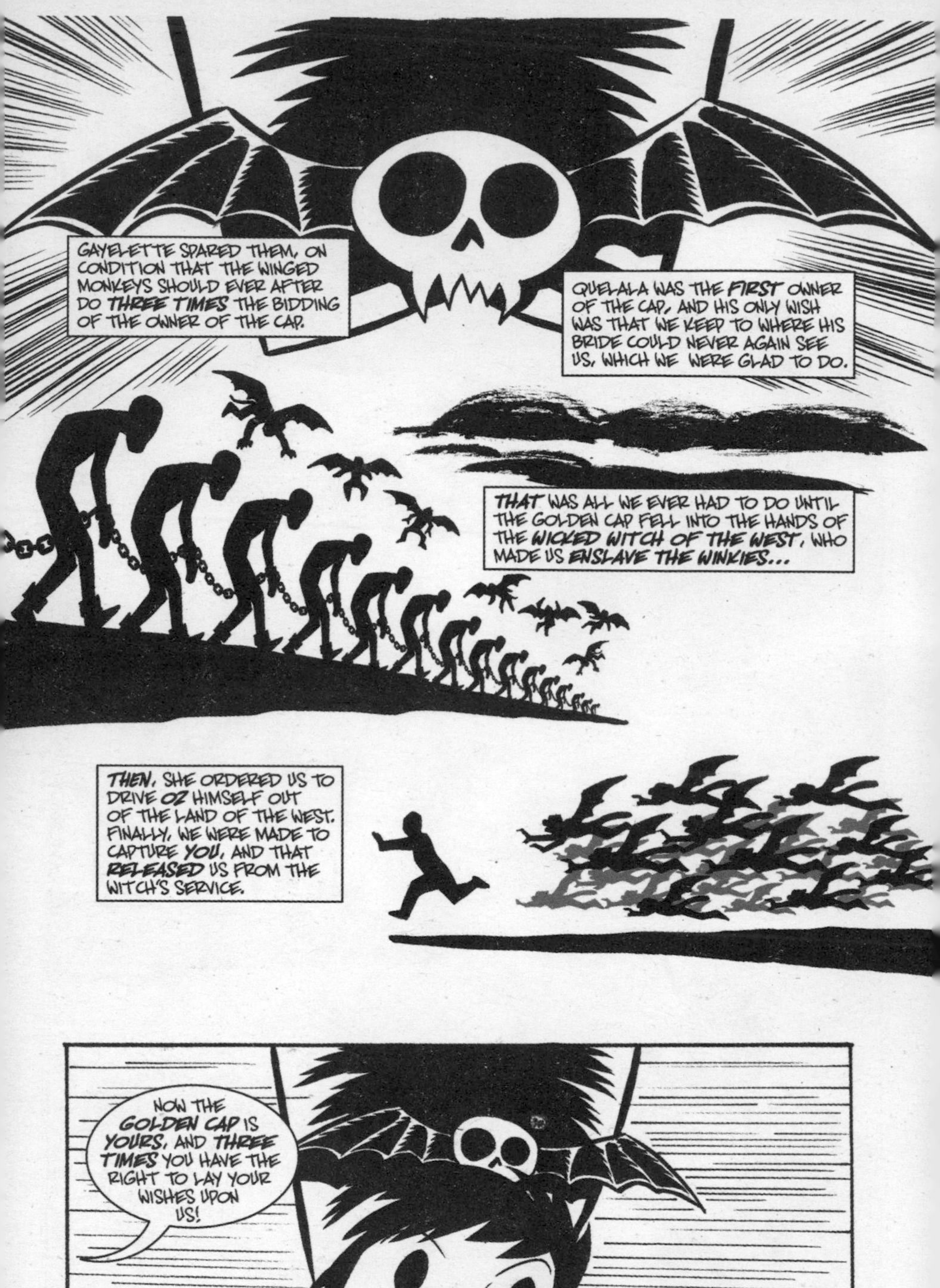
GAYELETTE SPARED THEM, ON CONDITION THAT THE WINGED MONKEYS SHOULD EVER AFTER DO THREE TIMES THE BIDDING OF THE OWNER OF THE CAP.
QUELALA WAS THE FIRST OWNER OF THE CAP, AND HIS ONLY WISH WAS THAT WE KEEP TO WHERE HIS BRIDE COULD NEVER AGAIN SEE US, WHICH WE WERE GLAD TO DO.
THAT WAS ALL WE EVER HAD TO DO UNTIL THE GOLDEN CAP FELL INTO THE HANDS OF THE WICKED WITCH OF THE WEST, WHO MADE US ENSLAVE THE WINKIES...
THEN, SHE ORDERED US TO DRIVE OZ HIMSELF OUT OF THE LAND OF THE WEST. FINALLY, WE WERE MADE TO CAPTURE YOU, AND THAT RELEASED US FROM THE WITCH'S SERVICE.
NOW THE GOLDEN CAP IS YOURS, AND THREE TIMES YOU HAVE THE RIGHT TO LAY YOUR WISHES UPON US!

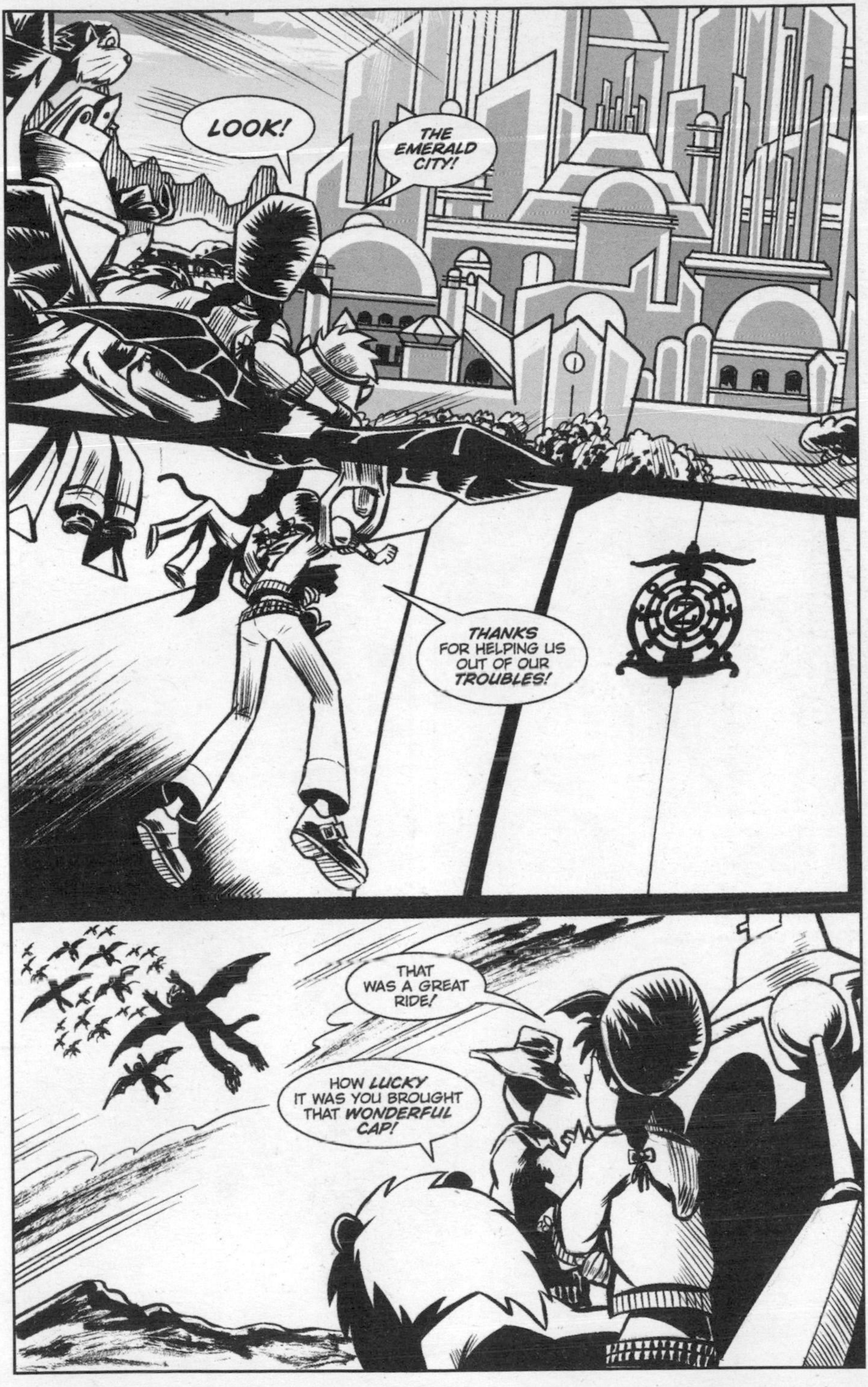
LOOK!
THE EMERALD CITY!
THANKS FOR HELPING US OUT OF OUR TROUBLES!
THAT WAS A GREAT RIDE!
HOW LUCKY IT WAS YOU BROUGHT THAT WONDERFUL CAP!

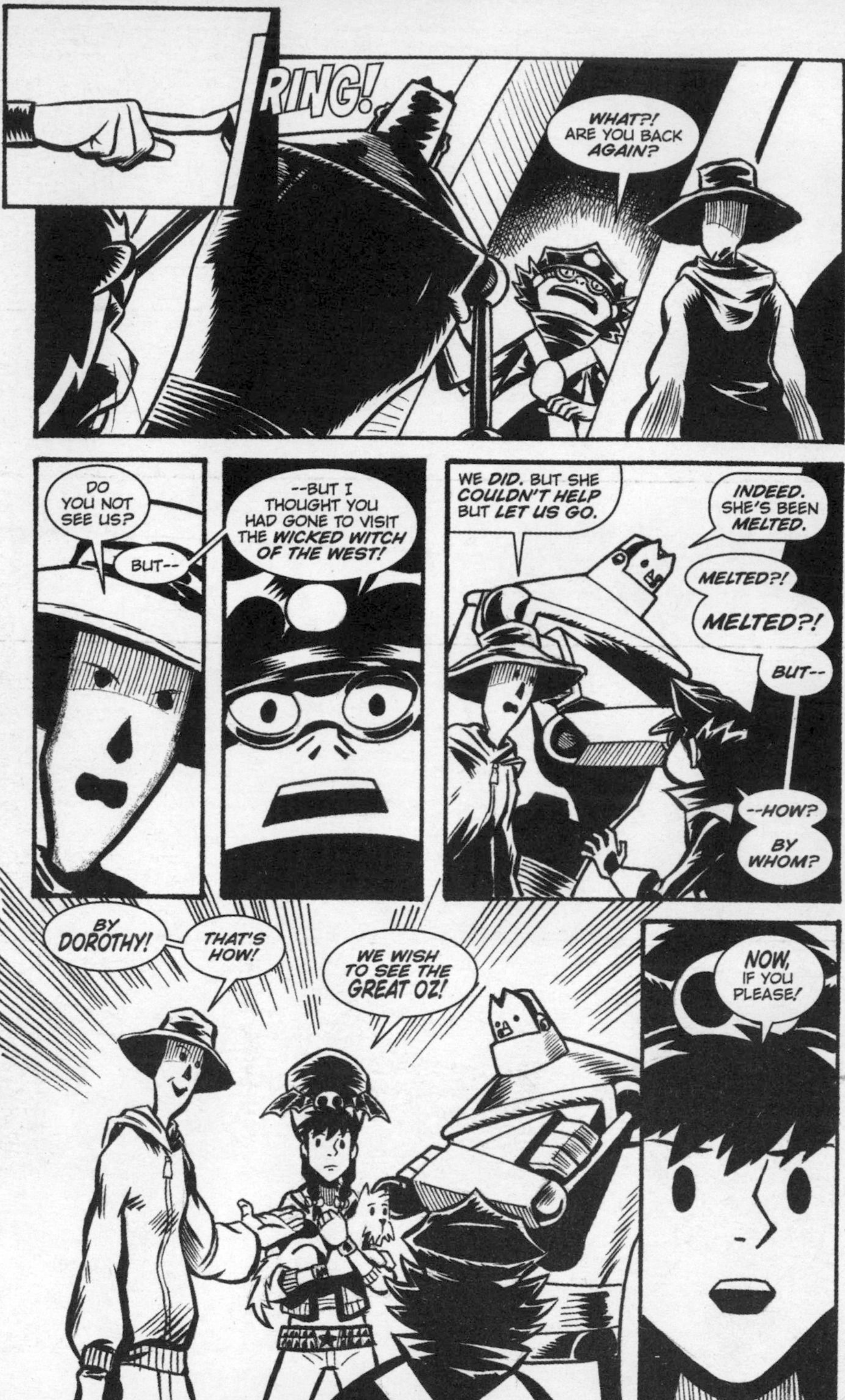
RING!
WHAT?! ARE YOU BACK AGAIN?
DO YOU NOT SEE US?
BUT--
--BUT I THOUGHT YOU HAD GONE TO VISIT THE WICKED WITCH OF THE WEST!
WE DID. BUT SHE COULDN'T HELP BUT LET US GO.
INDEED. SHE'S BEEN MELTED.
MELTED?!
MELTED?!
BUT--
--HOW?
BY WHOM?
BY DOROTHY!
THAT'S HOW!
WE WISH TO SEE THE GREAT OZ!
NOW, IF YOU PLEASE!

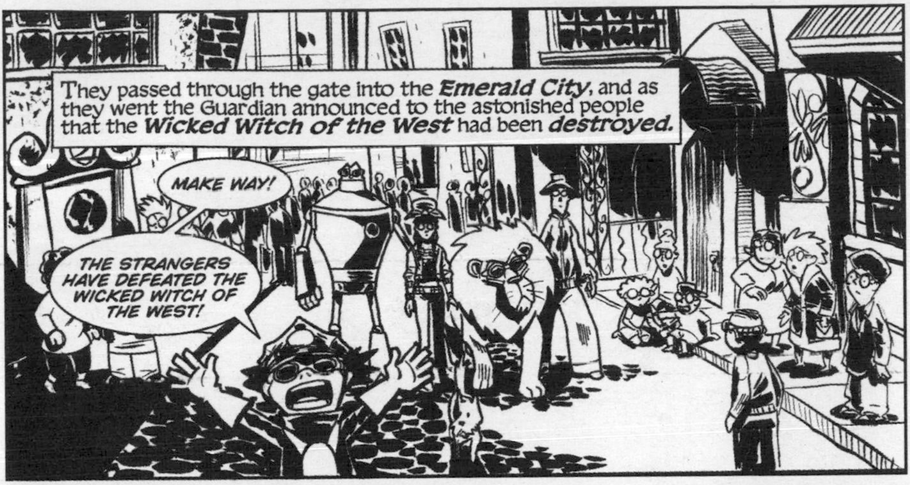
They passed through the gate into the Emerald City, and as they went the Guardian announced to the astonished people that the Wicked Witch of the West had been destroyed.
MAKE WAY!
THE STRANGERS HAVE DEFEATED THE WICKED WITCH OF THE WEST!

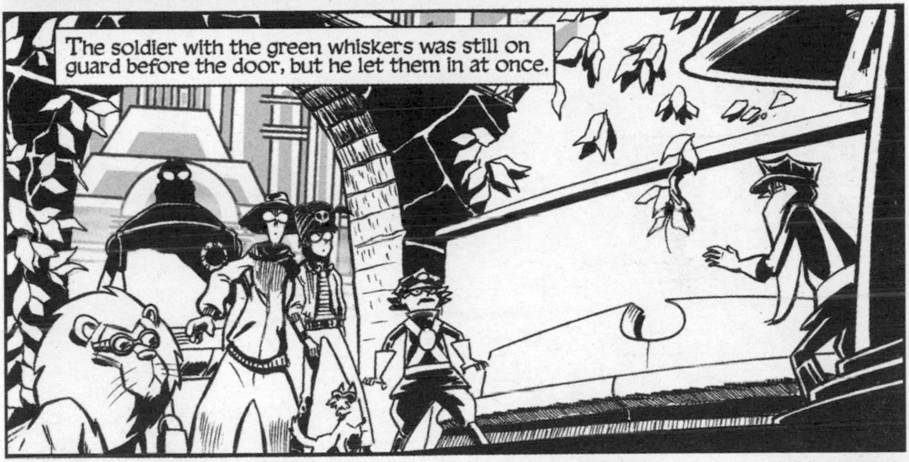
The soldier with the green whiskers was still on guard before the door, but he let them in at once.

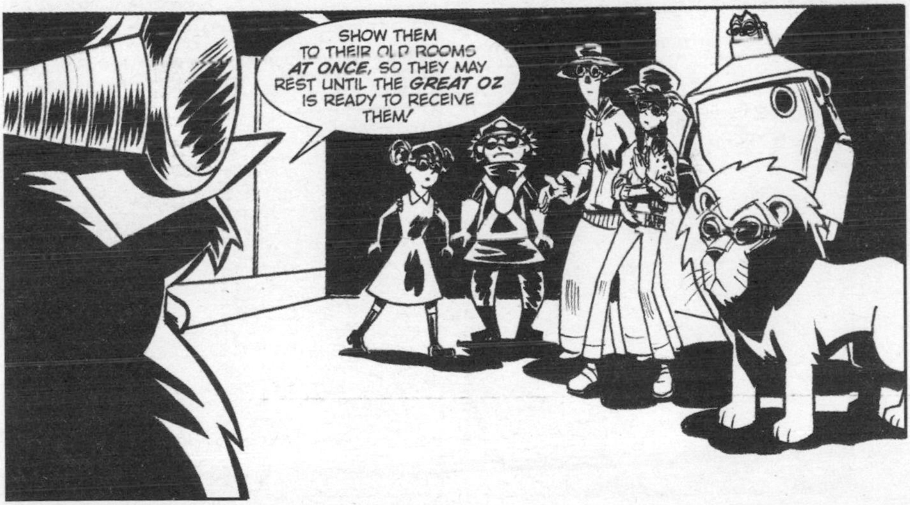
SHOW THEM TO THEIR OLD ROOMS AT ONCE, SO THEY MAY REST UNTIL THE GREAT OZ IS READY TO RECEIVE THEM!

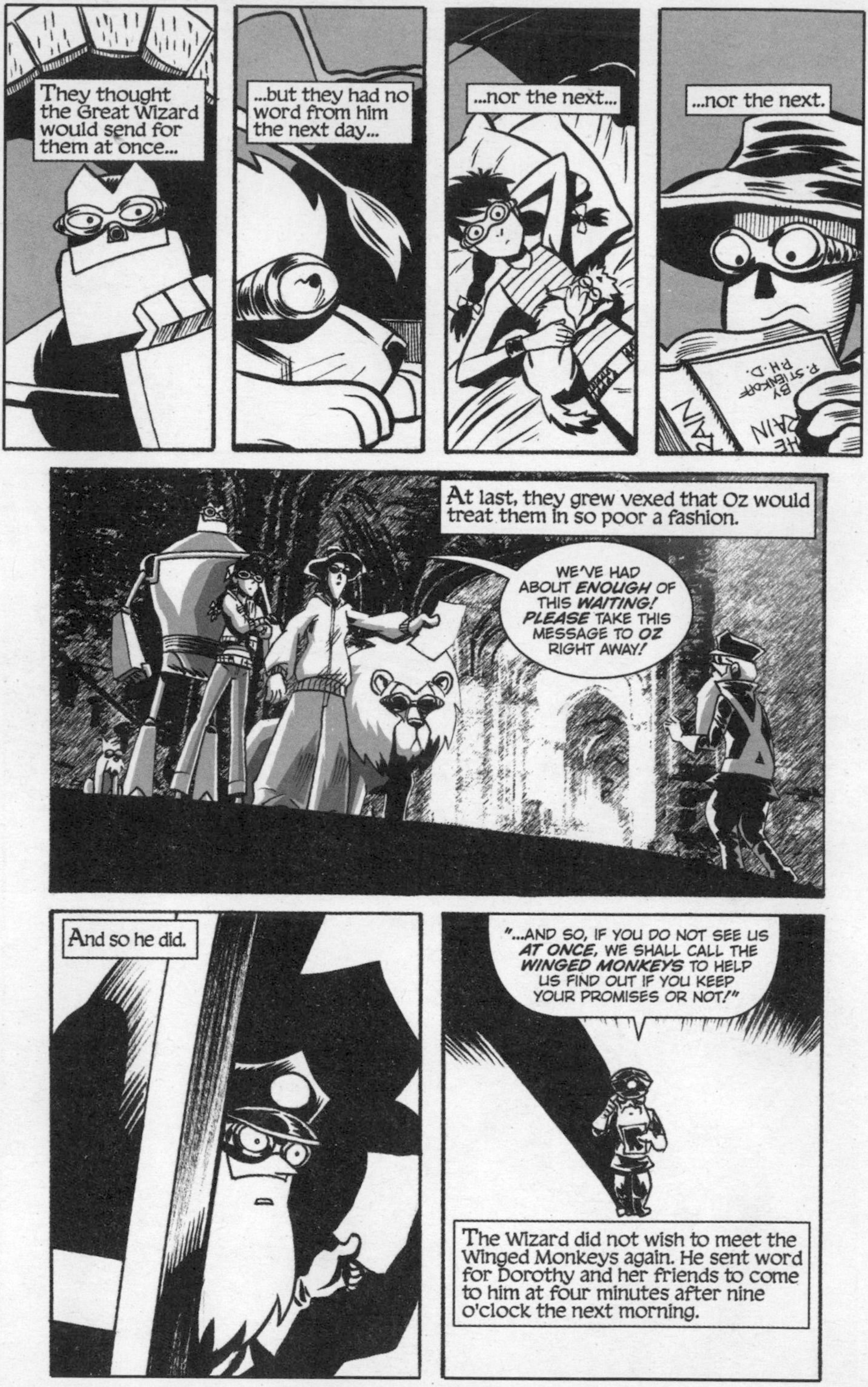
They thought the Great Wizard would send for them at once...
...but they had no word from him the next day...
...nor the next...
...nor the next.
At last, they grew vexed that Oz would treat them in so poor a fashion.
WE'VE HAD ABOUT ENOUGH OF THIS WAITING! PLEASE TAKE THIS MESSAGE TO OZ RIGHT AWAY!
And so he did.
"...AND SO, IF YOU DO NOT SEE US AT ONCE, WE SHALL CALL THE WINGED MONKEYS TO HELP US FIND OUT IF YOU KEEP YOUR PROMISES OR NOT!"
The Wizard did not wish to meet the Winged Monkeys again. He sent word for Dorothy and her friends to come to him at four minutes after nine o'clock the next morning.

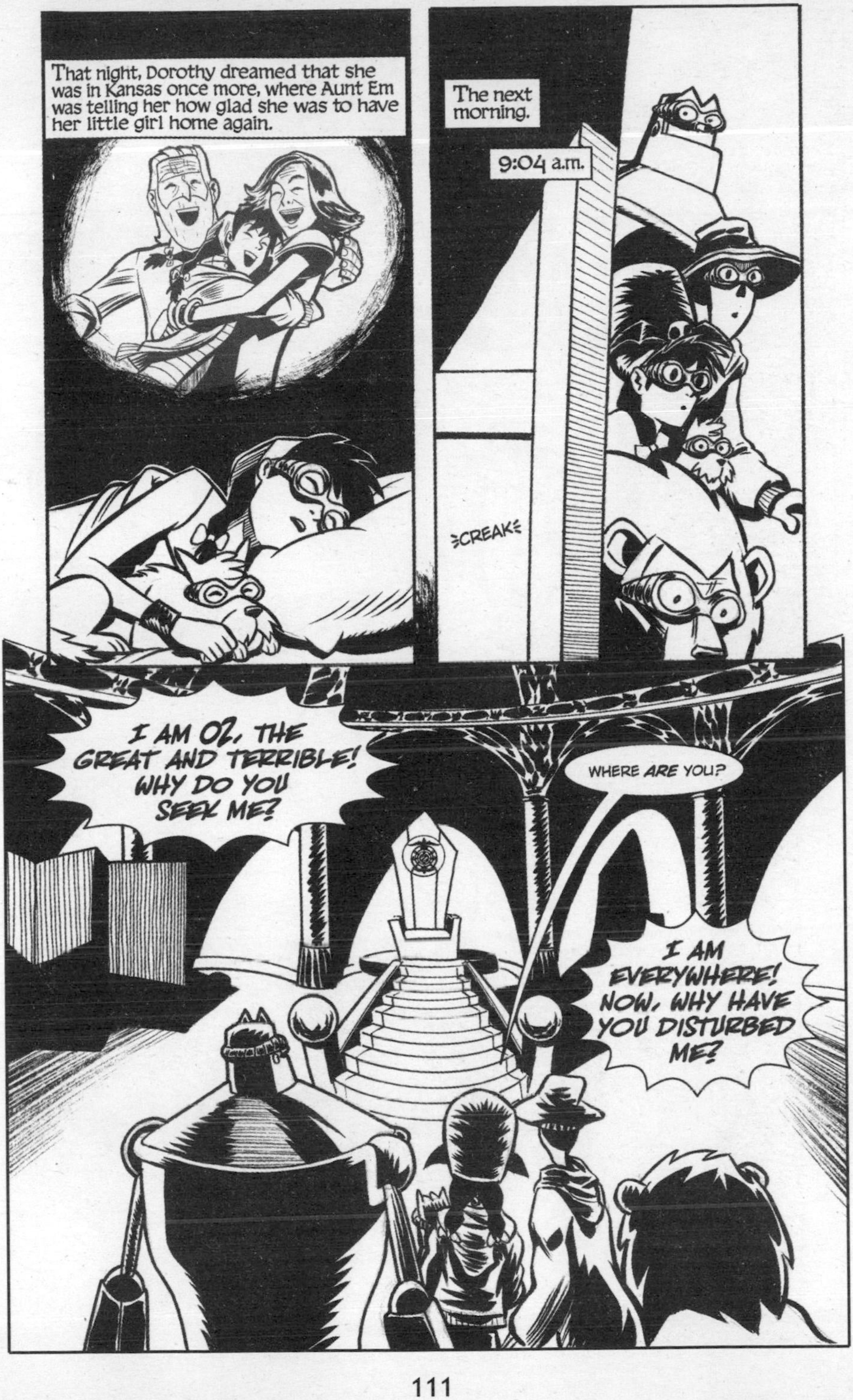

That night, Dorothy dreamed that she was in Kansas once more, where Aunt Em was telling her how glad she was to have her little girl home again.
The next morning.
9:04 a.m.
CREAK
I AM OZ, THE GREAT AND TERRIBLE! WHY DO YOU SEEK ME?
WHERE ARE YOU?
I AM EVERYWHERE! NOW, WHY HAVE YOU DISTURBED ME?

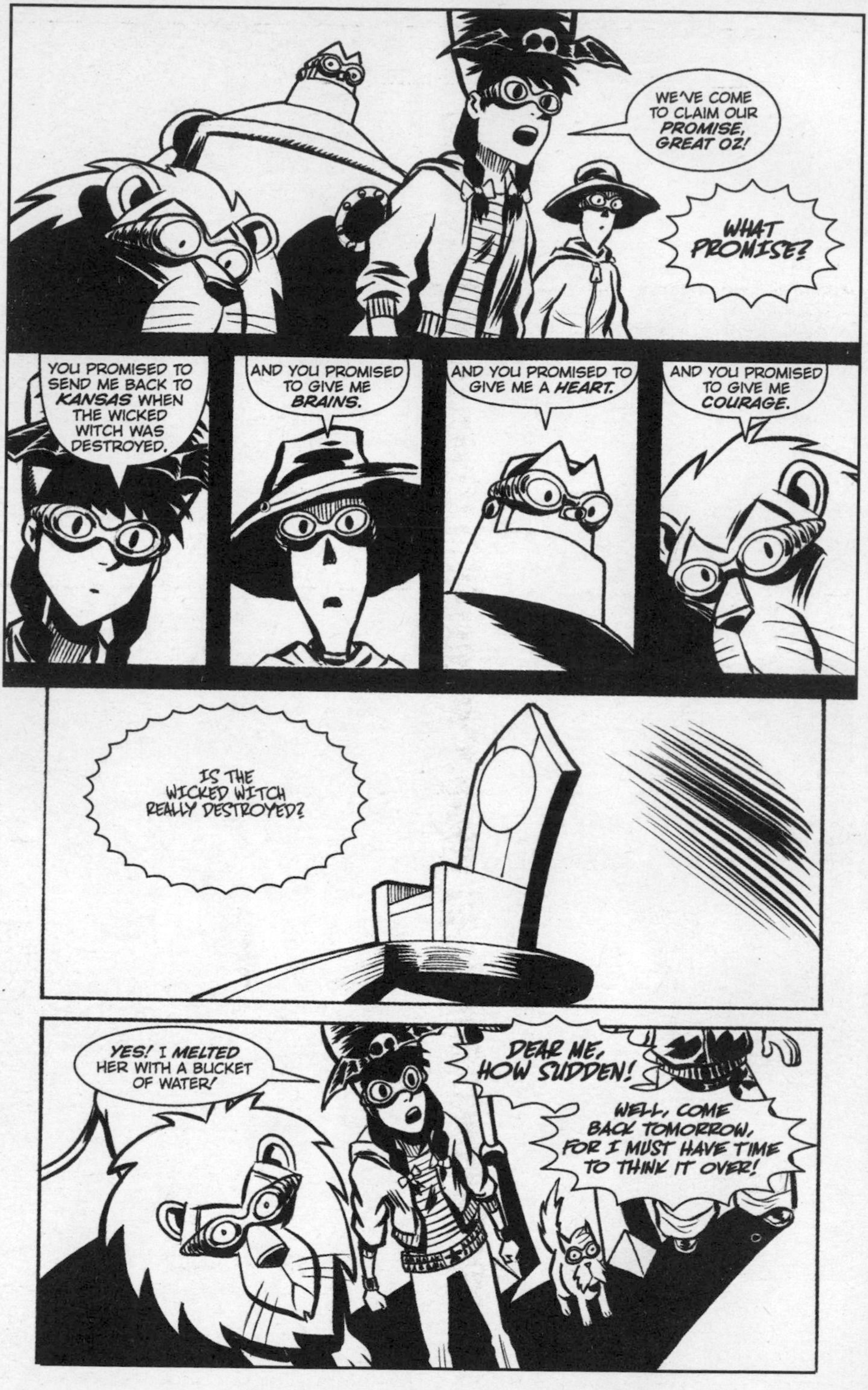
WE'VE COME TO CLAIM OUR PROMISE, GREAT OZ!
WHAT PROMISE?
YOU PROMISED TO SEND ME BACK TO KANSAS WHEN THE WICKED WITCH WAS DESTROYED.
AND YOU PROMISED TO GIVE ME BRAINS.
AND YOU PROMISED TO GIVE ME A HEART.
AND YOU PROMISED TO GIVE ME COURAGE.
IS THE WICKED WITCH REALLY DESTROYED?
YES! I MELTED HER WITH A BUCKET OF WATER!
DEAR ME, HOW SUDDEN!
WELL, COME BACK TOMORROW, FOR I MUST HAVE TIME TO THINK IT OVER!

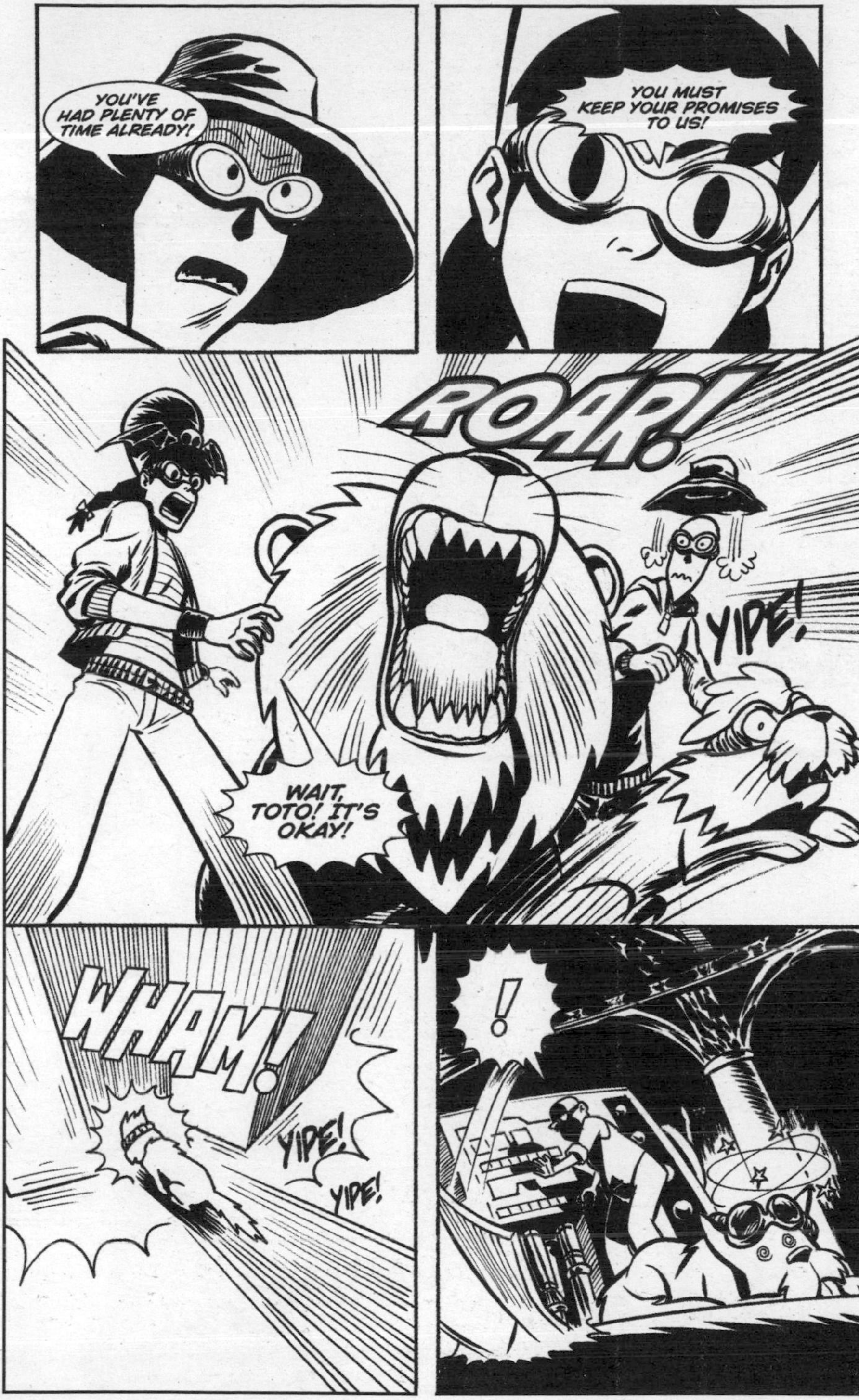
YOU'VE HAD PLENTY OF TIME ALREADY!
YOU MUST KEEP YOUR PROMISES TO US!
ROAR!
YIPE!
WAIT, TOTO! IT'S OKAY!
WHAM!
YIPE!
YIPE!
!

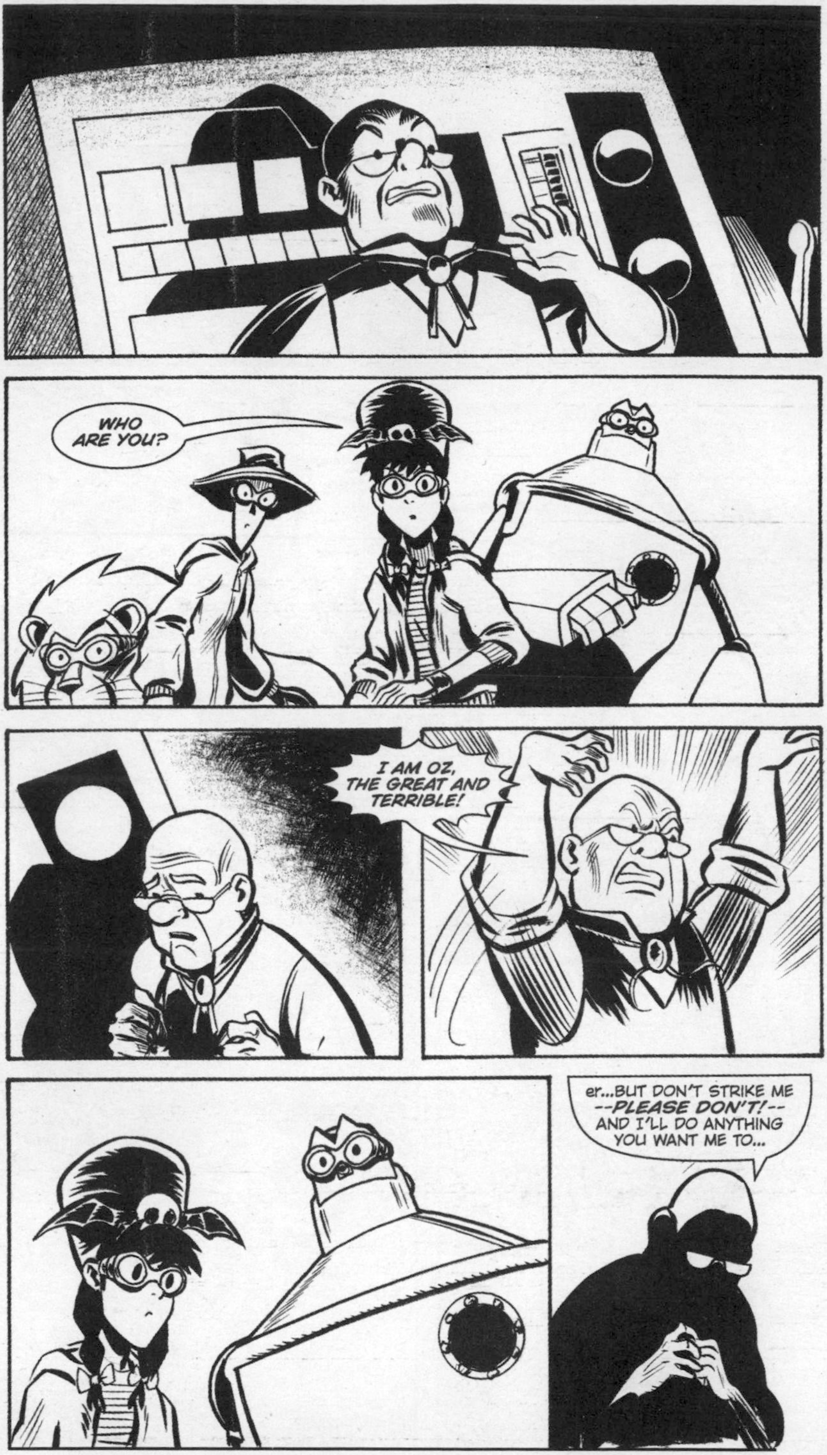
WHO ARE YOU?
I AM OZ, THE GREAT AND TERRIBLE!
er...BUT DON'T STRIKE ME --PLEASE DON'T!-- AND I'LL DO ANYTHING YOU WANT ME TO...

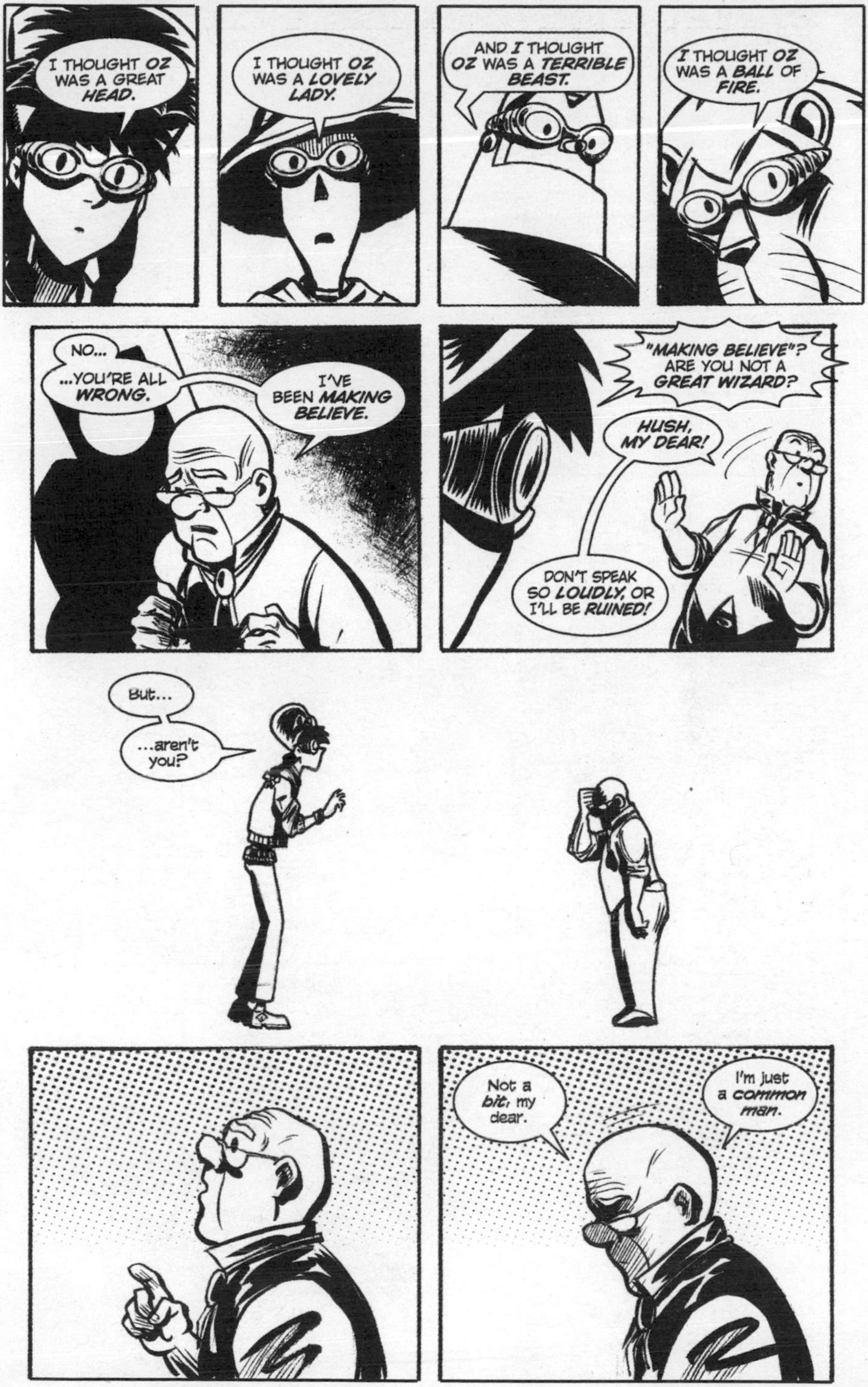
I THOUGHT OZ WAS A GREAT HEAD.
I THOUGHT OZ WAS A LOVELY LADY.
AND I THOUGHT OZ WAS A TERRIBLE BEAST.
I THOUGHT OZ WAS A BALL OF FIRE.
NO...
...YOU'RE ALL WRONG.
I'VE BEEN MAKING BELIEVE.
"MAKING BELIEVE"? ARE YOU NOT A GREAT WIZARD?
HUSH, MY DEAR!
DON'T SPEAK SO LOUDLY, OR I'LL BE RUINED!
But...
...aren't you?
Not a bit, my dear.
I'm just a common man.

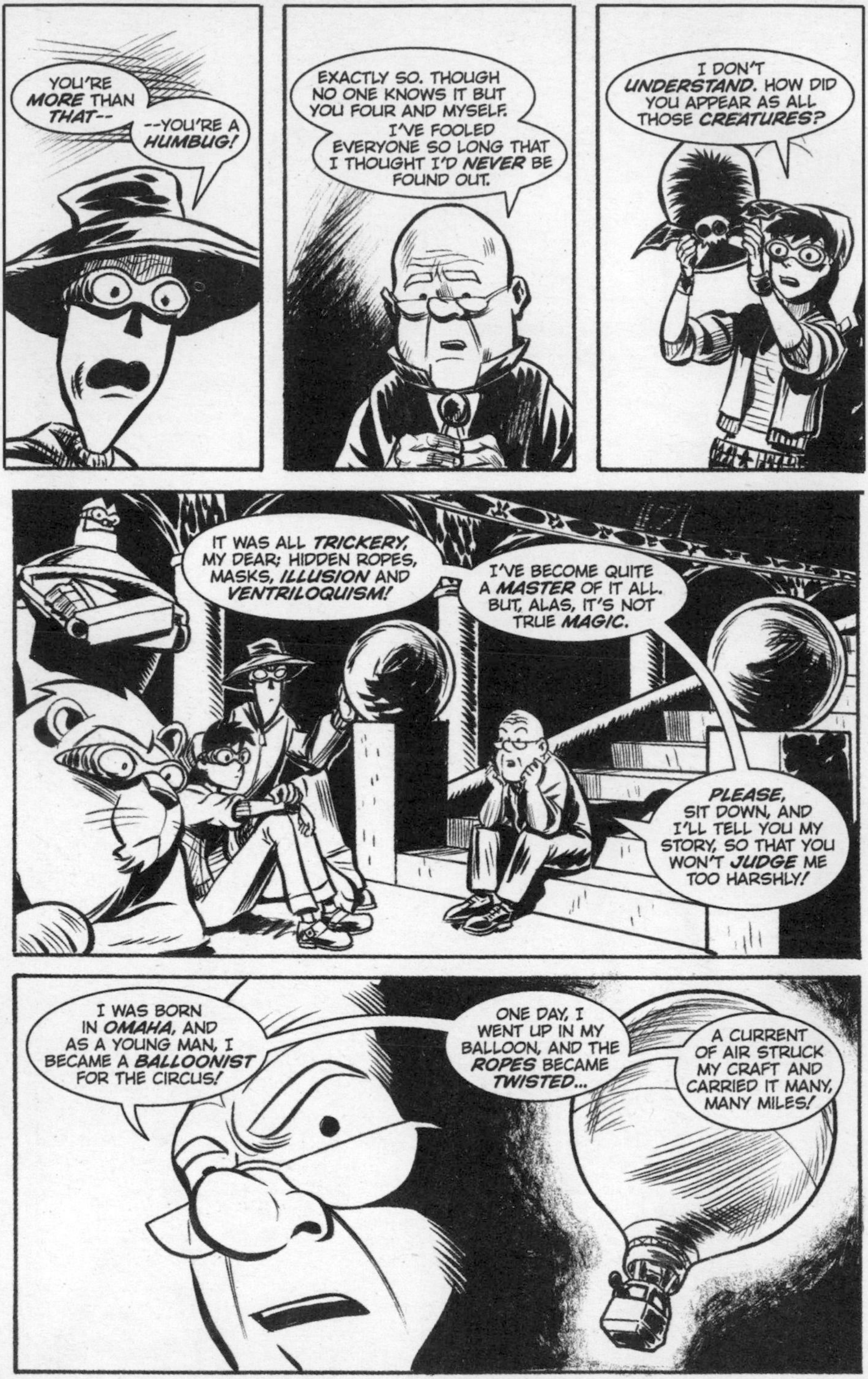
YOU'RE MORE THAN THAT--
--YOU'RE A HUMBUG!
EXACTLY SO. THOUGH NO ONE KNOWS IT BUT YOU FOUR AND MYSELF.
I'VE FOOLED EVERYONE SO LONG THAT I THOUGHT I'D NEVER BE FOUND OUT.
I DON'T UNDERSTAND. HOW DID YOU APPEAR AS ALL THOSE CREATURES?
IT WAS ALL TRICKERY, MY DEAR; HIDDEN ROPES, MASKS, ILLUSION AND VENTRILOQUISM!
I'VE BECOME QUITE A MASTER OF IT ALL. BUT, ALAS, IT'S NOT TRUE MAGIC.
PLEASE, SIT DOWN, AND I'LL TELL YOU MY STORY, SO THAT YOU WON'T JUDGE ME TOO HARSHLY!
I WAS BORN IN OMAHA, AND AS A YOUNG MAN, I BECAME A BALLOONIST FOR THE CIRCUS!
ONE DAY, I WENT UP IN MY BALLOON, AND THE ROPES BECAME TWISTED...
A CURRENT OF AIR STRUCK MY CRAFT AND CARRIED IT MANY, MANY MILES!

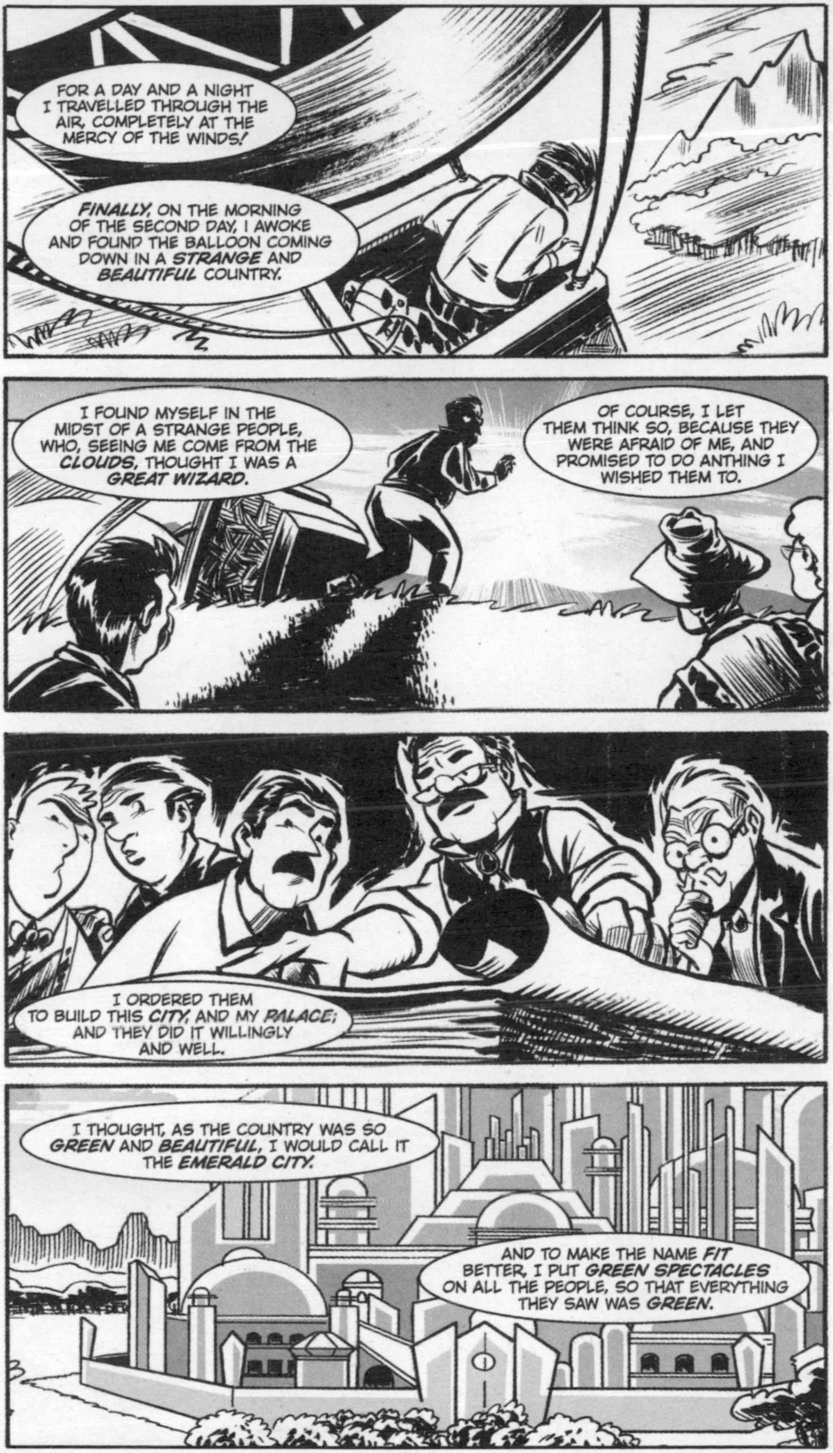
FOR A DAY AND A NIGHT I TRAVELLED THROUGH THE AIR, COMPLETELY AT THE MERCY OF THE WINDS!
FINALLY, ON THE MORNING OF THE SECOND DAY, I AWOKE AND FOUND THE BALLOON COMING DOWN IN A STRANGE AND BEAUTIFUL COUNTRY.
I FOUND MYSELF IN THE MIDST OF A STRANGE PEOPLE, WHO, SEEING ME COME FROM THE CLOUDS, THOUGHT I WAS A GREAT WIZARD.
OF COURSE, I LET THEM THINK SO, BECAUSE THEY WERE AFRAID OF ME, AND PROMISED TO DO ANTHING I WISHED THEM TO.
I ORDERED THEM TO BUILD THIS CITY, AND MY PALACE; AND THEY DID IT WILLINGLY AND WELL.
I THOUGHT, AS THE COUNTRY WAS SO GREEN AND BEAUTIFUL, I WOULD CALL IT THE EMERALD CITY.
AND TO MAKE THE NAME FIT BETTER, I PUT GREEN SPECTACLES ON ALL THE PEOPLE, SO THAT EVERYTHING THEY SAW WAS GREEN.

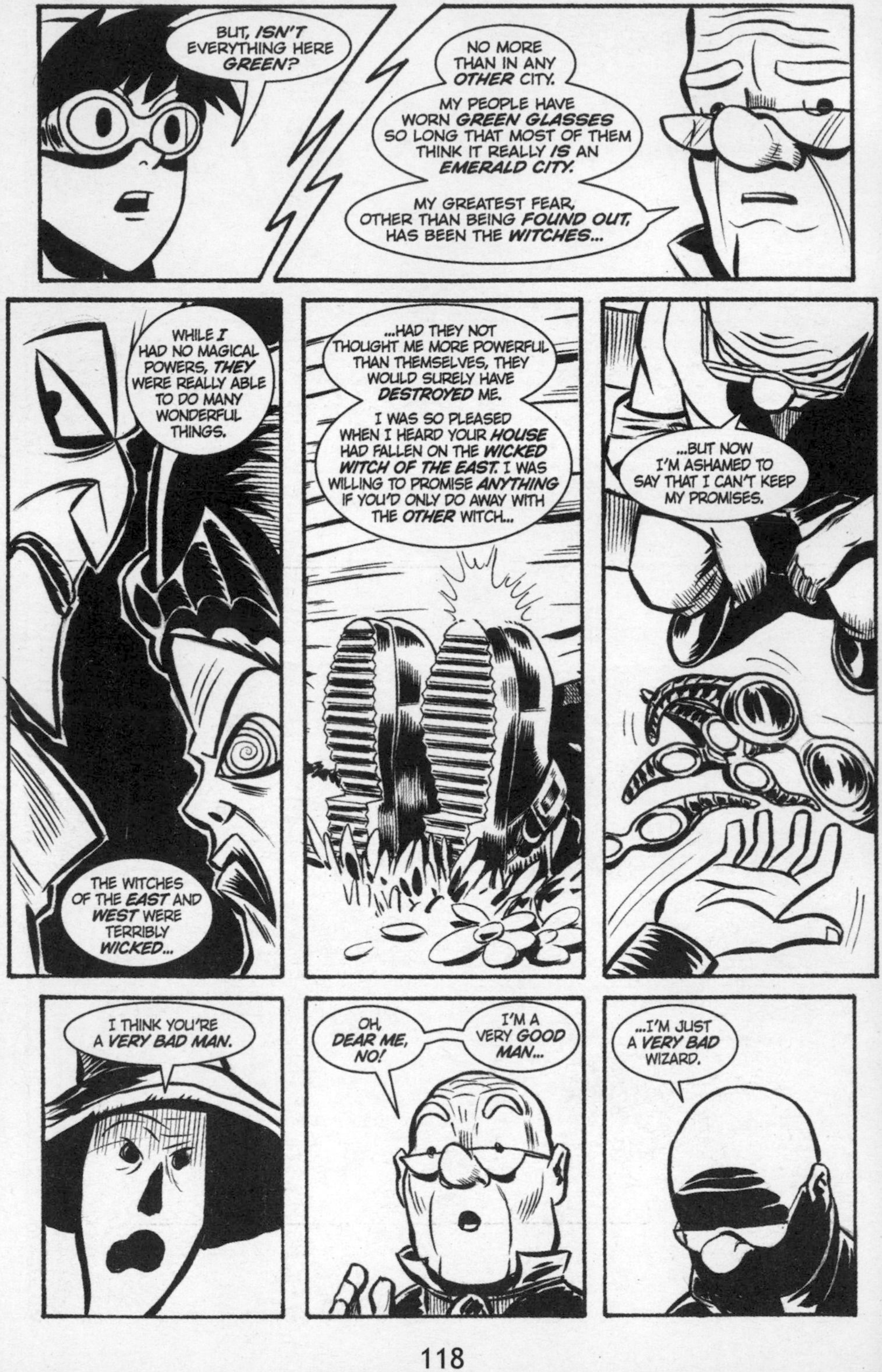
BUT, ISN'T EVERYTHING HERE GREEN?
NO MORE THAN IN ANY OTHER CITY.
MY PEOPLE HAVE WORN GREEN GLASSES SO LONG THAT MOST OF THEM THINK IT REALLY IS AN EMERALD CITY.
MY GREATEST FEAR, OTHER THAN BEING FOUND OUT, HAS BEEN THE WITCHES...
WHILE I HAD NO MAGICAL POWERS, THEY WERE REALLY ABLE TO DO MANY WONDERFUL THINGS.
THE WITCHES OF THE EAST AND WEST WERE TERRIBLY WICKED...
...HAD THEY NOT THOUGHT ME MORE POWERFUL THAN THEMSELVES, THEY WOULD SURELY HAVE DESTROYED ME.
I WAS SO PLEASED WHEN I HEARD YOUR HOUSE HAD FALLEN ON THE WICKED WITCH OF THE EAST. I WAS WILLING TO PROMISE ANYTHING IF YOU'D ONLY DO AWAY WITH THE OTHER WITCH...
...BUT NOW I'M ASHAMED TO SAY THAT I CAN'T KEEP MY PROMISES.
I THINK YOU'RE A VERY BAD MAN.
OH, DEAR ME, NO!
I'M A VERY GOOD MAN...
...I'M JUST A VERY BAD WIZARD.

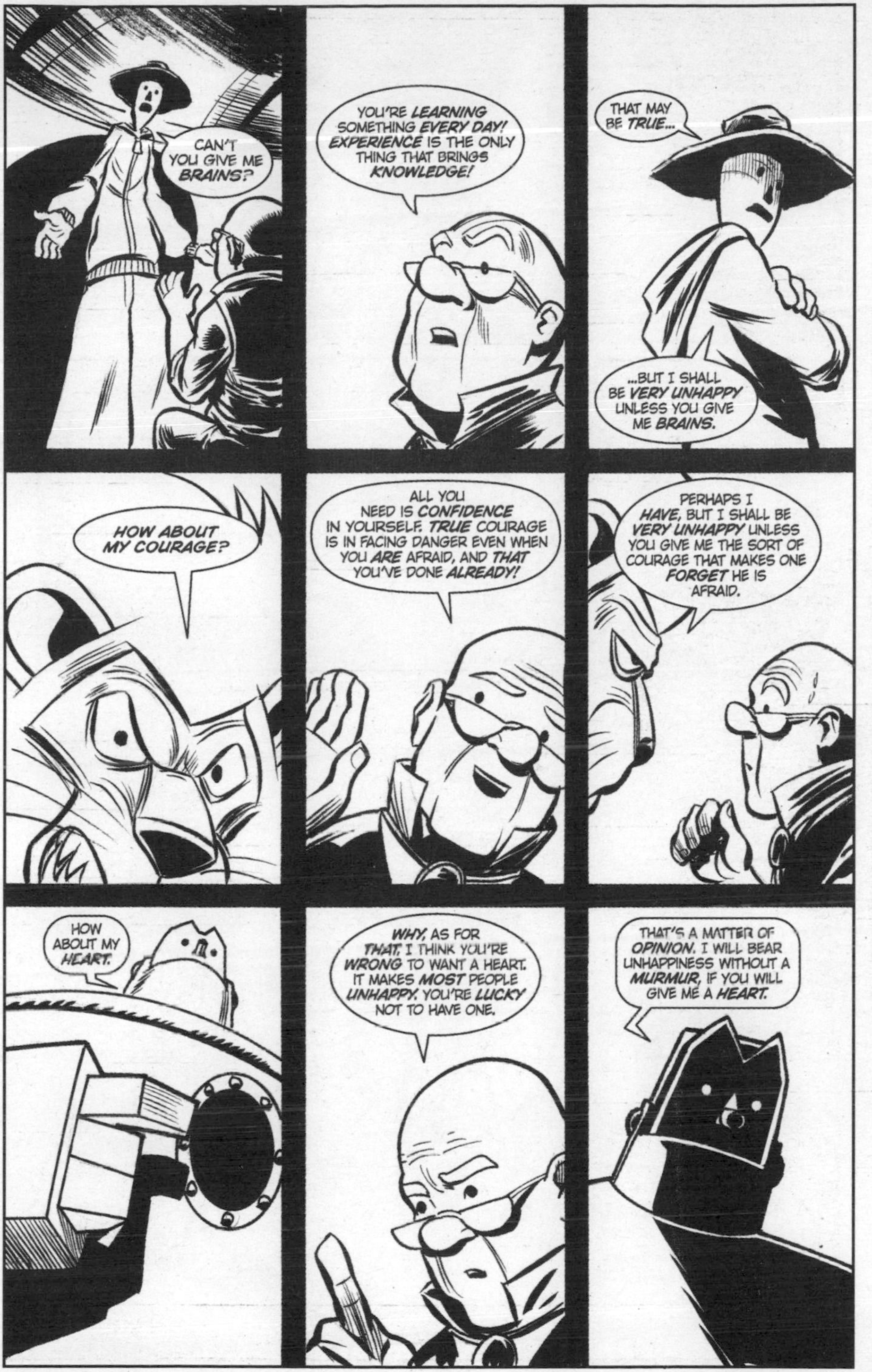
CAN'T YOU GIVE ME BRAINS?
YOU'RE LEARNING SOMETHING EVERY DAY! EXPERIENCE IS THE ONLY THING THAT BRINGS KNOWLEDGE!
THAT MAY BE TRUE...
...BUT I SHALL BE VERY UNHAPPY UNLESS YOU GIVE ME BRAINS.
HOW ABOUT MY COURAGE?
ALL YOU NEED IS CONFIDENCE IN YOURSELF. TRUE COURAGE IS IN FACING DANGER EVEN WHEN YOU ARE AFRAID, AND THAT YOU'VE DONE ALREADY!
PERHAPS I HAVE, BUT I SHALL BE VERY UNHAPPY UNLESS YOU GIVE ME THE SORT OF COURAGE THAT MAKES ONE FORGET HE IS AFRAID.
HOW ABOUT MY HEART.
WHY, AS FOR THAT, I THINK YOU'RE WRONG TO WANT A HEART. IT MAKES MOST PEOPLE UNHAPPY. YOU'RE LUCKY NOT TO HAVE ONE.
THAT'S A MATTER OF OPINION. I WILL BEAR UNHAPPINESS WITHOUT A MURMUR, IF YOU WILL GIVE ME A HEART.

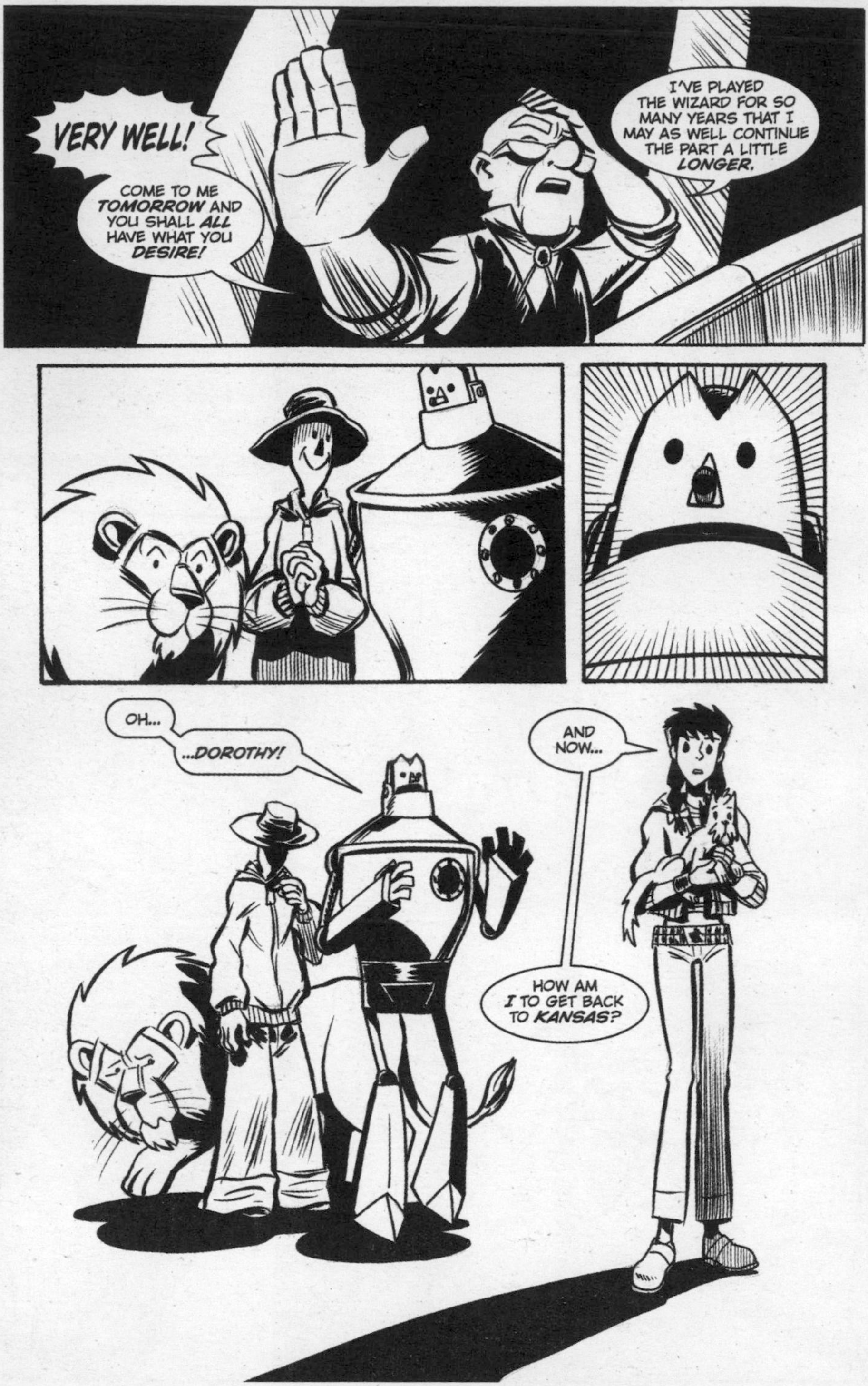
VERY WELL!
COME TO ME TOMORROW AND YOU SHALL ALL HAVE WHAT YOU DESIRE!
I'VE PLAYED THE WIZARD FOR SO MANY YEARS THAT I MAY AS WELL CONTINUE THE PART A LITTLE LONGER.
OH...
...DOROTHY!
AND NOW...
HOW AM I TO GET BACK TO KANSAS?

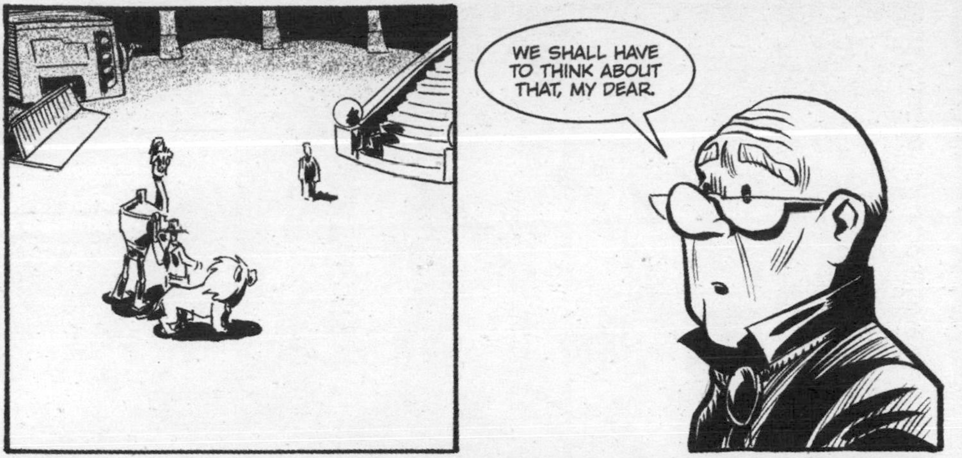
WE SHALL HAVE TO THINK ABOUT THAT, MY DEAR.

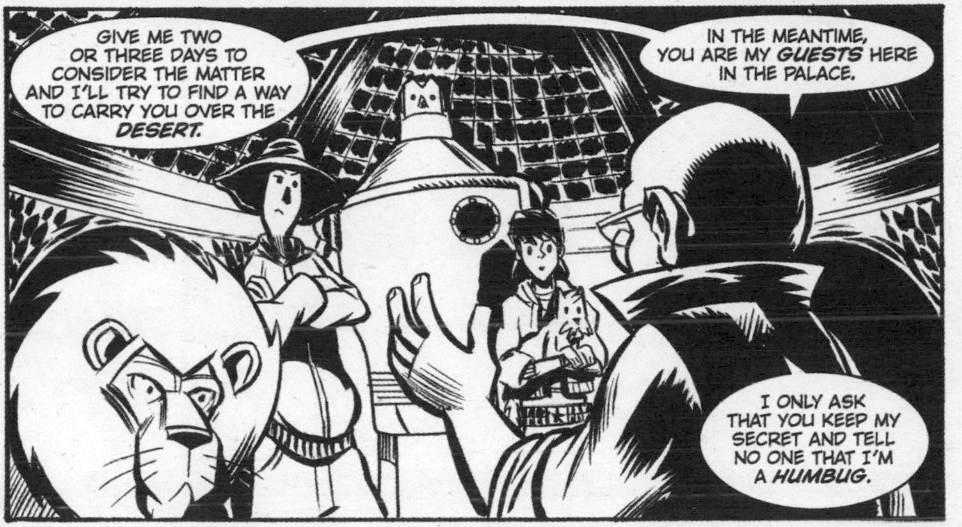
GIVE ME TWO OR THREE DAYS TO CONSIDER THE MATTER AND I'LL TRY TO FIND A WAY TO CARRY YOU OVER THE *DESERT.*
IN THE MEANTIME, YOU ARE MY *GUESTS* HERE IN THE PALACE.
I ONLY ASK THAT YOU KEEP MY SECRET AND TELL NO ONE THAT I'M A *HUMBUG.*

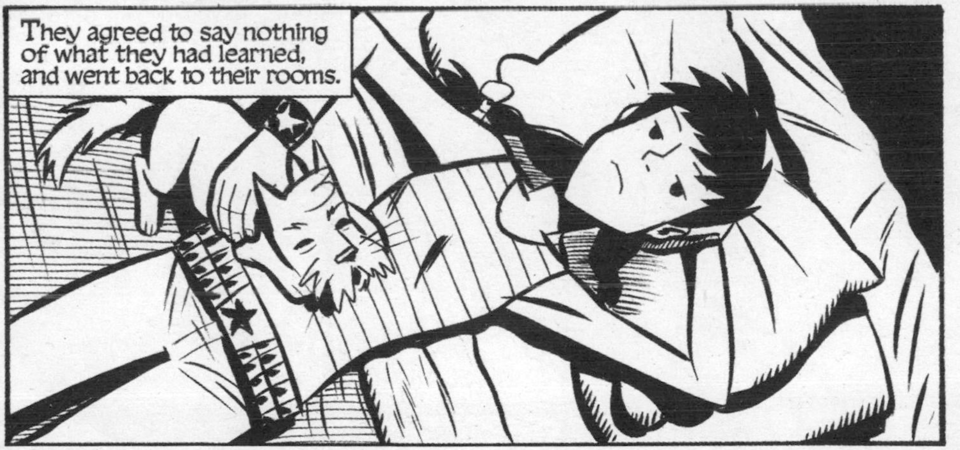
They agreed to say nothing of what they had learned, and went back to their rooms.

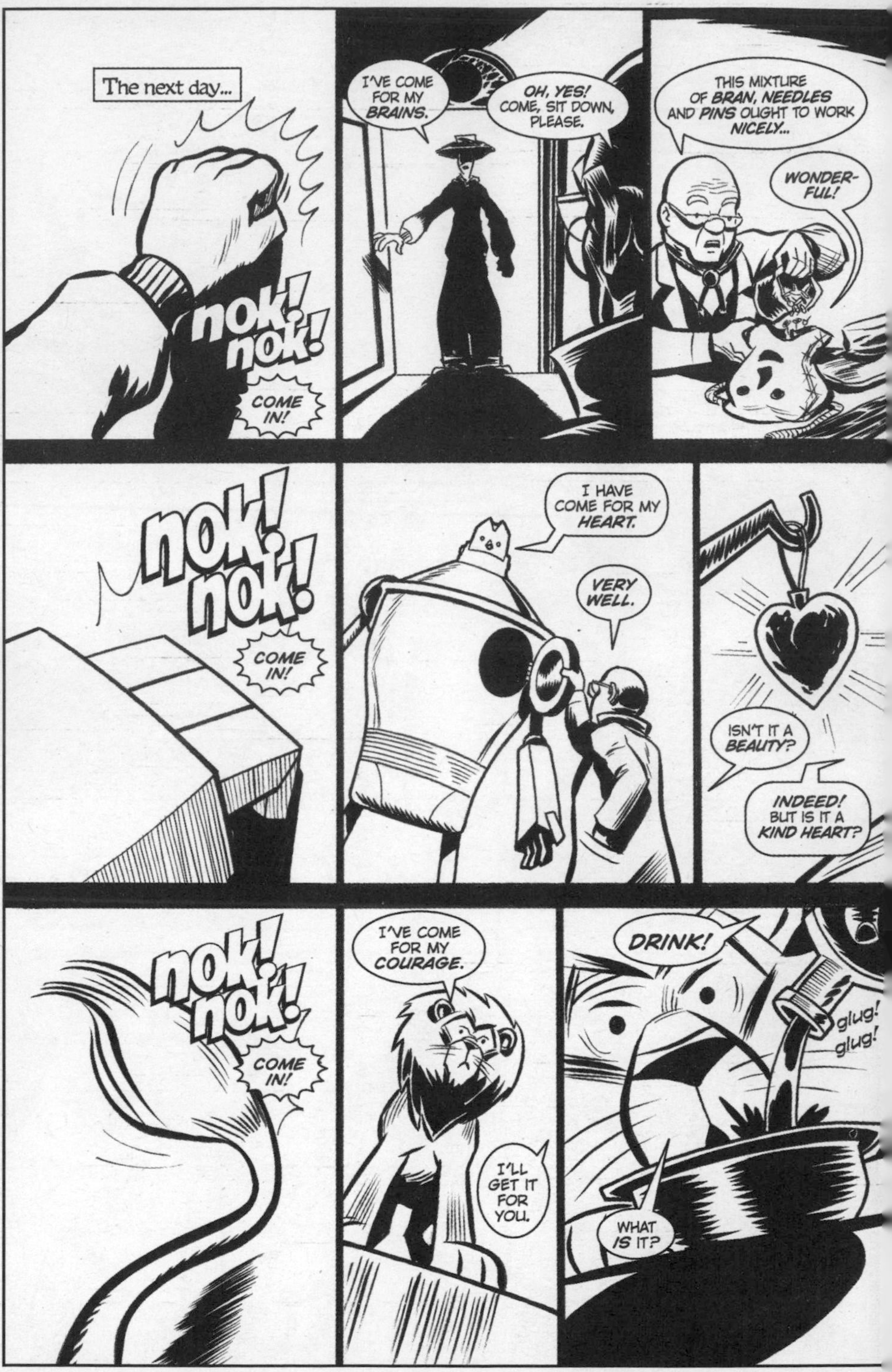
The next day...
nok! nok!
COME IN!
I'VE COME FOR MY BRAINS.
OH, YES! COME, SIT DOWN, PLEASE.
THIS MIXTURE OF BRAN, NEEDLES AND PINS OUGHT TO WORK NICELY...
WONDER-FUL!
nok! nok!
COME IN!
I HAVE COME FOR MY HEART.
VERY WELL.
ISN'T IT A BEAUTY?
INDEED! BUT IS IT A KIND HEART?
nok! nok!
COME IN!
I'VE COME FOR MY COURAGE.
I'LL GET IT FOR YOU.
DRINK!
glug! glug!
WHAT IS IT?

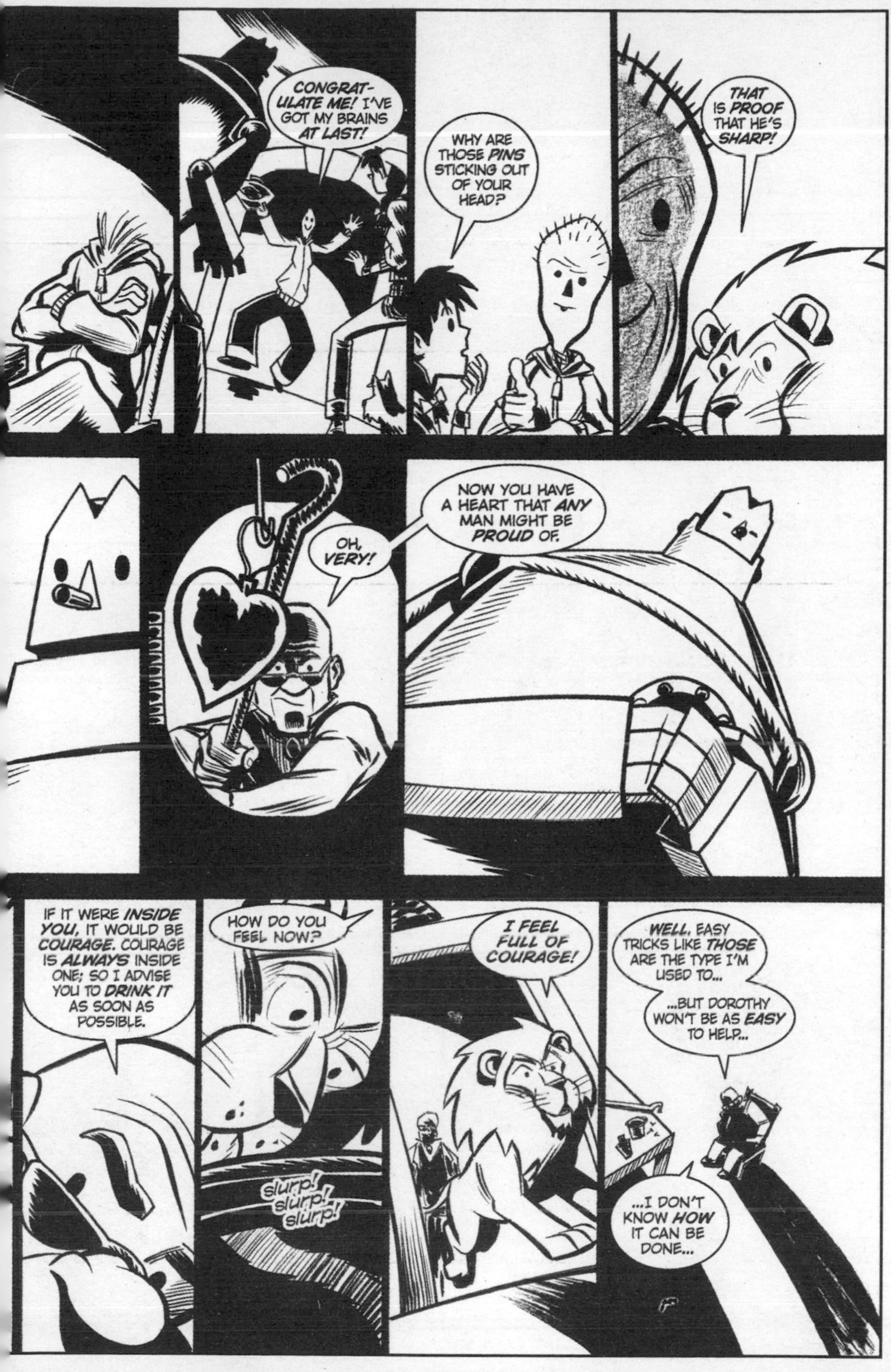
CONGRAT-ULATE ME! I'VE GOT MY BRAINS AT LAST!
WHY ARE THOSE PINS STICKING OUT OF YOUR HEAD?
THAT IS PROOF THAT HE'S SHARP!
NOW YOU HAVE A HEART THAT ANY MAN MIGHT BE PROUD OF.
OH, VERY!
IF IT WERE INSIDE YOU, IT WOULD BE COURAGE. COURAGE IS ALWAYS INSIDE ONE; SO I ADVISE YOU TO DRINK IT AS SOON AS POSSIBLE.
HOW DO YOU FEEL NOW?
slurp! slurp! slurp!
I FEEL FULL OF COURAGE!
WELL, EASY TRICKS LIKE THOSE ARE THE TYPE I'M USED TO...
...BUT DOROTHY WON'T BE AS EASY TO HELP...
...I DON'T KNOW HOW IT CAN BE DONE...

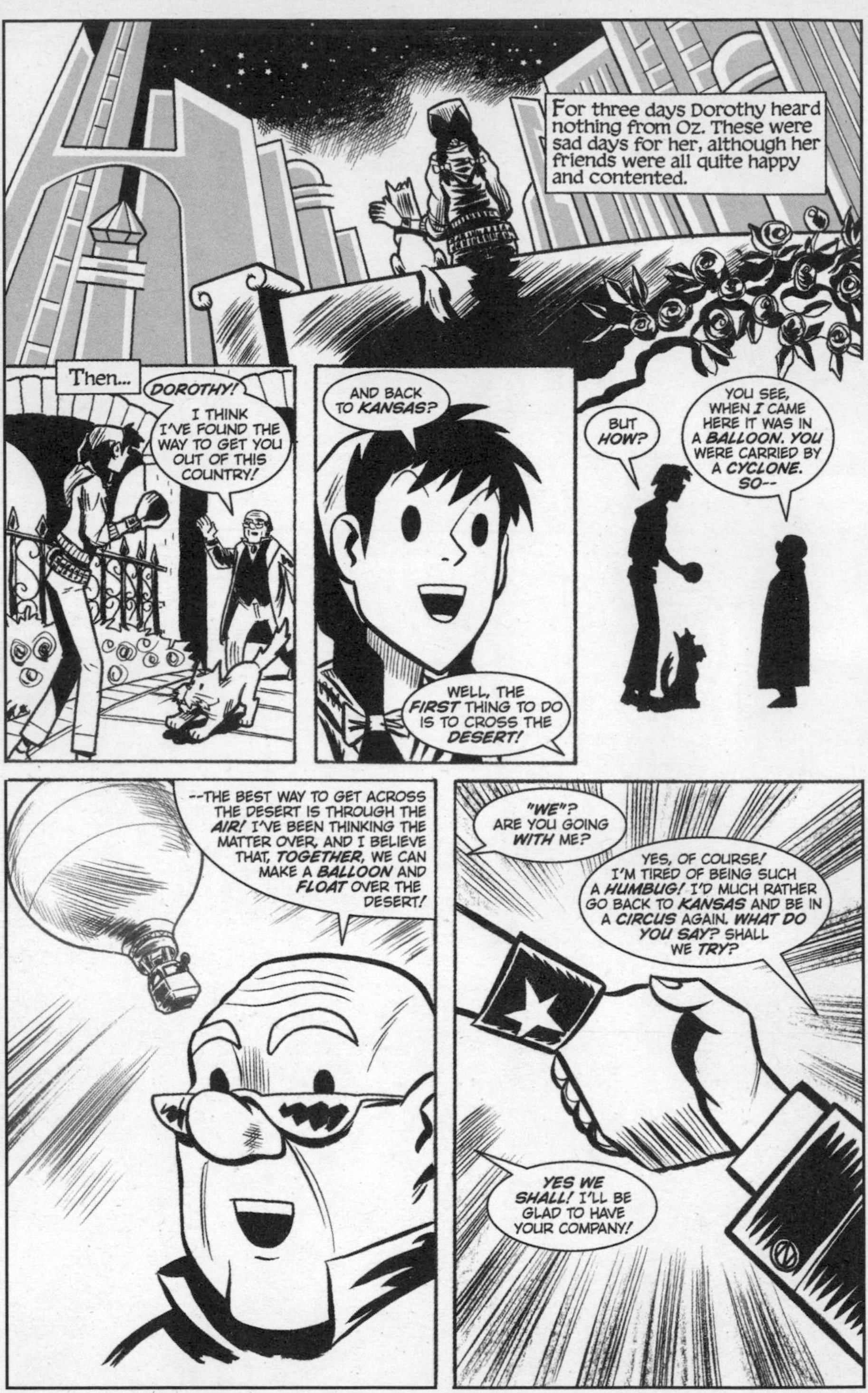

For three days Dorothy heard nothing from Oz. These were sad days for her, although her friends were all quite happy and contented.
Then...
DOROTHY! I THINK I'VE FOUND THE WAY TO GET YOU OUT OF THIS COUNTRY!
AND BACK TO KANSAS?
WELL, THE FIRST THING TO DO IS TO CROSS THE DESERT!
BUT HOW?
YOU SEE, WHEN I CAME HERE IT WAS IN A BALLOON. YOU WERE CARRIED BY A CYCLONE. SO--
--THE BEST WAY TO GET ACROSS THE DESERT IS THROUGH THE AIR! I'VE BEEN THINKING THE MATTER OVER, AND I BELIEVE THAT, TOGETHER, WE CAN MAKE A BALLOON AND FLOAT OVER THE DESERT!
"WE"? ARE YOU GOING WITH ME?
YES, OF COURSE! I'M TIRED OF BEING SUCH A HUMBUG! I'D MUCH RATHER GO BACK TO KANSAS AND BE IN A CIRCUS AGAIN. WHAT DO YOU SAY? SHALL WE TRY?
YES WE SHALL! I'LL BE GLAD TO HAVE YOUR COMPANY!

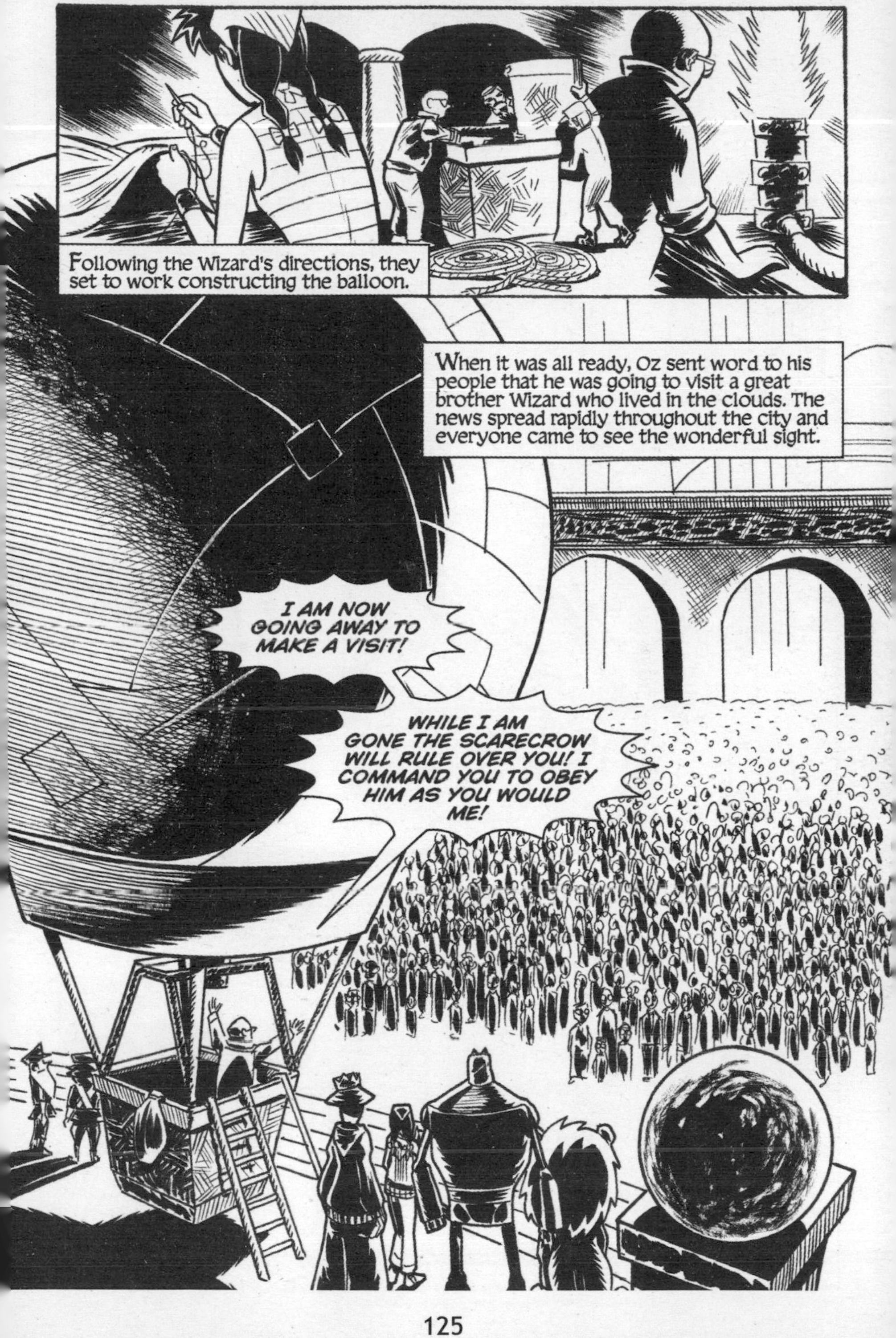
Following the Wizard's directions, they set to work constructing the balloon.
When it was all ready, Oz sent word to his people that he was going to visit a great brother Wizard who lived in the clouds. The news spread rapidly throughout the city and everyone came to see the wonderful sight.
I AM NOW GOING AWAY TO MAKE A VISIT!
WHILE I AM GONE THE SCARECROW WILL RULE OVER YOU! I COMMAND YOU TO OBEY HIM AS YOU WOULD ME!

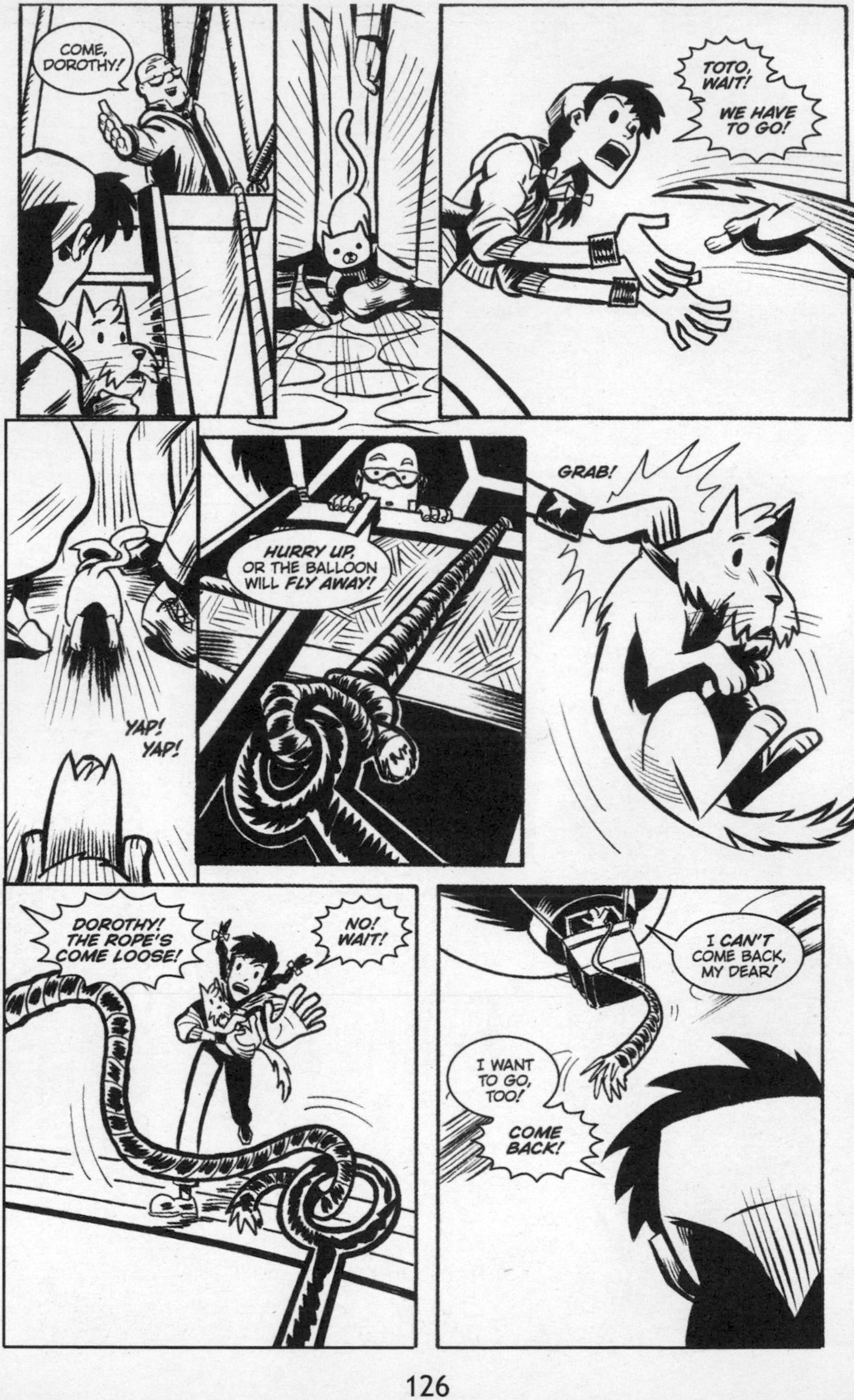
COME, DOROTHY!
TOTO, WAIT!
WE HAVE TO GO!
YAP! YAP!
HURRY UP, OR THE BALLOON WILL FLY AWAY!
GRAB!
DOROTHY! THE ROPE'S COME LOOSE!
NO! WAIT!
I CAN'T COME BACK, MY DEAR!
I WANT TO GO, TOO!
COME BACK!

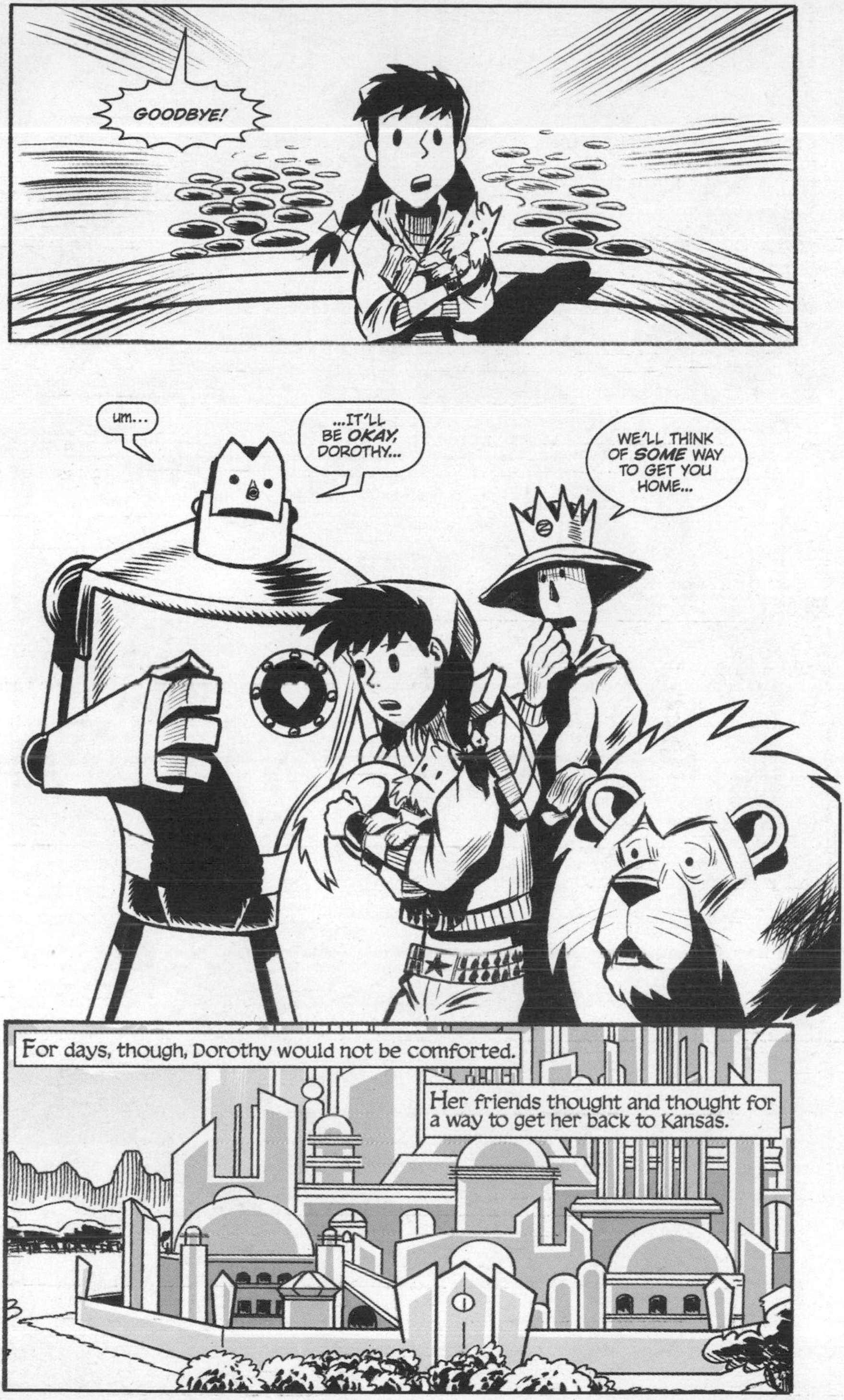
GOODBYE!
um...
...IT'LL BE OKAY, DOROTHY...
WE'LL THINK OF SOME WAY TO GET YOU HOME...
For days, though, Dorothy would not be comforted.
Her friends thought and thought for a way to get her back to Kansas.

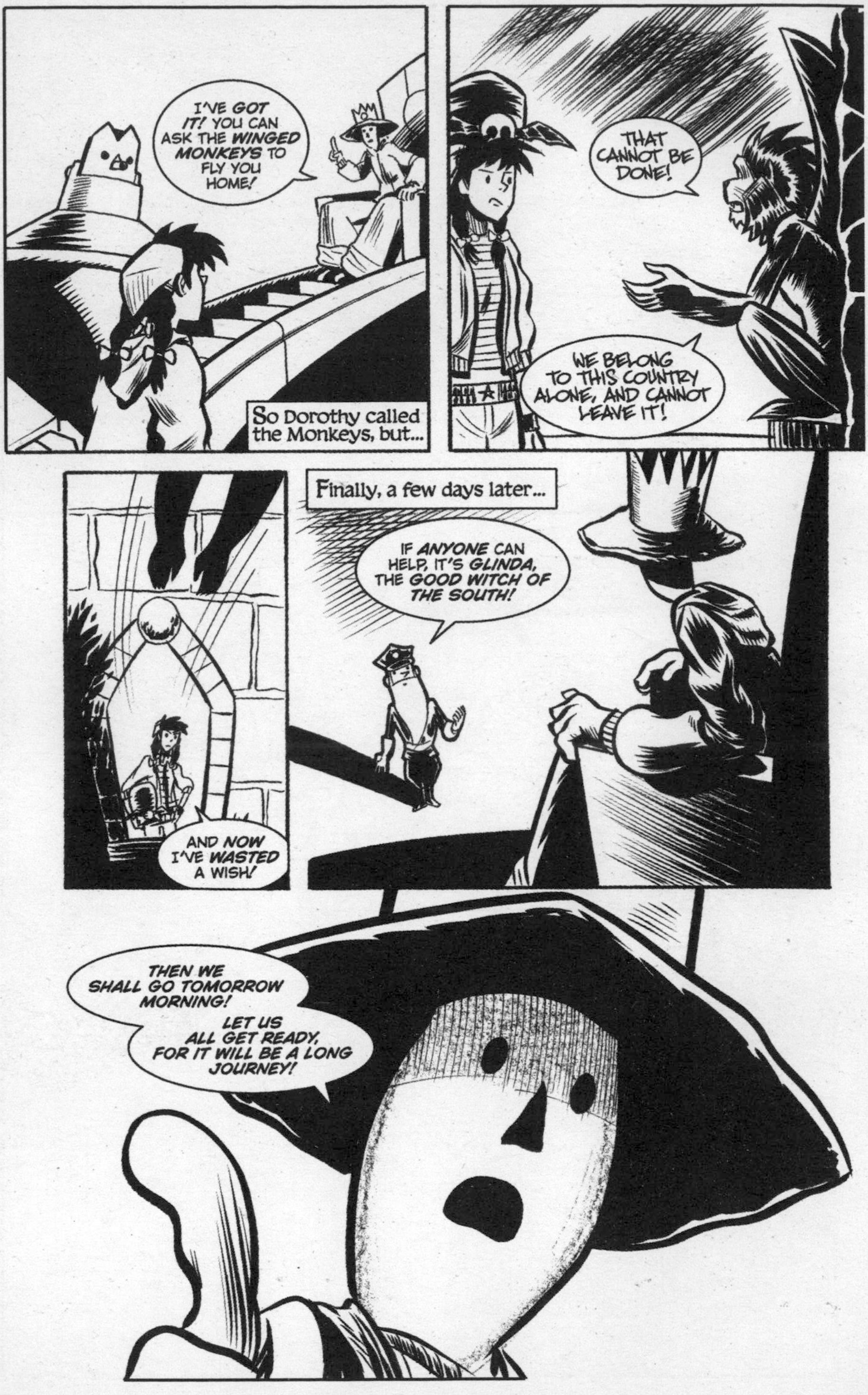
I'VE GOT IT! YOU CAN ASK THE WINGED MONKEYS TO FLY YOU HOME!
So Dorothy called the Monkeys, but...
THAT CANNOT BE DONE!
WE BELONG TO THIS COUNTRY ALONE, AND CANNOT LEAVE IT!
AND NOW I'VE WASTED A WISH!
Finally, a few days later...
IF ANYONE CAN HELP, IT'S GLINDA, THE GOOD WITCH OF THE SOUTH!
THEN WE SHALL GO TOMORROW MORNING!
LET US ALL GET READY, FOR IT WILL BE A LONG JOURNEY!

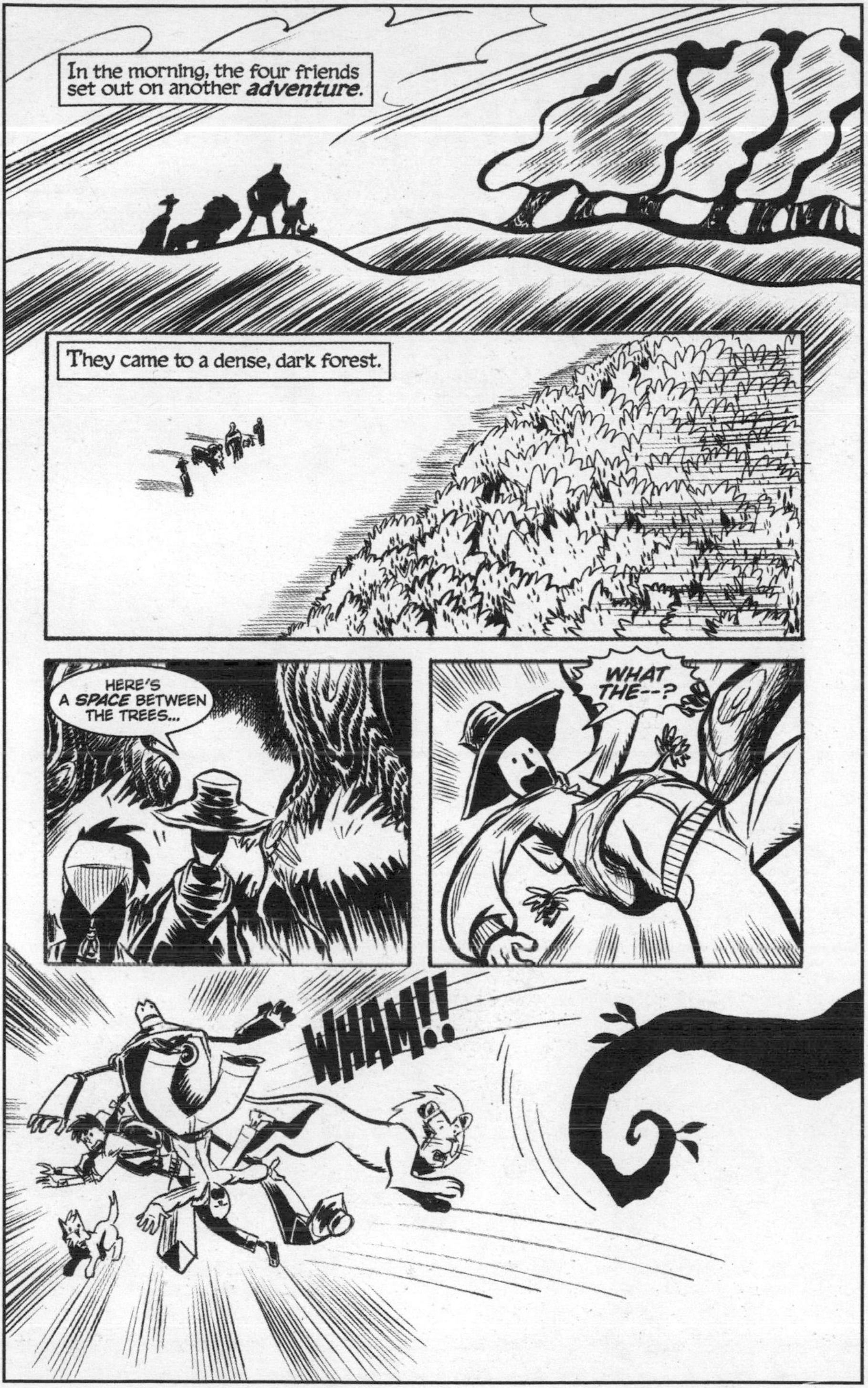

In the morning, the four friends set out on another *adventure*.
They came to a dense, dark forest.
HERE'S A SPACE BETWEEN THE TREES...
WHAT THE--?
WHAM!!

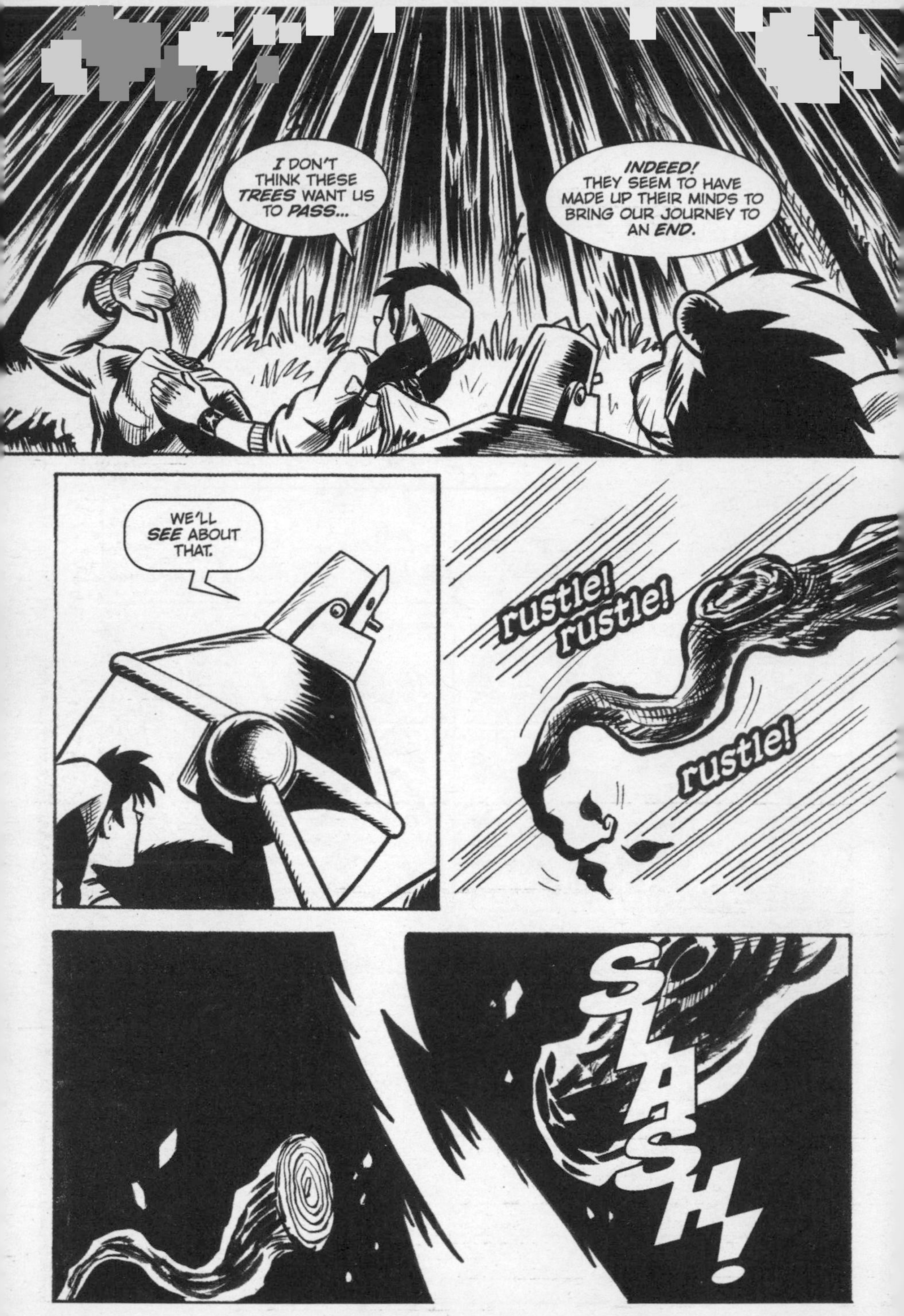
I DON'T THINK THESE TREES WANT US TO PASS...
INDEED! THEY SEEM TO HAVE MADE UP THEIR MINDS TO BRING OUR JOURNEY TO AN END.
WE'LL SEE ABOUT THAT.
rustle!
rustle!
rustle!
SLASH!

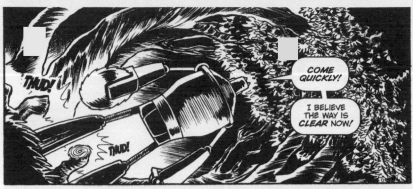

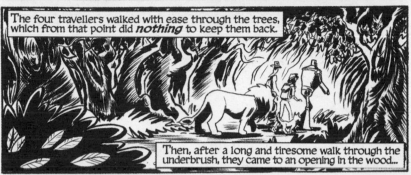

THUD!
THUD!
COME QUICKLY!
I BELIEVE THE WAY IS CLEAR NOW!
The four travellers walked with ease through the trees, which from that point did nothing to keep them back.
Then, after a long and tiresome walk through the underbrush, they came to an opening in the wood...
!

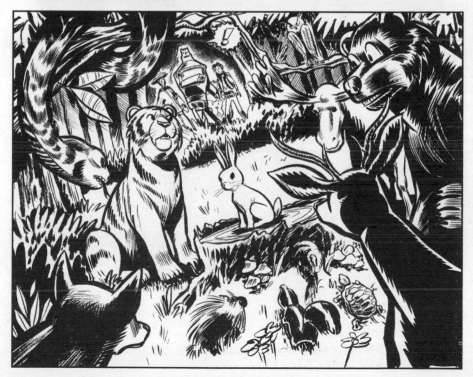

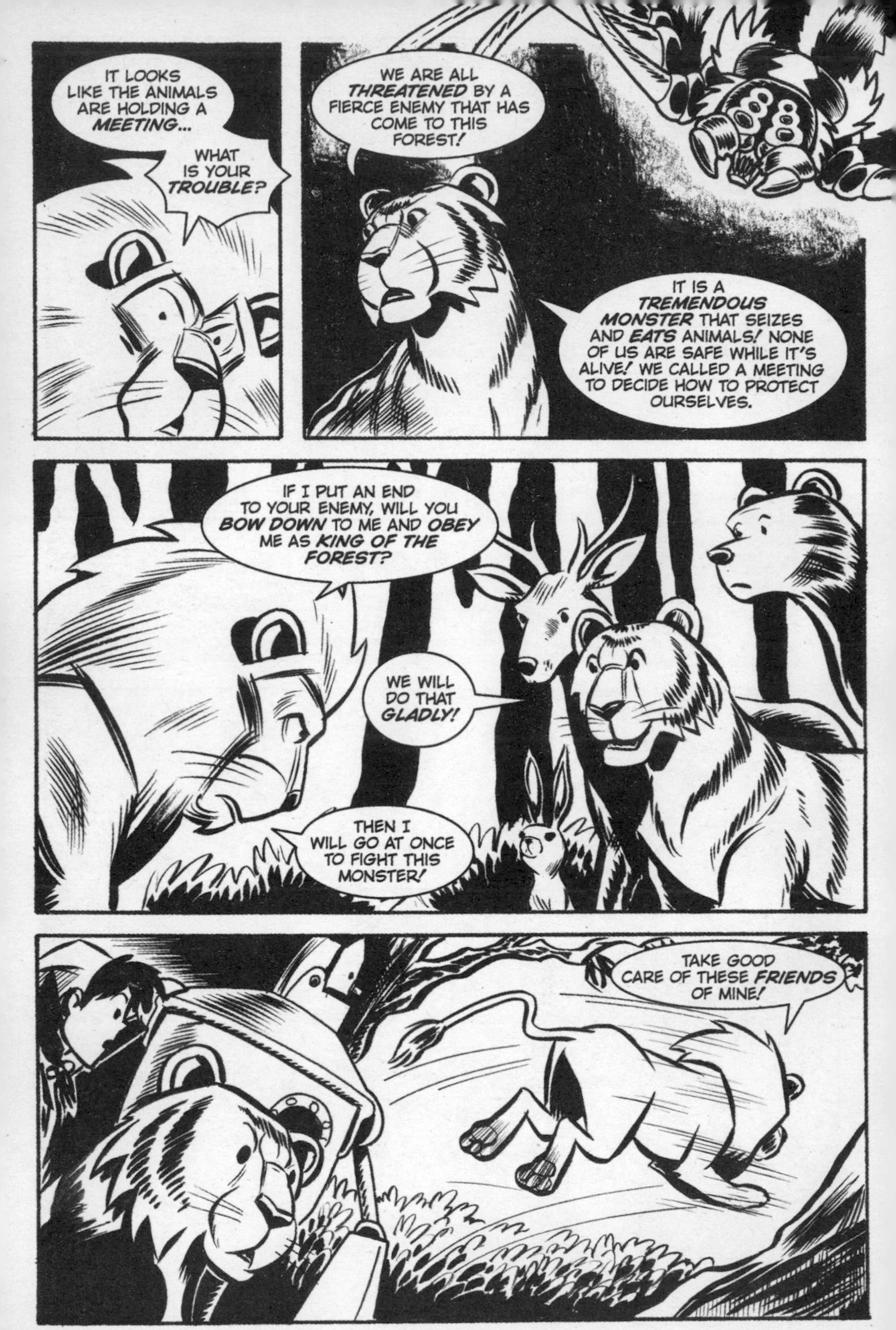
IT LOOKS LIKE THE ANIMALS ARE HOLDING A MEETING...
WHAT IS YOUR TROUBLE?
WE ARE ALL THREATENED BY A FIERCE ENEMY THAT HAS COME TO THIS FOREST!
IT IS A TREMENDOUS MONSTER THAT SEIZES AND EATS ANIMALS! NONE OF US ARE SAFE WHILE IT'S ALIVE! WE CALLED A MEETING TO DECIDE HOW TO PROTECT OURSELVES.
IF I PUT AN END TO YOUR ENEMY, WILL YOU BOW DOWN TO ME AND OBEY ME AS KING OF THE FOREST?
WE WILL DO THAT GLADLY!
THEN I WILL GO AT ONCE TO FIGHT THIS MONSTER!
TAKE GOOD CARE OF THESE FRIENDS OF MINE!

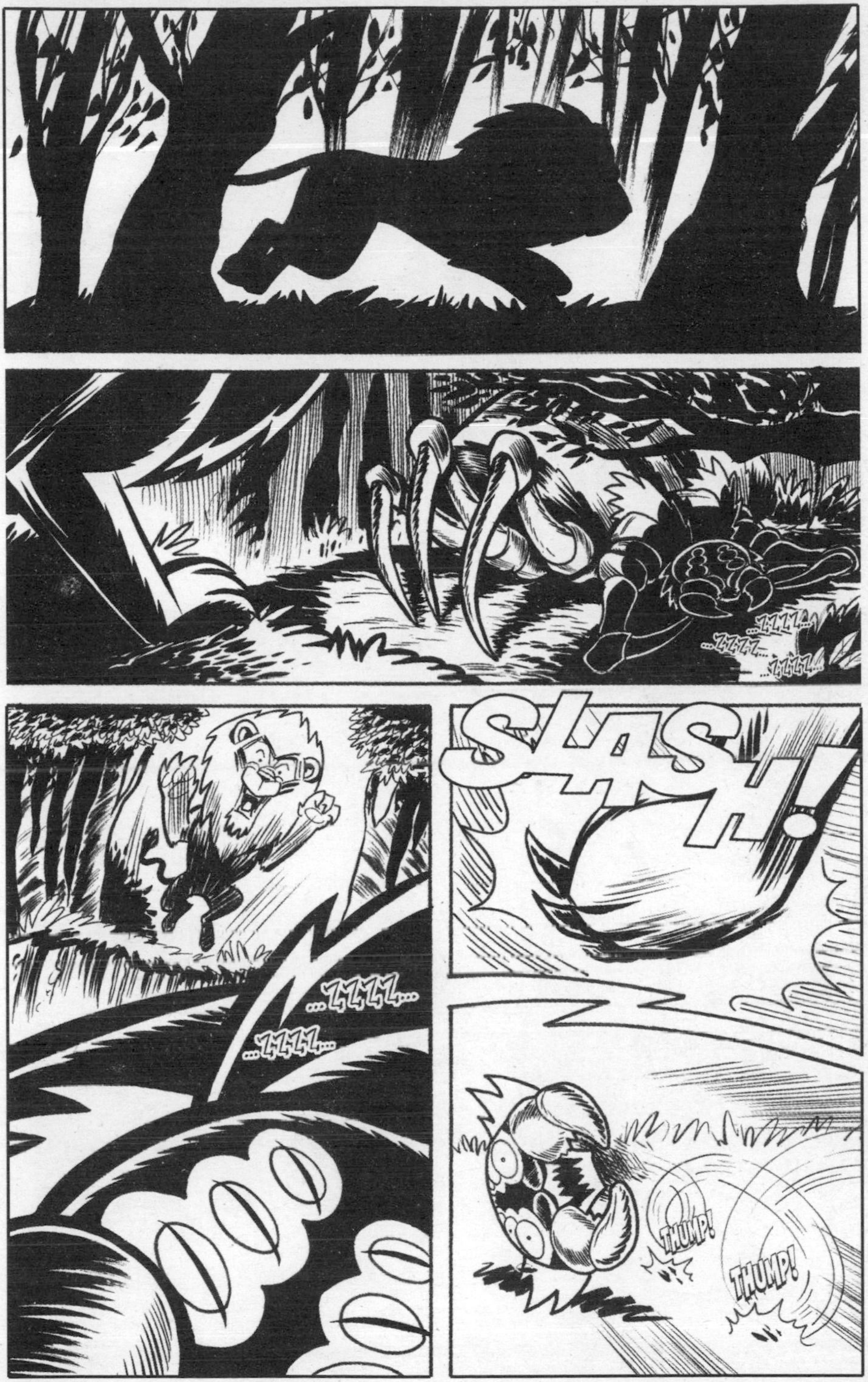

...ZZZZ...
...ZZZZ...
...ZZZZ...
...ZZZZ...
...ZZZZ...
SLASH!
THUMP!
THUMP!

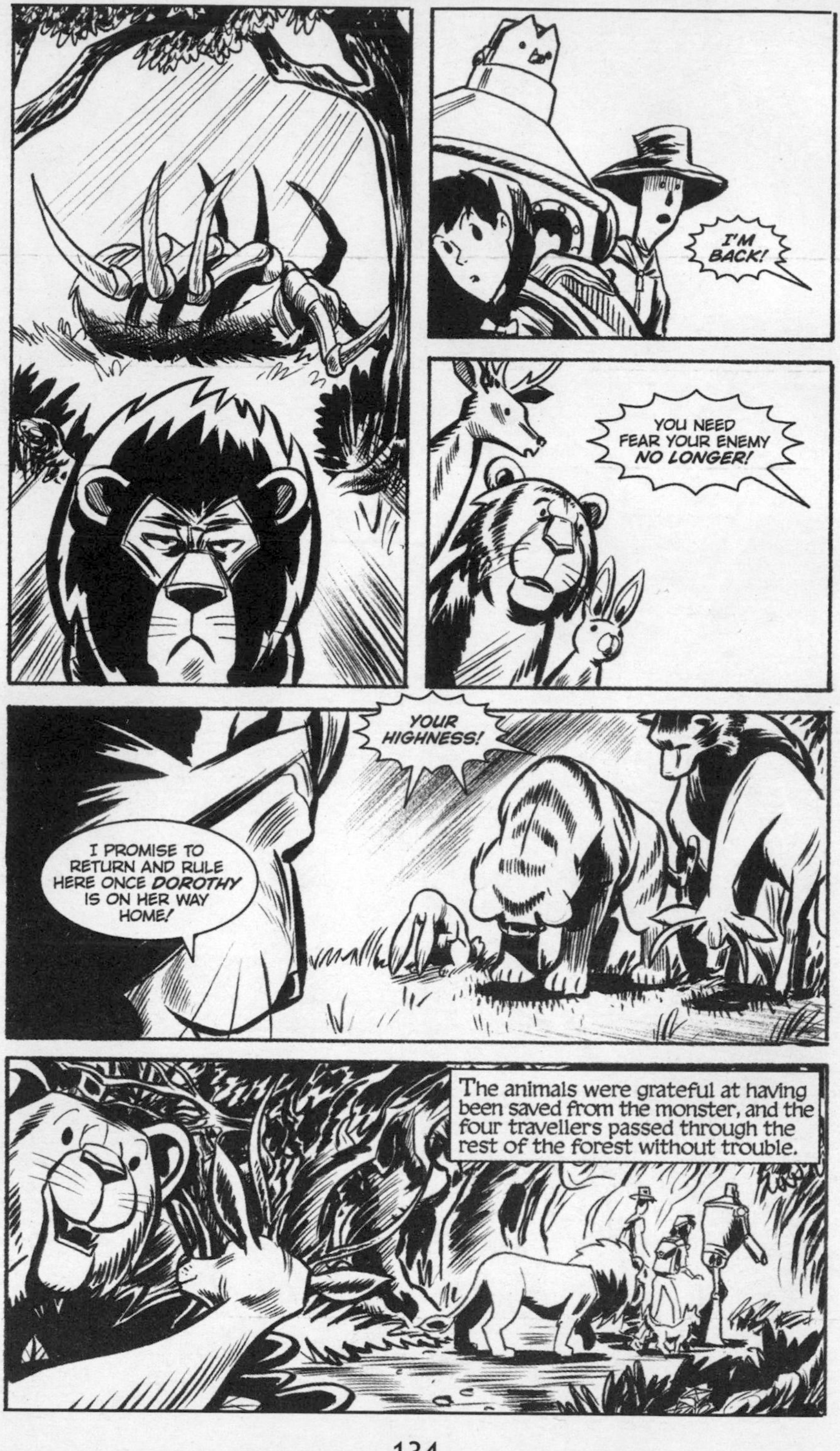
I'M BACK!
YOU NEED FEAR YOUR ENEMY NO LONGER!
YOUR HIGHNESS!
I PROMISE TO RETURN AND RULE HERE ONCE DOROTHY IS ON HER WAY HOME!
The animals were grateful at having been saved from the monster, and the four travellers passed through the rest of the forest without trouble.

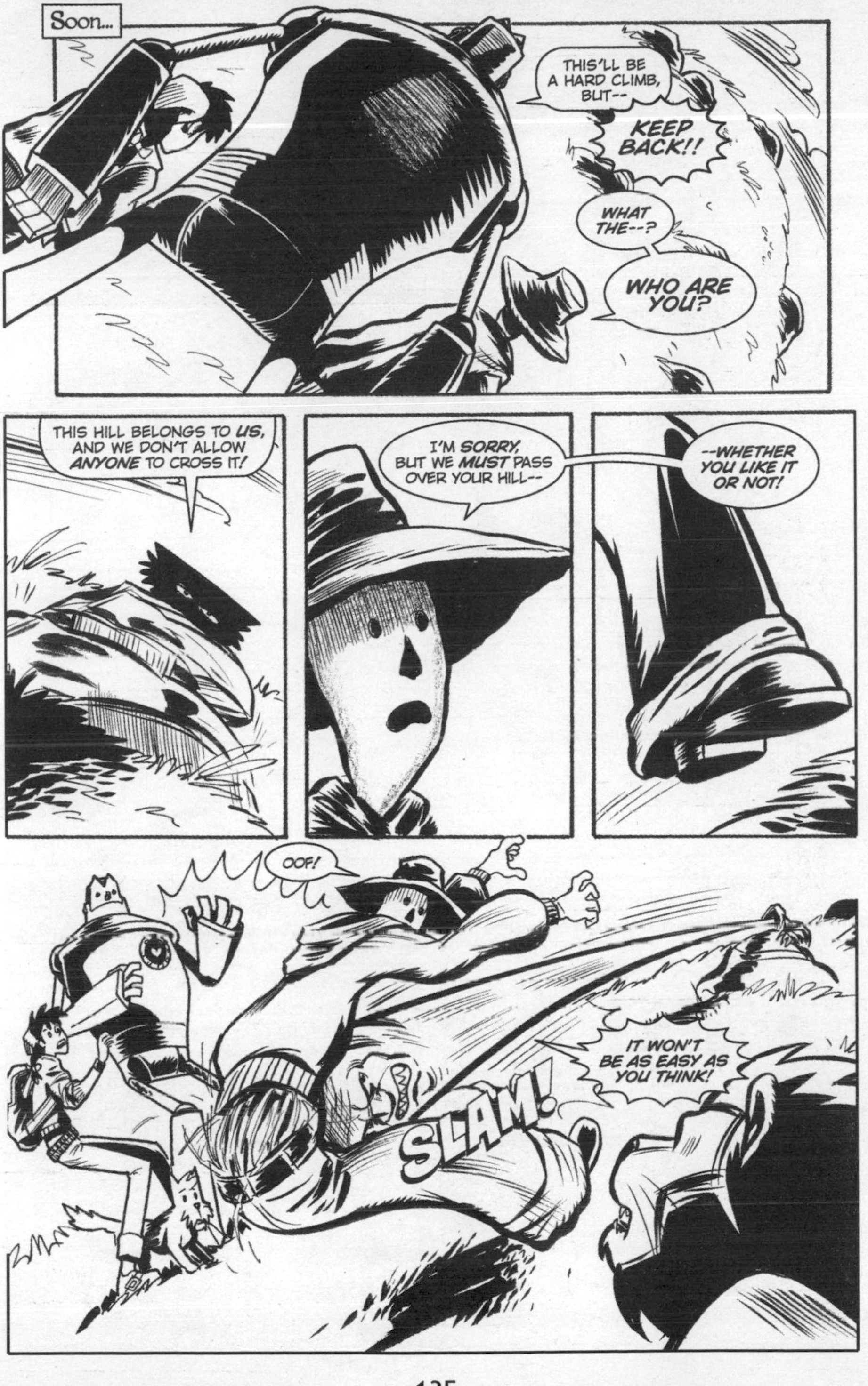
Soon...
THIS'LL BE A HARD CLIMB, BUT--
KEEP BACK!!
WHAT THE--?
WHO ARE YOU?
THIS HILL BELONGS TO US, AND WE DON'T ALLOW ANYONE TO CROSS IT!
I'M SORRY, BUT WE MUST PASS OVER YOUR HILL--
--WHETHER YOU LIKE IT OR NOT!
OOF!
IT WON'T BE AS EASY AS YOU THINK!
SLAM!

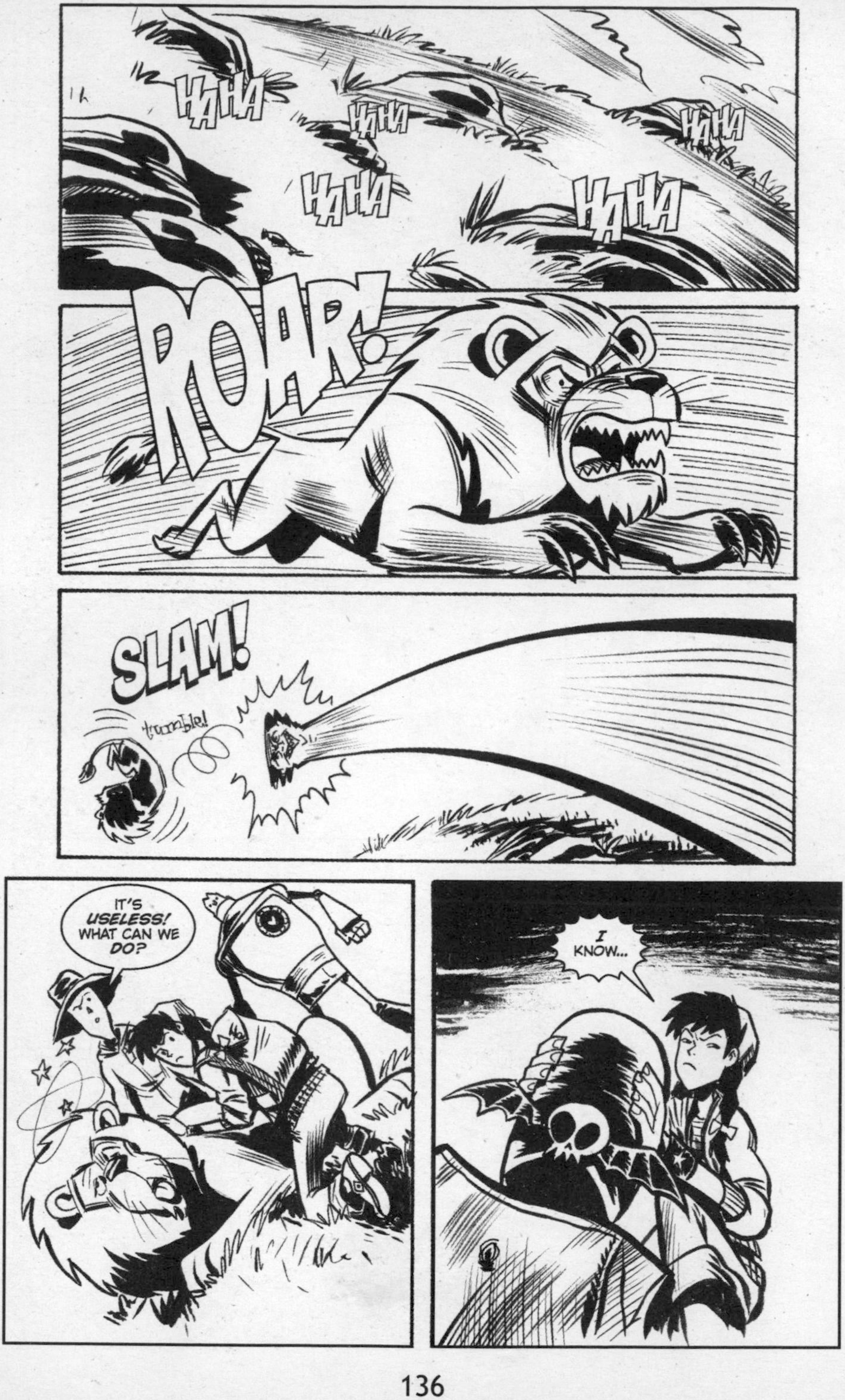
HA HA
HA HA
HA HA
HA HA
HA HA
ROAR!
SLAM!
IT'S *USELESS!* WHAT CAN WE *DO?*
I KNOW...

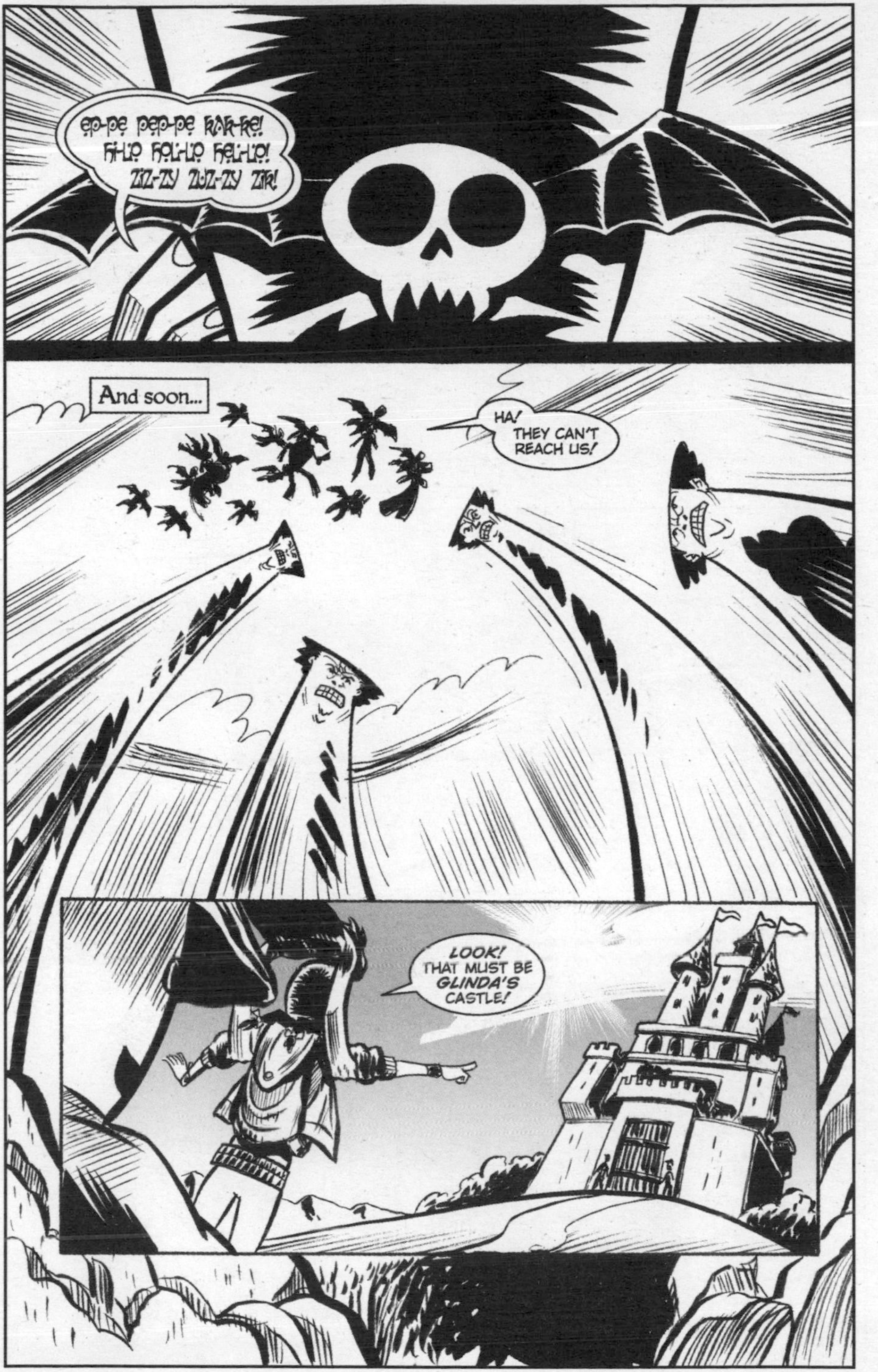
EP-PE PEP-PE KAK-KE! HIL-LO HOL-LO HEL-LO! ZIZ-ZY ZUZ-ZY ZIK!
And soon...
HA! THEY CAN'T REACH US!
LOOK! THAT MUST BE GLINDA'S CASTLE!

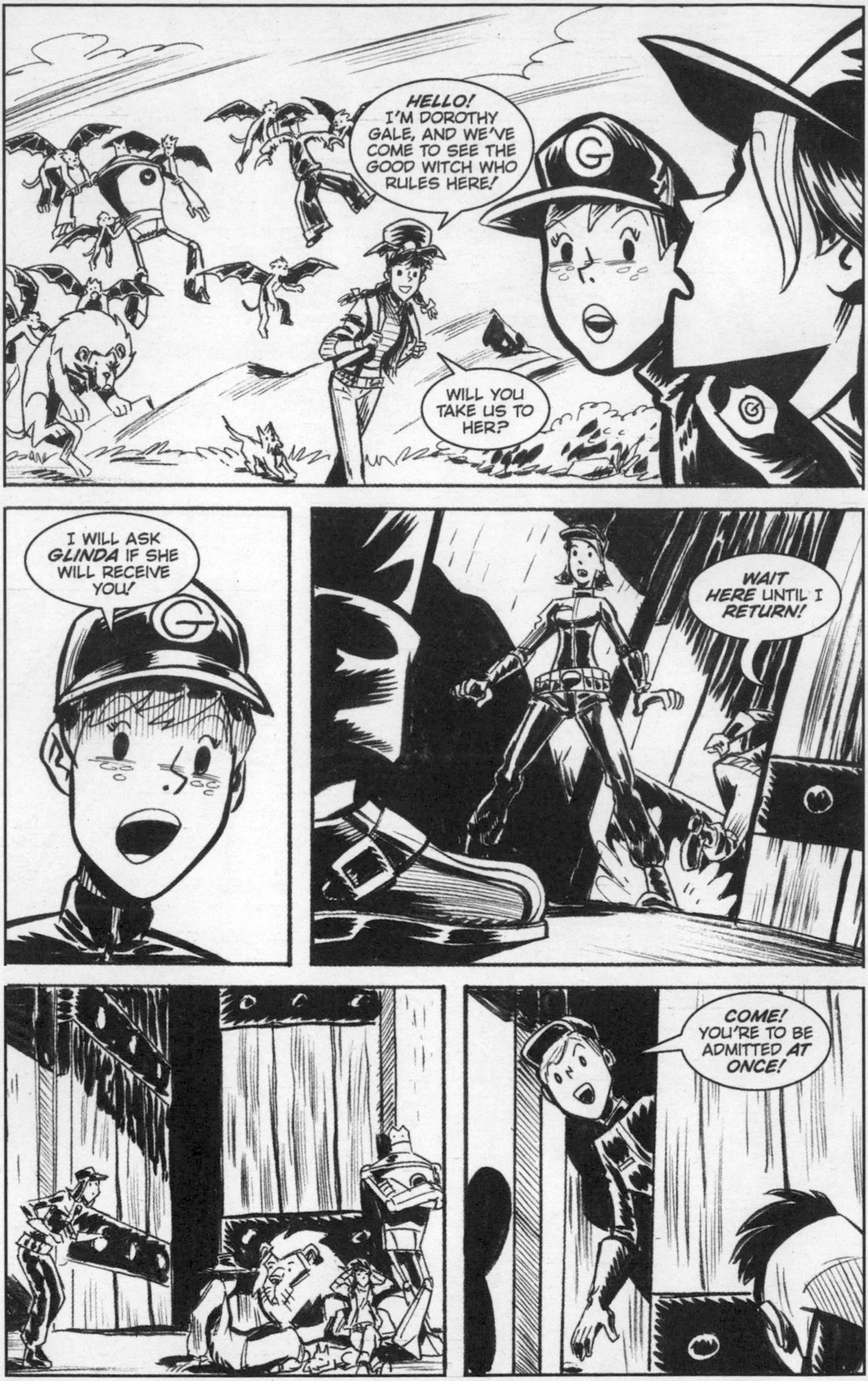
HELLO! I'M DOROTHY GALE, AND WE'VE COME TO SEE THE GOOD WITCH WHO RULES HERE!
WILL YOU TAKE US TO HER?
I WILL ASK GLINDA IF SHE WILL RECEIVE YOU!
WAIT HERE UNTIL I RETURN!
COME! YOU'RE TO BE ADMITTED AT ONCE!

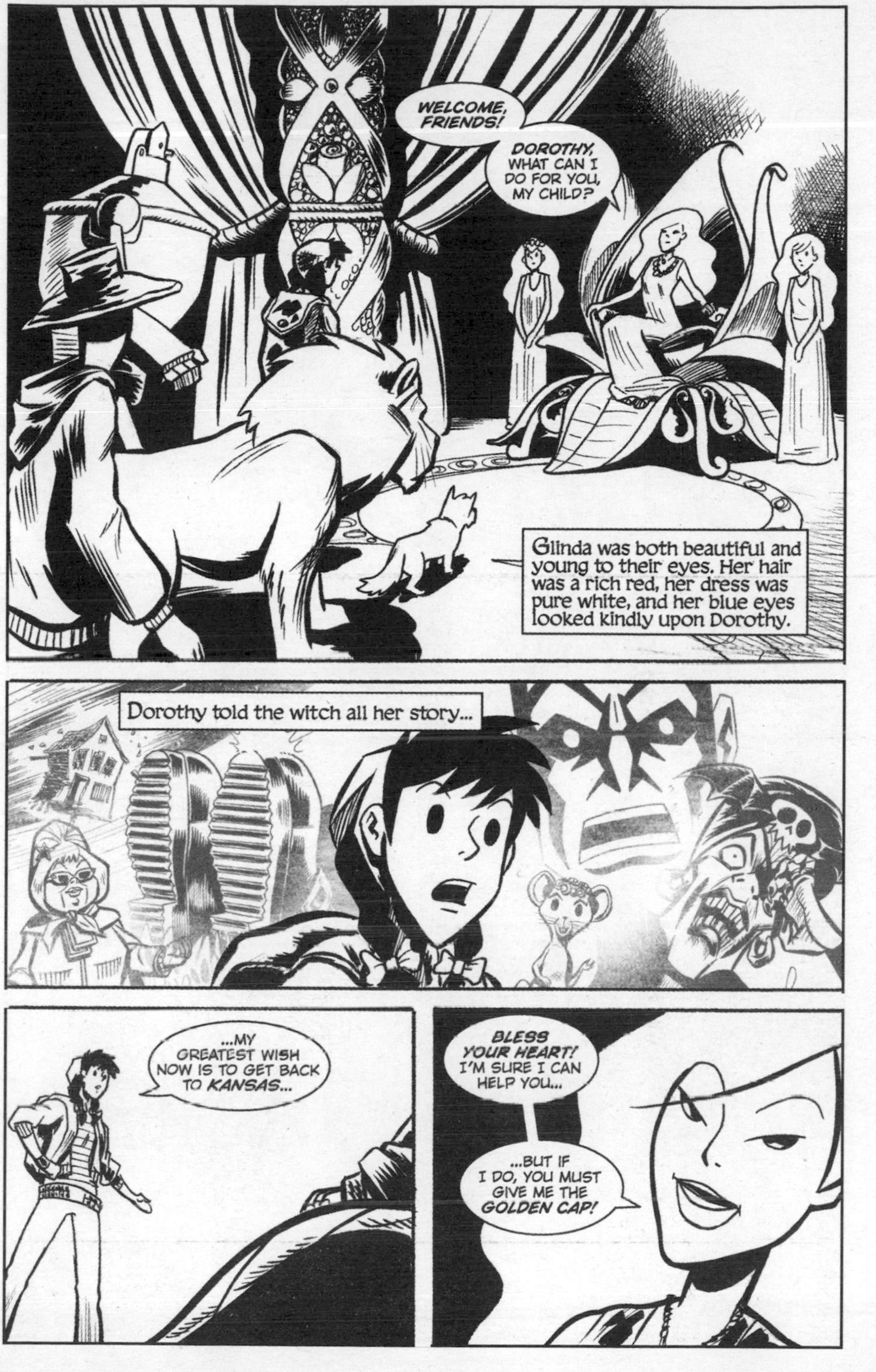
WELCOME, FRIENDS!
DOROTHY, WHAT CAN I DO FOR YOU, MY CHILD?
Glinda was both beautiful and young to their eyes. Her hair was a rich red, her dress was pure white, and her blue eyes looked kindly upon Dorothy.
Dorothy told the witch all her story...
...MY GREATEST WISH NOW IS TO GET BACK TO KANSAS...
BLESS YOUR HEART! I'M SURE I CAN HELP YOU...
...BUT IF I DO, YOU MUST GIVE ME THE GOLDEN CAP!

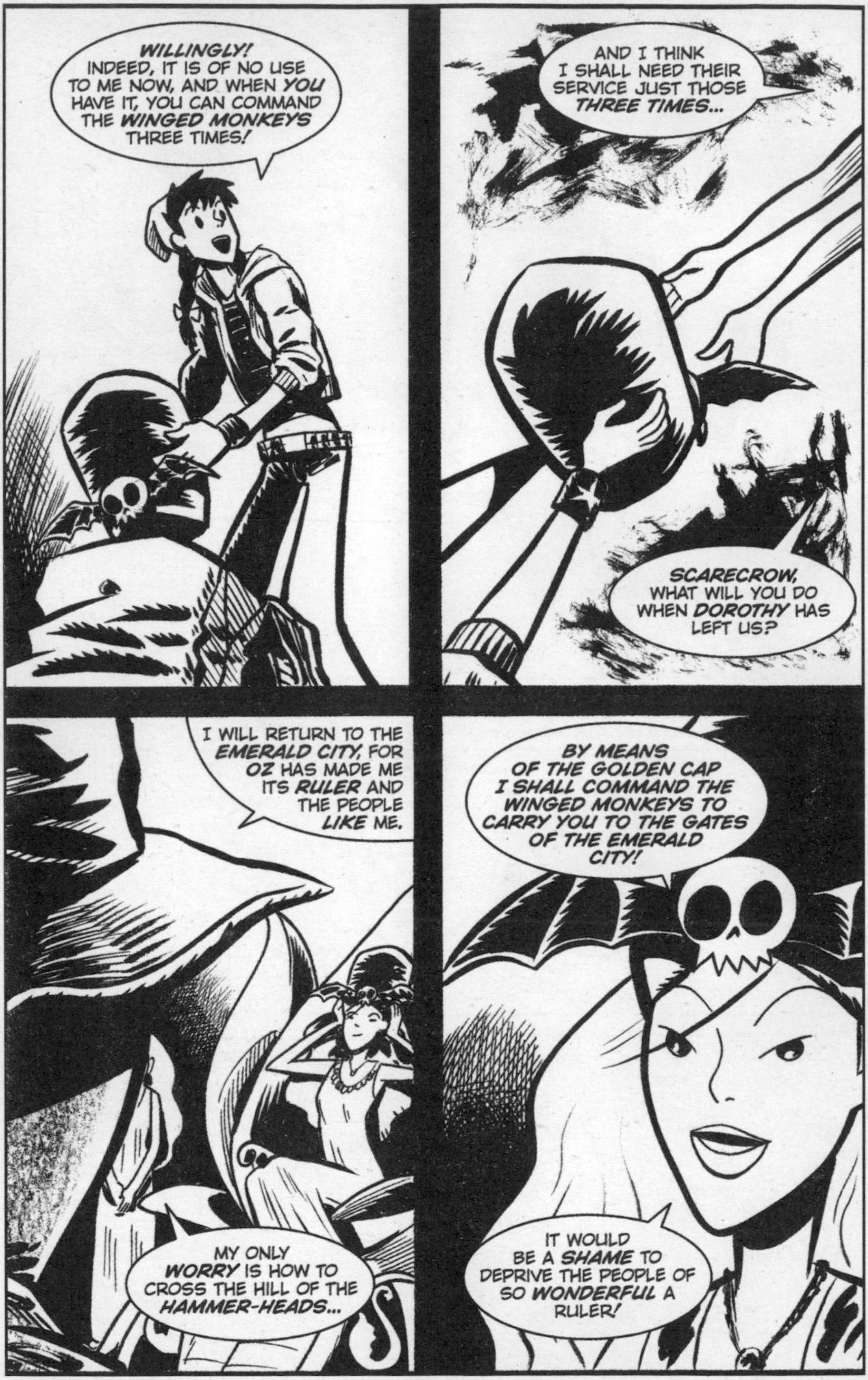
WILLINGLY! INDEED, IT IS OF NO USE TO ME NOW, AND WHEN YOU HAVE IT, YOU CAN COMMAND THE WINGED MONKEYS THREE TIMES!
AND I THINK I SHALL NEED THEIR SERVICE JUST THOSE THREE TIMES...
SCARECROW, WHAT WILL YOU DO WHEN DOROTHY HAS LEFT US?
I WILL RETURN TO THE EMERALD CITY, FOR OZ HAS MADE ME ITS RULER AND THE PEOPLE LIKE ME.
MY ONLY WORRY IS HOW TO CROSS THE HILL OF THE HAMMER-HEADS...
BY MEANS OF THE GOLDEN CAP I SHALL COMMAND THE WINGED MONKEYS TO CARRY YOU TO THE GATES OF THE EMERALD CITY!
IT WOULD BE A SHAME TO DEPRIVE THE PEOPLE OF SO WONDERFUL A RULER!

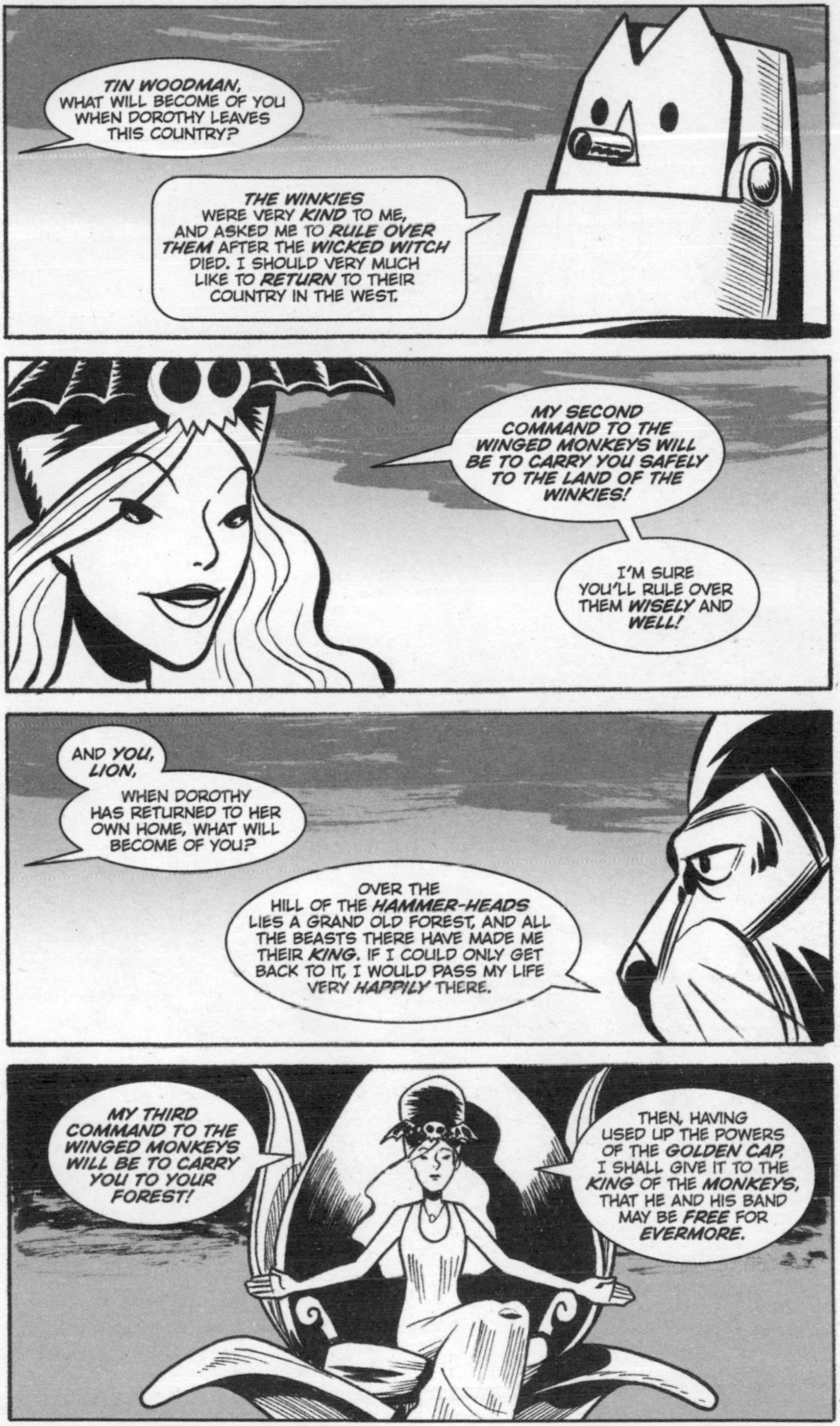
TIN WOODMAN, WHAT WILL BECOME OF YOU WHEN DOROTHY LEAVES THIS COUNTRY?
THE WINKIES WERE VERY KIND TO ME, AND ASKED ME TO RULE OVER THEM AFTER THE WICKED WITCH DIED. I SHOULD VERY MUCH LIKE TO RETURN TO THEIR COUNTRY IN THE WEST.
MY SECOND COMMAND TO THE WINGED MONKEYS WILL BE TO CARRY YOU SAFELY TO THE LAND OF THE WINKIES!
I'M SURE YOU'LL RULE OVER THEM WISELY AND WELL!
AND YOU, LION,
WHEN DOROTHY HAS RETURNED TO HER OWN HOME, WHAT WILL BECOME OF YOU?
OVER THE HILL OF THE HAMMER-HEADS LIES A GRAND OLD FOREST, AND ALL THE BEASTS THERE HAVE MADE ME THEIR KING. IF I COULD ONLY GET BACK TO IT, I WOULD PASS MY LIFE VERY HAPPILY THERE.
MY THIRD COMMAND TO THE WINGED MONKEYS WILL BE TO CARRY YOU TO YOUR FOREST!
THEN, HAVING USED UP THE POWERS OF THE GOLDEN CAP, I SHALL GIVE IT TO THE KING OF THE MONKEYS, THAT HE AND HIS BAND MAY BE FREE FOR EVERMORE.

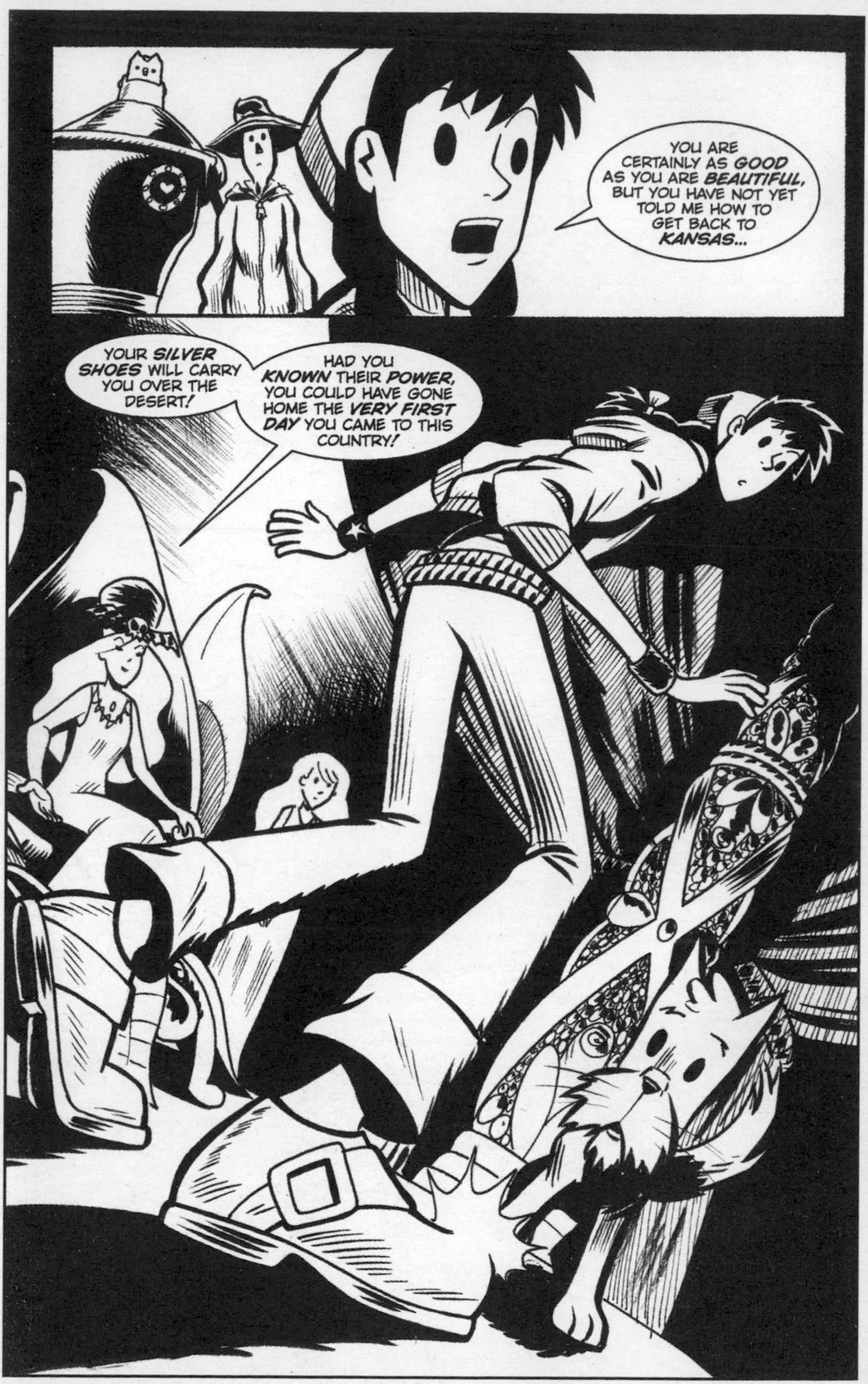
YOU ARE CERTAINLY AS GOOD AS YOU ARE BEAUTIFUL, BUT YOU HAVE NOT YET TOLD ME HOW TO GET BACK TO KANSAS...
YOUR SILVER SHOES WILL CARRY YOU OVER THE DESERT!
HAD YOU KNOWN THEIR POWER, YOU COULD HAVE GONE HOME THE VERY FIRST DAY YOU CAME TO THIS COUNTRY!

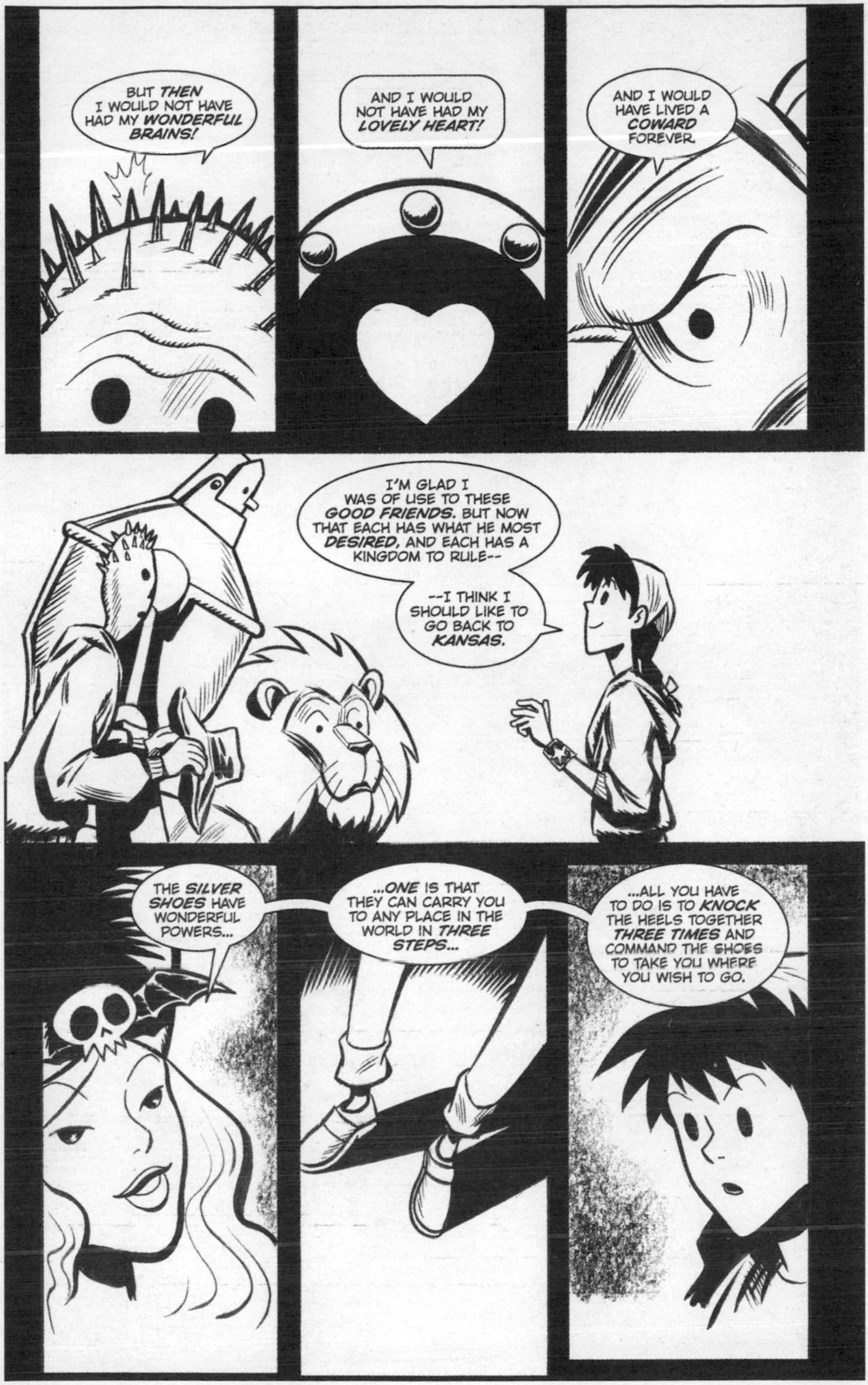
BUT *THEN* I WOULD NOT HAVE HAD MY ***WONDERFUL BRAINS!***
AND I WOULD NOT HAVE HAD MY ***LOVELY HEART!***
AND I WOULD HAVE LIVED A ***COWARD*** FOREVER.
I'M GLAD I WAS OF USE TO THESE ***GOOD FRIENDS.*** BUT NOW THAT EACH HAS WHAT HE MOST ***DESIRED,*** AND EACH HAS A KINGDOM TO RULE--
--I THINK I SHOULD LIKE TO GO BACK TO ***KANSAS.***
THE ***SILVER SHOES*** HAVE WONDERFUL POWERS...
...***ONE*** IS THAT THEY CAN CARRY YOU TO ANY PLACE IN THE WORLD IN ***THREE STEPS...***
...ALL YOU HAVE TO DO IS TO ***KNOCK*** THE HEELS TOGETHER ***THREE TIMES*** AND COMMAND THE SHOES TO TAKE YOU WHERE YOU WISH TO GO.

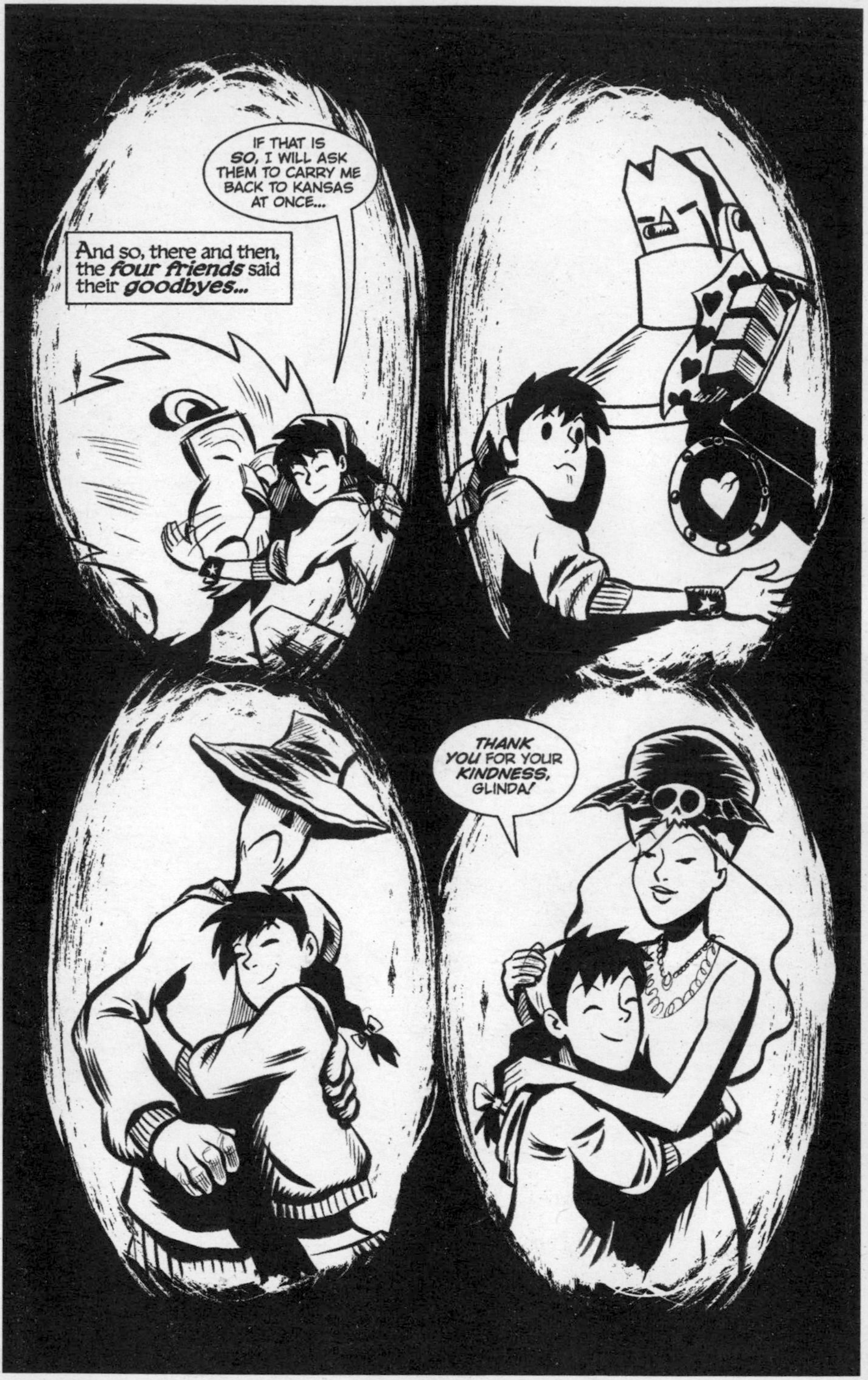
IF THAT IS SO, I WILL ASK THEM TO CARRY ME BACK TO KANSAS AT ONCE...
And so, there and then, the four friends said their goodbyes...
THANK YOU FOR YOUR KINDNESS, GLINDA!

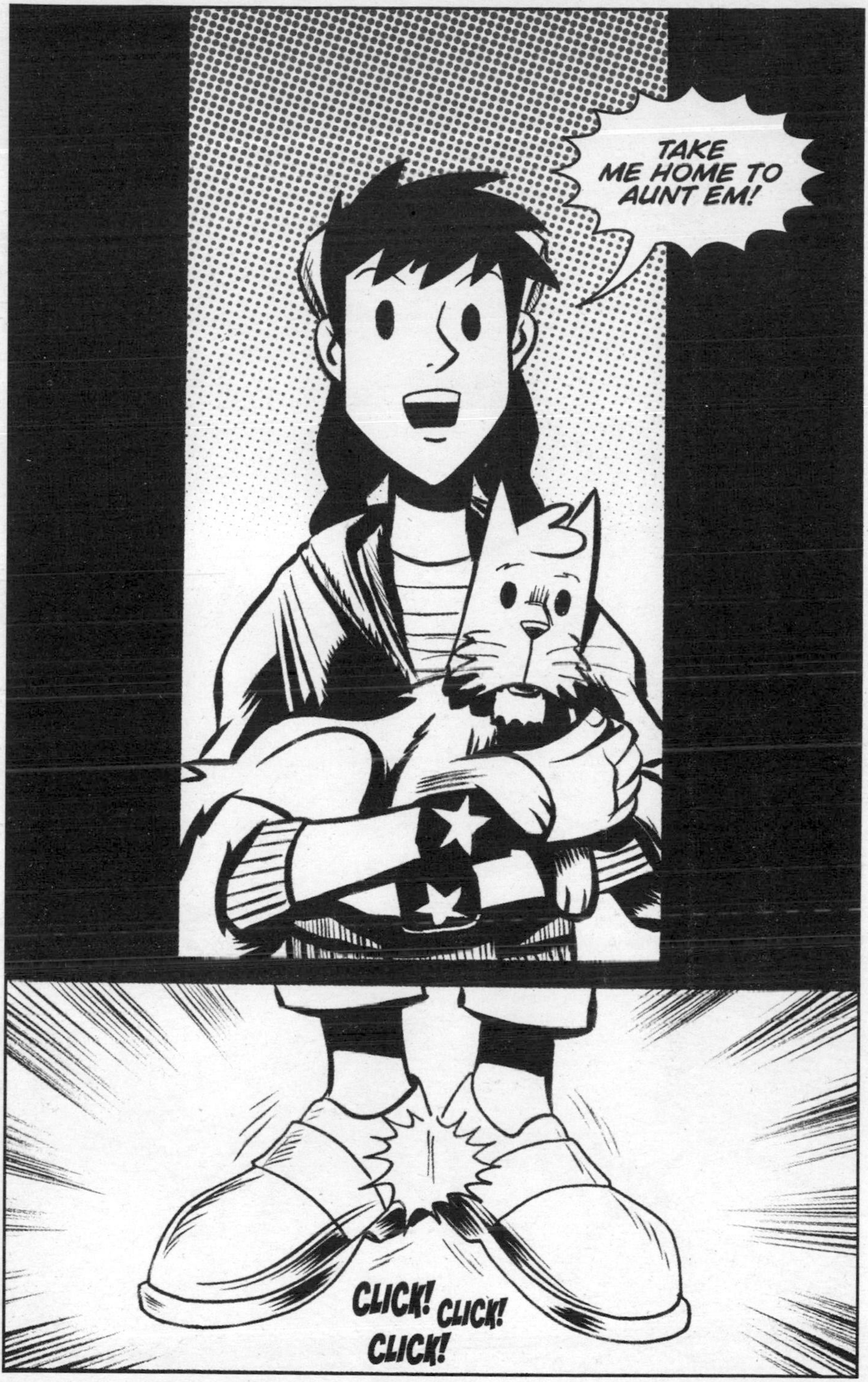
TAKE ME HOME TO AUNT EM!
CLICK! CLICK! CLICK!

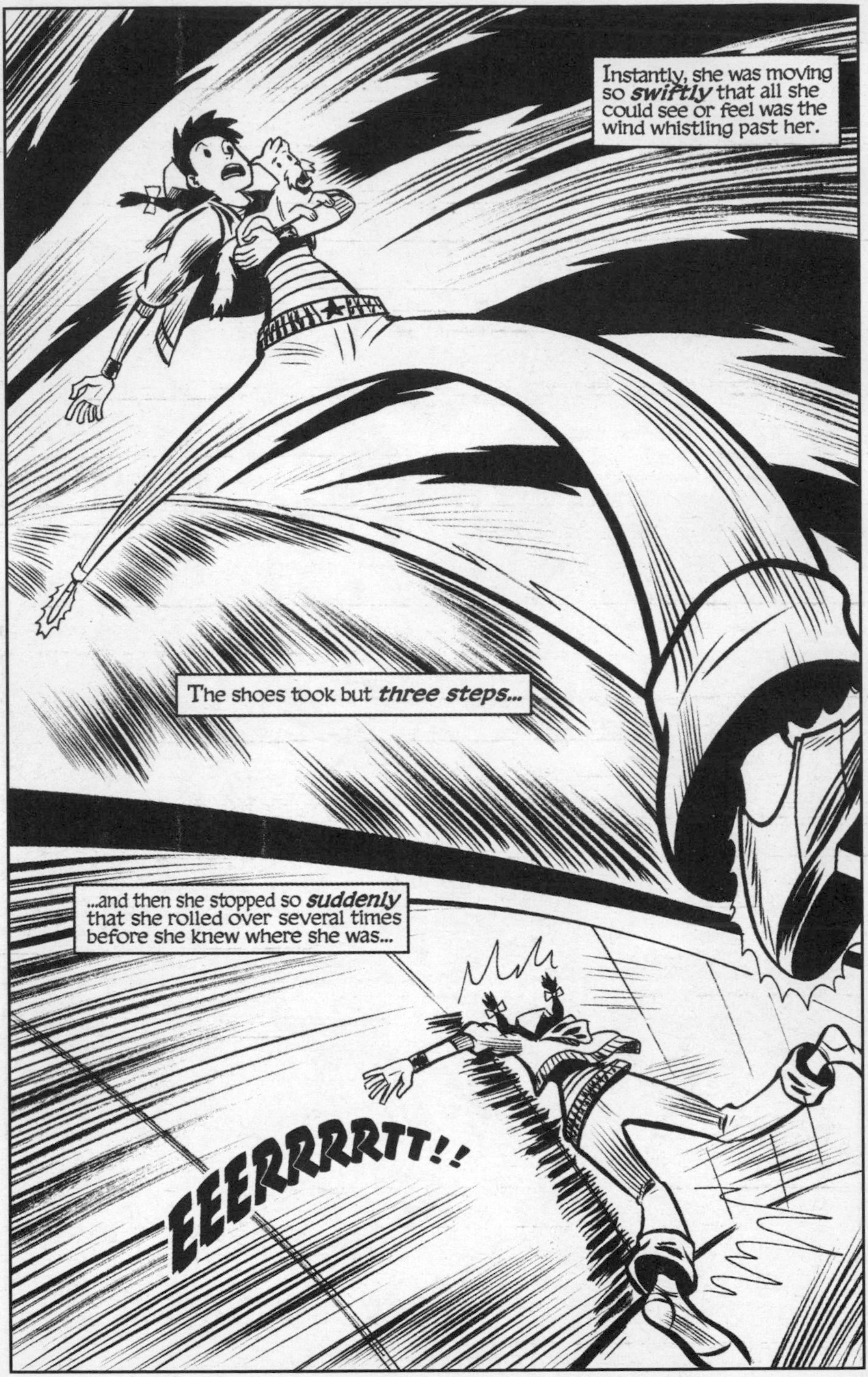
Instantly, she was moving so swiftly that all she could see or feel was the wind whistling past her.
The shoes took but three steps...
...and then she stopped so suddenly that she rolled over several times before she knew where she was...
EEERRRRRTT!!

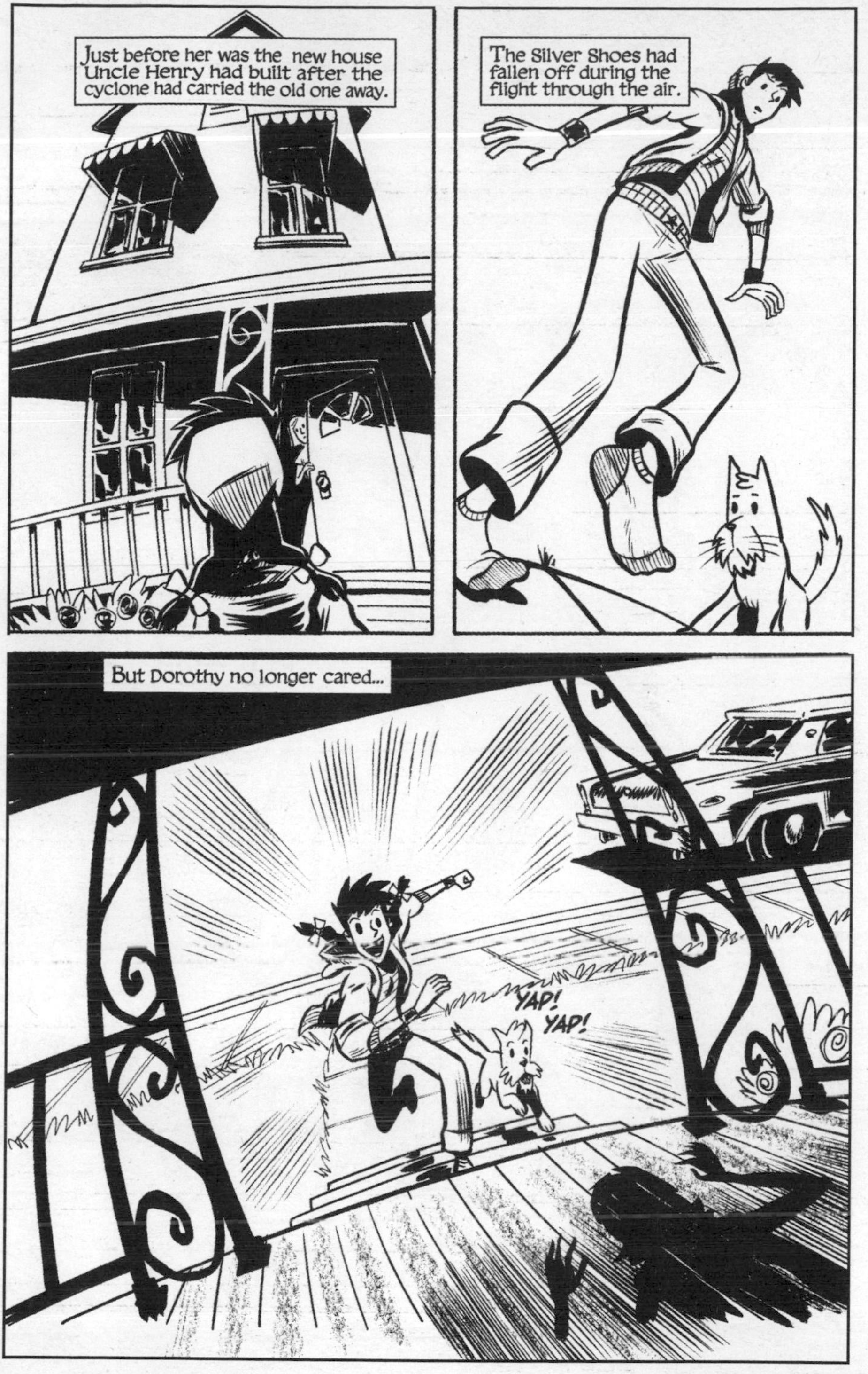
Just before her was the new house Uncle Henry had built after the cyclone had carried the old one away.
The Silver Shoes had fallen off during the flight through the air.
But Dorothy no longer cared...
YAP! YAP!

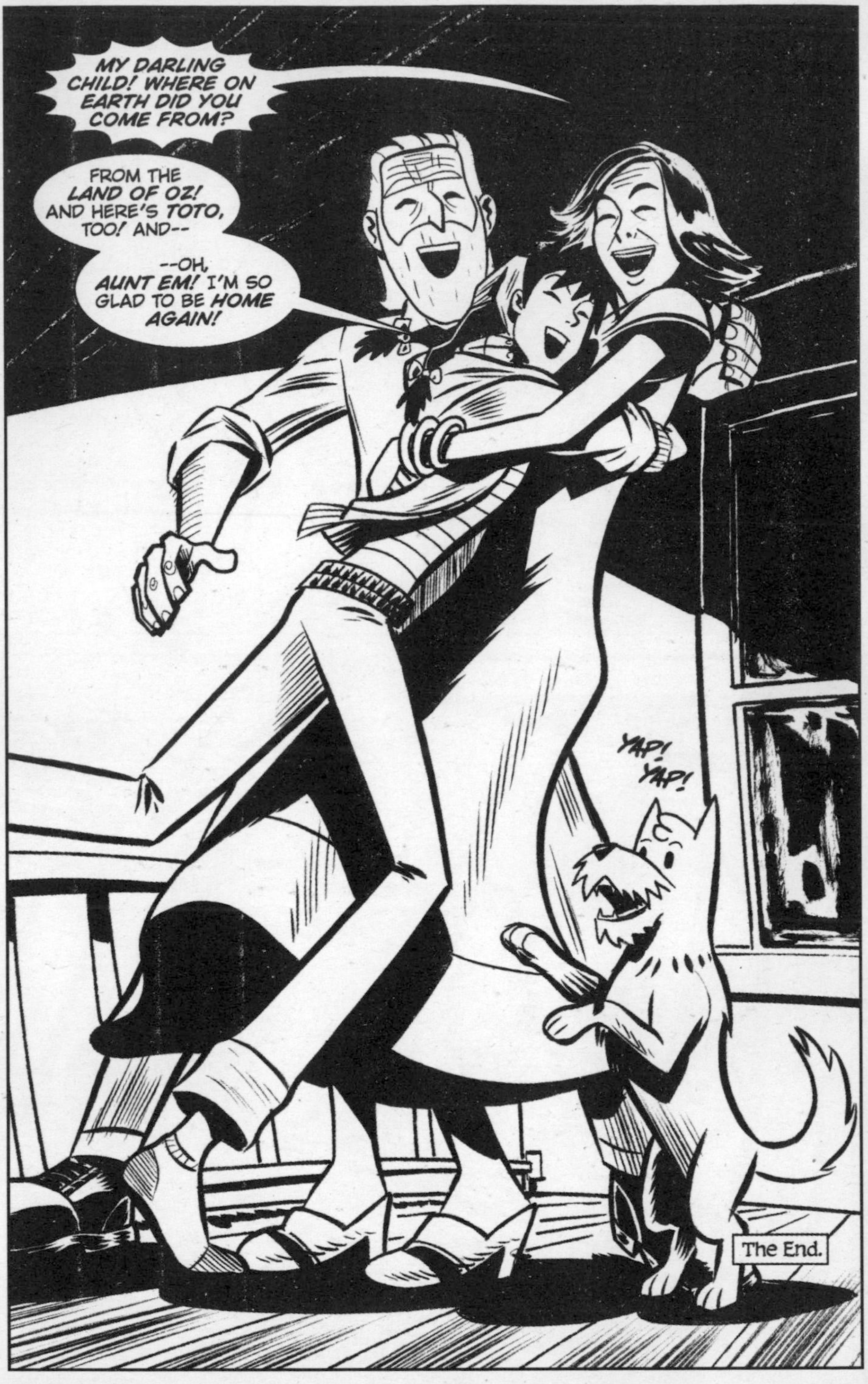
MY DARLING CHILD! WHERE ON EARTH DID YOU COME FROM?
FROM THE *LAND OF OZ!* AND HERE'S *TOTO,* TOO! AND--
--OH, *AUNT EM!* I'M SO GLAD TO BE *HOME AGAIN!*
YAP! YAP!
The End.

THE MAKING OF

L. FRANK BAUM'S

The Wizard of Oz

"Wizard exists somewhere down on the bedrock of that
creative field from which all later works of fantasy
have sprung. What an opportunity!"
—Michael Cavallaro

MICHAEL CAVALLARO TALKS ABOUT

L. FRANK BAUM'S

The Wizard of Oz

I've been an avid fan of science fiction and fantasy my entire life. I was seven years old when *Star Wars* was released. Later, I read all the Tolkien, Robert E. Howard, Edgar Rice Burroughs, and Michael Moorcock books I could find. Of *The Wizard of Oz*, all I knew was the 1939 film version, which, like most people, I loved. I had not read the book until I signed on to do this adaptation.

As I began reading the book, I was amazed to find how many bits, pieces, and nuances of L. Frank Baum's classic story had found their way into the works of the authors I had grown up reading. *The Wizard of Oz* exists somewhere down on the bedrock of that creative field from which all later works of fantasy have sprung. The more I read the story, the more I understood how easy it would be to spend a lifetime exploring the ground that L. Frank Baum laid out.

Immediately thereafter, though, anxiety set in. Knowing how much the story is loved by millions of people, I didn't want to be the guy that created the kind of adaptation that I would have hated as a child. I can't draw something that doesn't reflect my personality, but at the same time, *The Wizard of Oz* is not "mine."

In 1900, Baum wanted to create a contemporary American fairy tale. He filled the story with elements that were at once fantastic and yet recognizable to the children of the time: the tin man that tinsmiths used to advertise their trade, and the Emerald City, Baum's version of the White City of the 1893 Chicago World's Fair. I found that these and other elements in the story held up even now. Oz itself is a timeless place, and there was little to gain by "updating" it. If anything, the woods and fields of Oz and the simple lifestyles of its inhabitants stand in even starker contrast to the real world today than they did in 1900, and as such provide the perfect foil for Dorothy's gray and dreary home. It seemed simple and believable for Dorothy to throw on her sneakers and set them onto the Yellow Brick Road, but beyond that, the true strength of the story is the fact that it's as fresh today as it was a hundred years ago.

I tried to use my affection for the story as my polestar, while allowing my own personality as an artist to present a new depiction of Baum's world. I hope that my respect for his work shows through.

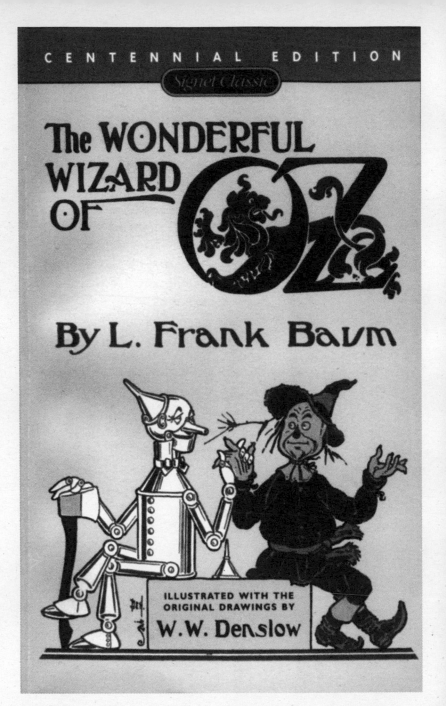

Signet Classic

The WONDERFUL
WIZARD
OF OZ

By L. Frank Baum

ILLUSTRATED WITH THE
ORIGINAL DRAWINGS BY
W.W. Denslow

Michael used the Signet Classic edition of *The Wonderful
Wizard of Oz* for this adaptation.

COVER GALLERY

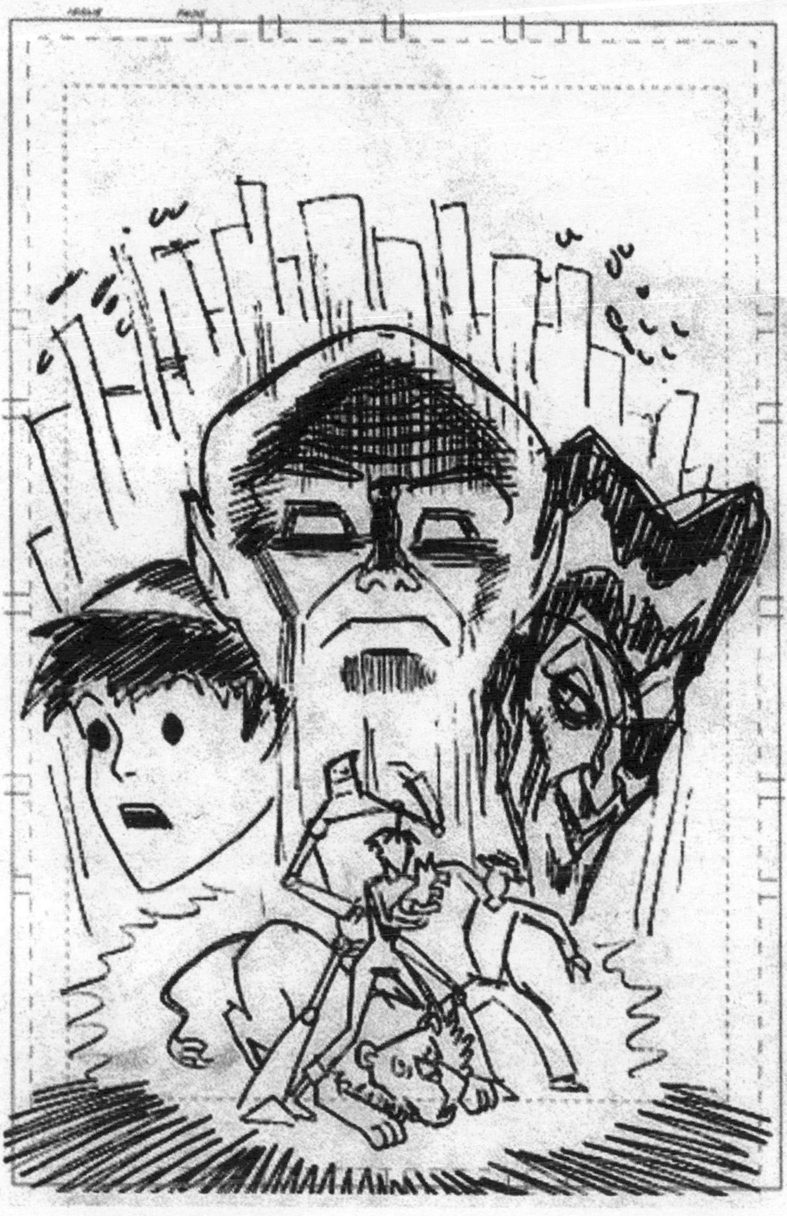

Initially, Michael did three cover sketches. The first is a symbolic design.

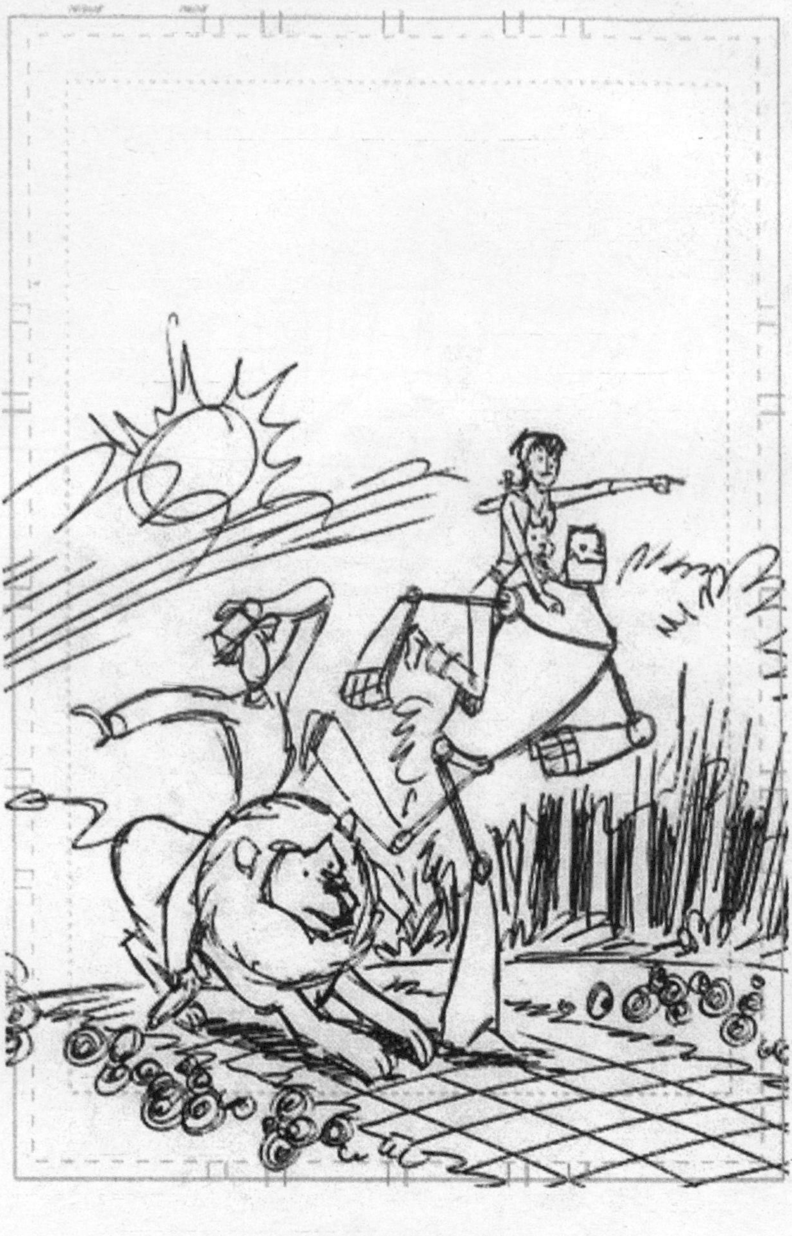

The second cover is more action-oriented.

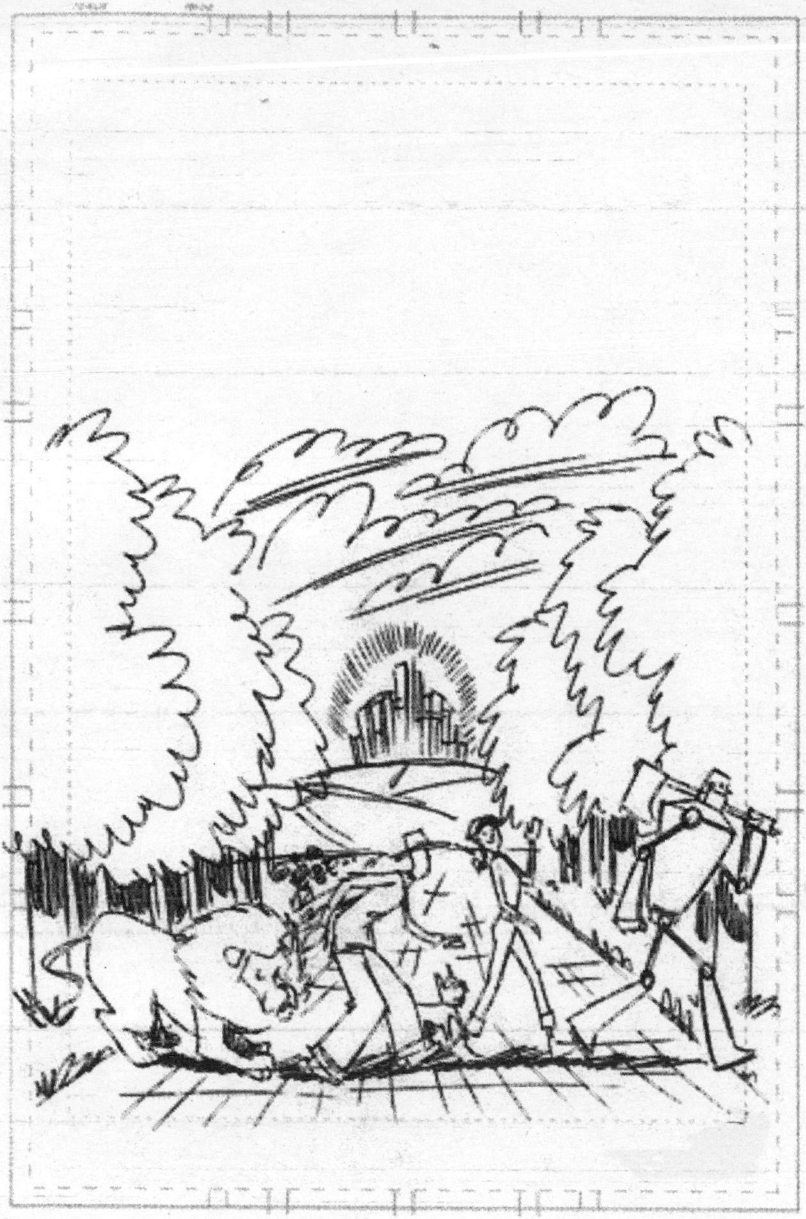

The third cover has a more light-hearted, fun approach.

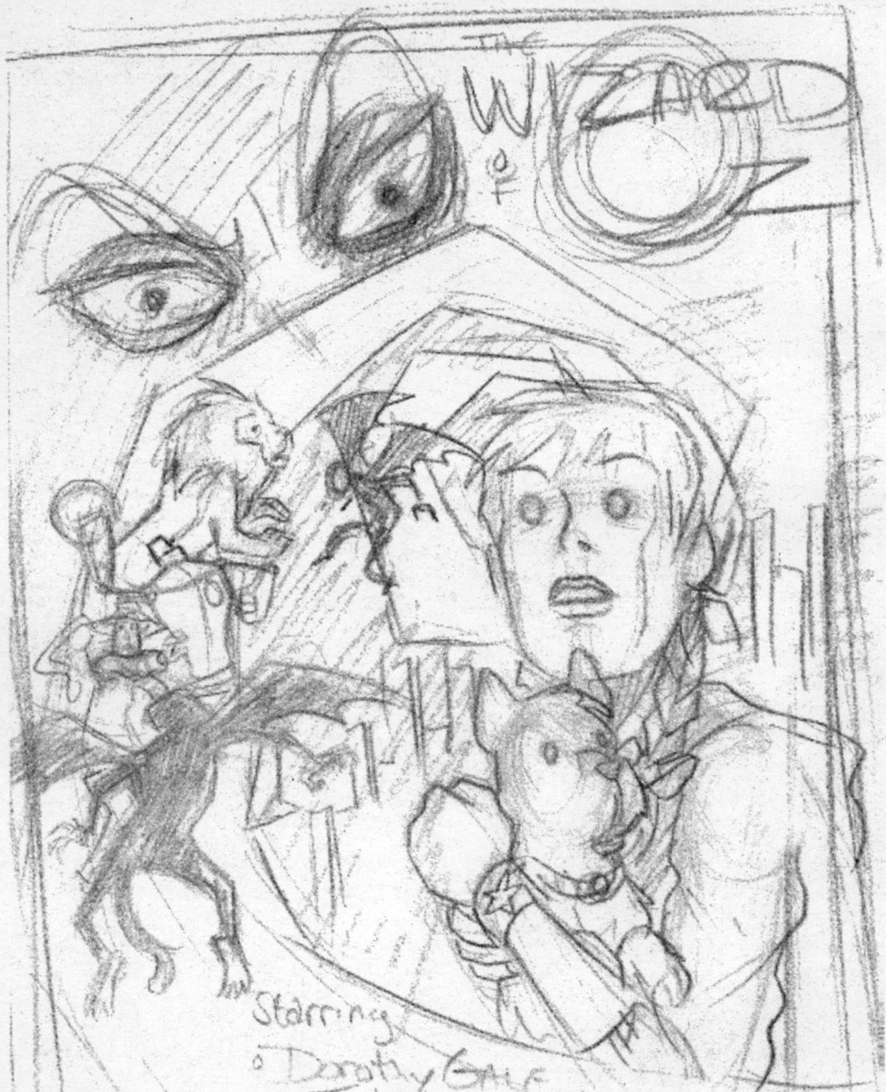
Starring
Dorothy Gale
Tin Woodman
Scarecrow

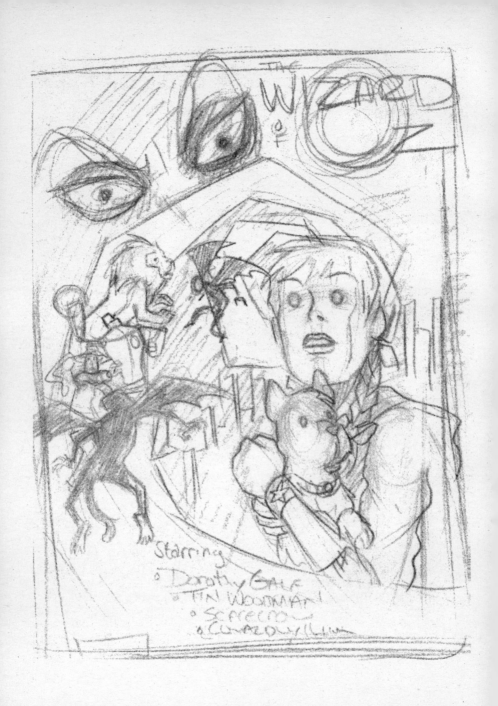

A movie-poster concept was suggested, and this is Michael's initial sketch.

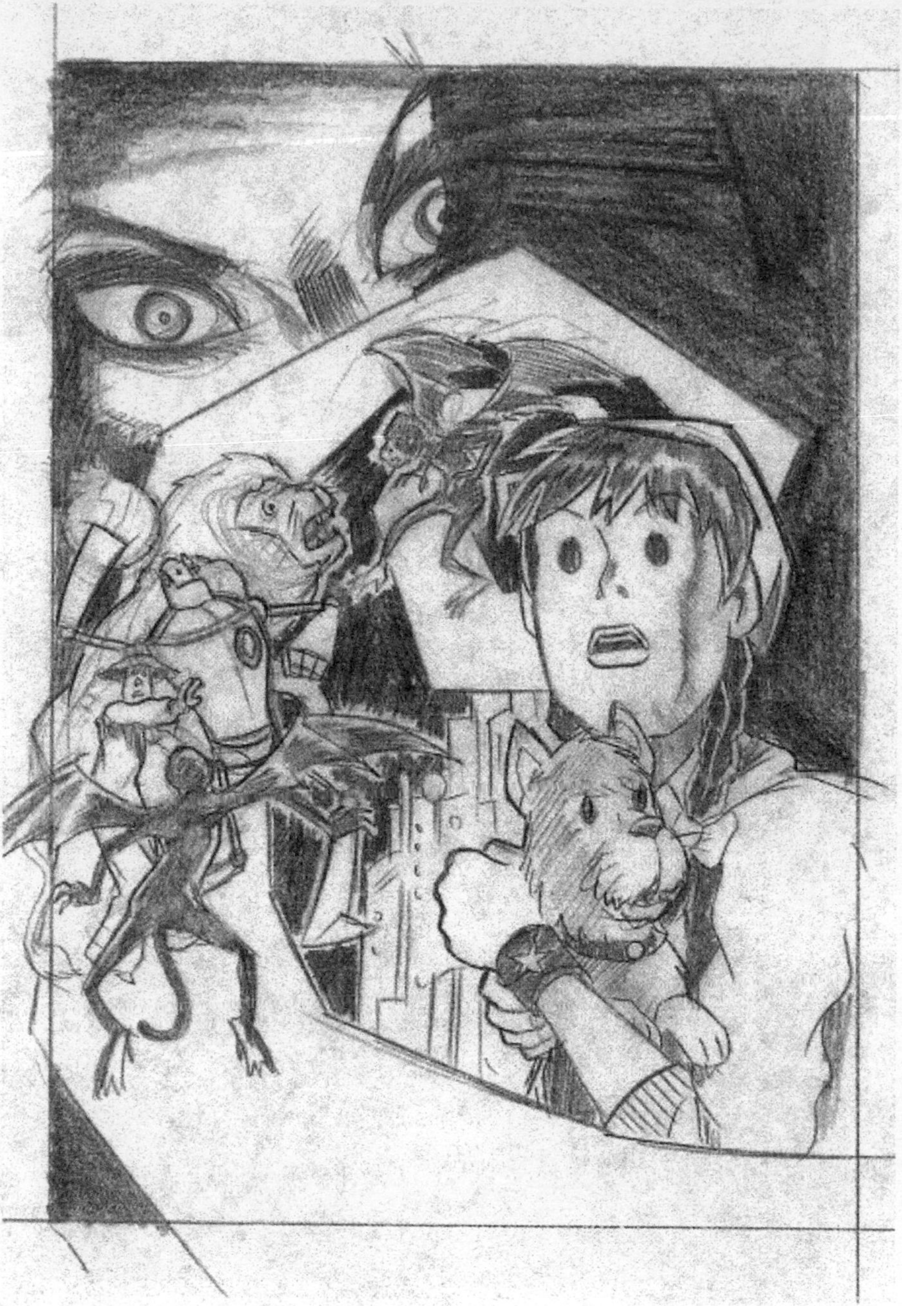

This is a tighter pencil version of the cover.

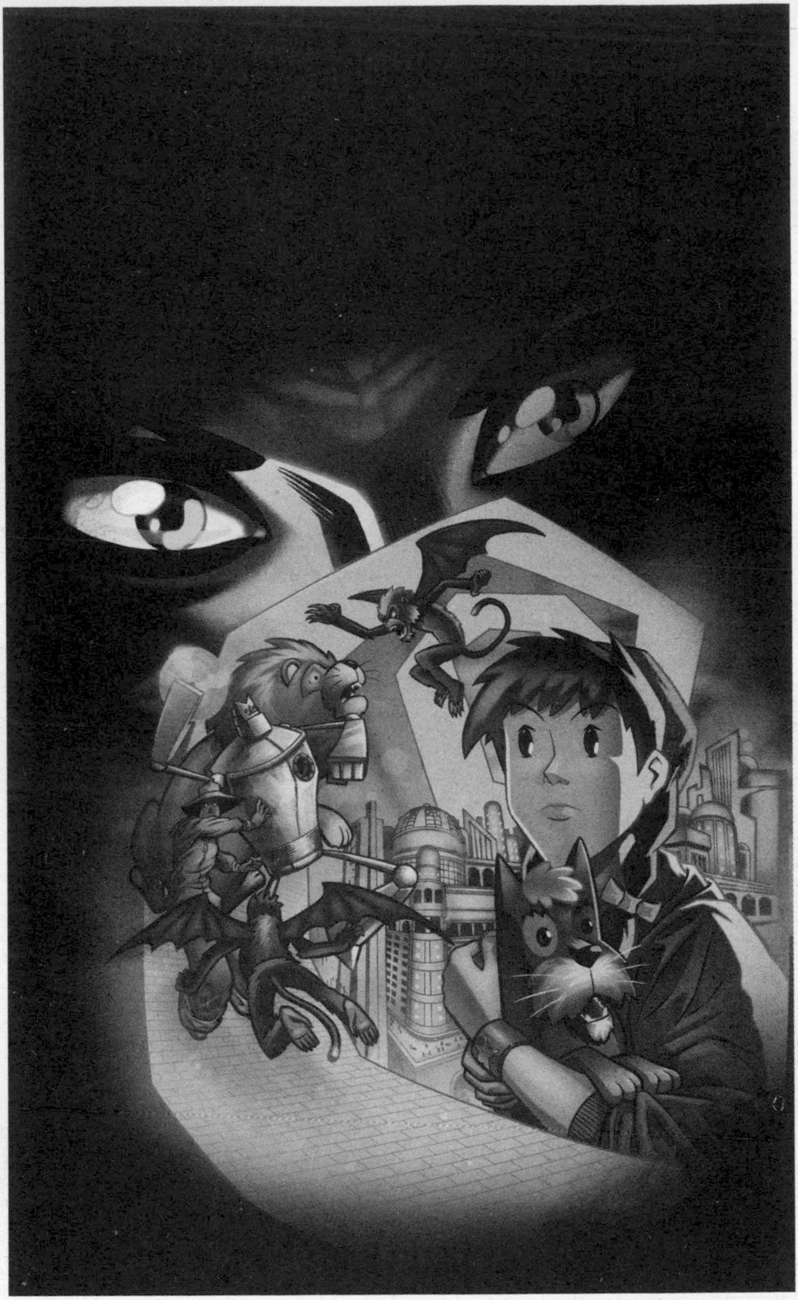

Michael then did four variations of the pencil design, each one slightly different from the others.

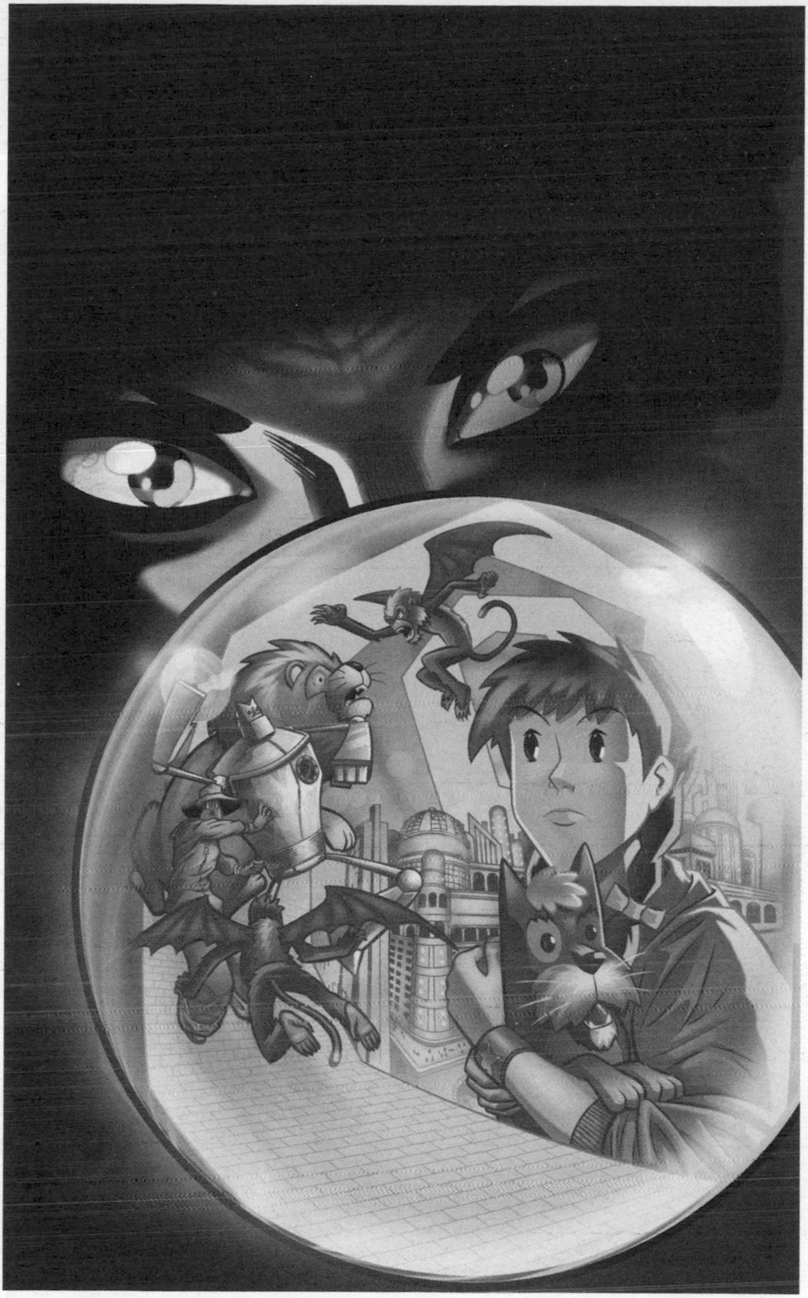

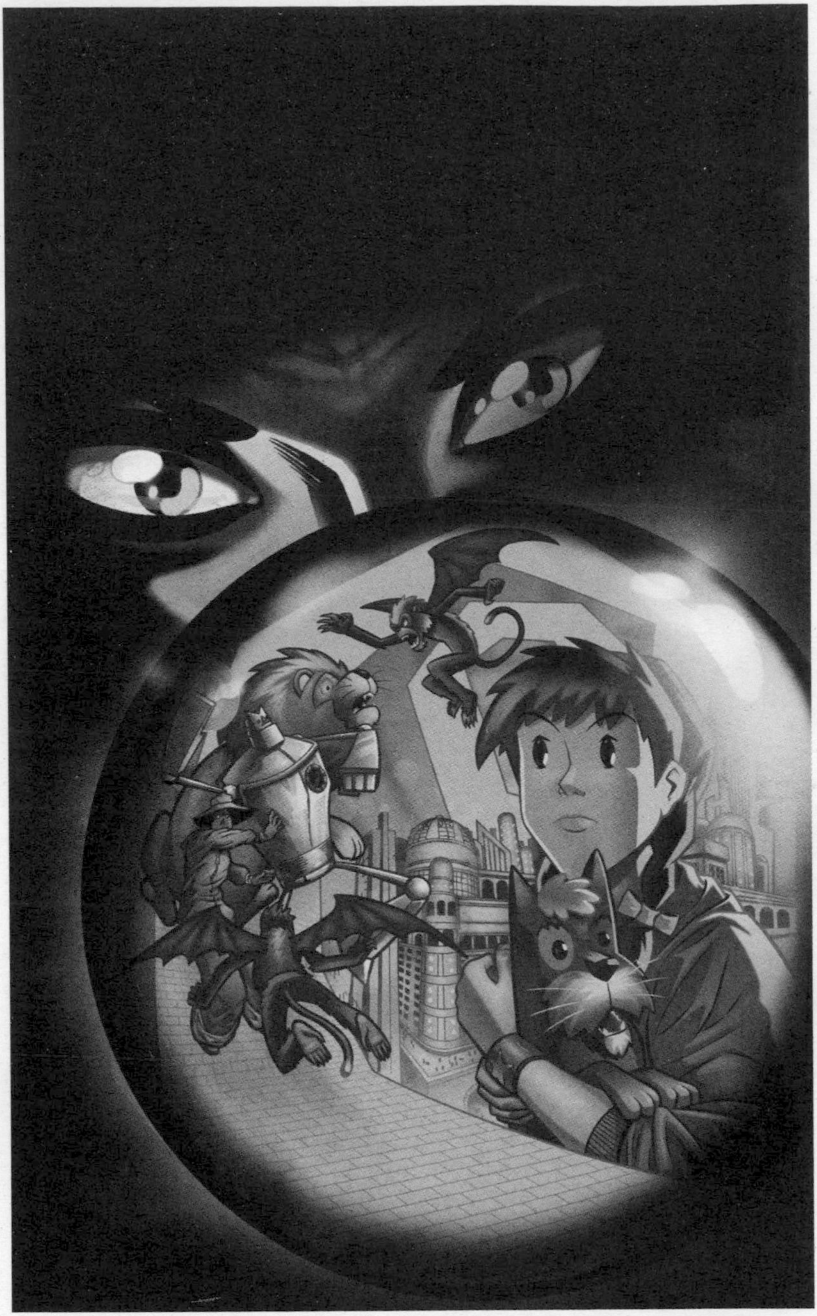

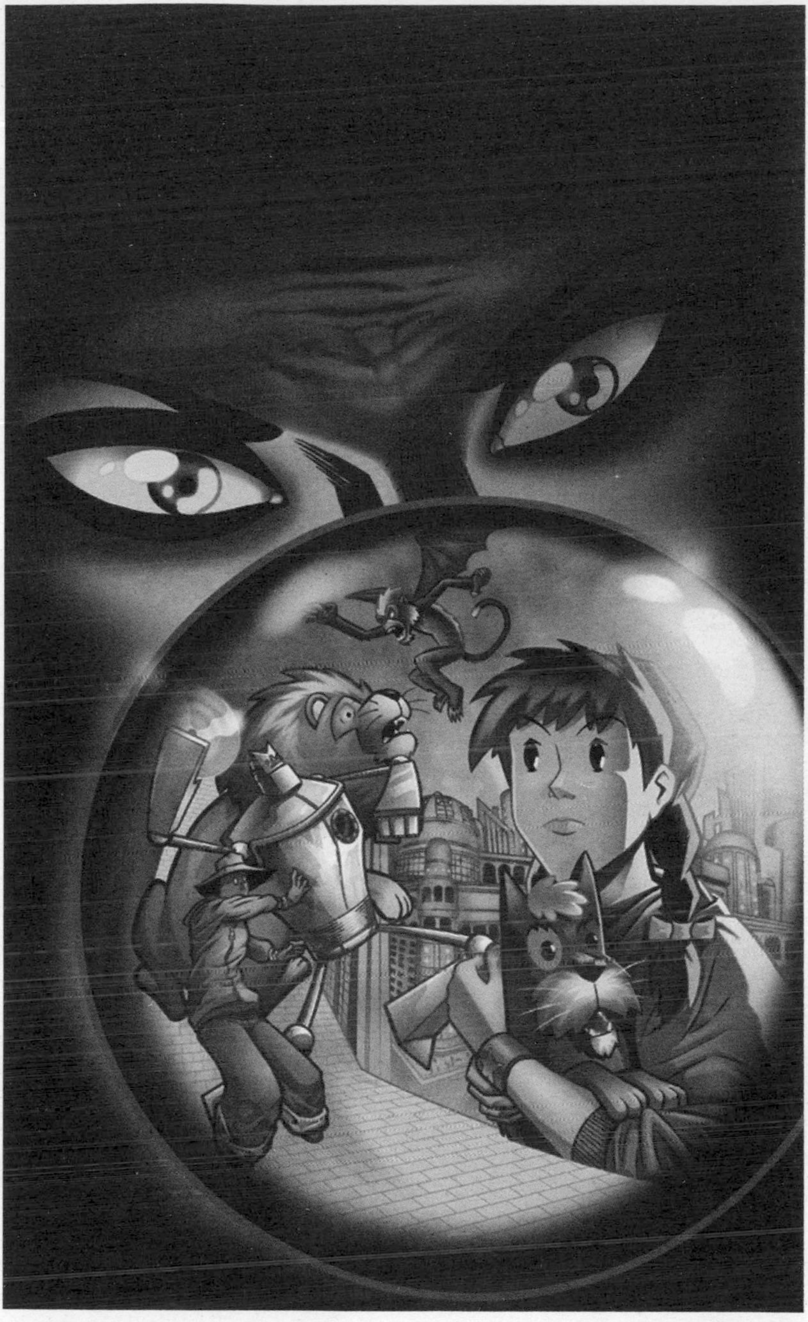

HOW MICHAEL WORKS

In creating the artwork for this book, I walked a line between traditional and digital techniques.

Every page begins as a rough blue pencil drawing. I scan the rough and add lettering in Adobe Illustrator. I may at this time resize elements of the artwork using Photoshop to accommodate the lettering. The lettering is removed and saved for use on the final, and then the rough is printed out very faintly on Strathmore 400 series smooth bristol board.

I refine the drawing right there on the final board until I'm comfortable enough with it to begin inking. For inking, I used an assortment of markers, mostly Staedtler Pigment Liner and Micron pens of various sizes. I use these mostly for panel borders and fine detail, like facial features or architecture. The mainstay of my inking, though, with which I do 90 percent of a page, is a Windsor Newton Series 7 #2 or #3 brush and Black Magic ink. Mostly, I free-hand everything and try to keep it loose, lively and fun.

After inking, I scan all the pages again and clean up any smudges or smears in Photoshop. On some of the pages, I added dot screens or gray tones on the computer. The lettering gets dropped back in place, and there you have it: a finished page.

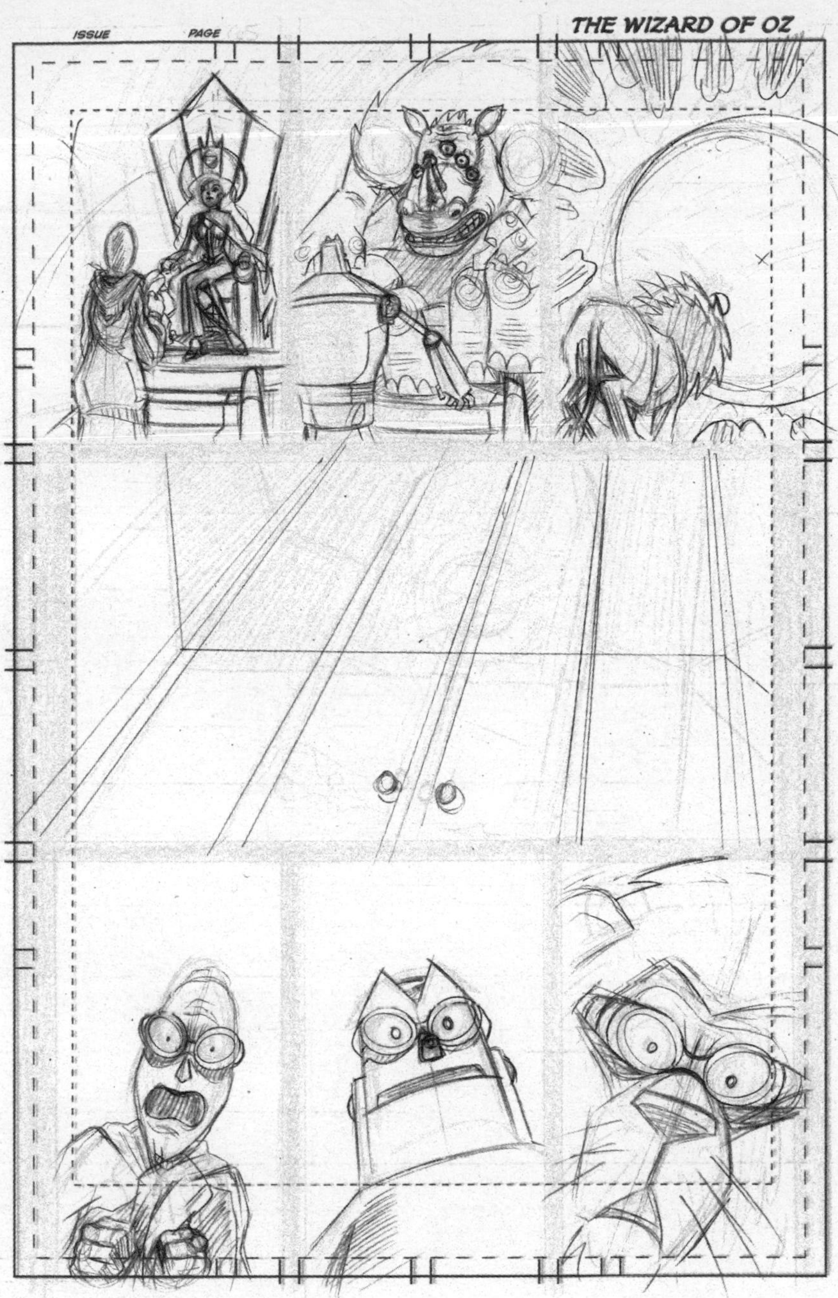
ISSUE
PAGE
THE WIZARD OF OZ

Michael's pencil sketch for page 69.

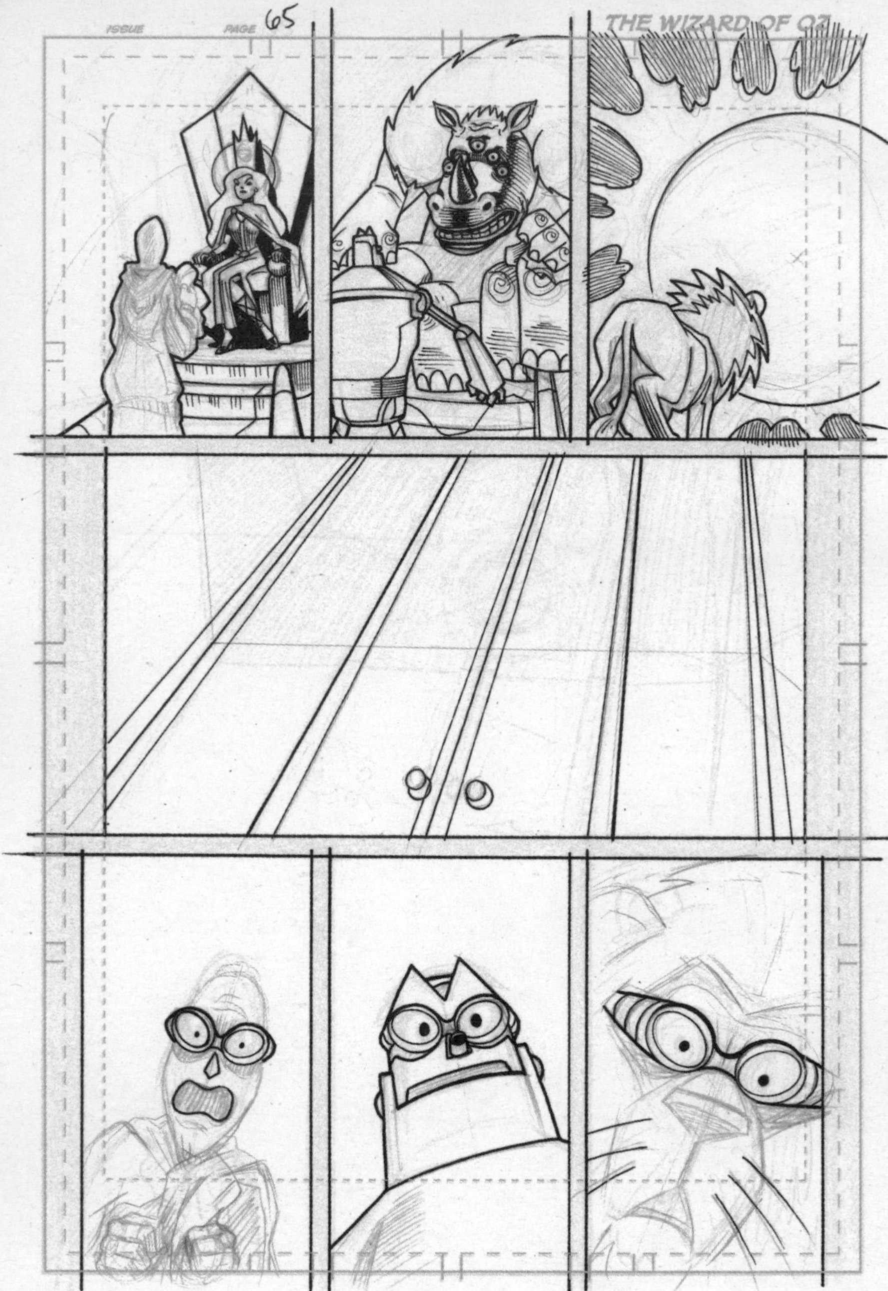
ISSUE
PAGE 65
THE WIZARD OF OZ

The same page in the middle of the inking process. Note the inked borders, and partially inked panels.

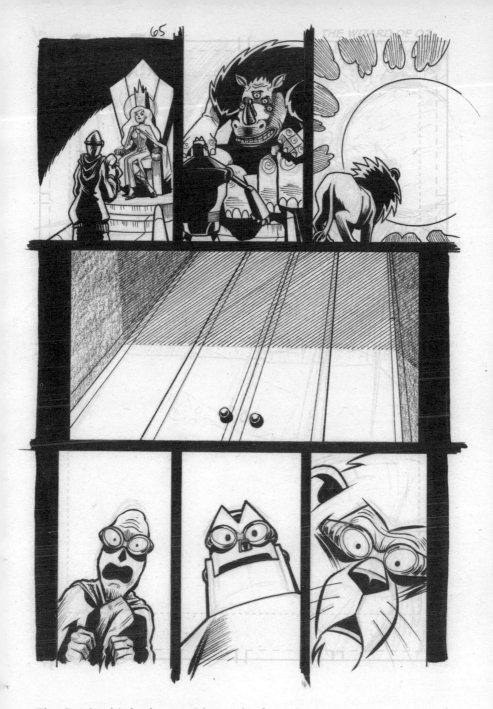

The finished inked art, without the lettering.

MICHAEL CAVALLARO'S PENCILS

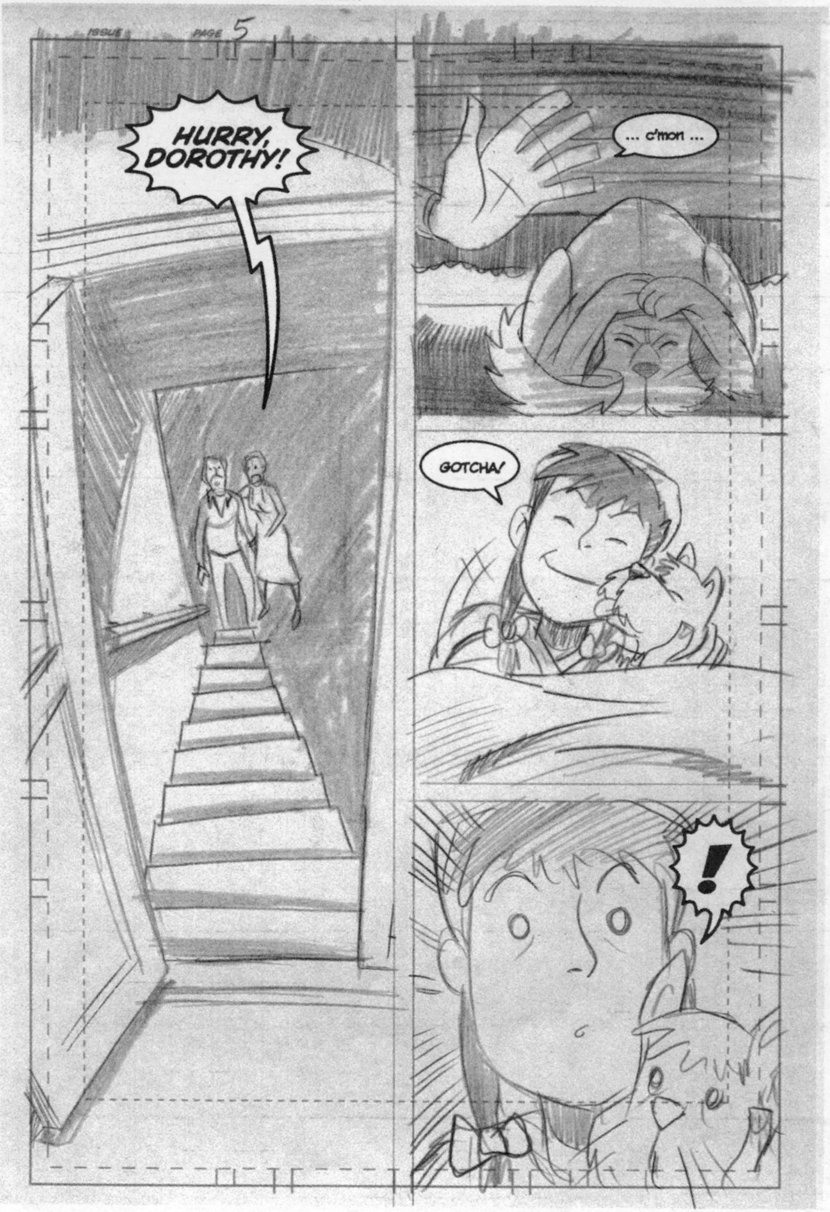
ISSUE
PAGE 5
HURRY, DOROTHY!
... c'mon ...
GOTCHA!
!

Here is a unique opportunity to see a sequence of pencil art from a graphic novel. These pages are taken from the opening scene.

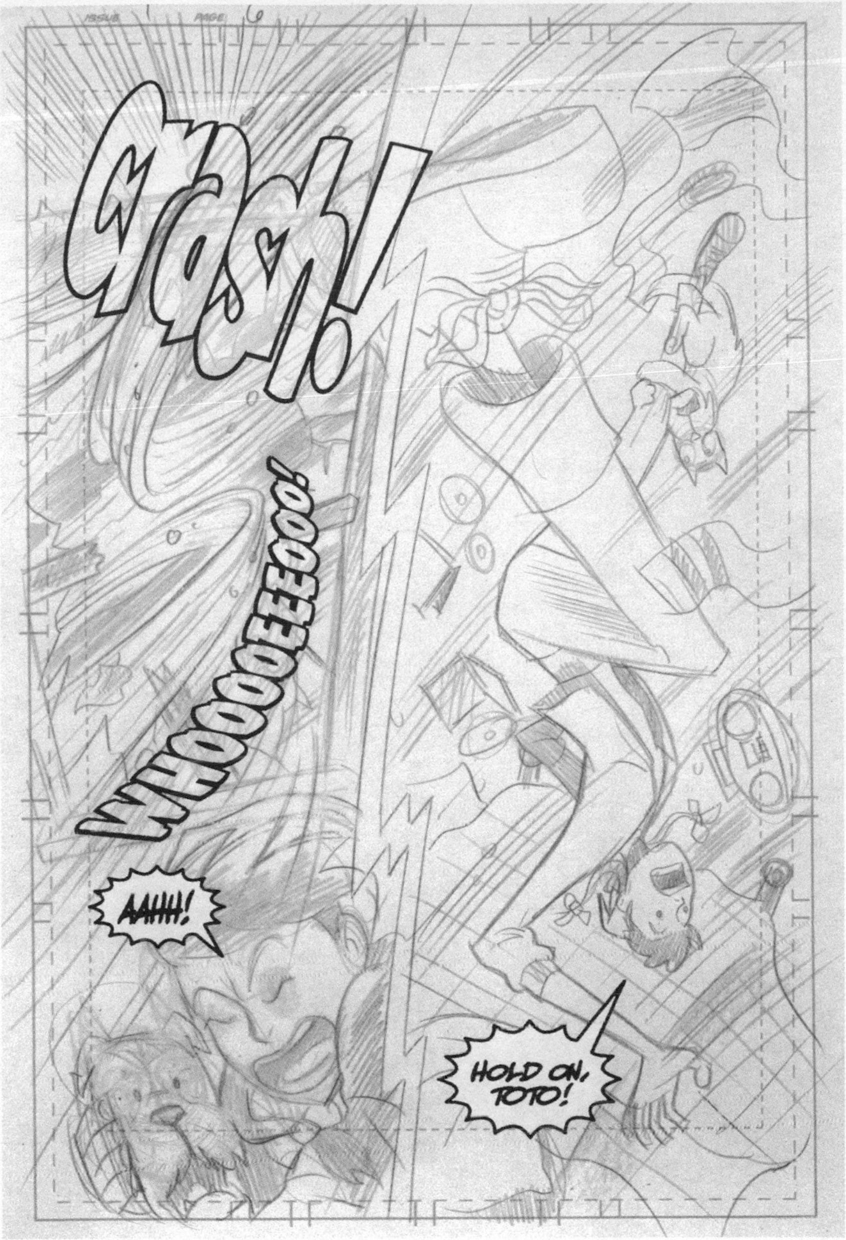
CRASH!
WHOOOOEEEOOO!
AAHH!
HOLD ON, TOTO!

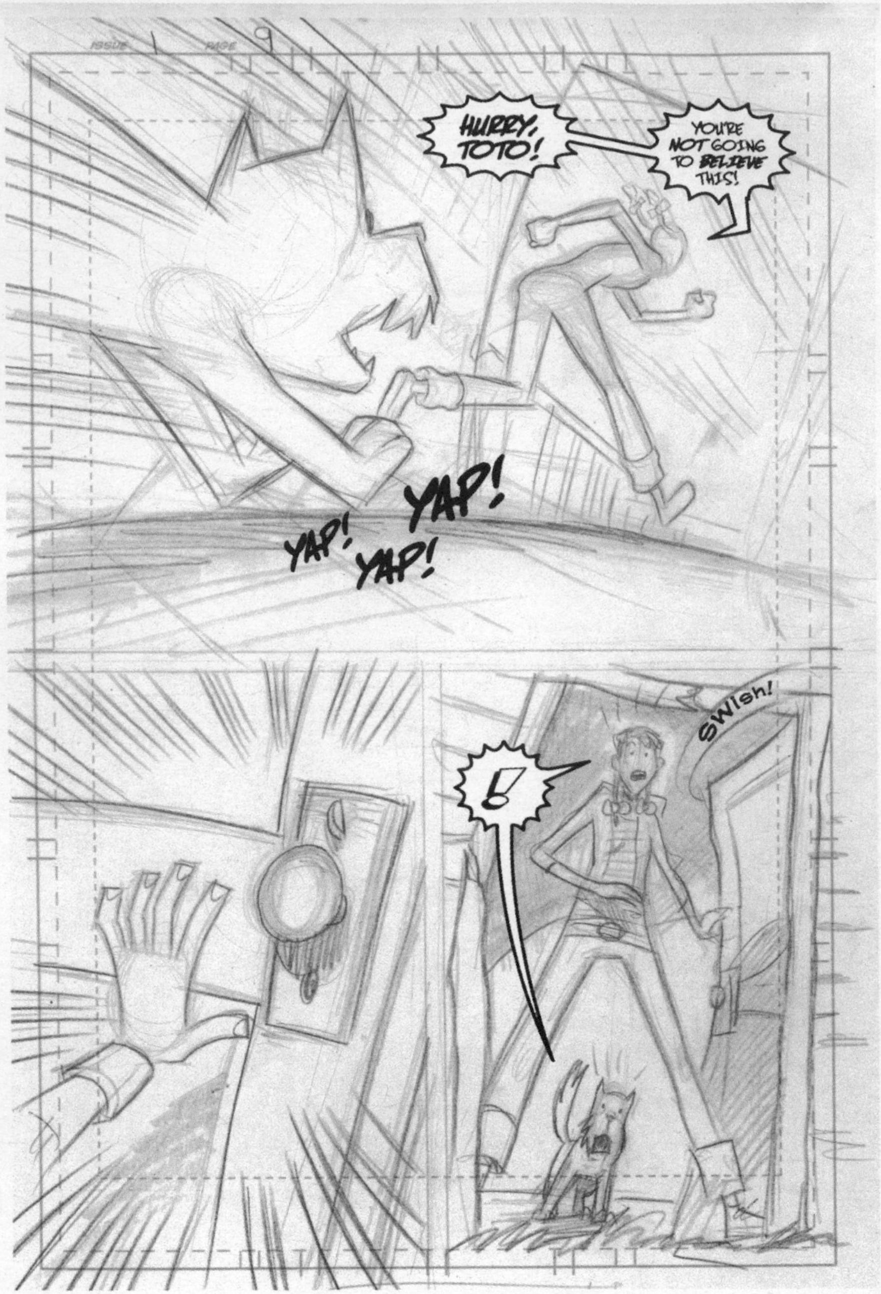
ISSUE 1 PAGE 9
HURRY, TOTO!
YOU'RE NOT GOING TO BELIEVE THIS!
YAP!
YAP!
YAP!
SWISH!
!

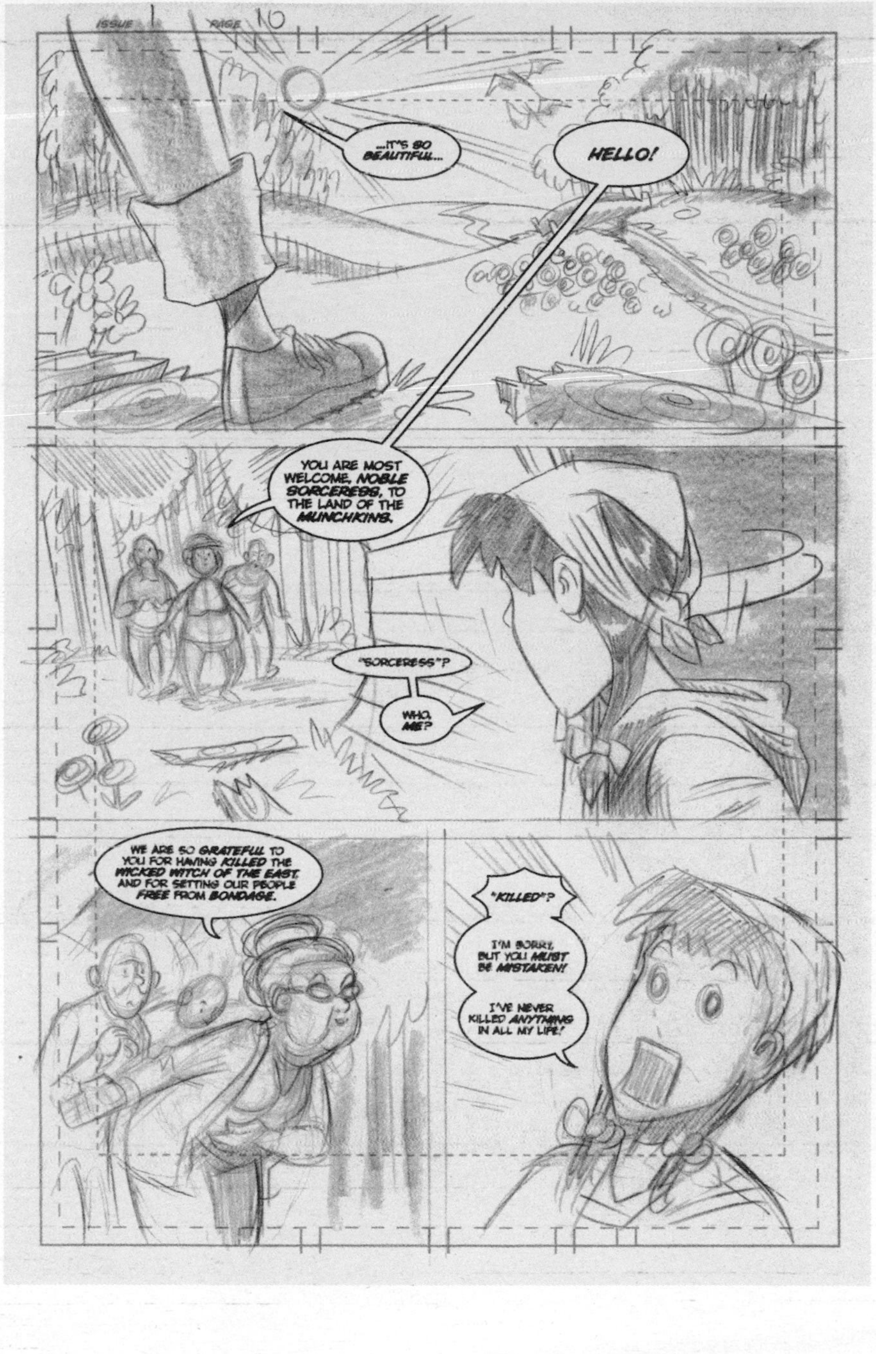
ISSUE 1 PAGE 10
...IT'S SO BEAUTIFUL...
HELLO!
YOU ARE MOST WELCOME, NOBLE SORCERESS, TO THE LAND OF THE MUNCHKINS.
"SORCERESS"?
WHO, ME?
WE ARE SO GRATEFUL TO YOU FOR HAVING KILLED THE WICKED WITCH OF THE EAST, AND FOR SETTING OUR PEOPLE FREE FROM BONDAGE.
"KILLED"?
I'M SORRY, BUT YOU MUST BE MISTAKEN!
I'VE NEVER KILLED ANYTHING IN ALL MY LIFE!

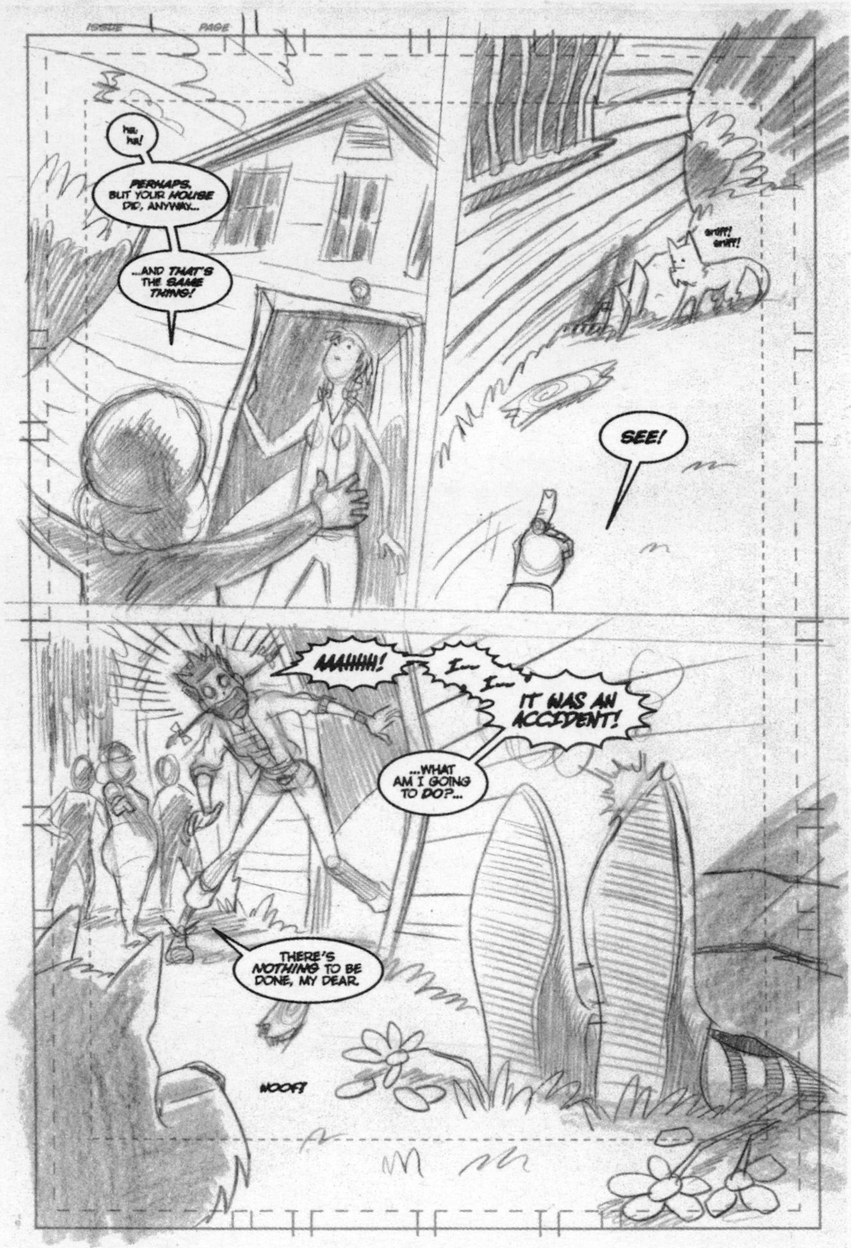

ISSUE
PAGE
ha, ha!
PERHAPS, BUT YOUR HOUSE DID, ANYWAY...
...AND THAT'S THE SAME THING!
SNIFF! SNIFF!
SEE!
AAAHHH!
I... I...
IT WAS AN ACCIDENT!
...WHAT AM I GOING TO DO?...
THERE'S NOTHING TO BE DONE, MY DEAR.
WOOF!

173

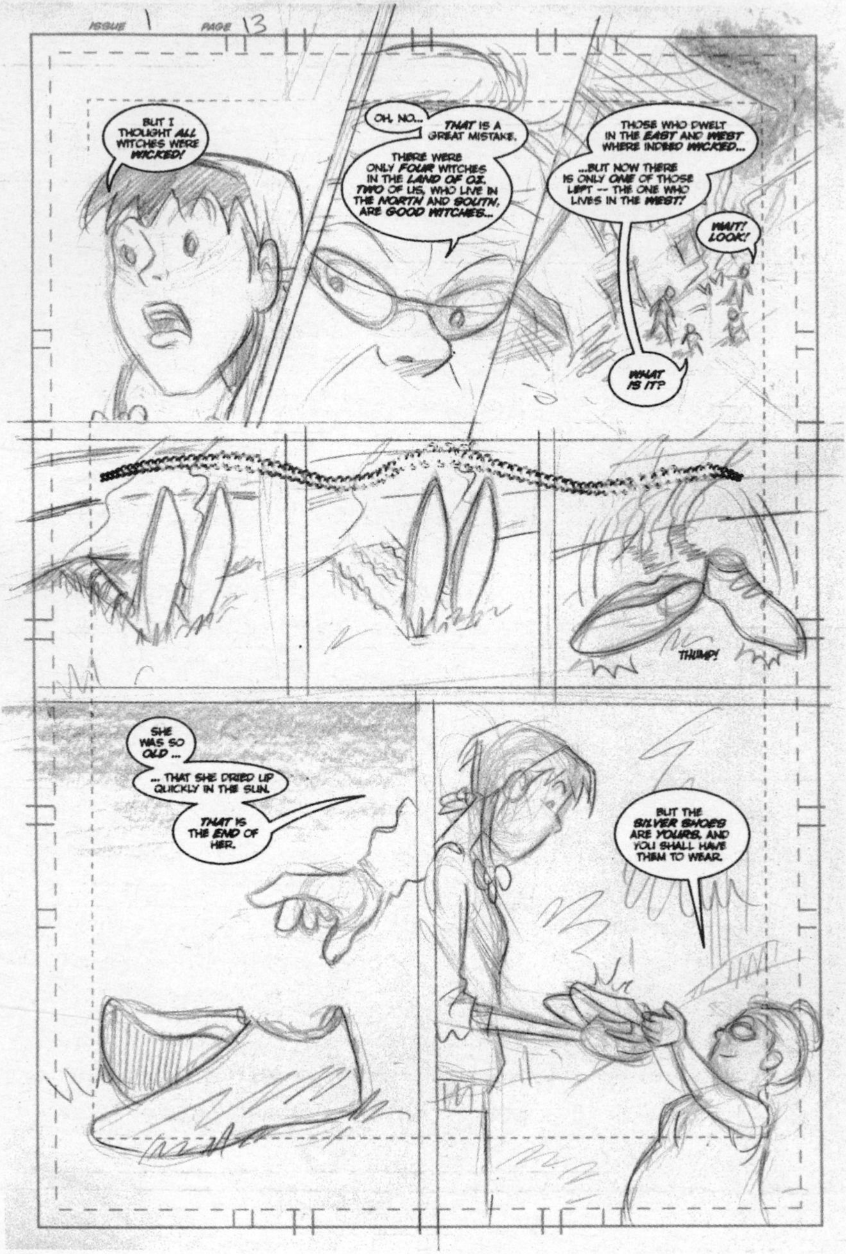
ISSUE 1 PAGE 13
BUT I THOUGHT ALL WITCHES WERE WICKED!
OH, NO... THAT IS A GREAT MISTAKE.
THERE WERE ONLY FOUR WITCHES IN THE LAND OF OZ. TWO OF US, WHO LIVE IN THE NORTH AND SOUTH, ARE GOOD WITCHES...
THOSE WHO DWELT IN THE EAST AND WEST WHERE INDEED WICKED...
...BUT NOW THERE IS ONLY ONE OF THOSE LEFT -- THE ONE WHO LIVES IN THE WEST!
WAIT! LOOK!
WHAT IS IT?
THUMP!
SHE WAS SO OLD ...
... THAT SHE DRIED UP QUICKLY IN THE SUN.
THAT IS THE END OF HER.
BUT THE SILVER SHOES ARE YOURS, AND YOU SHALL HAVE THEM TO WEAR.

LYMAN FRANK BAUM was born on May 15, 1856, in Chittenango, New York. During his childhood, he lived on a luxurious country estate called Rose Lawn as his father had made a fortune in the Pennsylvania oil fields. When he was fifteen, his father bought him a printing press, and for most of the rest of his life he was involved in drama, writing, or journalism.

In 1882, he married Maud Gage, the daughter of a leading suffragist, and after some financial bad luck, he made a romantic decision to move his family west to South Dakota. There he became publisher of a weekly newspaper filled with his own witty verse, editorials, and a column called "Our Landlady," which contained some of the imaginative ideas later developed in his story set in Oz. After losing the paper in 1891, the Baum family moved to Chicago.

In 1896, Baum completed his first two children's books. Now in his early forties, he decided to collaborate with a well-known artist and newspaper cartoonist, W. W. Denslow. Their first effort produced the successful *Father Goose.* Their next book was *The Wonderful Wizard of Oz.* Baum wrote thirteen more Oz books, but because of a disagreement with Denslow, all, except for the famous first one, were illustrated by John R. Neill. Before his death in 1919, Baum had written about sixty books for children, most of them very popular in his day, but none with the eternal appeal of his beloved masterwork *The Wonderful Wizard of Oz.*

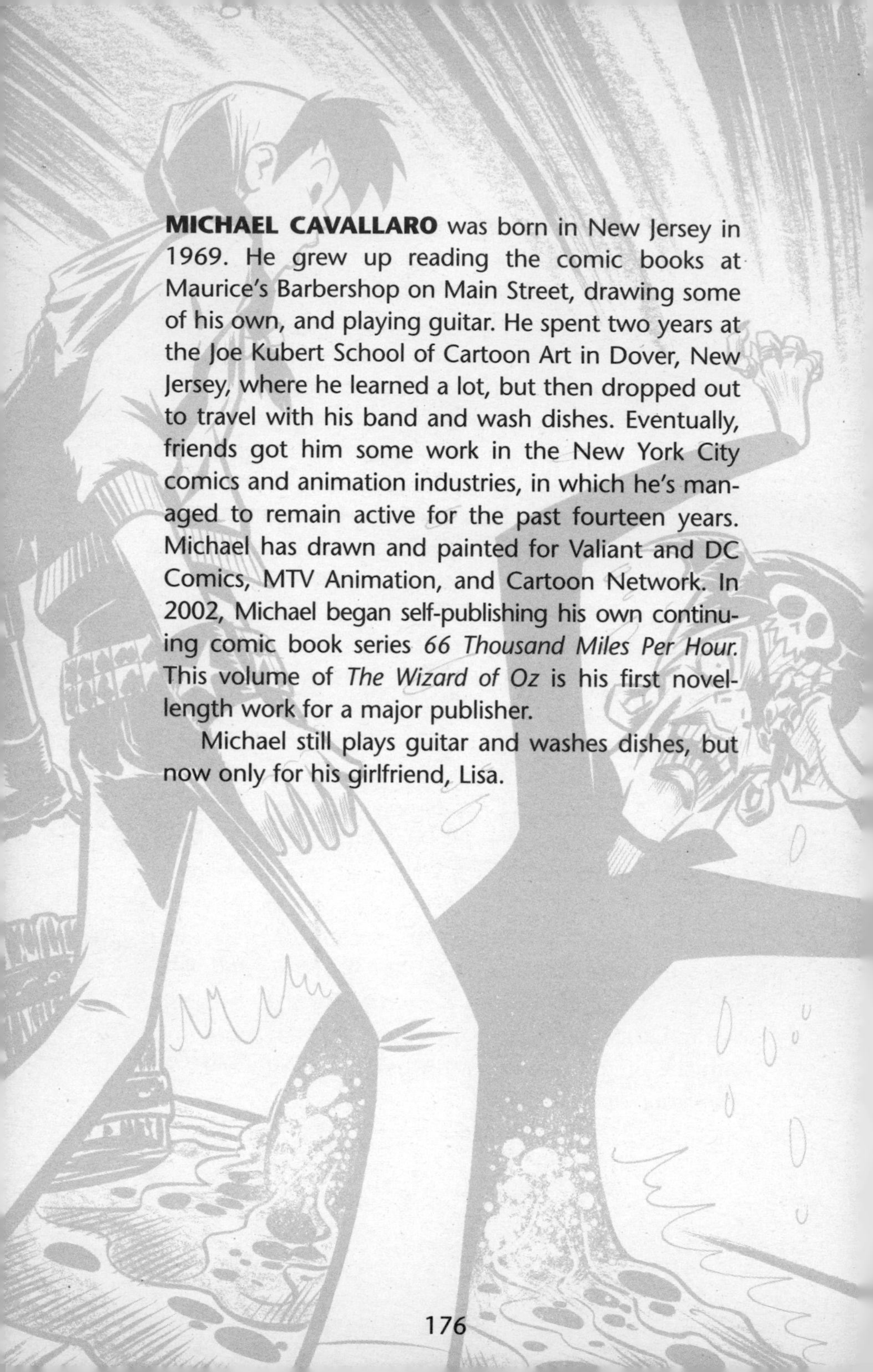

MICHAEL CAVALLARO was born in New Jersey in 1969. He grew up reading the comic books at Maurice's Barbershop on Main Street, drawing some of his own, and playing guitar. He spent two years at the Joe Kubert School of Cartoon Art in Dover, New Jersey, where he learned a lot, but then dropped out to travel with his band and wash dishes. Eventually, friends got him some work in the New York City comics and animation industries, in which he's managed to remain active for the past fourteen years. Michael has drawn and painted for Valiant and DC Comics, MTV Animation, and Cartoon Network. In 2002, Michael began self-publishing his own continuing comic book series *66 Thousand Miles Per Hour.* This volume of *The Wizard of Oz* is his first novel-length work for a major publisher.

Michael still plays guitar and washes dishes, but now only for his girlfriend, Lisa.